YOU *and* OTHER NATURAL DISASTERS

María Martínez

sourcebooks
casablanca

Originally published as *Tú y otros desastres naturales*, © María Martínez, 2019. Translated from Spanish by A. Nathan West.

Published by Sourcebooks Casablanca, an imprint of Sourcebooks
P.O. Box 4410, Naperville, Illinois 60567-4410
(630) 961-3900
sourcebooks.com

Originally published as *Tú y otros desastres naturales* in 2019 in Spain by Crossbooks, an imprint of Grupo Planeta.

Cataloging-in-Publication Data is on file with the Library of Congress.

Printed and bound in the United States of America.
VP 10 9 8 7 6 5 4 3 2 1

For Celia and Andrea. I gave you life, but you have taught me to live mine.

"There must be a limit to the mistakes one person can make, and when I get to the end of them, then I'll be through with them."

—Lucy Maud Montgomery,
Anne of Green Gables

Indecisive, adj:
1. Prone to indecision, hesitant. | 2. Of an incident or event: inconclusive. | 3. Not clearly distinguished, indefinite. | 4. Harper Weston

My grandmother used to say that time is the only exact measure of whether we've made the right decision. And she knew what she was talking about. Only as the days, the months, even the years pass can we know if we've made a brilliant choice or an idiotic mistake.

It seems like forever ago that I was admitted to the University of British Columbia in Vancouver, where I could have stayed to do an MBA at the Sauder School of Business, but instead I chose to attend the University of Toronto to study comparative literature.

My plan was to become an editor and eventually run a publishing company. I would be important and would leave my mark on the world as the one who'd discovered the successor to J.K. Rowling or Paula Hawkins or who'd unearthed the next John Green.

I couldn't settle for less if I wanted to prove to myself I hadn't been an idiot or a rebel trying to go against my father, disappointing all the hopes he'd placed in me.

Three years later, I had the best grades in my class and was interning at Simon & Schuster's offices in Toronto, thanks to a letter of recommendation from my creative writing professor. My responsibilities boiled down to fetching coffee, passing out mail, and running errands. But I knew as soon as I walked through the doors there that the risk I had taken had been worth it.

This year was busy as I juggled my studies and internship, but I didn't mind. I felt secure in what I thought then would be my future. I'd planned everything down to the last detail, step by step, with no room for surprises. One more year, and I'd have my degree. I had an editorial assistant post waiting for me in YA fiction and could pursue my MA at the same time. And when I had it, that would be my ticket to one of the top jobs in publishing.

Meeting my goals was just a matter of time. Time, and lots of work. And I was doing it on my own, without help from anyone else. I'd show my father that he'd been wrong about me—that I could do it all, and that his condescending attitude had only made me stronger.

What my grandmother never told me, though, was how to survive the time before making an important decision. A decision of the kind that can change your life forever. That's the hard part: struggling against confusion, doubts, and insecurities that make it impossible to breathe. Anxiety, insomnia, and the feeling that there's an abyss lying at your feet. Until, at last, the compass needle stops circling and points you in the right direction.

You don't have a choice; you just have to jump and hope you won't crash. Because even if uncertainty is still there tightening around your neck like a noose, all you can do is wait to see whether your choice was the right one.

The moments before jumping were torture for a person like me: indecisive, insecure, full of fear. If a therapist had seen me in his waiting room, he'd have rubbed his hands together with anticipation.

Choosing, deciding, taking the initiative, was like standing in front of an open window a hundred stories up. I was torn between my own desires and what others wanted for me. Scared to disappoint those who mattered to me, but at the same time scared of betraying myself.

I'd been like that since I was a girl, looking in the mirror and feeling like a stranger was looking back at me. It's hard to know yourself when all you've ever tried to be is someone else.

When you've spent your whole life trying to live up to others' ideals, forcing yourself to fulfill their expectations and never getting to know yourself, there's no way you can develop a personality of your own. And without your own personality, even choosing a dress can become an impossible task. Something complicated—like realizing what you thought you wanted was wrong, and having to decide what to do with the rest of your life—can knock you down completely.

And that's what happened to me.

All at once, my safety net was pulled away, and I was hurtling toward the ground. My perfect plan, the thing I thought I wanted more than all else, turned once more into doubts and insecurities. Because there's nothing scarier than when you're harboring a secret dream, and all of a sudden, it's fulfilled.

It all started with a letter, a gift, and a guy as lost as I was.

A book is a dream that you hold in your hands.

—Neil Gaiman

1

The Letter

Books are like life, and just like life, they hold secrets. They're like an ark full of treasures and hidden secrets, waiting for someone to open them up and air their mysteries.

I've always thought books are tiny confessionals where authors hide their most private thoughts. A way of telling the world what brightens or darkens their souls. The way they free themselves of all those burdens a person can accumulate over time. Tales of love, guilt, desire, and many other feelings twist together through the pages, expressing an urge to tell a story that couldn't be told any other way. Footnotes visible only to those who know how to look with their eyes closed.

This belief means I've always read with a slight excess of curiosity, making conjectures, with my feelings whispering to me that this or that passage may conceal a higher truth, may represent an act of atonement both real and impossible at the same time.

Books have a strange power, but not everyone knows how to appreciate it. For a time, we live in them, and after that, they live in us. It's a perfect symbiosis between reader and written word that makes both live more vibrantly than they could otherwise.

Books are little portions of happiness. Even when they're sad or frightening, they bring you memories that put a smile on your face.

Books are winter evenings sitting in front of the fireplace, spring mornings in the park, summer vacations on the beach, autumn walks crunching leaves underfoot.

They even smell good. I mean, isn't that the best smell there is? I can't understand why the famous perfume houses haven't thought of putting it on the market. What lover of reading wouldn't like a fabric softener that smells like a new book? A lotion that smells like ink and recycled paper. An air freshener that smells like a used book shop. Essence of first edition. Library-scented deodorant...

Imagine having those aromas around you all the time.

Books have always been my refuge when everything is going wrong. Taking one down from the shelf, opening the cover, glancing at the first page, is as bracing as a gust of fresh air after an eternity being unable to breathe. Books are the antidote to sorrow, worry, fear, even to a broken heart. I'd be willing to say they cure everything, as long as you can find the right one.

But not even that first page could give me the air my lungs needed when I was lying to myself, telling myself it would be easy to make a decision. And the page I was looking at wasn't just any first page; it was in a book by Alice Hoffman, one of my favorite writers. Even she couldn't save me from the confusing and hurtful thoughts that had been assailing me for days.

I put the novel back on the new release table and dragged my feet to the armchair in the corner of the YA section. I sighed and flopped down in it under the faint orange glow of a lead-crystal floor lamp. That was my favorite place in the bookstore, my favorite place in the whole world. I used to sit there when I was a girl and my feet didn't even touch the floor. I had practically grown up there.

My grandmother had bought the bookstore forty years before, when her husband, my grandfather, had abandoned her to go to the Yukon and look for gold. She never heard from him again.

She had a small inheritance she invested in a musty ground-floor space that was falling apart, but that soon became the most magical place on Montreal's Plateau. It wasn't easy at first, especially with a little girl to take care of—my mother, I mean, not me—but she managed to get ahead and built a future for them in those walls full of stories, novels, and manuals.

She called it Shining Waters—le Lac-aux-Miroirs. Like the famous lake that appears in L.M. Montgomery's books about Anne Shirley. *Anne of Green Gables* was always her favorite book, and my mother's, and mine, too. It was the first book my mother taught me to read, and its pages gave me the most wonderful gift anyone ever could: a passion for reading and a secret desire to write one day if I was ever brave enough to try.

I miss my grandmother.

I miss both of them.

"You can read it a thousand times, and the words aren't going to change."

I looked up and saw Frances staring back at me from the counter. She was surrounded by invoices and account books. She pointed and my eyes wandered down to the letter that had come out of my pocket and was once again in my hands. I had no idea how it had gotten there.

"I know, but I just can't understand why she did it. She knows better than anyone that my life is in Toronto. Coming back here isn't an option." I sighed and sank deeper into the chair. "It's not fair, what she's asking of me."

"She's not asking, Harper. She left you the most valuable thing she had, and she gave you the option of what to do with it."

"Why me, though? Why didn't she leave it to you? That would have made more sense."

"Because Sophia knew me, and she knew she was the only thing that kept me tied to this city. We talked it over many times, Harper, especially during the last months. If she went first, I'd go back to Winnipeg. My sister and my nephews live there. They're all the family I have left."

I rubbed the rough surface of the paper with my fingers.

"I thought I was your family," I said softly.

Frances came out from behind the counter and approached me. I couldn't look at her until I felt her hand on mine, calming my frantic fidgeting. She smiled gently, a slight tremble in her lips. I remembered I wasn't the only one who had suffered.

She had shared every second of her life with my grandmother for the last three decades. They had met when they were girls and had been inseparable ever since. They grew up together and remained side by side, supporting each other in everything. One day, that friendship turned to love. And she was still there when my grandmother left her.

Or maybe they had always loved each other and just weren't brave enough to admit it.

"Of course you're my family. I love you, Harper, but my place isn't here. There are too many memories."

I bit my lip, trying to hold back the tears. A week had passed since the funeral. Three days since the reading of the will, when Frances had given me the letter. I still couldn't believe I'd never see my grandmother again.

I felt sad and angry with her. For months, she had hidden from me the lymphoma that would take her away. She had hidden it from everyone. I could understand why, but her silence was still an open wound.

She didn't give me the chance to say goodbye. Or to tell her once again how much I loved her and how thankful I was for all she had done for me. She was the only one who helped me preserve my mother's memory, helped me get to know her in a way, because I was so young when she had to leave us. She was the only one who didn't forget her and who didn't forget me.

I squeezed Frances's hand and smiled back at her. Her brown eyes gazed into my blue ones, and I could see her broken heart. I couldn't break down in front of her, though.

"She loved you, Frances."

"I know. I loved her, too."

"When are you going to leave?"

"In a few weeks. Three, maybe. However long it takes me to get the accounts up to date, pay suppliers, get our orders straight. Sophia was a disaster when it came to practicalities." She touched my knee. "I'll leave everything organized so you won't have any headaches."

"I don't know if I'm going to stay."

She stood and returned behind the counter with its piles of papers.

"I talked to Mr. Norris, your grandmother's lawyer. He'll help you if you decide to sell."

Sell. That word made my mouth dry out and my spine stiffen. Getting rid of a place you consider your home goes against nature. But what else could I do? *Stay,* a voice in my head told me. I ignored it. I folded the letter and set it down.

My cell phone rang. It was probably my sister, reminding me again we were supposed to see each other that night. Hayley was a perfectionist, a control freak, and very punctual. Everything I wasn't. We creative minds are unorganized by nature. Or that's what I like to tell myself instead of admitting I'm a total disaster.

I reached into the back pocket of my pants and looked at the phone screen. My hair stood on end, and my entire body stiffened. My hand quivered as the phone rang and rang, almost as if I were being shocked.

"Aren't you going to pick up?" Frances asked.

I shook my head.

"It's Dad."

She waited, observing my horrified expression.

"Don't you want to know why he's calling?"

I stood up and put the phone back in my pocket. We all have our complexities, our weaknesses, and our eccentricities. Not answering my dad's calls was one of mine.

"I know why he's calling. The same reason as last night and yesterday morning. And the day before yesterday." I walked over to the wooden counter and leaned on my elbows in front of the cash register. It was a fossil, just like everything else there, and that's why I loved it. "He wants me to sell the house and bookstore and leave my life in Toronto. He wants me to quit school and my internship and take a job at his firm. He wants me on a short leash. And I don't understand why, honestly, since he can't even stand me and never has been able to."

Frances stuffed a pile of receipts in a box and wrote a note on the top.

"Did you ever ask him why?"

"Why what?"

"Why he can't stand you?"

"No," I replied meekly.

I had tried to, I really had, but at the last minute, the words always froze in my throat. I was scared he might answer. And that the answer might justify him always being so cold, so cruel with me. And just with me.

When I was little, I thought maybe I had broken or lost some prized possession of his. I always tried to imagine what it was. At home, I'd look all over trying to find traces of the mistake I'd made so I could repair it. Eventually I came to the conclusion that the fault lay with my wavy blond hair. His was black and straight, the same as my brother and sister's. I thought he probably didn't like people who were different, so I cut it with garden shears and darkened it with shoe polish. He got so mad he wanted to send me to a girls' boarding school in Ottawa. Luckily, my grandmother stopped him. When I grew up, I assumed the problem was me: I wasn't smart enough, or pretty enough, or refined, or strong… I didn't know how to do anything right.

Frances took a deep breath.

"Honey, you're a grown woman. You're twenty-two years old, and you've been on your own since you were eighteen. You need to stop being so scared of him."

"I'm not…" Her look was so penetrating that I gave up my pathetic attempt to lie to her. "It's just easier when I'm far away and don't have to see him."

"Yeah, but you're here, and tomorrow you'll have to see him, no matter what. Not answering his calls may not be the smartest thing for you, let alone the most mature."

I rested my head on the counter. Then I looked over at her and smiled naively.

"I don't have to see him if I pretend I'm sick."

Naturally, Frances shouted back, "Your sister's getting married tomorrow! You can't do something like that to Hayley!"

"I know, I know, I know… It's a dumb idea," I rushed to say, but that didn't mean I hadn't seriously considered it.

She looked at me skeptically, but a second later, I could see the compassion on her face.

"Your father can't force you to do anything you don't want to do, Harper."

"Nolan Weston never takes no for an answer, and he always finds a way to get what he wants. Sooner or later."

"Maybe not this time."

I smiled. I wanted to believe her, but a barrier of anxiety and intimidation warded off all logical thought, and my insecurities over-took every part of me as soon as I thought about seeing him the next day. Three days in one week, a record. We hadn't seen each other that many times all year. In fact, we hadn't seen each other at all.

Some customers came in, and Frances hurried to take care of them. I went back to my armchair, where I had left the letter from my grandmother. I grabbed it, meaning to put it back in its envelope, but I wound up lost in its words, even though I knew them by heart.

Harper:

If you're reading this, you know about my will.

You must feel confused right now, and angry, too, but you have to understand: I couldn't tell you. You would have left everything to come be with me, and I couldn't allow you to make that sacrifice.

I love you too much to let you watch this old woman fade away.

I also think a person has a right to decide how she wants to spend her last days, and that's what I'm doing, living them without regrets. This is how I want to go, free, not being a burden. It might seem selfish, but it's actually the most selfless thing I've ever done.

One day, you'll understand, and I know you'll forgive me.

You must have a lot of questions. Why did I leave everything to you? Why not to the others? The answer's simple. They're different. They've always been more practical, and if something doesn't make money for them…

My home and my bookstore are all I have. They're worthless, but they contain a whole life's worth of moments and memories and dreams.

I know you've struggled to make it where you are. I also

know you think you've got the life you've always wanted. But when I look at you, I still see that little girl who would rather put books in order on a bookshelf than go play with other kids. The one who enjoyed making recommendations and dreamed of writing her own stories one day. I still recognize her in you and I still see the flickers of that old wish in your eyes. And that's why I want to give you the chance to get that hope back.

Keep the bookstore. Your dream of writing lives on in it.

Why work publishing other people's books when you can show the world your stories? You've got talent. You always did. You shouldn't be scared of your dreams, because without them, much of what we are loses its meaning.

But if I'm wrong, and you go back to Toronto and to your life there, I'll understand. And if you do that, you won't be able to hang onto the bookstore. If that happens, find someone who will truly appreciate it, please.

I'm sorry if this old woman has made your life complicated with her last wishes. I could use my age as an excuse, or all those awful anxiety pills I have to take, but I'd be lying.

I'd like to think I'm not burdening you, that I'm liberating you.

Harper, I'm so proud of you and the woman you've become, and it makes me feel calm as I go to meet your mother.

We'll always take care of you.

Now you take care of yourself. You're perfect just the way you are.

I grimaced, with a sharp pain in my chest that I thought would never end.

I felt Frances's hand on my back and her caramel scent enveloped me. The weight of recent days came down on me all at once, and I started crying.

"Get it out, there's nothing wrong with showing you're hurting."

Her voice was so sweet, so absolutely hers, that I couldn't stop the tears from flowing. I hiccupped and looked up at her.

"It's just…Mom left me, and now Grandma's gone, and you're going to Winnipeg." I knew that was mean, but I couldn't help snapping.

She dried my tears, ran her hands over my hair, combing it with her fingers from the roots to the tips so gently that I started sobbing again.

"You'll be all right, Harper. You're stronger than you know. And this isn't a goodbye." She smiled at me, and I tried to smile back. "I'll always come running if you need me."

She hugged me, and I tried not to drown in the knowledge of how much I would miss her. She had always been there for me, her smile as warm and comforting as hot chocolate on a cold day.

I let her baby me until the door flew open and the store filled with the soft jingling of the bells hanging from the doorframe.

2

Facing an Unexpected Encounter

For the next two hours, the bells kept ringing as regulars came in and out and strangers peeked in to see what was on sale. On a table by the door there was always a pile of cards with the name of the shop on them in gold ink. I set out more and tidied them up, along with the bookmarks the publishers often sent us for free.

Then I dusted off the heavy walnut shelves that reached up to the ceiling. There were hundreds, maybe thousands of books in there in all shapes, sizes, and colors: deluxe editions with beautiful illustrations and engraving on their covers, new releases, classics, and paperbacks. Oscar Wilde rubbed elbows with Paul Auster on the bottom shelf, while Charles Dickens sat next to Jane Austen and Charlotte Brontë. Gabrielle Roy, Marie-Claire Blais, Danielle Paige… My grandmother had always had a weird idea of what order things belonged in.

I rubbed my forehead. I still had a headache, and my mind was tired. But I needed to be present.

"You feel like a coffee?" I asked Frances.

She nodded and smiled as she helped an older woman choose a book about submarines for her nephew.

I grabbed my bag and went outside. As usual, the Montreal

summer was noisy and full of movement. The scents took me back to special moments, reminded me of people who seemed to have been there forever: Beth, famous for her mint cakes and chocolate brownies, which disappeared from the shop window every day as soon as she lifted the blinds, or Percy, a street musician who'd played trumpet on the same corner as long as I could remember. I waved at them as I passed by and exchanged pleasantries with Meg, the florist.

Our bookstore was on Mont-Royal Avenue, on the Plateau, a neighborhood in downtown Montreal full of students, artists, and bohemians. When I lived there, I used to love walking its narrow, tree-lined streets with their pretty, colorful Victorian houses and their exposed spiral staircases. I was fascinated by the unique, multicultural mixture of stores and restaurants.

I walked slowly to Rue Saint-Denis. The sun shone through a thin layer of white clouds that were starting to darken the horizon. As I looked up, I prayed. The wedding was going to be held in my father's gigantic gardens in Léry. The rain could ruin everything, and Hayley didn't deserve that. She'd been planning the perfect wedding for months.

I turned right and walked on up the sidewalk to Café Myriade, my destination, which was on the next corner.

It was bustling. There wasn't a free inch on the terrace, and inside, people were lined up in front of the counter. I almost turned around and went elsewhere, but I had gone that whole way dreaming of their muffins of cheddar cheese and cranberries, and I wasn't going to leave without them and one of their wonderful lattes.

My caffeine addiction was one of the few things that gave meaning to my life.

I got in line and looked at the email on my phone. I had several messages from Ryan Radcliffe, the editor who was my direct superior. He wanted to know if I'd gone through the last manuscript he sent me. I ran my hand over my face, feeling guilty, and made a voice memo to remind myself I needed to download and print the document. I'd take care of it as soon as my sister's wedding was over.

I started feeling uneasy and wondered whether my stress about my job might not be an unequivocal sign that I wanted my life to continue as it had been. And then the opposite occurred to me: if I hadn't even looked at the manuscript, it might mean I didn't care about it as much as I thought. Or maybe, since my grandmother had just died, I simply didn't give a damn about the rest of the universe.

A voice broke through the fog, asking for my order.

I looked up and smiled at the barista apologetically.

"Two lattes and a cheddar and cranberry muffin, please."

I looked, distracted, at the people at the tables, and at a little boy who was eating a pastry with his hands behind his back, pretending to be a bird picking at it. I smiled when I saw his mother's desperation.

Scenes like that awakened my imagination. A wicked witch, a boy turned into a bird, and a moral… That was one more idea for the long list of books I'd probably never write.

"Harper?"

In that eternal second, as my name echoed in the air, the entire world slowed down and finally stopped. Well, that sounds nice, and it's probably a metaphor for something, but it isn't actually true.

In fact, in that eternal second, as my name echoed through the air, the entire world was engulfed by the worst natural disaster you could ever imagine.

Because that's what Trey Holt was for me, an earthquake, a hurricane, a volcano spitting lava, the perfect storm I'd never been able to survive. I had sunken into him before like a fragile wooden raft in the middle of a choppy sea, and he'd shattered me into a million splinters and left me drifting…

"Harper?"

I thought I'd turned the page. But four years after hearing him speak for the last time, I'd only needed one word to recognize his voice again. That's how deep a mark he left on me.

I turned, heart pounding in my chest, unsure how to keep my balance as I looked up and saw his beautiful eyes staring at me.

"It's you! I wasn't sure, but…my God, it's you!"

I struggled to convince myself he was really there in front of me after all that time.

He stepped back to observe me from top to bottom, and he must have liked what he saw, because he smiled until I could see wrinkles in the corner of his eyes. Then he bent down and surprised me with a hug.

"I'm happy to see you, Pumpkin."

I felt a tingle in my belly when I heard that pet name from my childhood. I was such a dummy that I closed my eyes when I smelled his scent, so unlike anyone else's.

I took a step back when he let me go.

"Hey, Trey," I said, my mouth dry.

He smiled. I wished I could do the same. I hated him for breaking my heart and sending my self-esteem whirling down the drain. I hated him. And at that moment I had to remind myself how bad he'd hurt me to escape the spiderweb of his mischievous, insolent smile, in which I was momentarily trapped like an insect.

He looked down, and his expression changed. When he glanced back up, his expression was graver as he tucked his hands into the back pockets of his jeans.

"Harper, I'm sorry about Sophia's passing, and I feel bad that I couldn't attend the funeral. When Hoyt gave me the news, I was outside the country, and there was no way to get back in time."

Despite myself, I grinned scornfully. "Don't worry, I didn't even notice your absence. Besides, it was an intimate affair, family only."

My cheeks burned as I replied. I'm not like that, curt, impertinent. But with him…with him, a very unpleasant side of me emerged.

I tried to feign indifference. Anxious lines appeared in Trey's forehead. He'd always had a gift for pretending to be the good guy.

"Yeah, of course, the family." The air around us turned dense, and I started to feel claustrophobic. After a pause, he added, "But the Westons are like my family, too, and I'd have liked to accompany you in that difficult moment."

I exhaled. Seeing him had reopened a wound. What he'd done in the past had marked me and my future, and there he was acting all innocent, and it didn't work.

"I'm sure Hoyt and Hayley would have appreciated your support."

He scrutinized me and licked his lips. "Them… Yeah, right."

His eyes were just as I remembered them: seductive, brownish-green, with thick, black lashes and dark brows. His jaw was square. His lips were attractive, the lower one fleshier than the top one. His hair was longer than the last time I'd seen him. That made him look more mature.

He was still the most handsome man I'd ever met.

He rubbed the back of his neck and smiled, as if pushing sorrow from his mind, and gestured toward me.

"You look amazing! You've grown… God, how long has it been since we've seen each other?"

Not long enough.

"Four years. I was eighteen then. I'd just gotten into college, and you were heading off to the United States."

"You're beautiful. You… You've let your hair grow out. It suits you."

"Thanks. You haven't changed a bit."

He smiled timidly as he examined my face. "Tell me, then, do you usually come here, or did I happen to get lucky?"

"I come when I'm in town. My grandmother's bookstore is close by."

"That's right, next to that store that sells comics and secondhand records. I haven't been there in ages. I love it over there!"

I looked over my shoulder. Where the hell was my coffee? I needed to get out of there. The air in the room kept getting thinner and thinner. I was nervous, my heart was palpitating, and I could feel the blood pumping in my head.

"Hoyt told me you graduated and got a job at a publisher."

"It's just an internship for now," I said impatiently.

"Well, it sounds brilliant, and I'm sure they'll end up hiring you. Hoyt says you've got a knack for it."

"I see Hoyt likes to talk." The frustration in my voice was evident.

"I ask him now and again how you're doing," he muttered, chastened. "He also told me you were thinking of going to grad school. So probably you'll head back to Toronto soon."

"I'd say that's the likeliest thing." Finally I had to look away. But I couldn't for long, not with that perfect smile I'd called up in my mind so many times. Did he really ask Hoyt how I was doing? Why would he? I never mattered to him. He ditched me the way you throw a cigarette butt on the ground and forget it.

"I admire you for that."

"Thanks."

"I finally graduated from MIT last year."

"So you're an architect. You always wanted that."

"Yeah. But now comes the hard part: getting a job. For now I'm back in Montreal working on my own things."

I lost it.

"Trey, what makes you think I care about your life at this point? I don't even understand why you came over to talk to me."

His expression was so disconcerted that I instantly regretted what I'd said. I tried to catch my breath, remembering that November morning and the last words that had come out of his mouth, those cold, hard, piercing words. The pain came back, and my body went numb. For four years, I'd been unable to face what had happened between us, what had happened after.

It was too humiliating.

I couldn't stay there any longer.

"Sorry, I've got to go."

I walked past him and outside without stopping. He said something else, but I don't know what. My steps took me back to the bookstore, but my head was still in the café with Trey. Seeing him again had upset me more than I'd have thought.

A million times, I'd imagined running into him, the different ways it might happen, the different scenarios. In all of them, I acted like an adult, and I was marvelous and interesting and living a life anyone would have envied. I'd see him, and he'd be standing there with regret in his eyes, contemplating what he could have had if he hadn't been so foolish. But I wasn't that lucky. Trey looked better than ever, and I…

I…

I saw my reflection in the mirror and wanted to die. My hair was ratty and the little makeup I'd put on that morning was smeared from the tears I couldn't control every time I thought of my grandmother.

Trey. Fucking Trey.

For a long time, he was my unrequited love. At first, in a childlike, innocent way, because I was too little to understand what love and desire meant. Later, with the passage of time, I did, and all my happiness hinged on him and on his smile and just one look from him could make my world stop turning.

I'd always felt something intense for him. Or at least that's how it seems to me now.

I was twelve the first time I saw him. He was sixteen and had just moved to Montreal with his father. The first day of school, the first time they ever saw each other, he and Hoyt came to blows in gym class. They both wound up in the infirmary and had to write a paper together on violence and its consequences. That same day, Trey came to my house to get started on their punishment.

I was on the floor in my bedroom with the door cracked, doing homework, when I saw him walk down the hall. He had a black eye and a fat lip, but he was the best-looking boy I'd ever seen. He looked at me, and his brief, almost imperceptible smile gave me a tingle. I was captivated.

Hoyt and Trey soon became best friends, along with Scott, who was my sister Hayley's boyfriend at the time. The four of them were inseparable. They spent all afternoon at home watching movies and talking. I would observe them with fascination, and I dreamed of being like them. Of belonging to their universe one day.

For the next two years, Trey was a constant in my life, a source of suffering and happiness. I suffered when I saw him go out with other girls, and I was happy when he noticed me, even if he only saw me as his best friend's little sister.

The summer I turned fourteen, the four of them went to Vancouver to college.

I thought my feelings would fade with the distance, but they didn't. I was still in love with him, in secret, for the next four years, and all the while I heard rumors about him going from girl to girl, from bed to bed, and I even saw him do it myself when he'd come back to visit or for the holidays. His charm was a weapon, and he used it without caring about whose heart he broke, whose life he destroyed. Even then, as I witnessed who he really was, I was incapable of hating him, of truly hating him.

Deep down, I wanted to be the girl he disappeared with every night instead of being the one who watched him disappear.

Then a day came when things changed. And I really did end up hating him.

"Where's my coffee?" Frances asked.

"What?"

I was so caught up in my own thoughts that I didn't realize I was back in the bookstore.

"I thought you were going to get me a coffee."

"I was! But, like, there were so many people out, and it was hot. And it's lunchtime. A coffee would have taken away our appetite, and I was thinking we could go to Schwartz's for one of those delicious sandwiches. What do you say?"

"It's only eleven," she told me with suspicion.

I hung my bag on the coatrack by the window and smiled.

"We could push lunchtime back an hour. Let's go crazy!" I exclaimed.

She laughed, and that sound made me feel better.

The bell chimed as the door opened, and when I turned around, there was Trey with a paper bag in his hand. The scent of coffee filled the room.

"You left this behind."

I was so surprised he'd followed me that I didn't know what to say. Trey looked at me, and I looked at him.

Frances cleared her throat and emerged from behind the counter with her brows knit. She smiled at Trey—not so much at me. *Traitor*, I thought, but I couldn't reproach her because I'd never told her about us. Not her, not anyone else.

"Hello. I'll take that. Thanks."

"You're welcome," he replied.

"We've met before, haven't we? I think I recognize you."

"Yeah, I used to come here with Hoyt. But that was a long time ago. When we were kids."

"Yeah, I remember you now. Your name's Trey. You were Hoyt's best friend."

"I still am, I think," he replied timidly.

Frances nodded, smiled, and glanced over at me. "Sophia liked you. She used to always say, *See that boy? One day he'll be proud of who he is and that scowl will disappear from his face. That handsome little face.*"

"Seriously? Why would she say that?"

"Son, have you looked in the mirror?"

Trey tried not to smile, at least not too openly, and I found that disarming. He was letting down his guard, and that helped me pull myself together.

"I meant the part about being proud of who I was."

"Who knows? Sophia saw things in people most of us overlook. Do you feel proud of who you are?"

That was Frances: always direct, no filter. Trey blinked and shrugged. His expression changed subtly as he reflected on the question.

"Yeah."

I believed him.

"What about before?"

"No."

Again, I believed him, and I couldn't help but see him differently because, for a moment, I had the feeling that the guy I knew was no longer there, that this was just someone who looked like him.

"There you have it, then. She saw something in you. Why? I don't know. Maybe that was just another of her many gifts," Frances whispered. She was clearly moved. "She saw something in me, too, and she wasn't wrong about it."

Trey must have realized then that she and my grandmother had a very special relationship, because he came close to her and squeezed her shoulder softly.

"I'm very sorry. She was always so kind to me."

A lone tear fell down Frances's cheek, and she nodded. Then she turned and left us alone, taking her coffee with her.

In the dead space afterward, I looked at the white canvas of his face, which showed no emotion, at least not at first. But then it changed as he reproached me, "What was that all about before? Do you have some kind of problem with me?"

Is that why he had followed me, to ask me that? I raised my chin, defiant, but inside I was feeling strange, meek, as though I had shrunken in front of him. His stare drilled into me as he waited warily for me to say something.

"Do I have a problem with you? You know the answer to that question."

But judging from his face, he didn't seem to.

"I do, do I? And what is it I supposedly know?"

I closed my eyes and my lips. Those words unsettled me even more than his presence. He knew as well as I did what the problem was, and him being there pretending to be innocent was a joke. I was hurting; he was digging up feelings I had buried as deep as I could.

I swallowed my frustration and walked toward the door. I opened it and held it, almost on my tiptoes, wanting to appear taller, more dignified, more…just more. Even that was absurd, pathetic, because Trey was a foot taller than me and a foot broader, and he looked like a grown man while I was still just a girl. I mean, I even still got carded when I went to bars!

He clenched his jaw at my invitation to go back where he'd come from. His expression was icy, livid. For a tenth of a second, he seemed to grin, and I saw the Trey I was used to: proud, sarcastic, selfish. The kind of guy I'd never get close to—the guy I'd fallen in love with before I knew who he really was.

He passed by me like a windstorm and disappeared.

For a few seconds, I stared at the ground, feeling something break again inside me. I pushed the door closed and leaned into it, covering my face with my hands.

I thought I'd gotten over him. I thought that when the time came, I could handle bumping into him again.

How naive I was!

3

People Say Time Heals All Wounds

I had agreed to meet Hayley at an Italian restaurant close to the Museum of Fine Arts. I got out of the taxi and saw my sister waiting for me by the entrance.

She looked stunning in her dark jeans, white shirt, and flats. She'd left her hair down, and it fell over her shoulders like a dark, shimmering cascade. My sister was beautiful, with a dark tan and eyes the color of obsidian. Her features were much more pronounced than mine: well-defined nose and cheekbones and a little dimple in her chin, just like Hoyt's. Of course, they were twins.

I waved at her from the sidewalk, and we hugged when I reached her. I had never gotten used to how much I missed Hayley, no matter how many years we'd spent apart. We talked on the phone often about whatever—usually stupid stuff that helped us stop thinking about our worries at work and with life in general. But those calls didn't make up for all the time we spent hundreds of miles away from each other.

"Hayley, you look great!"

"You, too, little sister." She seemed worried. "You look thin, though."

"Don't start. I'm not dying of hunger."

"Are you sure? Because you know your body needs a proper diet to feel happy."

I rolled my eyes so hard I was worried they'd get stuck there.

My sister was like one of those mothers who can't stop worrying about their children's weight or whether they're getting enough vitamins. But since she didn't have kids, she focused on me.

"Hayley…" I warned her.

"I just want to make sure you're okay. There's nothing wrong with me wanting you to take care of yourself, eat right, get enough sleep… That's an older sister's job."

I tried to look irritated, but the dam broke, and I said, "You know you're the best sister in the world, right?"

"Someone reminds me of it from time to time." She smiled and leaned her head on my shoulder.

The host told us we could be seated and guided us to a table on the patio courtyard. We sat there smiling, and it seemed strange to me that I'd never been to the place before. The patio was between two buildings and had cobblestone flooring and lots of brightly colored flowers: hanging baskets, hibiscus, oleander. Precious. I'd never have found it if it weren't for Hayley. This is another secret in a city that's full of them.

We ordered crepes with cheese and saffron sauce as an appetizer and pasta pomodoro for a main course, with red wine and olives and onion bread.

The waiter soon returned with our first course.

"Are you nervous?" I asked. The next day, my sister would no longer be a single woman.

"Incredibly. It's been hard for me to sleep these past few days."

"What are you doing here, then? You should be resting up for the big day."

Hayley smirked and reached across the table to take my hand.

"No! I want to spend some time with you. I haven't seen you since the funeral. Tomorrow I don't have a second to spare and Sunday I'm taking a plane to French Polynesia with my brand-new husband. But this night is ours, Sister. Just for the two of us."

Then, with a serious demeanor, she looked down into her glass.

"Hayley, are you okay?" I asked.

She looked almost mournful, and tears seemed about to fall from her eyes.

"I feel like it isn't right for me to go ahead with the wedding. Like I should wait a while, leave it for later. It hasn't even been a week since she died."

I shook my head and bent over the table.

"Don't say that. You know she wouldn't want you to…"

"I know, but still…"

"It was her last wish, and you want to get married. You've been planning this day for months, Hayley. You shouldn't feel bad for going ahead with it."

"You really believe that?"

"Of course I do. Don't let anything spoil one of the happiest days of your life. Grandma wouldn't want that. You know how she is. I mean, how she was…"

She nodded and looked me in the eyes.

"What about you? Do you know what you're going to do?"

I swirled my wine and thought it over.

"I don't have the least idea what to do. It was so hard to make the decision to move to Toronto and study literature, and I convinced myself it was my life's dream and no one would take it away from me. That city's home now, and I have everything I need there."

"But…?"

"I'm not sure anymore if what I need and what I want are the same thing. I try to imagine another life, getting up in the mornings and going to the bookstore. I see myself putting books on the shelf, making recommendations, and writing my own stories."

Hayley smiled.

"It sounds nice. You could become a famous writer, sell millions of books, and turn them into a series on Netflix. Or a movie! And Charlie Hunnam could be the main character in all of them."

"Yeah...or maybe not. It's hard. Only very few people make it to that level. Most are just scraping by."

"You could also be happy with a more modest vision. I still remember you pounding on that old typewriter of Mom's and repeating like a parrot that you would be a writer one day. You wanted it with all your heart."

"I know, but I've grown, and I see things differently now." I took a sip of wine and tried to smile. "If I compare that with what I have now, I feel like I'd be taking a step backwards. I've struggled to make it to where I am now, Hayley. And if I keep going, I can do big things. In a few years, I could be working for one of the most important publishers in the world. If I'm lucky, I could really be someone."

"You've never cared about a degree or a fancy job, though. You always appreciated less superficial things."

"And I still do. It's just that..." I closed my eyes a moment. "I think this is a big opportunity, the kind that only comes along once in a lifetime and that you have to grab hold of. I want to show I can be the best."

"If you're so certain, then what's the worry?"

Good question. I was convinced I had some kind of syndrome that kept me from being a determined, decisive, resolute person.

"I don't know."

"Maybe it's because of Dad?"

I clenched my teeth.

"I've been making my own decisions without thinking of Dad for a long time."

"We both know you care what he thinks, though."

I looked away.

"I really don't care if it matters to him. I'll never be the person he wants me to be. I could leave Toronto and come home, sell the bookstore, take a job in his company, and it still wouldn't be enough for him. I could be the prime minister of Canada and it wouldn't mean a thing to him. Because I'm the problem. I always have been." I laughed mirthlessly. "What did I do, Hayley?"

I felt a tingle in my nose and had to blink to keep from crying. I was relieved when the waiter appeared with the pasta and saved me from breaking down. I could tell from Hayley's stare that she understood.

"Honey, nothing, you did nothing. Dad's a complicated man, and since he lost Mom…" She shook her head. "Listen, you don't have to do anything you don't want to do. You're obviously upset and confused. Just forget all the rest and think about you and where you see yourself in ten or twenty years."

It seemed simple when she put it like that. But it wasn't.

"I don't know, though. That's the problem. I don't know what I want and I don't know where I see myself years from now. I thought I did, but now I don't!"

I was frustrated.

"You think about things too much and you end up complicating matters for yourself, Harper. A coin only has two sides, and most questions are the same way: is it yes, or is it no?"

Hayley was my opposite, and I envied her for it. She was practical, methodical, and saw the whole world in primary colors. For me, there were infinite variations in tone, and they depended on the light, the shadows, the perspective… For Hayley, blue was blue. When I looked, I saw ice blue, grayish blue, indigo, turquoise…and in all those possibilities, I got lost.

When I pursed my lips, she set her fork down on her plate.

"Deep down, you do know. You know what you want, but you also know you'll be disappointing someone who matters to you: Grandma, Dad, your teachers, the editor you work for… Whatever you decide, someone will end up angry with you."

She rolled up some spaghetti and brought it to her mouth. I knew she was right, but no matter how deep inside myself I dug, I didn't manage to feel anything that would tell me what path to take.

"Hayley, I don't know, I swear. I don't know what to do."

"Well, fortunately you don't have to decide tonight. All you have to do is get drunk with your big sister."

I grinned, happy the conversation had changed course. I adored Hayley. She knew me well enough to know when I needed a rest.

"We can't get drunk. Imagine the bride and her maid of honor with hangovers." I savored my pasta. "And poor Scott! You want that to be your husband's memory of the big day?"

"Fine, no alcohol, but you'll be wishing you'd ordered shots of Everclear when you hear what I'm about to tell you."

I stopped chewing and raised an eyebrow.

"Which is…?"

"Dad sat you next to Dustin at dinner."

"What? Why? He knows we broke up. I can't sit there with my ex-boyfriend. He shouldn't have even invited him!"

"I said that, too. But he thinks you're acting like a fussy baby."

"Fussy!" I couldn't believe it.

"Remember what Dad said though: 'That Dustin's a smart cookie, and he's got a promising future at the Weston Corporation. He suits you, and he'll know how to take care of you the right way.'"

Evidently, my father and I hadn't dealt with the same person.

I first met Dustin at a café close to college...

"Critical theory, sounds fascinating."

I looked up from my notes and frowned at him. "Law, how original!"

"How do you know I'm studying law?"

"Your pleated pants gave you away."

He laughed and sat at my table, raising his hand to get the server's attention. He had blond hair, big green eyes, and a pleasant smile. "My name's Dustin. Dustin Hodges."

"Harper Weston. A pleasure," I responded, shaking his hand.

Almost without realizing it, we started going out. I liked how I felt when I was with him. Everything was easy and natural. Comfortable. He was always so sweet. His kisses, his caresses, and the way he made love.

Until that moment, I had only really fooled around with people. And my one-night stands never turned out the way I'd hoped. With him, I thought I could break out of that pattern and open myself up to other things.

After a year, Dustin started talking about our future together. I wasn't sure what that future meant, and I also didn't feel we were ready for it.

"Just think it over. We sleep together almost every night. I have more clothes here than I do at home..."

"I'm only twenty-one, Dustin. I'm not ready to live together."

"Not even to have a stable relationship," he mumbled.

"Why can't you just be happy with what we have?"

"Because I don't feel like we *have* anything. Not anything solid, anyway. We've been going out for a year, and I don't even know your family. I feel like you view what we have as a passing phase, and that worries me, because I do see you in my future."

As always when I'm disappointing someone who matters to me, I gave in. "Would you feel better if I introduced you to my family?"

I took him home for Christmas, and Dustin met my father.

He went back to Toronto with a job offer that only a crazy person (or someone with principles) would turn down. That was how the distance between us started. His priorities, his dreams, his ideas all changed. Even the way he looked at me.

He pressured me for weeks to make our relationship official and move with him to Montreal. He wanted the whole shebang: rings, wedding, home, kids… I got tired of arguing, of having to defend my need for space and the life I'd chosen, and I broke up with him. Not that it did much for me. Dustin refused to accept that we were done, and he made up a different reality in which we were just taking a break before reconnecting.

Fortunately, he accepted the job at the beginning of April and left.

I couldn't stand his insistence and his condescending attitude. Him looking at me with pity and his stupid belief that one day I'd recognize my errors and rush into his arms.

Well, he could keep waiting.

I poured us both a bit more wine. "So he suits me and he'll know how to take care of me the right way," I repeated.

My sister nodded and took a sip. "His words, not mine."

"He thinks that because Dustin's turned into his lapdog. Dustin wags his tail and sits every time Dad tells him to. Jesus, he's probably in love with Dad instead of me. I'll bet he looks at a photo of him when he masturbates."

Hayley laughed so hard the spaghetti shot out of her mouth, and little pieces of it hit me in the face.

"Hayley!"

She laughed even harder as I tried to wipe myself off with my napkin.

"I…I'm sorry. You, uh…you've got a piece in your hair, too." She hiccupped. "I don't think I'll ever get that image out of my head. Dustin thinking of Dad while he… Ugh!"

I ended up laughing, too. We were both making a scene. But with that eternal smile, that eternal good cheer, what else could I do? I felt a tingle in my chest. She was my hero. When I was with her, everything seemed to fall into place. I stopped pretending to be someone else and could live as Harper.

After dinner, we went dancing at a fancy club. We wound up in the park looking up at the starry sky, listening to the music that wafted over from a nearby balcony, all alone for that instant. Until the sprinklers turned on and we got soaked as we ran barefoot through the grass, still laughing.

Hayley slipped. I tried to catch her, and we both fell and rolled over. We stayed there, immobile, holding hands under the fine mist.

"I wish so bad she'd be with me tomorrow, helping me dress, telling me everything would turn out okay."

"You mean Grandma?"

"No…Mom."

I bit my lip to keep from crying. Hayley was ten when our mother died, and her memories were clearer than my own. If her absence hurt me, I didn't want to imagine what my sister must be feeling just then.

"She'll be here," I said, resting my hand on her chest.

Hayley turned on her side. "You look so much like her…"

Everyone who had known my mother said the same thing, that we were so much alike. But in my memories, her face was always blurred.

I licked the drops of sprinkler water from my lips and tried to push those distant memories away. They were so vague that they almost seemed to belong to someone else.

"I don't want to be sad," I said. "You shouldn't, either."

She smiled and squeezed my hand tight before lying on her back again and looking up. I did the same. The stars were twinkling in the dark sky.

It was late when my sister and I said goodbye. I watched her ride off in the taxi, and as I did so, I felt lonelier than ever. I recalled that life goes on, people come and go, they take detours, they grow distant… And there I was, still waiting. But for what? The saddest thing of all was that I had no idea.

I walked back to my grandmother's house on Laval Avenue at a leisurely pace. It wasn't far away. I had moved in there after the funeral because the idea of being in the same place as my father, if only for a few days, was unbearable.

Frances was asleep. I tried not to make noise as I brushed my teeth and undressed. I got into bed, too nervous to sleep, hugged my pillow, and closed my eyes.

A few seconds passed, and then he reappeared. He always did. Days, weeks, months… Sometimes he took a while, sometimes it was like he never left, but I could always count on the memory of him showing up to catch me off guard.

Trey.

People say time heals all wounds. It's not true. Time is like the tide. Sometimes it's low, soft, calm. Other times it rushes up and floods everything around it. That night, remembering our encounter, I felt it wash over me and drown me. In that dark room, the notion that I'd had him in front of me was so unreal that I hoped it had just been a bad dream.

4

Dad Is...Just Dad

"You're still in bed? Do you have any idea what day it is?"

I opened my eyes and saw the outline of a person. I blinked and pushed my tangled hair out of my face. Frances was standing at the foot of my bed holding a cardboard box. Confused, I tried to force my brain to work.

"What are you doing?"

"I told you I was going to visit friends in the Eastern Townships this weekend. They're taking some stuff off my hands."

That was true. She'd told me several times that week, but my selective hearing had filtered out and suppressed any information related to her departure. I sat up in bed, still groggy. The reds and pink of dawn were gone. Now the bright, white light of day was pouring through the window.

"What time is it?"

"Noon."

Noon?

"Oh my God, oh my God. Hayley's going to kill me. I promised I'd get there early."

I jumped out of bed, showered, and threw on some clothes. I didn't bother putting on lotion or drying my hair. I drank a nasty cold coffee and hugged Frances goodbye. I tried my best to get into the taxi without wrinkling my maid-of-honor dress, which was on a hanger in a protective plastic covering.

The taxi driver, a gaunt man with a weary face, smiled at me in the rearview mirror. I gave him the address, and he drove through the city without saying a word.

I rested my head against the window and observed the bright, cloudless sky as it appeared between the buildings. As we left the city behind us, the calm, the traffic whirring by on the highway, and the car's soft movements made me close my eyes for a few minutes.

Our family home was in Léry, thirty or so kilometers outside of Montreal's center, on the other side of the St. Lawrence River. We crossed the Mercier bridge to the South Shore, passing Kahnawake, the Mohawk reservation on the coast, and through Châteauguay. Not long after that, we were on the avenue that led to the Weston property.

Once through the checkpoint, we drove up to the house. There were a few soft clouds in the sky. It was the perfect day for a wedding in the garden.

In the parking area were countless vehicles belonging to the wedding planners, the caterers, the florists, the band…

"Well, this is really something! Is there a party here?" the taxi driver asked.

I smiled and nodded. "My sister's getting married this afternoon."

"Congratulations! I wish her the best of luck."

I thanked him and got out, feeling flushed and trying to remain relaxed as I walked slowly, mechanically, concentrated on pushing everything else from my mind.

I stood a moment at the front door, stretching out the time before I had to walk into that house that seemed ready to pounce on me. It was an elegant, classical stone structure on the tip of the peninsula, with views of Lake Saint-Louis. Built in the early twentieth century, it had been renovated several times and was now a modern mansion: sophisticated, beautiful, and cold.

Only I knew how alone I had felt, how invisible, within those walls.

I walked in with a self-assured stride. The vestibule was like a subway station at rush hour, full of people I'd never seen, all of them in the same uniform: black pants, white shirt. They were walking back and forth under the orders of a woman with a headset and iPad who pointed where they should go. She looked me up and down before noticing my bag with the dress.

"Are you from the dry cleaner's?" she asked.

I almost said yes, dropped the dress, and ran out. But instead I forced a smile.

"No. I'm Harper, Harper Weston. Hayley's sister."

"Oh! Of course! I apologize for the confusion." Her stiletto heels echoed off the wooden floor as she approached to give me her hand. She squeezed so hard that I had to shake out my fingers afterward to make sure they still worked. "I'm Minerva Compton, event planner. It's a pleasure to meet you. Weddings are my specialty. Hayley told us to send you to her room. We'll take care of your hair and makeup there, and Howard, my assistant, will give you the rundown on how the ceremony's going to go and where you'll need to be at any given time. Sound good?"

"Yeah, sure."

"Since you weren't able to attend the rehearsal, it's very important that you pay attention so we don't have any mix-ups. You can organize everything perfectly, everything can flow right along, but if there's one simple mistake, the press will jump all over it, and it'll be the only thing you read about in the society pages."

Listening to her, I thought: one thing this woman isn't good at is making others feel calm.

"I'll pay attention. No one wants my sister's wedding to be perfect more than I do."

"Lovely, dear." She brought her hand to her earpiece and shouted, rolling her eyes, "Does nobody know how to do anything around here?" With a gracious expression, she said, "Nice to meet you, Harper."

As she departed, I stood there by the staircase like a deer in headlights before closing my eyes, taking a deep breath, and going upstairs, not stopping and not looking back. Hiding, the way I always had in that house.

The hallway was empty, and I tiptoed over the carpet to keep from making noise. The door to the master bedroom was open and I stopped. I don't know how long I stood there frightened in front of it, waiting for my father to pop out. I tried to avoid letting these visceral feelings get the best of me, but I never succeeded. They were instinctive and rose up from deep inside.

My pulse slowed when I'd convinced myself he wasn't there.

Pathetic, I know.

I hadn't been in that room in years. If I asked myself, I'm not sure I could have given a detailed description of it. And now, for some strange reason, I felt the powerful urge to go inside. Against my better judgment, I glanced around to be sure I was still alone and stepped over the threshold.

The wooden floor creaked under my feet, but all I could hear was the blood rushing through my temples. I forced myself to stay calm. To breathe, which I kept forgetting.

I felt like I was six years old again. Glimmers of the past returned to me: blurry, disconnected images. I saw myself running to the bed where my mother rested. She was always resting. I didn't know then that her days were numbered. I didn't understand she couldn't do the same things with me she'd done before. I didn't understand why she slept so much. Why her skin smelled like medicine instead of flowers.

I felt nervous as I walked between those walls where every piece of furniture, every nook and cranny, awakened memories I thought I'd forgotten. They were like sparks: her sweet smile, the feel of her kisses on my cheeks, her voice whispering stories to me in the darkness. The vibrant echo of her laughter. All of it warmed my heart now, but at the same time, it made me feel I was dying inside.

It's funny how we can feel happiness and pain at the same time and with the same intensity, and how we end up unable to really say where one feeling begins and the other ends.

I walked toward a table by the window covered in photos in frames of various shapes and sizes. There was an order to them: my brother and sister on their birthdays, at dances, graduating from school… And there were many images of my mother. Pregnant. With Hayley and Hoyt in her arms. Making a snowman with them. Opening Christmas presents by the tree. Sunning themselves on a sailboat.

She was so pretty!

How funny they were, those moments I couldn't remember. But then I noticed something, and the good feelings disappeared and I couldn't see any of those faces anymore through the tears. I closed my eyes and bit my lip till it hurt and I could taste blood on the tip of my tongue. But that was better than the ache in my chest that was making me feel faint.

There wasn't a single photo of me.

Not one.

I took a sip of my second glass of champagne, but without the desired effect. I didn't feel anything at all. Well, apart from nausea and a slight feeling of vertigo that might have been the result of not eating a single bite at the banquet. But I couldn't help it.

I stirred in my chair and smiled back at the girl seated across from me, as though to say, *What a wonderful night! Isn't it a shame that it has to end?* I looked the way the bride's sister was supposed to look, making a titanic effort to do so.

That table of photographs went on torturing me. I could think of nothing else, and it filled me with questions. I had a right to my place there. I had been a part of the story represented there on that surface with four carved legs. That was my family. Why the hell wasn't I…

Stop it for once! I told myself.

A band was there to liven things up, and now they were playing "When You Love Someone" by James TW. Hayley and Scott walked out on the dance floor amid applause. She was radiant, precious, and my brother-in-law looked at her with such admiration that I wondered if there had ever been a man so deeply in love.

I got misty-eyed and felt like a dumb little girl.

Hoyt was at the bar talking with a work colleague he'd invited along as his date. Megan, I think her name was. She seemed to have her wits about her, but she came across as a little cold. Nothing like the girls my brother usually went out with. And yet, he seemed absorbed in their conversation and pleased to be with her.

He liked her.

And I liked seeing him take an interest in someone normal.

As I looked away from them and down at my nails, trimmed short, I felt it. A shiver that made me turn. I got that feeling in my chest like when you jump off a cliff, and you feel dizzy and you flail around for something to hold on to. Trey had passed my table on his way to the bar, sucking up the entire space like a black hole nothing can resist. And that included me. I couldn't take my eyes off of him, but I was terrified at the same time that he'd notice me.

All evening, I thought I'd seen him, but when I blinked, he'd be gone. So I wasn't certain if he was actually there or if my subconscious was just incapable of letting him go.

He was dressed in a classic tux, with cuff links but no bow tie. He didn't need any accessories to look perfect. Given cover by the distance, I saw how little the four intervening years had changed him. His hair was a little longer and was starting to curl, and the golden flecks in his green eyes reminded me of molten caramel. He had a tan, his jaw was square as ever, his hands just as big. When he swallowed, his Adam's apple moved slowly up and down, and under his carefully trimmed beard I could see the little scar on his chin, his curved lips… Well, I couldn't see all those details, but I'd memorized them, and time had done nothing to soften their edges.

Resentment burned my soul. Four years of yoga to try to channel my wounded emotions had gone to hell in just over one day.

"Miss, more champagne?"

I raised my glass to the waiter who had stopped next to me. I'd drunk my entire glass without realizing it. I shook my head and sank in my chair, frustrated that I felt so terrible.

It was a party, dammit, and there I was looking pathetic!

The problem was that I struggled to have fun when my senses were on alert. It's like when you walk down a dark street and you don't dare look back because you're afraid there's someone creeping up behind you…

"You feel like a dance?"

I looked up at Dustin with disdain. I was angry with him for allowing my father to seat us at the same table. Angry because he was still pretending we were together. Angry because he was acting like I was a sad little girl who didn't know what was best for her. And angry with myself, above all, for not knowing how to put him in his place.

"I don't want to dance at all, and certainly not with you."

"Come on, Harper, try and make an effort. You've been ignoring me all night, and it's starting to feel nasty. People are noticing," he whispered in my ear.

That was true. My sister's friends were very interested in what was going on. That was understandable: the tension between us was palpable.

I wanted to get up and run out. So I did. I said a soft *sorry* and went off to find somewhere I could relax and put back together the shattered pieces of my mask of happiness. The fact is, whether our situation is good or bad depends on our perspective, and my perspective was unstable, shifting constantly between highs and lows. Sometimes I was calm, sometimes frantic. My whole life was that way, and it was exhausting.

Up all of a sudden.

Down just as fast.

On my way across the garden, I felt as though the waves were dragging me out to sea.

"When are you going to stop being so irresponsible?"

Dustin had followed me out there.

I needed a few seconds to take in his words. Then I turned around and gave him a stare that could have struck him dead. "What did you say?"

"Come on, Harper. This was funny at first, and I even found it attractive, you being so rebellious. But now you're taking it too far."

I tried to control my nausea and my urge to explode. Then again, I thought, I could just puke all over his designer shoes. I guess things weren't going bad for him if he could afford them. "I'm taking it too far?"

"It's been months now. You've made your point. Now it's time to take your future seriously."

"What future?"

"What do you mean, what future?" he said, as if I were an idiot. "Your future, our future…our family's future."

"Our family? You mean the Westons? *My* family?" I didn't try to hide my sarcasm.

He knit his brows and his ears reddened. I could see the muscles tensing in his jaw. "Yeah. I mean, no." He looked exasperated. "You understand perfectly what I mean."

With a humorless smile, I placed my hand dramatically over my heart. "Of course I understand. You made it perfectly clear the last time you called me, and the time before that, and the time before that… And the response is still the same. I'm not getting engaged to you, Dustin. I'm not getting married. I'm not going to turn myself into your baby factory to guarantee you a spot at my father's firm kissing his ass for the rest of your life."

He went pale.

"That's not what I…"

"Isn't it?"

"No! What the hell's up with you? We were good together!"

"According to you we were. And it did work back when you were fun and had principles and wanted to be a good person and save the world. Back when you respected my ideas and understood my aspirations and wanted to be with me. With me alone."

"That's still what I want," he said, reaching out toward me and stepping forward.

I blew him off. He didn't understand me, not because he didn't want to, but because he couldn't. He never had been able to, even if there was a time in our relationship when I thought otherwise.

"Don't make me laugh, Dustin, and don't take another step, because I'm about to puke all over your pretty little suit."

Actually, I would have liked that. He scowled at me, accusingly.

"You're intoxicated? At your sister's wedding, of all places?"

I laughed and stumbled.

"I'm not intoxicated, I'm drunk. Maybe you don't know there's a difference, but there is."

"Jesus, Harper. Imagine if someone saw you like that. Your father…"

"Oooooh, my father! If I say his name in front of the mirror three times, will he appear like the boogeyman? Bloody Nolan, Bloody Nolan…"

"Behave, there are people watching us."

The words *Fuck you* danced on the tip of my tongue, but I swallowed them, and they stung going down.

"I used to like you. I really did. I thought you were a sweetie. But you've changed…"

"I haven't. I'm still the same guy." He ran his hand through his hair and looked around at the garden before settling his eyes on me again. "But I see things differently now. I'm more realistic. And if you weren't so proud and hardheaded, you'd get that. You'd realize that…"

That flipped a switch in me.

"Proud? How…how can you…?"

Those words were barely audible when I saw my father striding toward us. I had managed to duck him all day, and there was a part of me—an immature part, I admit—that thought I could make it out without seeing him. My father was the type of man who managed to make everyone and everything around him shrink, to the point that even the air around him seemed to grow thinner.

"Harper." His voice was thundering. "Do you think I have the time and patience for these stupid games? To have you here acting like a spoiled child? You've been ignoring my calls. Don't do it again."

"I was busy," I murmured.

"Busy with what? Wasting your time on nonsense?" He shook his head and a few dark hairs fell over his forehead. He pushed them aside and glared at me. His eyes were bottomless black pits. For a moment, I thought he was vacillating, but no—my father was incapable of that. He didn't know what self-doubt was. He was cold, distant, a rock covered in jagged edges. He took a card from his pocket and handed it to me. "Here."

I couldn't move at first. I had to squint when I grabbed the card to see the tiny shiny letters that seemed to float over the paper.

"What's this?"

"Call that number. It's a real estate agent who's done work for us. Set up a meeting with him and give him whatever he wants. Keys, documents, whatever he needs to sell the house and the bookstore ASAP. He'll make it a priority."

The alcohol, which had made everything feel dull before, now evaporated through my pores like a cold sweat. My heart sped up as I found the courage to look him in the eyes.

"I haven't decided yet. On that, or on anything else…Dad." This last word tasted bitter on my lips. "I need to take my time and think about it."

"There's nothing to think about. You aren't keeping that woman's house, let alone the bookstore."

"*That woman* was my grandmother."

"*That woman* made the Antichrist look charming."

Rage like hot lava flowed through my veins. He was talking about the person I'd loved most in the world. The person whose absence made my soul ache inconsolably. I clenched my fists.

"You have no right to talk about her that way. You don't…"

"Me?" He shouted me down. "That woman's the one who filled your head with all those stupid ideas. I gave in when you decided to waste your life studying literature…"

"That wasn't a waste. Mom did the same thing…"

Sweat pearled on his forehead as he stepped even closer to me.

"How dare you mention your mother?"

I breathed in and out slowly and tried to stop trembling. I could feel his eyes burning holes in me, searing my skin, my muscles, charring my bones. He was making a tremendous effort to keep his cool. He always had to when he was with me. I wondered what would happen if one day he couldn't, if his rage just kept growing and growing. I suppose the whole world would explode.

I would disappear.

And he'd be happy.

He looked at Dustin as if he'd just noticed his presence. Then he focused on me again and slowly, the color drained from his face.

"Grow up, Harper. Forget literature, editing, writing your little stories, and the rest of that junk. Come home, sell the bookstore, and know your role. You're a Weston! Do you understand what that means? The responsibility you have to this family, to me, to your brother and sister? Jesus, stop being such a baby."

Why did that word always sound so humiliating coming from him? He was the very embodiment of contempt.

"I'm not a baby."

"Dad, that's enough." My brother appeared behind him and put a hand on his shoulder. I hadn't realized he was there until I heard his soft voice.

"Hoyt, don't tell me…"

My brother came around between us, and I took shelter behind his back. That's what Hoyt meant to me: safety. He was the closest thing I had to a real father figure, even if he was only four years older than me.

"Dad, Hayley and Scott are about to leave, and they're waiting for you to see them off. That's what matters tonight."

For a few long seconds, Dad said nothing. Then, almost imperceptibly, he nodded. "Try to get your sister to listen to reason. My patience is running out with her. Either she does her duty, or she can forget about this family."

He turned around and walked toward the house. Briefly, the tension he'd brought to the atmosphere lingered behind him, and it felt cold and humid. Or maybe the night really was that way because of the air rising off the lake. But I've always been imaginative and dramatic. No one's ever called me *simple*.

"Harper, your dad's right—" Dustin started to say.

Hoyt turned to him. "Shut your mouth if you don't want me to shut it for you."

"I'm just worried about her. She's my—"

My brother grabbed his lapels and narrowed his eyes. His mouth was a thin, tense line. He'd never liked Dustin, and he'd have no problem showing that now.

"Let's see if you can understand me, blockhead. She's nothing to you. Now scram."

Dustin hurried away, glancing back several times over his shoulder. His wounded ego was evident in his eyes.

Hoyt turned to me. I smiled, shyly at first, as though wanting to say *sorry*, and then without regrets.

"Blockhead?"

"I don't know. I didn't want to swear. In my head I was calling him a piece of shit and telling him I'd tear him to bits."

"Now that's more like it," I replied.

He reached a hand and cupped my cheek, looking worried. "You okay?"

I shrugged. No, I wasn't. I was the furthest thing from okay. The week before, all kinds of things had happened I'd have preferred to forget. The straight line of my path, my everyday life, the future I had told myself lay before me, was now full of potholes. I couldn't see it clearly. All I saw were shadows that told me where the road once lay, the way traces of letters remain on a chalkboard after you've erased it. And there I was, lost in a pile of chalk dust.

Hoyt tried to smooth out the wrinkles between my eyes.

"You know Dad … He's just Dad. You don't have to pay attention to him if you don't want. You need to make your own decisions."

"It's easy to say that when you're not the one who's always disappointing him."

"I've disappointed him lots of times."

"That's not true," I moaned. I felt like a loser. I almost always did, and yet I had no idea what I was doing wrong. "He's always loved you. You and Hayley. But me… I–I mean, who am I even?"

"You're my little pumpkin." He hugged me tight and kissed my forehead and added, "He's a tough man, but he loves you. I know he loves you."

There was no point in arguing about it.

Since I'd refused to spend the night there, Hoyt insisted on driving me home. The party was still going even after the newlyweds and many of the guests had gone.

"What's up with your date?"

"She'll stay in one of the guest rooms. Don't worry about her."

"One of the guest rooms?" I wasn't so sure about that. I'd seen how they'd looked at each other. "Yeah, right."

With a sly smirk, he said, "Don't look at me like that. I'm being serious! She's different, and I–I want to take it slow. I don't want to spoil things."

I nodded. I was happy for him. He kissed the crown of my head and said, "I gotta go get the car keys. I'll be right back."

"Sure."

I followed him up to the house and waited in the vestibule while he went up to his room. Looking out the windows, I could see couples dancing to the soft rhythms of sensual soul music that echoed faintly where I stood. Past the dance floor, there were other couples listening to the lapping of the waves and watching the stars. The house was in a beautiful location with a strange enchantment, and the lake views made it almost perfect.

I turned toward the door. I was tired and my feet were killing me in those new high heels, which I would never have agreed to wear on my own. I saw my reflection in the mirror over the console. God, I looked horrible! My hair had been in a bun, but now strands of it were falling everywhere. I walked closer and started pulling out the hairpins with their little jewels until my hair fell over my face and shoulders. Then I ran my fingers through the little knots and tried to relax. The night was all over.

That's when I saw him.

I didn't move. I couldn't.

Our eyes connected in the mirror.

And as we looked at each other, I felt everything vanish. His expression was dark, hard, defiant.

Nervously, I found the energy to leave. With firm steps, I walked outside, and the humid air hit me in the face, so dense it was almost impossible to breathe.

"Are you running away from me?"

Glancing back over my shoulder, I saw Trey had followed me out. "How observant of you." I walked downstairs and to the fountain. He came to a stop next to me.

"What the hell is up with you?"

"Like you don't know," I said.

I felt his fingers suddenly grab my wrist, forcing me to turn toward him. His hand trembled in contact with my skin, or maybe it was my arm that was shaking.

"I don't like riddles, Harper. So if you have a problem with me, just spit it out."

I pulled away. "I've got nothing to say to you."

"That's not what it seems like. And judging from your face, there's a whole speech inside you just waiting to be delivered."

"One you've already heard before."

"Here we go again," he grunted.

I sighed loudly and tried to hide as best I could how little control I felt over the situation.

I watched myself through his eyes, and for some strange reason they looked sincere as he lied to me, acting like he didn't know the origin of the gulf that separated us. For a moment, I saw myself as he saw me. A spoiled, whiny little girl who used silence as a punishment. Stupid, immature, and a bunch of other things I didn't want to think about just then. It was true, too. That was how I was acting, and I didn't know why.

I should have screamed at him. Should have let it all out, one detail at a time. What it feels like when you break into a million pieces and nothing can put you together again. How hard it is to admit that you meant less than nothing to someone. The hatred, the pain and dis-appointment I felt when I saw him fall off the pedestal where I'd put him. It would have made me feel better, but I said nothing because my heart needed him to open that door. I needed him to say sorry, to repent, and he hadn't done it. I needed to know why. Perhaps that would erase from my mind what he'd said to me back then.

Insolently, I said to him, "Isn't there something horrible you should be doing?"

He clenched his teeth audibly, and a faint grin appeared on his face, venomous. My hair stood on end as he bent down over me, invading my personal space. He knew how to get my attention, and he knew how to intimidate me.

"Doing horrible things is my day job. By night I like to drive girls like you crazy."

He'd hit the button. I tensed up. I hated that word; I hated it with all my might.

"Are you calling me a girl?"

"Yeah, a whiny little girl," he whispered, so close I could smell his breath. "I don't know what the hell is wrong with you, but just so you know, I couldn't care less."

"Fuck you."

"Fuck you."

"Very mature response."

"You're one to talk about maturity, Pumpkin."

"You have no right to call me that," I said.

"Pumpkin!"

"Shut up!"

"Or what?"

Just then, I heard another voice shout, "There you are!" It was Hoyt, now walking out the door. He had changed out of his suit into a pair of jeans and a T-shirt. Trey and I separated, but we were still eyeing each other as if we were in a duel and whoever blinked first would lose. I remained firm until he shook his head, smirked, and started walking away.

When he reached us, Hoyt said, "Hey, Trey, are you going?"

"Yeah, I'll call you in the morning."

"You okay, man?"

Trey raised his hand with a thumbs-up on his way to the parking lot beneath the orange light of the lampposts and of the Tiki torches lining the path.

"I'm great," he shouted back. "I'm going to try to find a cat to kick or a baby whose pacifier I can steal. Who knows? Maybe I'll even push an old lady into traffic while I'm at it."

I blushed. Maybe I'd gone too far in what I'd said.

Lines appeared across Hoyt's forehead. "Did something happen between you guys?"

"No."

"Are you sure?"

I looked away before answering. "Yeah, we just talked. I mean, he wanted to talk, and I didn't really feel like it."

"When's the last time you saw each other?"

"Four years ago."

He opened his eyes, surprised. "Four years?"

I felt a twinge of guilt. Actually, we'd talked two days before, twice, but I wasn't going to tell Hoyt that. Just like I wasn't going to tell him what happened between us. I wasn't such a bad person that I was willing to ruin Trey's friendship with my brother just to get revenge. I loved Hoyt too much for that, and Hoyt loved Trey.

"Yeah," I responded with more energy than I thought I had.

"And you didn't feel like talking to him after all that time? I thought you two liked each other."

"That's debatable."

Hoyt looked anxious as he rubbed his face and passed an arm over my shoulder on the way to the car. "What's going on?"

"Nothing."

"It didn't look like nothing."

"I just don't feel like talking to him. I realize he's your best friend and all, but he's not a good guy, and you know that. He's an idiot." As I saw the sarcasm in Hoyt's expression, I continued, "It's true! I didn't realize it when I was little, I even thought he was nice, but I've grown. Now I see people the way they are, and I just don't want anything to do with Trey."

Once we reached the garage, my brother hit the remote, and the door lifted to reveal several cars. The lights on his Jeep blinked. I got inside and took off my shoes. Hoyt put it in gear and we left Léry without a word, him thinking his thoughts and me thinking mine. Eventually, after those tense hours, I fell into a not unpleasant lethargy.

"Trey isn't the same guy he used to be," my brother murmured after a while.

I opened my eyes and looked away from the window I'd been leaning on. My face was starting to feel numb. "That's what you say."

"That *is* what I say." His tone led me to think he might be irritated with me. "He's *not* the guy he used to be. And he hasn't been for a long time."

"You're telling me he's no longer a womanizer and a moron?" That stung him. Whatever I might have thought or felt, Trey and he were close. I almost regretted my words.

He looked as if an immense weight were burdening him. "He's changed. We all have a right to change. And all of us do change with time. Some more than others. Don't you think?"

I nodded, but I wasn't really sure. To tell the truth, I wasn't sure at all. Many people never even tried to change, either because they didn't believe they could have a better life or they didn't want one. Whether that meant being a better person or…just anything. Why would Trey Holt bother changing if he'd always had the world at his feet?

My brother cleared his throat.

"I've learned some things these past few years. First, appearances can be deceiving. Second, when we judge someone based on past prejudices and not firsthand, we're often mistaken. And if we refuse to look beyond the surface, if we refuse to dig any deeper, then maybe the problem is *us* and the way *we* see reality."

My cheeks reddened, and I felt like a student caught cheating on a test. My brother was young, but still, he had more or less raised me. Since our mother left us, he had simply accepted that I was another of his obligations. He worried about my grades, my friendships, my behavior, and he wasn't shy about chewing me out or putting limits on me if necessary.

I was grateful for all that, for him giving up a part of his adolescence to make sure mine could be as normal as possible. That meant I couldn't bear disappointing him. And just then, it seemed that I had.

His words made me feel bad about myself. At the same time, there was fury burning in my chest, and the fire refused to go out. I couldn't accept that Trey had changed, that he was no longer who I thought he was. It's easy to hate the bad guy in a movie. But when he repents or redeems himself or dies, that hatred turns to pity, and pity into forgiveness. And I didn't know if I could forgive him. But I didn't forget what my brother said.

5

I Closed My Eyes and Jumped

Thump, thump, thump...

I opened my eyes reluctantly, just a crack. Enough to make sure the sun hadn't risen.

Thump, thump, thump.

It wasn't a dream. It wasn't my imagination. Someone was knocking on the door. Or trying to beat it down, to be exact. I looked over at my alarm clock blinking on the bedside. It was five in the morning. I'd barely slept. I got up and crept over to the peephole.

"Hayley? What the hell are you doing here?"

I opened the door and she stumbled in, falling on top of me. She'd had her ear pressed tight to the door. As we hit the floor, we dragged down a coatrack full of jackets and sweaters no one ever bothered wearing, and one of the wooden hangers hit me on the head.

"Ow!"

"Oh jeez, Harper, I'm so sorry. Are you okay?"

My hand on my forehead, I stared at her. I was going to have a serious bruise. She crawled over to take a look.

"I'm sorry," she repeated, then grabbed my arm. "But why did you open up without saying anything? You almost killed us."

"Why did I what? The better question is, what are you doing here at five in the morning? You scared me to death! Shouldn't you be in an airplane on your way to your honeymoon?"

"I've still got two hours."

I got up and went to the bathroom to check myself out in the mirror, and Hayley followed me. When I turned on the light, I saw a pale, haggard face staring back at me with a red mark over the right eyebrow that was starting to swell up. I ran water over a hand towel and pressed it down on the bruise.

"Sorry. Does it hurt?"

"I'll survive. What are you doing here? Is everything okay?"

"Yeah, don't worry, I just wanted to see you and give you something before I left." She felt her clothing as if trying to find it. "Wait, it must have fallen out."

She ran to the door, and I followed her in time to see her bend over and pick up a white envelope. She handed it to me.

"Here, this is for you."

"For me?"

I opened it and took out an airplane ticket. For a moment, I thought she wanted me to accompany her on her honeymoon. Had she lost her mind?

"What's this?"

"A present."

"A present? My birthday was weeks ago, and you already gave me one."

"This is a very special present. The most important one I've ever given anyone," she replied solemnly.

"Hayley, look, I love you, but if you don't start explaining yourself, I'm going to scream. It's early as hell, I'm tired, and you're supposed to be at the airport with your husband. This is weird!"

She grabbed my hand and guided me to the sofa, sitting down and motioning for me to do the same.

"It's an airplane ticket to Prince Edward Island."

"For me?"

"Yeah."

"Why?" I stared at her, goggling.

"So you can go there."

"Why?"

"Shut up!" I nodded as she went on. "Remember the house on Petit Prince that was Scott's engagement gift?" I nodded. I'd only seen it in photos, but I remembered it being gorgeous. "Well, you're going to take a vacation there."

"What?"

"Since we talked the other night, I've been thinking over things about the bookstore, the house, your studies… You have important decisions to make, and you need calm to do that, with no one else there to put pressure on you. That includes me. So I think it's best for you to leave for a few days and meditate on it so you can figure out what to do on your own."

I was skeptical. "On an island in the middle of nowhere?"

"It's not in the middle of nowhere."

"There's nothing there!"

"Exactly! Nothing except the sea, beaches, and tranquility. It's the perfect place to think. Harper, you can't just drag this situation out forever, even if, knowing you, that's what you'd like. I mean, it takes you forever to decide whether or not to use real sugar in your coffee."

I looked down, embarrassed. "I can't just up and go like that. The fall semester's around the corner, I have deadlines for projects and reports, books to edit, assignments to turn in…"

"So you're going to stay in Toronto?" she asked.

"No."

"You're going to stay here and keep the bookstore, then?"

"No." I shook my head.

"Are you going to work for Dad?"

"Never!"

She'd said her piece, and sat there now with that impenetrable expression meant to show that she knew everything about me and I knew nothing. I sank back into the sofa, exasperated.

"Can't I just think it over here?"

"With Dad stressing you out and Dustin all over you?"

I knew she was right. Time was passing, and I couldn't just sit on my hands.

If only there was some way to avoid choosing and have everything turn out right. But my father had stopped helping out, and the little inheritance my mother had left me had disappeared into school fees, books, rent, and the basic necessities over the last four years. My income was already barely enough to live on.

I had to decide. "Is Scott okay with me using your house?"

"Scott has no idea. Let's be honest: he's not the best at keeping secrets. But you don't need to worry there. He loves you almost as much as I do."

"I'm not sure, Hayley. I appreciate what you're trying to do, but I can't just up and disappear to some island. I have things to do! I can't pause my whole life for this."

"You can!" I saw the pleading in her big, expressive eyes. "You can do whatever you want. You're not chained down. For once, just make it up as you go along. Do something even you didn't dare imagine."

"It's not that easy." I tried to hand the tickets back to Hayley. With a sad smile, she refused. After checking her watch, she stood and said, "I need to go."

"Fine."

"Your plane leaves Monday. Please, think it over. You've got time. If you decide to go, the key to the house is in that envelope along with some useful directions."

"Thanks. I'll consider it."

"Promise me."

"I promise."

We hugged goodbye and swore to stay in touch.

I couldn't fall back to sleep, so I put on some coffee and walked around the house, shooting glances at the envelope on the couch. It was an attractive thought, getting away from it all for a few days. Disappearing somewhere until my head was clear. Without pressure.

Just being gone.

Vanishing.

What a word. It was scary and fascinating at the same time.

But I couldn't.

Or could I? Maybe.

No, it was impossible.

The story of my life.

The door to my grandmother's room was cracked. I looked inside and noticed most of Frances's things were gone: her first editions of classic books, her paintings, the armchair where she used to sit and read by the window...

As I walked in, I turned the key that had locked my heart up tight those last few days so I wouldn't fall to pieces. I felt too much; that was my problem. I experienced everything with an intensity that knocked me over. I had always been that way. I could hardly manage my own emotions. I sank into them, analyzed them without ever managing to understand them, let them drag me around, feeling strong at one moment, vulnerable at another, sometimes resolute, most of the time timid and insecure.

A heart like mine has cracks in it, and they're impossible to seal shut, so whatever I try not to feel still seeps in like water between your fingers.

I opened the closet. Part of it was empty; part of it still had my grandmother's things hanging inside. Sorrow overtook me as I smelled her perfume. I touched the dresses, shirts, and jackets, sank my face into a wool sweater. I took it out and put it on, wrapped my arms around myself and tried to imagine she was hugging me.

Frances had already chosen which things of my grandmother's she wanted to keep. I had to figure out what to do with the rest. The best option was some charity. That's what she would have preferred, but it hurt me to think of getting rid of all that forever. When these things were gone, her scent, her memory would be gone. It would mingle with the air and disappear forever, because a day would come when I wouldn't remember what her hair smelled like anymore, or her skin...

I spent that Sunday shut up in the house, eating chocolate and popcorn and watching old movies. At night I took a hot bath that lasted an hour. I liked the water covering me up, ducking my head under, and holding my breath with my eyes closed, as though I were surrounded by a magic crystal that isolated me from the rest of the world. A slight pressure in my ears, a rushing of blood pumping over the silence.

Later, I got in bed and took my copy of *Anne of Green Gables* out from underneath my pillow. When I was a girl, I always kept it with me wherever I slept. Other people hugged their stuffed animals to feel less alone. I cuddled up with books. It was my most valuable possession, not because it was a first edition from 1908, but because my mother had given it to me as a present on my fifth birthday. It had belonged to her before that, and to my grandmother before that, and a long, long time before, it had been my great-grandmother's. She'd found it at a secondhand shop in Quebec.

I reread it when I was down, and it always brought out the most positive side of me, the side I hadn't managed to find for days.

My mother used to tell me I was like Anne, because I felt everything and I lived as if it were my last day on earth. And I was chatty like her, and full of imagination, and I believed in myself.

Personally, I didn't remember ever being that way.

On Monday, I woke as the first rays of sun were brightening the sky, and the darkness of my room receded into shadows. I made myself a coffee and turned on the computer.

My email inbox was bursting. Ryan, the editor I worked with, had written me every day since I was gone. There was also a message from the department head with information about classes that might be of interest to me and a possible candidate for my thesis advisor. I decided to call him later and thank him personally. It was rare for those classes to have an opening, so I really should sign up and then…

And then…

Nothing.

The thought of going back depressed me.

The thought of staying made me feel guilty.

Because I didn't know what to do with my life.

I shut my laptop. I felt an uncomfortable pricking in my chest. Anxiety.

I grabbed my purse and went outside, trying to dodge the thoughts piling up in my head. I liked walking when I felt unhappy or ill at ease. That alone—walking nonstop—would cool my head, ward off despair, help me to actually think things over.

My steps took me to La Fontaine Park. I loved getting lost on its tree-lined paths, riding a bike on its trails, sunning myself by the lake there. But that morning, I couldn't find the peace I needed.

My phone rang and startled me. After a glance, I put it away. It was Dustin. Ugh. He called back ten minutes later, then two more times over the next half hour. The next time I looked at my phone, I had three voicemails and five text messages. I had to admit he was tenacious, but I was getting sick of him.

I took a winding route home. I was hungry and in the mood for a bagel with butter and marmalade. I loved that. The sweet flavor, the scent of freshly baked bread, all that took me back to those winter afternoons when I'd have hot chocolate at my grandmother's house with my brother and sister. Fairmount was the place with the best bagels, and I was the first in line when they opened.

My phone rang again while I was waiting for the light to change at a crosswalk. I ignored it and took a deep breath when it went silent. *Leave me alone!* was all I could think.

My steps sped up. I was anxious to get home and hide away in a corner. The city I'd always loved was starting to stress me out, and I was surprised to find myself missing my little place in Toronto. I was so absorbed as I walked the last block that I didn't notice Dustin there waiting for me by the door. He came toward me.

Instead of stopping, I sidestepped him, reaching into my bag for my keys as if he weren't even there.

"Harper, we need to talk. This is ridiculous. Your father called me in a rage because he says you won't pick up the phone."

I opened up, went inside, and shut the door in his face.

"What the hell? You're acting like a baby." The wooden door didn't muffle his voice. "Harper? I promised him I'd take you to see him."

I felt myself sinking to the floor and had to catch myself against the wall.

Frances was back, I realized. She looked over at me from the kitchen door.

"What happened to your forehead?"

I touched my bruise. It hadn't looked so bad when I saw it in the mirror, but it hurt like hell.

"Nothing, a little slip. How long has Dustin been here?"

"He got here around an hour ago and hasn't moved. I doubt he'll give up, but if you want me to send him packing…"

I smiled. It was comforting, having her there.

"They aren't going to leave me alone, are they?" She shook her head. I raised my arms, exasperated, and let them fall to my sides. "Why is this so important to Dad? It's a personal issue for him, me getting rid of all this, like he wanted me to cut the last ties I have to Grandma. I know they never got along well, but going to this extreme…?"

Frances looked irritated, or perhaps she knew something she wasn't telling me, but instead of responding, she just groaned.

"What happened between the two of them?" I asked.

"They started fighting when your mother got sick, and they went on doing it until one day they just stopped talking."

"Yeah, but there had to be a reason. Something major, something that would justify all that hate."

In Frances's eyes, I could see the beginnings of a storm, dark, somber, but then it disappeared. She shrugged as if she didn't know or didn't care and as if I shouldn't, either. Then she turned back to the kitchen.

"You want coffee?"

"Please."

I sat down on the sofa. Through the window, I could see the blue of the sky over the roofs of the homes across from us. It was going to be a beautiful, sunny day.

Minutes later, Frances was back with two cups of coffee. She handed me one and sat down next to me as elegantly as a ballerina. Age had made her prettier, if that was possible. She was thin, with high cheekbones and snow-white hair. She could have been anything, a model, an actress, but she'd chosen a calm life by my grandmother's side. Something crunched beneath her, and she hopped up. Pushing the cushion aside, she found the envelope Hayley had given me.

"What's this?"

"A present from my sister."

"Hayley gave you a present?" I nodded. "Why's it hidden under a couch cushion?"

I told her the whole story, even the incident with the coatrack, as we drank our coffee.

"You should go," she said.

"I can't."

"Do you know what you're going to do, then?"

"Not yet," I admitted.

Leaving my coffee on the table in front of us, I noticed the tension in her back and shoulders. It was my fault. She turned to me. "Harper, I'll be leaving soon. And I'll be gone too long to help you with this."

I knew that. I'd been unable to stop thinking about it.

The doorbell rang and my heart stopped a second. I was scared to death. I heard the knocker strike twice afterward.

"Harper, please, open up. You're acting like a child," Dustin shouted from outside.

"Go away."

"I can't. Your father and the real estate agent he recommended are coming here. Please, open the door. We just want the best for you."

The best for me? By forcing me to do something when I didn't know if it was what I wanted?

My pulse was racing, and I whimpered like a child afraid of the dark, like someone shut up in a dark dungeon. Once again, Frances started to say something. But perhaps there was nothing to say.

Then she looked down at the envelope and back at me. And at that instant, I did something I'd have never thought I could do. Without thinking, without weighing the consequences, I made a decision. I closed my eyes and jumped. I felt the emptiness beneath my feet, the fear, but I didn't try to reach out for something to hold onto.

I just held my breath and kept falling.

And I liked it.

That I exist is a perpetual surprise which is life.

—Rabindranath Tagore, *Stray Birds*

6

We Would Be Shadows of Ourselves

The plane landed in Charlottetown at three in the afternoon. According to Hayley's letter, the easiest way to travel would be to get a car there and drive to the coast, where I could catch the ferry that would take me to Petit Prince.

As I left the parking lot headed for Souris, I felt my heart pick up a bit. Until then, I had been so impossibly composed. You could almost say I was numb.

I rolled down the window on my rented Honda Civic to get some fresh air. It was cool and smelled good and made me briefly calm. But soon I was nervous again.

To tell the truth, I was barely aware of what had happened just a few hours before and what repercussions my decision would have. I had packed my suitcase in a matter of minutes and vanished into a taxi, much to Dustin's perplexity. I didn't think twice, and I definitely didn't mull it over. At that moment, I was incapable of dealing with more complications, so I ran away.

After an hour's drive from Charlottetown, I was in Souris, a charming little town of twelve hundred people. The ferry that would take me to Petit Prince didn't leave until six thirty, so I decided to find somewhere near the port where I could eat. I hadn't had a bite since breakfast, and my stomach was growling constantly.

I asked a fisherman cleaning out his traps where to go, and he recommended a nearby restaurant called 21 Breakwater. It was right by the road, a two-story house with a wraparound porch. I ordered a cheesecake and a tea with milk and had them outside.

Someone had left a travel magazine in one of the chairs, and on the cover was the teaser for an article on Prince Edward Island and the Magdalen Islands.

I paged through it as I devoured my cake. I liked how small this island was. You could go from the east side to the west in three hours by car, and you could cross it from north to south in less than an hour. It was practically impossible to get lost. If I could have gotten a hotel, I'd have stayed there instead of taking a ferry for two hours to a tiny island far out in the sea.

I was starting to worry about things. Was there a supermarket on Petit Prince? What about restaurants? A pharmacy? I hadn't left Montreal with anything but clothes and some toiletries, and I had no idea about the place where I was going.

As I walked around the port, I tried to find some information. I punched the name of the island into my phone. Just a dozen links appeared, with no details that would be useful to me. The internet told me what I already knew: there was nothing there.

Brilliant.

A few minutes later, on the deck of the ferry, my willingness to spend a few days on the far edge of the world flagged, and the reality of what I was about to do overcame me. For six years, I'd been so indecisive that I'd been using the same brand of shampoo, even though I didn't like it, just to avoid having to choose another one. The devil you know is better than the one you don't know. After all, in the blink of an eye, everything can go downhill, so why bother helping the process along?

If my thoughts were a reflection of myself, I was pathetic.

The ferry docked in the port sometime after eight thirty. I was the only person who got off.

That wasn't exactly an auspicious beginning.

The orange ball of the sun was descending rapidly, and shadows were falling over the landscape. I started the engine and reread Hayley's instructions. They included a not-very-detailed map that I turned round and round twenty times before finally deciding which part of the island was north. I needed to go south, then turn right at the third crossroads and pass through what looked like a stretch of woods. Once I thought I had that down, I took off, departing the town, or what I thought was the town: just a few streets with buildings scattered around in no particular order.

The moon rose, and a pale light bathed everything. Not enough to see clearly, but enough to guess at the height of the trees, the outline of the hills, and the houses here and there.

I stopped a few times to check the map, comparing the lines on it with the terrain illuminated by my headlights. Nothing I saw matched, and I was starting to get nervous. I was tired, I was hungry again, and to make things worse, clouds had covered the moon and I could barely see.

I kept going in the hopes of seeing a sign somewhere. But after three miles of driving, none had appeared. After four, it was the same story. Then six. Then eight. I didn't even think the island was that big.

I was about to give up when at last I saw some lights in front of me. Finally! Electric lights! Civilization!

"No way!" I shouted.

I recognized the post office and the violet house next to it. I was back where I had started.

I got out, angry with myself, and kicked the back wheel, like it was the car's fault.

Somewhere behind me, I heard music and voices, but then they faded out. I walked in that direction. Past a few houses, I found another street. To my left, I saw a square building with a sloping roof and a wooden sign over the door lit by a bare bulb. It read, simply, EMMA'S PLACE. RESTAURANT.

Inside, I smelled fried fish, and my mouth watered in response. It wasn't a big place, but it was homey. It looked old and musty, untouched for decades. The walls were covered in black-and-white photos, little paintings of ships, and fishing tackle hung up wherever. Decor was clearly not their strong suit.

The people at the tables were talking over music coming from a classic jukebox, and there was a woman behind the bar. She was drying glasses with a rag. I hoped she would notice my presence, but when she didn't, I said, "Hey, excuse me."

She was around my age, maybe a little older or a little younger. Looking not particularly friendly, she responded, "Yes?"

"Could you tell me how to get to Old Bay from here?"

"This isn't a tourist office. We've got food, and we've got drinks. Order something or hit the road."

I couldn't believe it. I guess hospitality wasn't the islanders' strength. I tried to make some witty reply to put her in her place. Something that would piss her off even worse, if that was possible. But nothing occurred to me, and in frustration, I asked, "If I order something, will you tell me how to get there?"

She shrugged and leaned her hands on the bar. I pushed my hair out of my face and smiled tensely.

"A vanilla latte, please."

"Jesus!" She rolled her eyes. "This isn't a Starbucks!" she snapped. "We got coffee, coffee with milk, and raw sugar if you're really feeling frisky."

Where in the hell was I? I started to get up and tell her to go piss up a rope, but before I could open my mouth, a guy appeared beside her carrying two plates of food and dropped them off at the bar. He was wearing a ball cap with a few coppery curls poking out from under it. He looked me up and down and then glanced at the bartender.

"Carlie, take this to table six."

Her eyes were murderous, but she picked up the dishes and did as he said.

I couldn't help but be amused to watch her walk off, cranky and grumbling.

"Your employees here could use some customer-service training. She's terrifying."

He smiled. "She's not my employee, she's my sister."

"Oh. Sorry."

"No worries. She's pissed off because she's being punished. Don't pay her any mind."

I settled down on my barstool, more relaxed now. I wondered how old the guy was, but he had one of those eternally young faces that made it hard to tell, plus a beard.

"So you punished her because she's so charming, or…?"

He shook his head and smiled. "Carlie's going through a tough time and my parents decided it would be good for her to spend some time with me. They live in Dartmouth."

"You mean Dartmouth in Nova Scotia?"

"Yeah."

"What brings you here, then?" I asked with surprise.

"I could ask you the same thing."

I looked down, wondering if I'd offended him, and my ears suddenly felt hot. I'm not usually nosy. I was just curious, and I didn't think such an innocent question would bother him, even if we had just met. I mean, I didn't want to be rude; it was just weird that a guy from the city would wind up behind the bar on an island in the Gulf of St. Lawrence. According to the sign I'd seen next to the church, Petit Prince had six hundred twenty-three inhabitants. And to judge from the customers at the table, the average age must have been around fifty. If you rounded down.

"Someone loaned me a house on the island, and I've come for a couple of days. For vacation, you know."

"Just you?" He sounded a little skeptical.

"Yeah, why do you ask?"

"We get tourists here, but they're usually groups or families. Rarely just one person on their own."

"I'm not a tourist. You could almost call me a resident. It's my sister's house."

"Well, then… It's a pleasure to meet you, neighbor! My name's Ridge, and this is Emma's Place, my home and my business. I doubt there's a better spot on the whole island, if you don't mind me saying. Welcome to Petit Prince!"

He was so enthusiastic that I couldn't help laughing. I shook his hand and nodded with feigned seriousness.

"Glad to meet you, Ridge. My name's Harper, and I hope you can tell me how to get to Old Bay. That's where my home for the week is."

"Old Bay? That's on the other end of the island."

I took the map out of my pocket and smoothed it out on the bar so he could look at it.

"I've got these directions my sister gave me, but I'm not sure if they're right."

"Did you try following them?"

"Yeah, and I went in a gigantic circle and ended up here."

"Well, you were lucky to even be able to do that. This is all wrong. It's not a big island, but that doesn't mean you can't get lost if you don't know it well, especially at night."

YOU AND OTHER NATURAL DISASTERS 79

"Do you have a decent map, then? A real one?"

"I've got something way better. Me."

"You?" I smiled when I realized he was offering to come along. I threw my bag on my shoulder, ready to get up. "Thanks!"

"No problem. But I can't take you until I close up here."

I fell back on my seat. I'd been awake for nineteen hours, and I was tired. Each minute felt like an hour, and for some time now, my pants and shoes had felt like they were cutting off the blood flow to my legs. Not to mention, I badly needed to brush my teeth.

"When's that, then?"

"A couple of hours. During the week, people don't stick around very late. In the meantime, are you hungry? Thirsty?"

I nodded and my mouth started watering. I'd never been so hungry, and the scent of food was so tempting I could hardly think of anything else.

"I saw those dishes you brought out... They looked pretty good."

"Fish and chips, plus mussel sauce. I promise you've never tasted anything better in your life."

"I'll take five," I joked.

He chuckled and looked me in the face, and I saw something in his eyes that made me nervous. You know the story: boy meets girl, boy likes girl... Well, it wasn't that. He looked interested in me, actually *interested*, curious, somehow knowing, as if he could already sense I was running away from something and wanted to know what and why.

He served me a plate overflowing with fish and potatoes topped with an orange sauce with aromatic herbs. The first bite was divine. The second, third, and the rest I swallowed so quickly that I was hardly able to taste them.

When I was done, he gave me a piece of apple pie and a cup of coffee on the house. By then, I was satiated and could take my time with them. I actually didn't need either, but turning them down would have been rude. The pie was delicious. It tasted like real apples, not that gooey brown mush I was used to at the cafeteria at university.

Ridge smiled from the other end of the bar, where he was closing out his last few guests. I smiled back. He was a nice guy, extroverted, and nothing like his sister, who'd been glaring at me the whole time while I tried to ignore her and be empathetic. I guess if someone had forced me out of my city and made me move in with my brother in the middle of nowhere with no better distraction than fishing, I'd probably be that hateful, too.

I closed my eyes. Thinking that, I suddenly felt that my situation wasn't that different from Carlie's. I mean, there were differences, obviously—big ones—but in the end, it was the same thing: she was there because she'd been pushed to go, and so was I.

I smiled at her when she came over to clear my dishes. I wanted to be nice. I thought that would make her act nice, too. But instead she lifted an eyebrow and frowned. "Sucking up to me won't make my brother sleep with you. You're not his type."

I sat up straight as a ramrod. So much for friendliness. She was a bitch. I was about to tell her where she could stick her attitude, but Ridge beat me to the punch.

"Carlie, what the hell is up with you? Are you trying to scare off all my customers?"

"If it gets me off this goddamn island…" she replied, walking off.

Ridge pinched the bridge of his nose as if he had a headache and looked at me apologetically. "I'm sorry. I don't know what to do with her." With a humorless smile, he asked, "Any advice?"

"A pair of cement boots and a bottomless pit?"

He laughed. "Don't tempt me," he replied as he pulled off his apron. "We can go now."

I got into the car and started the engine, and a few seconds later,

Ridge pulled up next to me in an SUV and gestured for me to follow him.

It was desolate on those narrow roads leading out of the center of town, and just as silent as it was dark. I started to ask myself what Hayley and Scott had seen in that no-man's-land that had made them want to buy a house there. Ridge's left blinker started flashing, and he turned soon afterward. After a couple more yards, he stopped. I braked next to him and managed to make out the outline of a house against the sky.

"Here it is," Ridge said, getting out.

"Are you sure?"

"There are just three other houses in Old Bay, and I know the owners of those. They're islanders, and they've all been here forever. So this is the only one it can be."

I tried to glimpse some detail that might remind me of the few photos I'd seen of the place, but I only remembered them vaguely.

A trail led around the house to the front door, which looked out onto the sea. With one foot on the first step, I drew a tense breath, gripping the key tight. Ridge had left his truck running with the high beams on so I could see, and he'd told me he'd come in with me just to make sure everything was all right.

The lights didn't work.

Ridge told me to wait as he walked inside, using the flashlight on his phone to light the way to the fuse box. A few minutes later, I could hear a slight hum in the walls, and the overhead bulbs turned on. I blinked a few times until my eyes got used to it.

The walls were white, a contrast to the burnished caramel brown of the doors and window frames. What few furnishings there were had a solid and robust appearance and were honey-yellow to match the brass of the fireplace with its protective glass pane. A few paintings added color to the room, as did the upholstery of the sofa and chairs and the cushions and curtains. It was simple but pretty. I liked it.

Ridge smiled as he reappeared. "You've got electricity and water now. And I wrote my number on the chalkboard in the kitchen in case you need anything."

"Thanks, but you don't have to…"

"Everyone here knows everyone else. And you can never predict when you might have an emergency or need help. Besides, your nearest neighbor is a mile away south."

He didn't need to say more to convince me. A strange feeling of apprehension brought me to a shiver. I had been living alone, sleeping alone for years, but I'd always been surrounded by people right next door. Solitude was relative in a big city. Here it was real and intimidating, and it felt eerie.

"Thanks."

"Of course. Well, it's getting to be that time when I need to go home before Carlie steals a boat and rows off. Are you good here?"

I looked around and nodded, trying to appear convinced. "Yeah, I'm fine."

I followed him out and heard something that frightened me again. Ridge had left his radio on, and a shrill voice was giving what seemed like a meteorological report. Ridge turned the volume up, looking worried.

"*The approaching storm will be one of the strongest in years, my friends, with constant winds of up to sixty miles per hour and occasional gusts up to ninety. We can expect rain and hail, so those of you who haven't covered your gardens should try to, and fishermen should bring in their traps and stay indoors. Don't worry, the crabs and lobsters won't go anywhere. Remember, this could drag on for several days, so people should make sure they have enough food, water, and whatever else they need. The rain will start Wednesday on the northern coast and will continue southward in the hours afterward. We are urging maximum caution…"* Now another voice took over: *"Well, you heard the man. Thanks, Terry, for looking after us, and we look forward to you keeping us up to date. This is Kevin Brooks at Petit Prince Radio. Have a good night."*

Suddenly my throat felt dry. "What storm is he talking about?"

"They've been going on about it for days. The atmospheric temperature dropped rapidly for the season and the ocean's still warm. High pressure in one place, low pressure in the other…"

I closed my eyes and tried to organize my thoughts. I knew how storms worked and what caused them; that wasn't what I meant. I shook my head, unable to accept that a storm would hit as soon as I'd reached the island.

"This morning while I was at the airport waiting for my flight, I looked at the weather for the week and it was supposed to be fine, just one little storm north of the Magdalen Islands that was due to bypass us to the northwest."

"Yep. Well, it looks like they got it wrong."

"How could they get it wrong? It was a national meteorological service report. They have all kinds of equipment at their disposal. You think this Terry knows more than them? Where did he study?"

"Terry? I doubt he even went to high school, but he's got lots of experience and a funny knack for knowing these things."

"Instinct? He just told everyone to take cover, like a Category 4 hurricane was about to strike."

Ridge tried not to laugh, and that bothered me. This was no joke, and I wasn't sure how serious the situation was.

"Listen, I've been living here for three years, and the first thing I learned was to pay attention to the locals when they tell you what the weather's going to be. They're rarely wrong. They may not have fancy equipment or satellites, but they have experience, and they know how it was in the past. I'd be willing to bet that storm's coming on Wednesday, and we'd better be prepared."

He sounded so convinced I had to nod and ask myself what the hell I was going to do. I was born under a cloud, and all I could think was that this was just the beginning of something much, much worse. The domino effect had been one of the guiding principles of my life, and once the first piece fell, others tended to follow.

I imagined all the possibilities: a leaky roof, the house lying directly in the flood path, me getting appendicitis in the eye of the hurricane… I brought a hand to my chest and leaned against the car.

Ridge could probably tell what I was thinking. He came up next to me, not close enough to make me uncomfortable, but not so far away that I felt alone. That told me a lot about him—above all, that he was a good person.

"Can I ask you something personal?"

"I guess so." I shrugged.

"What are you doing here?"

"Wow! Are you always this direct?"

"I don't want to get into your personal business, but I look at you, and…you're a city girl. You don't belong here."

I concentrated on the house, all brightness and shadow under the headlights. "I have to make a big decision, and my sister thought I could find the peace I needed to do it here."

He nodded, seeming to understand, and I almost asked him for advice. Maybe he was right; maybe it didn't make any sense for me to be here.

"Is it important, this decision?"

"Very." I could tell he was curious, but he didn't inquire further, so I decided it was my turn. "Was it easy for you to leave Dartmouth and come here?"

He crossed his arms.

"Coming here was easy. The hard thing was deciding whether or not to stay." Responding to my look of confusion, he smiled and turned his head toward the sky. "I came with a group of climate activists. We stayed for two weeks, we organized with the Climate Action Network, and…I just ended up falling in love with the island and the people here. Lots of people leave for the mainland. It's only a few who come here and stay."

"Does your family mind you wanting to be here?"

"They didn't get it at first. I left behind a good job, my studies, a great girl, and now what have I got? An old bar with a bunch of surly customers." He laughed and shook his head. "My father eventually understood, but he never misses a chance to tell me I'm ruining my future. My mother's still so mad at me that she barely talks to me."

"And yet here you are, taking care of your sister."

"I'm more like her prison warden. Carlie was running with a rough crowd, hanging out in bad places, and here that's not an option. She spends all day angry and hating everyone, but at night, she sleeps safe in her bed. That's all that matters now. And it's one thing my parents and I can agree on."

"So you did what you wanted, even though everyone was against it. Weren't you scared of losing them?"

"Not if I lost them because I was living the way I wanted to live. I mean… People have lots of defects, and one of them is telling everyone else what they should do, and how, and when, and where. I can't stand people trying to get mixed up in my life when I never asked anyone's opinion."

"Still, what if that *anyone* matters to you?"

"I don't care if *anyone* means my parents, my friends, my girl-friends." He straightened up and tucked his hands into his pockets. "Can I tell you something?" I nodded, concentrating on him and his words. "No one will ever live your life for you. And if you don't, then what do you have?"

I reflected on his words, trying to savor them in my mind. "Nothing, I guess…"

"Exactly. Nothing. And you can't make your mark, live your life, with nothing."

His words touched me deeply. Ridge was an interesting guy, and what he said reminded me of a paragraph I'd written the last time I tried to start a novel. That had been a strange moment in my life, but now it made sense. I had thought those words were just nonsense, a momentary inspiration, but they were the answer to a question I hadn't let myself formulate. And without realizing it, I'd held on to them in my private collection of thoughts.

"*We would be shadows of ourselves. Empty shells others have filled with their desires. Sad beings without motivation. Entities walking wherever others push us. Tempus fugit.*" I recited these words exactly as I'd written them.

Ridge grunted in reluctant acknowledgment. "I prefer carpe diem, seize the day, enjoy yourself. Dum vivimus, vivamus."

I giggled, pleasantly surprised and timid at the notion that I was sharing such private sentiments with a stranger. And yet, it didn't feel that way. It felt like we had been friends our whole lives.

After a moment's pause, Ridge said, "I hope you find what you came here looking for, Harper."

"So do I."

I looked at the house apprehensively. He bumped shoulders with me. "You sure you'll be okay?"

"Yeah. I think so."

He nodded and stroked his beard.

"Listen, I've got a couple of rooms I rent to tourists. If you need one…if you don't want to be here when the storm hits…just call me."

"Thanks, Ridge. I'll keep that in mind."

7

Where the World Ends

"Everything started with a woman who wanted to put her life in order." If my adventure in that part of the world had been a novel, it would have begun with those words.

When I awoke, the sun was coming through the half-drawn curtains and leaving little quivering circles of light on the ceiling. The light penetrated every corner of the room, so bright and white that for a few moments, it blinded me. Blinking, I checked the time on my cell phone and was surprised to see it was after nine.

I jumped out of bed, feeling rested for the first time in ages. I opened a window, and fresh air shook the curtains. A blue jay flew just a few inches in front of my face and scared a yelp out of me.

Just beyond the porch was an explosion of color: a blanket of green grass, a beach of reddish sand, a blue sea with shimmers like diamonds. The sky was a softer blue, the scattered clouds were white, and the entire scene left me speechless. It was stunning!

I couldn't wait to go closer.

I dressed in blue shorts and a gray T-shirt and pulled my hair back into a ponytail. I was worried about what I'd find on the island—not the landscape, the air, or the neighbors, but rather what I'd find inside myself when there was nothing outside me telling me what I should be or forcing me in any direction.

It was time to be honest with myself.

To be me, just me.

But my enthusiasm waned when I found the empty pantry and fridge. There was nothing in the cabinets, not even a can of soup. I would have eaten anything just then. So I changed my list of priorities, moving saving myself from starvation to the top. When I went outside, the salty air struck me in the face, and I heard the loud sound of breaking waves as droplets of foam touched my lips and cheeks.

The house was prettier than in the pictures, with its cedar shingles so dark they were almost black. The rest of it was of a yellowish wood, except for the white pine of the gables, the windows, the columns, and the stair rail.

Now I knew why Scott had fallen in love with the place despite its seclusion, and why it had meant so much to my sister. It looked torn from a fairy tale and plopped down there. It was magic, perfect.

I took a few turns in the car, some wrong, and managed to make it to town. I parked in front of Ridge's bar and opened the door. The air inside smelled of rich coffee, bacon, cinnamon and sugar. During the day, with natural light coming in, the bar wasn't as fusty as it had seemed the night before, and I realized my mood had colored my first impressions. In fact, the place was clean, well lit, even pretty by island standards. I guess the word that would best describe it is *authentic*.

Ridge came out of the kitchen and waved when he saw me. I smiled back at him as I approached the bar.

"Hey! I see you found your way back."

"Not without difficulties, but yeah, here I am."

"Did you sleep well?"

I nodded. "Yeah. It was hard to get used to the silence at first, but I was so tired that I crashed almost immediately." Only now did I notice how handsome and dreamy his eyes were. "You think you could fix me some breakfast?"

"Sure, what would you like?"

"I don't know. What have you got? Never mind," I said before he could respond. "Just surprise me."

"Sure. Take your pick of the tables. It'll be out soon."

I sat next to a window with a view of the port. The boats and ships moored there shook with the breeze, now softer, now harder. Clouds were crossing the sky, mingling, leaving behind white strips as they broke apart.

I was scared of the storm that was coming. If it was really about to strike the island, I'd need to buy lots of stuff: water, food, a flashlight, batteries, candles. Or maybe just a ticket for the next ferry to PEI, where I could change the date on my airplane ticket and go back home.

"There you go."

Ridge set down a plate of eggs and bacon, toast, and sauteed mushrooms. He'd sprinkled something on them that smelled delicious. I thanked him and bit into a strip of bacon as he sat down across from me. I closed my eyes and inhaled deeply.

"This is delicious!"

Ridge smiled, somewhat startled. "Thanks. You can have seconds if you like. On the house. I think you're the most enthusiastic customer I've ever had."

I smiled and kept chewing. I like to eat, and even though I've never had a talent for cooking myself, I can tell when someone else does, and he did.

"Who's Emma?" I asked. "This is called Emma's Place, right?"

"Yeah. She's the old owner. When I decided to stay here, the first thing I did was look for a job. Emma lived by herself on the island.

Her whole family had moved to Quebec, and she was starting to feel the years and wasn't keen on running the place on her own. She hired me for three months on a trial basis and then signed the place over to me."

"Just like that?"

"Yeah, it surprised me, too. I tried to pay her, and she threatened to break the deal, so I shut my trap."

"Smart."

"Emma's still on the island, though. I always ask about her family and when she's going to join them, and she always says next spring or next summer, and she's been saying that for three years now."

I stopped chewing and asked, "Are you sure she has family? That it's really that she *doesn't want* to go?"

"Yeah, they've come here a few times trying to take her back with them, but it's impossible. You know what? You might end up meeting her. She comes around often to give me a hard time."

I laughed and had to cover my mouth to keep from spitting out my breakfast.

Ridge didn't seem in a rush to get back to work, and he told me more about his life. He'd studied marine biology at Dalhousie University, specializing in marine mammals and habitat preservation.

During his last year, he was invited by a group of ecologists to take part in a program about climate change in the arctic tundra and its impact on the oceans. Seeing the risks of deglaciation firsthand made him realize this was his calling, and after graduation he committed to the struggle against global warming.

He felt guilty about leaving his girlfriend behind, but even though it took him a long time to get over her, he eventually realized he'd made the right decision. Through the distance, his perspective on their relationship changed, and he finally had to admit it had never worked between them. They were different. They had different dreams.

Three years ago, soon after his twenty-fifth birthday, his life changed again. He fell completely in love with Petit Prince and its inhabitants. And now he was happy. Sometimes—not often, but sometimes—he felt a little lonely. But he didn't regret a thing. He hadn't given up, and he'd wound up where he wanted to be.

I finished my eggs and toast, enchanted by the way Ridge's eyes lit up as he told me about the islanders and their life there. He said there were no supermarkets on Petit Prince, just a few shops owned by families or individual residents where you could find almost anything you needed. There was a pharmacy, a post office, and even a bank with an ATM, which must have been a major step forward, given how enthusiastic he seemed about it.

I had the feeling I had stepped back to a previous era, that I might be accused of witchcraft if I pulled out my cell phone.

As Ridge told me about his neighbors, spicing his story up with a bit of gossip, he served me more coffee along with some oatmeal and cranberry cookies he had baked himself.

He was so nice that it seemed almost false. And he was handsome—not cute, but handsome. Every time he smiled at me, his charm hit me like a warm wave. But then I'd cross eyes with Carlie. As she wiped off the tables, the look on her face told me she might die of boredom at any second.

By the time I left, I knew practically everything there was to know about the place.

I felt less worried about being far from civilization. In the daylight, the place looked very different. I saw big green fields, houses painted in bright colors—green, yellow, red, white, gray, blue… Unpaved roads twisted off in every direction.

My cheeks were hurting from so much smiling. I didn't remember the last time I had smiled for so long.

I still wasn't quite oriented, and as I drove away, I tried to memorize every crossing and building. I soon found the main road, the only one that was paved and the only one that led to the port. Ridge had told me it passed through the center of town, and most of the businesses bordered it.

There was a little shop with a wooden sign nailed to a post in front and a parking lot to the right where I stopped.

When I pushed the glass door, I heard some bells ring. The air inside smelled of smoked fish and cheese. The owner had an inviting expression as she sat behind the counter talking to two of her customers about the storm. Soon a chorus of voices was wishing me a good morning. I smiled at their warmth and their peculiar accent. It was funny, the way one island was so different from another. The people on this one had their own special tone.

I grabbed one of the baskets stacked by the door and paced past the shelves of beans, canned goods, soaps and cleaning products, pet food, newspapers, and magazines, filling up on anything I thought I might need. I continued toward the cash register, where I saw a little display of chocolates. That's my second addiction, right after coffee. I grabbed a couple of bars, and five minutes later, I was traveling back to Old Bay.

I put everything away and inspected the house more closely, discovering that there was a pair of double doors in the back leading to a small garage where I could park my rental car. I had been worried about it getting damaged if the storm was as bad as everyone said.

There was dust everywhere, and the garage smelled of damp. There was a gas-powered generator back there, and a couple of cans of fuel—of course there would be! A bike was hanging on one wall: yellow, old, with a wicker basket on the handlebars. With nothing better to do, I took it down, thinking I might go for a ride. But when I got it down, I abandoned the idea because the chain was broken.

I went inside, and the feeling of boredom was soon eating at me.

No one ever told me how hard it is to do nothing. And I mean nothing at all. I had free time. I wasn't in a rush. And I was used to running around everywhere: from home to school, from school to work, with an endless flood of jobs, classes, exams...

I entertained myself putting candles all over the house, each with its own matchbook next to it. I had also bought a flashlight and batteries, which I left in a drawer in the kitchen. I eyed the wood-burning stove, wondering if that was going to be something I needed to figure out. Then I went upstairs and unpacked my suitcase.

Hayley had left some clothes in the closet: long-sleeved shirts, a knit sweater. If it got cold, I'd have something to wear. I'd only packed summer clothes.

I made a sandwich and ate it standing up in front of the window in the living room. On the table next to me, my cell phone beeped. It was running out of battery. I plugged it in and stared at it, wanting to check my messages and missed calls, but I forced myself not to. I was on vacation!

Vacation!

I tried to hold on to that idea and to remind myself why I was there.

Come on, Harper. Get it together! You've only got a week to decide what to do with the rest of your life.

8

Mermaids' Tears

Maybe it was because I was there and not somewhere else.

Maybe because it was too late to run away.

Maybe because deep down, I hoped to find the answer I was looking for. Because I'd heard a million times that life was unpredictable, that everything changes when you least expect it, and I wanted to believe that was good. So I stopped running away from it.

You can't escape what you are unless you try to pretend you're someone else.

Maybe I'd spent too much time pretending.

I opened my eyes and looked at the ocean. A cool, soft breeze, smelling of algae, caressed my skin. I could taste the salt in the air on my tongue. I walked to the shore, opening my senses to the space around me. Soon, colors, sounds, and aromas enveloped me. It was as if I were looking at the world for the first time. And I loved what I saw. An isolated, untamed part of the planet.

I walked for a long while. The soft sand of the beach gathered in undulating dunes that led to a cliff of bloodred rock. I climbed to the top and looked down, panting. Below me was an endless pebble beach. Stretching as far as the eye could see, it was lashed by foam-capped waves.

A gust of wind knocked me backwards. In the north, the after-noon sky had turned gray. The beach was empty except for a house that looked tiny in the distance and a few surfers in their neoprene outfits. I jogged down a path to the shore.

The water bubbled as it rose around my feet. It was chilly but bracing as I waded through it. I found a shiny red stone among the pebbles. I bent down to pick it up and it twinkled in my fingers under the sunlight. It looked like glass.

"Nice job. You don't usually find them that big."

I shouted in surprise and looked up to find a woman grinning at me. Where the hell had she come from?

"Sorry if I scared you," she said.

"No problem, I just didn't see you coming," I said, standing up straight.

The first thing I noticed about her was her dark hair with coppery tones, which fell to her waist. Her skin was slightly tanned, her eyes turquoise green. She was pretty in her baggy white dress, which was thin and gave a view of her body. I couldn't say exactly how old she was. Her face was girlish, timeless, despite her crow's-feet.

Ethereal, I thought as I looked at her, bewitched.

She pointed to my hand.

"What are you going to do with it? It's perfect."

I looked at the pebble, not understanding what she meant. "What am I supposed to do with it?"

She seemed surprised at my question. "Oh, when I saw you, I thought you… You don't know what it is?"

"A stone?" I guessed.

The amused gleam in her eyes only confused me further. "It's a mermaid's tear," she responded.

A what? Did she mean a mermaid-mermaid, like a woman with a fish's tail and a crab for a best friend? Look, I've got an open mind.

You never know, after all. I believed in the tooth fairy until I was eleven, and I'm ashamed to admit I still gaze longingly at the fireplace when Christmas comes. Who am I to judge anyone for what they do or don't believe?

"A mermaid's tear? You mean like…a real mermaid?" I asked, feigning indifference.

She laughed a sweet, musical, throaty laugh. Her accent was French, not the usual accent of the French Canadians or the islanders. Hers was much softer.

"No, dear. People have different names for them: mermaids' tears, sea crystals… They're actually just bits of glass thrown up by the ocean. My name's Adele, by the way."

"Nice to meet you. I'm Harper."

"Nice to meet you as well, Harper. I haven't seen you around here."

There was kindness, but also caution in her approach.

"It's the first time I've been to the island. I got here yesterday on the last ferry. The, uh…the yellow house in Old Bay belongs to my sister."

She nodded, and her shoulders relaxed. I don't know why, but my answer had relieved her.

"Yes, I know it. It's a beautiful place. My friend Molly used to be the owner. She inherited it from her parents and turned it into a cute little bed-and-breakfast, but then she got sick and had to put it on the market. Poor Molly. She left us not long ago."

"I'm so sorry."

"Yes, it was a major blow for all of us who knew her. She's the one who taught me how to look for mermaids' tears."

I smiled awkwardly, unsure what else to say, thinking maybe our conversation was at an end, but she continued to study me with no apparent thought of going anywhere.

"Why do they call them that?" I asked to break the silence.

"There's a legend behind it…"

A gust of wind hit, blowing up sand around us, and I blinked to keep it from getting in my eyes. Another, more violent one followed, and the waves rolled in up to our calves. When they broke, the sound was deafening, and I noticed the white and gray clouds rushing across the sky. The weather was getting worse.

"Are you in the mood for a tea? I live in the blue house on the cliff. It's close by. And it's been forever since Sid and I had anyone over. It would be nice to talk with an outsider for a while."

"Who's Sid?" I asked, surprised at the invitation.

"My husband."

I didn't think it was a good idea. I knew nothing about that woman or her husband. Think of all the stories that begin with an innocent invitation and end with a girl chained up in a basement. Okay, sometimes my imagination gets the better of me. But it was getting windy. *I should probably go back home before it gets worse and I can't*, I thought. But then the image of that empty, lonely house with no distractions depressed me.

"It would be a pleasure to have tea with you," I responded.

Adele's house was deep blue with white window frames, two stories, with an attic and a dark slate roof. From outside, it was hard to tell how bright and spacious it was inside. I followed her to the kitchen and sat at the table while she put a kettle on the stove and brought out two antique-looking cups from a cabinet. On the counter was a jar of butter cookies. She served a half dozen of them on a plate.

Outside, over the roar of the wind, I heard a rhythmic pounding, as if someone were cutting firewood or maybe felling trees. Inside, I heard the ticking of a clock. Adele, I realized, didn't mind long silences the way some people did. As for me, they made me nervous.

When I was with other people, I felt I simply had to fill the air for reasons even I didn't really understand, and when I had nothing interesting to say, that only made it worse. Often, my mouth kept moving even when my mind told it to close. I could feel this about to happen again as I started to tell her how pretty her house was, but she cut me off with a mysterious expression on her face.

"Legend has it that mermaids are born with the power to control nature. They can change the ocean's currents or the direction of the wind. They can even provoke storms. But Neptune, the god of the sea, forbade their doing it. One cold, tragic night, a horrible tempest was unleashed, and a ship traveling the ocean found itself in the midst of a hurricane. The captain and his loyal sailors fought the wind and waves for hours to stay afloat. He remained at the wheel, and not even the tearing of the sails or the creaking of the masts broke his nerves. Finally, a powerful wave struck and he lost his balance and fell into the sea."

She paused when the kettle started to whistle, taking it off the stove and pouring the boiling water into two cups with tea bags. When she sat back down in front of me, she put two lumps of sugar into hers. Then she continued. "A mermaid had been watching the captain from the distance, admiring his strength and courage. Never before had she seen a man so daring, and she fell in love with him without realizing it. When she saw him struggling not to drown, she felt forced to break Neptune's rule, and she calmed the wind and the waves, allowing the captain to make it back to his vessel safely."

I was enraptured by her tale and the sound of her voice, and a strange feeling that I had seen Adele before grew in me as I listened.

She continued, "Neptune found out what the mermaid had done. Angry, he exiled her to the furthest depths of the ocean, never allowing her to surface again. She accepted her punishment and swam far away from the captain who had stolen her heart, crying endlessly in despair, eaten up by sorrow. And ever since that day, her glimmering glass tears wash up on the shore as an eternal reminder of her love."

She stirred her tea elegantly, with a smirk. Once again, I told myself there was something familiar about her.

"What a beautiful story. It's so sad though!"

"I got so angry the first time I heard it. I thought it was so unfair what happened to the poor mermaid, and that she didn't rebel or fight back. But later I came to realize there are times when love just doesn't have a future, and you have to make sacrifices, and those sacrifices are another form that love takes. We think if you love someone crazily, that's enough to overcome all obstacles, but it isn't like that. Sometimes, painful as that is to admit, there's just nothing you can do. The mermaid and the captain didn't even belong to the same worlds. There was no future there. She knew that. But still, she sacrificed herself for him."

"And the man never knew she existed or how much she had done for him," I whispered. Then I took a sip of tea, thinking about what all that had meant. "Why are we women so stupid? We fall in love and turn into idiots. It's like 'Okay, goodbye, brain!'"

Adele observed me from behind her long black lashes. "I sense some resentment behind those words, and I must say, you're very young to be talking that way."

I shrugged. "You're never too young to have your heart broken."

"That's true."

There was warmth in Adele's curiosity, and I wondered if she saw the same things in me that I saw when I looked in the mirror. I was like an eggshell, cracked, empty, but I longed to be full of something, and not just neediness. I worried she'd end up asking me about that broken heart, and I hurriedly changed the subject, setting my crystal on the table. "So this is just a piece of glass?"

"That's right. Before plastic was invented, almost every container people used was made of glass: bottles, plates, glasses, jugs, lamps. And lots of those things wound up in the ocean. Not to mention all the ships that sank at different times with their cargo of alcohol. Just think of all the bottles of beer, whiskey, and gin that ended up down there… The sea currents break them into little pieces and slowly polish them. One like yours"—she pointed at the table—"might take thirty or forty years to get to that shape and wind up on the shore. Some of them are centuries old."

"That's incredible!"

"Yeah. They can be very valuable, depending on the color. The gray ones, or pink or red. They're getting harder to find, too. There are fewer and fewer of them left. What washes up on the beach now is mostly plastic."

"What do people want with them?"

"They collect them, make jewelry out of them, decorative objects, all kinds of things."

"So that's why you asked me what I was thinking of doing with it," I said, picking it up and rubbing it between my fingers.

"That's right."

"How do you know so much about all this?"

She winked and stood. "Come here, I'll show you something."

I followed her through the house to an open door on the second floor. When I walked into the room, what I saw took my breath away. It was full of jars of sea glass in every color imaginable. In the center of the room was a square table with tools, glue, wire, a tiny anvil, a magnifying glass, and boxes with tiny compartments with even more bits of glass inside, organized by size. An unfinished piece was on another table under a window, and there was a glass case with finished jewelry: rings, pendants, bracelets…

"You do all this?" I asked, unable to believe it.

She blushed. I could tell she was proud of what she did. And she was right to be. Every object I saw in there was a work of art. On the table I found a nearly finished bracelet. The silver bezel holding the crystal was minutely shaped to match its form. She smelted and molded the metal herself. I couldn't hide my admiration.

"You're a true artist!"

She tried to wave me off. "I'm an artisan at best. But I do enjoy my work." Then her face lit up. "He's the artist."

I turned around and found a man covered in sawdust and wood shavings who was looking at me with curiosity. He must have been well over six feet tall, and his shoulders were nearly as broad as the doorframe. His hair was black and straight and shimmered under the bandanna tied around his head.

"Honey, this is Harper. We met on the beach, and I invited her up for a tea."

"Hi," I said, a little reserved.

"Happy to meet you. I'm Sid, Adele's husband."

He offered me his hand, and I shook it.

"Sid's a sculptor. He carves wood. His creations are the real artworks in this house."

Sid laughed.

"I'm the more modest of the two of us," he said.

Adele's expression showed feigned irritation, but it was evident that she loved him deeply. Their back-and-forth went on for a few minutes and ended in a kiss that I looked away from to give them their privacy. Sid said a pleasant goodbye and went to make a coffee for himself before returning to work.

"I adore that man." Adele sighed.

"You make a wonderful couple."

She tried to shrug off my remark, but admitted she felt incredibly fortunate to be with him, and also that he'd been a hard man to win over. That seemed strange, because Adele's personality was irresistible. She was a good storyteller, and as she walked through the room chatting away, I found myself more and more enchanted with her.

I looked at the photos hanging on the wall, some of which showed a much younger Sid. He was a member of the Mohawk nation, as evidenced by the flag he was waving in one of the snapshots. There was a long history of the Mohawk people fighting for their rights to the land they had tended for time immemorial.

I stopped in front of another black-and-white photo, peeking closely, with the persistent sense that I knew her from somewhere. And then I remembered, and yelped with surprise. It was her! My goodness, that teenager posing with a César Award was her!

My heart was racing as I turned around, and I hoped I wouldn't faint.

"You're Adele LaCroix!" I exclaimed, hardly able to speak. "I loved your movies when I was a girl. I loved-loved-loved them! I loved you!"

"Thank you!"

"I saw your first movie when I was nine, and right away you became my favorite actress. I bought every magazine you were ever in."

"How sweet of you."

"Jeez, I know I'm acting like a lunatic, but I can't help it! It's you!" I shook my hands in the air. "I cried so much in that movie where you became an orphan… It meant so much to me back then."

"That was my favorite."

"Mine too! I just admire you so much. I even wrote you a letter. Did you get it? I mean, I'm sure you didn't. Why would I even think such a thing… You must have gotten millions of them." Please, God, shut me up. Make my mouth stop moving. "I swear I'm a normal person. It's just that…it's you! I'm sorry, I promise I'll be quiet now."

Adele burst out laughing.

My legs were shaking. My whole body was. I tried and failed to suppress a nervous giggle. I couldn't stop looking at her. I was in the same room as my girlhood idol, I was in her house, I'd even had tea with her.

OMG!

She watched me patiently, with a pleasant look on her face, while I grew increasingly embarrassed by my childish response. Taking a deep breath, I tried to act like an adult who wasn't dying to get her autograph.

"I hope you don't mind the question, but why did you stop making movies? You utterly disappeared."

She sat on a stool and seemed to size me up, as if not sure whether it was worth it to respond. Finally, she motioned for me to sit down beside her. I almost ran over as she began: "I just lost interest in it. I mean, it's more complicated than that. My mother was an actress, my father was a director, and everyone just took it for granted that I'd follow in their footsteps, but with time, it stopped making me happy and turned into something almost mechanical, thoughtless. I was acting, but there was no passion in it, you know? So I quit. This wasn't the life I wanted; it was the one the people around me wanted for me. And that wasn't fair."

"Did your friends and family support you?"

"Not at first. They thought the glamour life was all there was, and couldn't understand how a person might want anything else. They were worried about the press and what people would say about me. In the end, it's all about sensationalism and how many newspapers they can sell, and no one cares if what they write is actually true."

"Yeah, I remember the headlines," I said softly.

"They published horrible things, stories about airplane crashes, rehabilitation clinics, unwanted pregnancies… I just tried to laugh it off. What else could I do?"

"How'd you wind up here, then?"

Her facial muscles relaxed.

"Some scenes in my last movie were filmed here. And I fell in love with the place, the people. I met Sid. He's the most wonderful man in the world."

"Was it love at first sight?"

The question made her blush a little.

"For me, it was. I had never seen a man as…impressive as him."

"And you stuck around to be with him? I think my heart's going to explode!"

She rested a hand on mine. I was so surprised by the gesture, I flinched. When she noticed this, Adele squeezed tightly.

"I'm sorry to disillusion you, but it wasn't quite like that. Nothing happened that time. It couldn't yet, and I knew that. The filming ended, and I went back to Paris, back to my life, the debut, the parties. But I realized that wasn't me, and all I could think about was how I'd felt here. Happy. Free… Like myself. Three months later, I came back to stay."

"What a story!"

"It's not a story, it's my life," she responded, content. Then she stood and walked a few steps, as if she couldn't be still for too long. "So what about you?" she asked. "Where's home for you?"

Before I could tell her, a shutter struck the window, frightening me. The wind's whistle was almost deafening. I waited a few seconds for my pulse to slow back down.

What had she asked me? Oh, right!

"I live in a rented apartment in Toronto, but I'm from Montreal."

"That's far from the island. Are you here for vacation?"

"No. I mean, sort of. It's a long story."

She could sense the worry in my voice, and she leaned her head to one side before saying, "I love long stories."

I shrugged.

"The fact is, this trip was sort of out of the blue. I should be back home, taking care of things at my internship and getting ready for the upcoming semester, but my grandmother died not long ago, and since then, it's like the whole world has stopped. Everything's falling apart." I paused to take a breath of air. "She brought me up, and…"

Adele's once cheerful demeanor changed all at once, and she grabbed both my hands. "I'm so sorry, Harper. I know what it means to lose a loved one."

"I miss her so much."

"Of course you do, dear." She wiped away a tear I hadn't been able to suppress. "Come on, let's go sit in the living room where we'll be more comfortable."

I followed her to a yellow sofa in the middle of the room facing a fireplace. I sat next to her, feeling abashed that I'd fallen into the same old trap of giving explanations no one had asked me for, personal details I wasn't sure anyone wanted to hear. I was always justifying myself, and I hated myself for doing it. I hated that constant need for approval.

Keeping my trap shut, that was the simplest, easiest way to avoid others' judgments. But for some reason, I had never learned how to do it.

"Sorry I asked. I didn't want to upset you."

Her soft voice was comforting. I cleared my throat before responding.

"Don't apologize. You're being so sweet. You barely know me and you opened your home to me. Besides, I asked you first. It's only normal that you do the same."

"Yeah, but don't feel forced, Harper. You only have to tell me what you want. But if you do feel like talking, I'm not a bad listener."

Adele seemed genuinely worried, and I smiled, trying to ease her mind. I told her in broad strokes about my situation. Something told me she understood, and I started to feel she could see who I really was, and this feeling grew the more I confessed to her.

"I need to make an important decision, and I'm hoping to find the answer I need here. That's it in a nutshell."

As she thought over what I'd said, I brought a hand to my chest, nervous. I'd heard what I thought was thunder far off, and clouds were starting to cast shadows over the light flooding through the windows.

"I hope you find your answer, too, Harper. I wish I could give you some good advice, but I'm someone who made a lot of mistakes before I managed to make the right decision."

"How did you know it was the right one, though?"

"Because it made me happy. It was as easy as that."

"I'm scared, Adele. I'm scared of being wrong."

"Dear, we're all scared of making mistakes. I am, still, because even the right decision may not be the most sensible one, and just because it's right for now doesn't mean it always will be in the future. It may only make you happy in that moment. And maybe that's enough, but still, it's normal to worry about that. Fear is natural—it keeps you on your toes, it pushes you to struggle, to survive. The problem is when fear turns into panic. Panic attacks the fragile parts of you. It can smell them out like a predator, and it eats you up inside because it knows you're weak and can't fight back. And it's easy to just let life drag you along, but if you get caught in the current, you might drown."

What she was saying made sense, and that weakness she spoke of, that current, was something I could feel in myself. That panic was paralyzing me. It had been there forever, like a worm inside an apple. From the outside, the apple looks perfect, but when you cut it open, you can see it's full of holes and starting to rot.

I wanted to cry, but instead I tried to put on a happy face. I rebelled against my sorrow, stopped slumping over, raised my chin up as if defying my own insecurities. They wouldn't get the best of me. Not this time.

9

And That Hurts

Something occurred to me as I said goodbye to Adele: things pile up and pile up, and eventually something tips the scale. Even the most trivial things weigh something. And when you feel the balance shift, it can change the whole course of your life. On that island, I could tell the balance was starting to shift.

I was taking a turn, and all around me were signs that fate or some higher power or who knows what was trying to tell me something. That fascinated me, but it was also an enigma. Since arriving in Petit Prince, I'd met two people who had given everything up for a new start there. They'd left behind a secure, comfortable, and stable life where they were just puppets, letting others pull the strings, because they'd wanted to follow their dreams and truly be happy. And that's what happiness is: a possibility that exists but that not everyone achieves—only those who accept the risk, no matter how far away their dream might seem. Because a dream that doesn't involve sacrifices isn't a real dream.

And I needed to find out what my dream was. That's why I was here. To find what it was that made my heart beat strongest.

I needed to start being who I really was. I needed to stop wasting my life trying to live up to the image others had of me; to know what I wanted, where it was and how to achieve it, and go for it.

Harper, don't be scared to start over, Adele had told me when she hugged me.

All right, then.

The air smelled of rain—that was my favorite scent—and it felt charged with electricity. A dark mass had covered the sky. I walked faster. The wind was howling and blowing sand into my hair, my eyes, my clothes. All around me was ocean, gray and foamy, whispering to me of the storm to come. The pebble beach had virtually vanished underwater. There was just a narrow stone path along the steep wall of the cliff.

For a few seconds, I thought I'd gotten lost. I didn't recognize the sinuous dunes that stretched out before me. They changed, rose up, and vanished before my eyes, shaped by the violent winds.

A gust brought salty sea spray up into my face. I looked at the sky, the coal-dark clouds, the glow of lightning. One bolt followed another, and a few seconds later, thunder reverberated in my head.

The first raindrops hit my hands and face. Soon afterward, the storm began in earnest. I took off running as fast as I could in my strappy sandals. A curtain of water devoured the remaining light. Every definite shape around me started to blur, as though fading into darkness.

At last, I saw my house, vague on the horizon. By the time I reached the porch, I was out of breath and my lungs were on fire. I wiped my damp hair back from my forehead and entered.

I was shivering nonstop, and my teeth were chattering. I ran to the bathroom and tore off my soaked, sandy clothes. From the coast, the wind struck the walls mercilessly. I could hear the crack of thunder and see the glow from the lightning crossing the sky. If this apocalypse was just the beginning of the storm, I didn't want to imagine what was coming next.

I filled the tub with hot water and exhaled as I submerged myself.

Slowly my body warmed up, and I played with the soap foam rising around me, thinking about Adele and what a coincidence it had been that I had met her. It was almost like a dream, and for a moment, I wasn't sure if it had been real.

But of course it had been! And I hoped I would see her again before I left.

I stayed soaking a long time, until the skin on my fingers and toes started to wrinkle. Then I put on underwear and an old T-shirt and went down to the kitchen for a sandwich and an herb tea. I ate by the windowsill to watch the storm, feeling safe behind the double-glazed windows. Knowing my sister, they must have been her idea.

I felt maudlin when I thought of her and how I missed her, and I picked up my phone to give her a ring. But because of the damn storm, I didn't have service!

An hour later, I was lying in bed, looking at the ceiling, nervous as I listened to the moaning and howling of the night outside. The rain struck the roof like drops of lead, so hard you could hear it echo in the walls. A few times, the lamp on the nightstand flickered. Then it went out and darkness filled the room.

I curled up under the blanket, hugging my book. I never went anywhere without it. In a situation like this, Anne would have invented one of her crazy stories, facing her fear and loneliness with the help of knights and princesses, shouting her head off to frighten whatever creature was lurking in the shadows and hurling lightning bolts that made the bedroom sparkle with blue.

Marilla would shout from the kitchen for her to quiet down, telling her that was no way for a lady to act, and Matthew would rush to her defense, amused at her imagination.

I closed my eyes and imagined I was six again. Six-year-old Harper, with Mother, not Marilla, coming to kiss me good night.

But the worst of imagining things is that the time comes when you have to stop, and that hurts. And I did hurt as I fell asleep.

A noise awakened me. I opened my eyes, startled, certain there was someone downstairs. I reached for the light switch and clicked it over and over, but nothing happened. Then I tried to grab my phone, but I remembered I'd left it in the living room.

When I think about it now, I don't know where I found the courage to get out of bed, but I did. On the dresser was a pair of wooden candlesticks. I grabbed the biggest one and held it like a baseball bat. Then I tiptoed down the stairs, trying not to make noise.

However closely I listened, I could hear nothing over the noise outside. For a moment, I told myself I was imagining things. It wouldn't be the first time my mind had played tricks on me.

Only when I was about to go back to the bedroom did I hear a thud and the voice of someone cursing.

I froze.

My legs went weak. Still, with the candlestick tight in my grasp, I kept walking downward. I didn't know what I'd find, and I could hear my pulse pounding, but I knew I had just two options. One: Catch the intruder off guard and whack him on the head. Second, probably wiser: Reach the door and take off running. I could do it, I thought.

On the bottom step, I heard a whisper. It was coming from the basement, I was certain of it. A flash of lightning brightened the ground floor, and for a moment afterward, I saw gleams and shadows dancing on the walls. Then the thunder came, so loud it drowned out my frightened cry.

The door was just a few feet away now. I gathered my courage, even as a little voice inside me told me I was just hearing things. I knew this was the perfect setting for a panic attack, and those vague sounds whose origin I couldn't identify could easily be inside my head.

I kept walking. I was covered in sweat, and my toes almost slipped across the wooden floor.

I heard heavy steps hurrying up from the basement, and my hair stood on end as I realized my ears hadn't deceived me. Someone was there, and they were right behind me. I looked at the door in desperation. It now seemed miles away.

I jumped just as the intruder entered the room. Instinctively, I raised the candlestick and brought it down as I screamed. It slipped from my hands and struck the wall.

"What the hell?" a hoarse, threatening voice shouted.

I screamed again, and the figure took a step back. Another lightning bolt lit up the room, and I managed to make out the man staring at me, his face surprised and confused. For a moment, I was speechless.

"You?" I shouted when my voice returned.

"You?" he hissed.

"Sometimes fate is like a small sandstorm that keeps changing directions. You change direction but the sandstorm chases you. You turn again, but the storm adjusts. Over and over you play this out, like some ominous dance with death just before dawn. Why? Because this storm isn't something that blew in from far away, something that has nothing to do with you. This storm is you... But one thing is certain. When you come out of the storm you won't be the same person who walked in. That's what this storm's all about."

—Haruki Murakami, *Kafka on the Shore*

10

You Broke My Heart

I was about to explode, with no idea when or how I would get over the fright. For a fraction of a second, I had seen myself dying at the hands of some psychopath. The police taking away my body. The headlines telling how I'd tried to defend myself with a wooden candlestick. Pathetic! My funeral full of strangers murmuring the usual clichés: *How sad! She was so young! She had her whole life ahead of her! If only she'd had better aim!*

I breathed in and out, trying to control the adrenaline that was shutting down my body. I pinched my arm, wondering if I was hallucinating. That was the only explanation.

Probably I had caught a cold from running so long in the rain. And now I had a fever, and I was actually still in bed, suffering an out-of-body experience, on the verge of death. That would explain why I was seeing *him*—that loose end I needed to tie up.

Good Lord, thanks to him, I was trapped between the world of the living and the dead! Or perhaps I'd died and gone to Hell, because if that happened, I had no doubt he would be there.

I blinked, and when I recovered, I stared daggers into him. Him. Trey Holt.

"What are you doing here?"

As if emerging from a trance, he responded, "The real question is what are you doing here?"

"This is my sister's house, and she lent it to me for a few days. What about you?"

"None of your business."

"Excuse me?"

He picked the candlestick up off the floor and weighed it in his hand. "Were you going to hit me with this?"

"You should be grateful I missed," I murmured.

"You couldn't hit the broad side of a barn," he said, not even trying to hide his amusement. My blood was boiling, and it occurred to me that I still had time to hit him with something else, like maybe the table lamp there to my left. The temptation was enormous. I pointed to the door.

"Beat it."

"I'm not going anywhere."

"You have to! I got here first, and there's no way I'm going to stay here under the same roof as you."

He pointed at the window. "Have you seen how hard it's coming down out there?"

As if to strengthen his argument, the rain started pounding even harder, and lightning brightened the room. His clothing was soaked, and there was a puddle forming at his feet. His hair was stuck to his head, and he had to push it out of his face. A part of me softened, seeing him shivering there, but I remained firm. He didn't deserve anything more than that.

"You think I care about that? You can sleep in your car. I'm assuming you brought it with you?"

Through his dark lashes, his eyes were icy as he clenched his jaw. Without a word, he turned toward the door. I smiled, thinking I'd gotten what I wanted, but instead, he picked up his suitcases and headed toward the stairs. I had to stand back to keep from being run down, and I turned to him, my jaw hitting the floor.

"This is a hijacking, Trey! This house is already occupied! By me!"

He replied sarcastically, "Occupied! You mean hijacked! I don't know if you've noticed this, but I have a key. Given to me by Scott, for your information." He lifted his hands. A tiny metal key ring hung from one of his fingers. "Scott, maybe you've heard of him, is the owner, and in case you forgot, he's my friend, too." He continued upstairs and, when he got there, shouted over his shoulder, "Don't get all excited. You being here is the last thing I wanted, too."

I rolled my eyes. "Well, at least we agree on something. But since I got here first…"

With a snort, he shot back, "I'm not going anywhere, but feel free to kick and scream all you want. Just try to keep it at a reasonable volume. I'm tired and I need some sleep."

At that, he slammed the door and vanished, muttering curses and probably even worse. I did the same on my way to my bedroom before getting into bed. Then, realizing I'd let him off easy, I got up, opened the door, and slammed it shut a second time.

That was more like it.

Still gripping the knob, I leaned my forehead against the wood and closed my eyes. I didn't want to think. If I did, this craziness would make me lose my mind.

I got back in bed and massaged my temples. And I felt my forehead, just in case I did have a fever, but it was cool.

I couldn't believe this was really happening.

I woke, hoping the night before had just been a dream. But the sounds coming from the ground floor dispelled my illusions like a needle popping a balloon.

I grunted and got out of bed with determination. I needed answers: how, why, for how long... The problem was, I couldn't stand to be in the same room as Trey, and that was going to cause problems for any conversation we might have.

I thought of myself as an adult, someone mature enough to deal with whoever. I knew how to adapt, how to find the best way to talk to everyone as an individual. But with him, I went back to being an eighteen-year-old. It was as if I was anchored in that time, as if I were a girl and not a woman and hadn't learned a thing in the intervening years.

I mean, I'm not sure about that—I was as insecure as ever, that's what this whole story's about—but you all know what I mean.

It was still storming all over the island, and the wind and rain were striking the windows. The sound made me nervous. When I looked out, I saw a curtain of water concealing everything and strips of fog obscuring the trees and hills.

I'm not sure how long I stood there watching the water bead and drip down the glass until I finally admitted I was hiding and that shutting myself up in that room forever was ridiculous. I put on a strappy dress that hung to my ankles and threw one of my sister's sweaters over my shoulders. The temperature had dropped, and the radiators weren't working. I tried to turn on the lights. Nothing. What else could go wrong?

I cleaned up and brushed my hair, looking in the bathroom mirror. Then I stood there as the reality hit me: the last ten years of my life could be summed up with reference to one person. And that person was under the same roof with me now. Ten years of loving him and then hating him. And I still hated him. I had gotten so good at hating him that it was an art.

It took all the courage I had to go downstairs.

I found Trey in the kitchen, barefoot, in dark jeans and a ratty gray sweatshirt. His hair was sticking out every which way, as though he'd just crawled out of bed.

He looked up when I entered, and for a moment, we stared at each other. Then we made a point of ignoring each other. I walked over to the tap and poured myself a glass of water, drinking it in tiny sips. I watched from the corner of my eye as he fired up the woodstove. I was relieved that at least we could cook and even boil water for a bath if things got really bad.

He put on a pot of water and grabbed the instant coffee from the cabinet. My instant coffee. Without thinking, like a spoiled little girl, I said, "That coffee's mine. You can't use it without my permission."

"That coffee isn't yours, it's mine."

"I don't think so. I bought it yesterday in the center of town."

Bitterly, he responded, "What a coincidence…so did I!" And he turned around, dumping two spoonfuls of it into the water.

When I smelled coffee, I nearly closed my eyes from pure ecstasy.

"Seriously. I get that I'll have to put up with you while you're here, but hands off my stuff!"

I noticed the tension in his shoulders. He reached out, opened a second cabinet, took out a second jar of coffee, and set it rudely on the table. It was exactly as it had been when I bought it the morning before. His things were in the next cabinet over. He must have put them there when he got in at night. That explained the noises that woke me.

But I couldn't say I was sorry, so I turned around and hurried out, sitting on the sofa, unsure of what to do. Outside, the storm was raging mercilessly, but it was nothing compared to the hurricane inside me. I was frustrated. I wanted to go home.

I closed my eyes and concentrated on the plinking sound coming from the roof. Then I heard a thud. Slowly, I opened my eyes and saw Trey walking up the stairs. On the table, he'd left a steaming cup of coffee.

Now I felt guilty.

The hours passed with agonizing slowness. There was no thought of going out, and inside, there wasn't much to do. I had fled Montreal so quickly that I had forgotten to bring anything to read—just *Anne of Green Gables*.

I tried to satisfy myself with the one book I did have, but I knew every word on every page and could even recite them in my mind, so I closed it and left it on the table.

Trey never showed himself again that morning. Only at midday did he come out to get some lunch. Whenever he appeared, I scurried off to the furthest corner of the house. We played this cat-and-mouse game all afternoon, not even bothering to try to be cordial. When night fell, our cold war had turned glacial.

After dinner, I lay down in bed and covered myself with the comforter. The temperature kept dropping. It was hard for me to believe it was late August. My head was starting to hurt, I felt something drilling into my brain, and finally I went down to the living room to get an aspirin from my purse.

Trey was kneeling in front of the fireplace. He'd lit a fire, and I could just feel the heat from where I stood. The flames glowed orange on his face, drawing out shadows and making him look slightly cruel. He turned his head to the side. There was something deep and firm in his stare. I held his eyes for a moment, but then I weakened and gave up.

I was nervous as I crossed the room to the chair where my purse stood. I felt around for the pill bottle and went to the kitchen for a glass of water. On the way back, I tried to pretend he wasn't there, buttoning up my sweater, shivering. I was freezing.

"Harper, this is ridiculous."

I stopped on the first step and turned around. Trey was looking at me with an expectant, almost anxious expression as he rubbed his chin and stood. His presence took up so much of the room that I felt I could hardly breathe.

"We're acting like children. You obviously have a problem with me, and I don't like the situation we're in any more than you do. But this is how it is, okay? We're going to be stuck here until the storm lifts, and it's up to us not to turn the hours we have left into a living hell."

I hated to admit it, but he was right. "So what do you suggest?"

"I don't know. Let's at least try to pretend we don't want to kill each other every second of every day. You avoiding me like I have a contagious disease kind of gets to me, if I'm honest."

"You're doing the same."

"Dammit, of course I'm…" He stopped himself. I guess he was trying to calm down. "You're right. But look, it's cold and we still don't have power, so why don't you stay here by the fire and we'll try to act civilized?"

He sounded sincere, so I replied in a whisper, "Sure."

Trey sat on the sofa, and I settled down as far as I could from him and watched the fire. As the minutes passed, my mood fluctuated between tension and anger. This was, without a doubt, the most uncomfortable situation I'd been in for as long as I could remember. The fire was crackling. Trey was shaking his leg nervously. Each second that passed was like an eternity. At last he sprang up and said, "I'm in the mood for a tea. You want one?"

Before I could respond, he'd vanished into the kitchen. A few minutes later, he was back and setting two cups down on the table. I shivered with disgust as he fell back on the sofa. It was one thing to put up with us sharing the same space. It was another to have tea with him like we were the best of friends, when I had to bite my tongue not to scream at him like a banshee. "I don't want any tea."

"Don't drink it, then."

My thoughts were a raging river, and the air was thick with tension. This was no good for either of us, so I decided to break the silence. "Are you staying here for long?"

He looked at me askance. I didn't think he was going to respond, but then he shrugged.

"It all depends on how long it takes."

"On how long what takes?"

"We're planning an addition. Scott wants to renovate the house. But he doesn't have the blueprints—apparently the only ones that exist are at the government offices on the island here—and I need them. We also need to check the state of the foundation and the retaining walls to see if the project is viable."

"If that's true…"

"Are you calling me a liar?"

"All I'm saying is, if that was true, Hayley would have said something to me. The idea was that I would get some alone time here."

At that moment, briefly, I saw interest in his face, a desire to talk that he immediately snuffed out.

"Your sister knows nothing about this," he said. "It's supposed to be a birthday surprise for her."

I tried not to smile. My brother-in-law was the most adorable guy on the planet. I brought my feet up under me on the sofa and hugged my knees.

"I didn't know you did home renovations," I said.

"I don't. It's a personal favor."

"Sure."

Nothing we'd said those past few minutes had eased my nerves. Having him there made me relive everything I'd felt for him, good and bad, with intense clarity. It was as if all those feelings had been lying dormant, waiting for their moment to come out. He turned, and I saw the flames dancing in his eyes.

"What are you doing here?" he asked.

"Vacation."

He looked skeptical. "You've picked a hell of a time for it."

"The storm caught me off guard. No one told me the end of the world was this week."

He nodded in agreement, as though to tell me he hadn't seen this coming, either. He leaned back and sipped his tea. It must have gotten cold by now. I did the same, just to busy my hands with something, and because if I looked down into my cup, then I'd stop looking at him, and I'd stop trying to remember what that short beard felt like rubbing against my skin.

I hated being so weak.

He spit his tea into the fireplace.

"Ugh. That tastes like cat piss."

"You seem pretty certain about what cat piss tastes like." A giggle escaped me, and his look of repulsion changed to one of amusement. But then I remembered I wasn't supposed to like him, and I froze. This got his attention, and he seemed to be sizing me up. I felt the room grow smaller and smaller the longer he did so.

"You're nothing like the nice little girl I remember."

"Maybe because I'm not a little girl," I replied belligerently.

"Or nice, it seems."

I stared at him, defiant, as though daring him to say something else.

And he did. "That's enough! Just spit it out!" I looked away, not wanting him to see how this outburst had affected me. "Are you this stupid with everyone, or just with me? Because if it's just with me, I think I have a right to know why." He pointed at me. "And if you tell me I already know what the problem is, I swear I'll…"

"You'll what?" I got up, ready to return to my room, but he jumped between me and the stairway.

"Don't even think about it. You're not running away this time."

"Move, Trey."

"No."

"Let me by."

"Not until you tell me what's up with you."

I turned around. I couldn't deal with this. My heart ached and he was acting like nothing had ever happened between us, trying to force out of me answers he already had.

That made me angry. Very angry.

I love a good dramatic scene in a book, but in real life, there's nothing worse. And yet there we were, giving a marquee performance.

"What's up with me? What's up with me is that you…you…"

"I…"

"You're…"

"Jesus, just spit it out."

"You're an idiot! I used to think you were a puzzle, but I've got you figured out, and I should have from the first time I met you. You're selfish, heartless, a dickhead. And you're an awful person for pretending nothing happened between us. You take advantage of people without thinking about how you might hurt them; you pretend your little games don't have consequences. You don't care about anyone or anything, just yourself. You use people. And you're cruel."

"Harper…"

I couldn't stop myself. "You used me. You were mean to me. And it hurt, because I thought I mattered to you. There was a time when I really believed that. Then you threw me aside like I was a wadded-up napkin. You pushed me out of that room and out of your life, and you didn't even blink. You hurt me, and I'll never forgive you. Never. Understand?"

My words were ruthless and bitter, and they remained floating in the air around us after I'd said them. Trey was frustrated. I could tell there was a storm brewing inside him, and feelings I couldn't really guess at. He seemed to have been looking back in time, and suddenly, he understood.

"Are you talking about that morning in the dorm room where I was living with Hoyt? About when I asked you to leave?" His voice was thin, surprised. And I didn't like it one bit.

"You didn't ask, you yelled at me to get out!"

"That's why you're acting this way with me?"

I didn't reply. I just scowled. He brought his hands to his head and sat on the bottom step, looking humiliated and incredulous. "That's why you've been treating me like a cockroach?"

"You are a cockroach."

"My God, Harper, of course I told you to go. I had woken up with the worst hangover in human history, and the first thing I saw was you standing there naked in my room. I was out of it. All I could think about was Hoyt tearing my head off if he found you there. Try to understand that. You're his little sister!"

I couldn't stand to hear another word. I turned around, but he stopped me.

"You were just a girl! I shouldn't even have been looking at you! I'm sorry if I was curt or if I said something rude. I wasn't thinking; I just reacted. But you have to understand that I couldn't let your brother find us like that. I can't imagine what he would have thought."

I tried to get past him, and again, he stopped me. I could see the tension in his shoulders and the doubts in his face. I laughed sarcastically, hoping it would keep me from crying and giving my feelings away. "So that's your justification? There were a thousand different ways you could have let me know, and you picked the absolute worst one because that's what was easiest for you. At no moment did you think of me." My legs started shaking. "If we'd gotten caught, I–I... Look, I'd never have let Hoyt figure out what had happened between us. Never. But you didn't care what I felt. What we did simply didn't matter to you."

Trey blinked, confused. "What we did?"

"It meant so much to me, and you throwing me out after what we shared was humiliating, absolutely humiliating. It destroyed me."

"Wait a minute. Did you say something about Hoyt catching us? And what do you mean by *what we did*? We didn't *do* anything, Harper."

I wrapped my arms around myself to keep from falling apart. My feelings and I needed some space. "I know. I know it was nothing to you. But to me, it was. It mattered. And you broke my heart."

I saw a muscle twitching in his neck. "Harper, what the hell are you talking about?"

"Trey, are you fucking with me?"

"No!"

"Are you really implying that you don't remember?"

"Remember what?"

"I can't believe you're such a bastard that you'd pretend. You're an adult. An adult is someone who takes responsibility for their actions. It won't kill you to admit you acted like a dog. I'm over it now anyway."

At last, I managed to make my way into the stairwell.

"Harper, I swear on my life I don't know what you're talking about. All I remember is getting up that morning. I don't know how else to tell you that."

The despair in his voice was so intense that it made me pause. I turned around to look him in the face. He was about to cry. And I felt even more apprehensive than before.

"Please," he said, "you're starting to scare me. What happened between us?"

"You really are serious."

"Yes, dammit, yes! The last thing I remember about the night before is my grandfather calling to tell me my mom had died of a heart attack. I felt like the worst son in the world. I was a coward, a jerk, someone incapable of facing my problems, so I got drunk to keep from thinking and I smoked Preston's entire stash of weed. After that, everything's a black hole."

I knew he was telling the truth, and this realization threw the whole world off its axis. I had no idea his mother had died. I hadn't even known she'd existed for him. As long as I'd known him, he'd lived with his dad, and he'd never mentioned any other family members.

"I'm not lying to you, Harper."

I believed him. So I told him the truth. "We slept together that night, Trey."

"Come on, that's not funny."

"I'm not kidding."

"No. That can't be true."

"It is. We slept together. That's why I was in your room with no clothes on." I stopped trying to hold back the tears. "It was my first time."

A nightmare gathered around me as Trey took in my response. I had no idea what he was thinking. I had never seen anyone's expression change so quickly, from bitterness to sorrow to shame…

So I waited. I waited for him to face up to the challenge my words presented. I watched him try to put the pieces together, struggling to remember but unable to. Endless emotions tussled on his face as he tried to find reasons not to believe me.

But he couldn't. He did believe me. I could tell. And now he was lost. My words had been a spark. And now there was a fire burning inside him.

He couldn't even look at me as he walked out the front door. Before I could react, he disappeared into the darkness, into the storm.

11

Not the Memories. Not the Desire.

With the passing of time, I learned that life is just a sequence of moments. Just that. Some mean nothing, others change everything. Life is unpredictable, and the fact that we were both there just then showed it. It was a mere coincidence, but it wound up becoming a turning point.

I stood there staring, trying to process what had just happened. My thoughts changed color, shape, tenor. I had imagined that conversation taking place many different ways, in many different places, but the reality had been utterly unexpected.

I had built four years of my life around something that had never existed. I'd put up a wall of resentment and disappointment, adding bricks to it day after day. Calling it a misunderstanding was too trivial, because part of who I was now was because of what happened that morning in Trey's room. A buildup of circumstances that had led to disaster.

There was no way to get distance, a perspective on his reality and mine. They were so mixed up that it was impossible to say where one began and the other ended. But there was a crack, and feelings were seeping through it, feelings I'd been carrying around for years and that were getting heavier with each passing day.

Feelings I didn't know how to deal with.

Didn't know how to face.

And that I couldn't just keep bottled up.

He'd left the door open, and the wind was blowing in the rain. I hurried over to shut it. I looked out the window, consumed by worry. Where the hell did he think he was going in that weather?

So many hours passed that I lost track of time. My nerves kept getting more frayed. This situation was ridiculous. I had come to that house to find myself, and now I felt more lost than ever.

I buttoned up my sweater and listened to the crackle of the dying fire before going to the kitchen for more candles. When I returned, Trey was in the doorway, wet and shaking. The shadows under his eyes were so dark, I couldn't see the bright amber glow of his irises. I crossed my arms, first relieved that he'd made it back, then angry that he'd left in the first place.

"Have you lost your mind? How could you do such a thing in this weather? Where the hell were you?" I shouted.

"I'm sorry."

"You had me worried!"

"I'm sorry."

"You already said that."

"I'm so…"

I almost smiled. Almost.

The floor creaked as I walked over to him. My mind was still occupied with the bad memories, which were clear as day and all too real. Even learning the truth hadn't made them go away. I took a deep breath. I didn't want the emotions bubbling up under my facade of calm to betray me.

"Come here, you need to dry off or you'll catch pneumonia."

I took his hand and forced him to follow me to the fireplace. He kneeled down while I went upstairs for towels. I went into his room for dry clothes, too. He needed them. On the bed, I found pants and a shirt.

Downstairs, he was trying to warm up in front of the fire. I crouched down beside him, uncomfortable in the silence, wanting some kind of reaction on his part.

"Here, let's take this off," I whispered, sliding my fingers under his T-shirt and pulling it over his head.

He hesitated for a moment, then let me. With the wet fabric tossed aside, I couldn't help but notice his tanned skin, the firmness of every inch of his torso, his beautiful hands with those long, masculine fingers. Touching him was a warm pleasure, and I instantly regretted how quickly he'd broken down my barriers.

I dried his hair with the towel as best I could, then ran it over his neck, his shoulders, his stomach. Then I stopped. He was watching me, and his breath was speeding up.

It was hard for me to look back at him, but I did. I even tried to smile, timidly.

"Maybe you should do the rest. I'll turn around while you take off your pants and put these dry clothes on."

I stood and walked away, feeling an unwanted warmth in my chest. Memories of the first and only time I'd touched him tugged at my heart. Our secret caresses. It was all I could think about just then.

"Done."

Finally.

I turned around. The space between us seemed blocked by all the things we couldn't say. There was a fragility in his expression, and something that hinted at feverish thoughts. He shook his head, kicked his damp clothes aside, and sat on the sofa, sinking his head in his hands.

"I'm sorry you lost your mother," I said.

"Thanks."

"I didn't know she… I mean, I never heard you mention her, and…"

"I can't talk about that, sorry." He cut me off gently.

They should make maps of people so you don't get lost in them. Each person should be born with an instruction manual that tells other people how to deal with them. Everything would be much easier that way.

"Where'd you go?" I asked.

"For a walk."

"A walk?"

"You dropped a bomb on me, okay? And I…" He leaned back and pursed his lips. "I don't know how to take it, Harper. And when I don't know how to deal with something, I turn distant."

He squinted and bit his lip, and I sensed he was on the verge of giggling.

"What's so funny? I can't believe you're laughing at a time like this."

"I can promise you, I find this situation anything but funny… Still, though. You've spent four years hating me, and here you are worried about me."

Whatever. He'd caught me. My heart was foolish. I was foolish. And I could turn on a dime. I sat down next to him to be closer to the fire. The wood was smoldering. Soon there would be nothing but embers.

"I'm not a bad person. And you didn't even know what happened that night."

"Don't try and justify what I did." He cut me off.

"Fine. You're a douchebag, and for all I care, you can go outside and stand there till a lightning bolt splits you in half. Feel better now?"

He chuckled and I turned away to keep from letting his eyes hypnotize me. No matter how many times I'd reproached him in my mind, no matter how thin the line was between love and hate, no matter how many times I'd jumped back and forth over it, torn between attraction and contempt, I couldn't help what I was feeling now. I laughed along with him.

"I need you to tell me," he said, gazing at me intently.

"What?"

"What happened that night. Everything."

I nodded, even though what I was thinking was *no*.

I had never talked about that with anyone. I had kept it to myself like a humiliating secret, and it was so shameful that just the memory of it brought blood into my cheeks. For some stupid reason, I'd convinced myself that if I just ignored it, if I never shared it with anyone, it would disappear, and it would be like it never happened.

But it didn't.

I never managed to leave it behind.

Not the memories.

Not the desire.

For him.

October 31. Halloween. Four years earlier.

The news had opened up a hole inside me. He was going to America. MIT had let him into its architecture program, and he hadn't hesitated to say yes to finishing his degree there. I wasn't happy for him. I couldn't be. It meant that for the next three years, there would be hundreds of miles between us.

I wouldn't see him anymore, even if I hadn't seen him often before then, and the thought of it killed me. Those brief moments when we crossed paths had meant everything to me.

I was a girl and I acted like it: dramatic, silly, immature. I couldn't accept an unrequited love. I was as invisible to him as all the girls he slept with. Even more. And they had gotten something I could only dream of: knowing what his lips tasted like. Even knowing he'd gotten around didn't stop me from hoping pathetically that something would happen between us one day, too.

And one day he noticed me.

One day, he actually looked at me.

That day, I would be brave, for both of us.

That day, I would become his entire world.

That day ended up being a catastrophe.

Hoyt and Scott had organized a farewell gathering for Trey in their dorm in Vancouver. It would take place on October 31, three days before his departure, and that would be my one chance to see him. I used all my savings to buy a plane ticket.

Once my morning classes were over, I caught a plane to Vancouver. Hoyt was waiting for me at the airport. When I arrived, we went straight to his place.

I was excited, but also nervous. I'd never been to a college party before. I'd never been to any party since I'd turned eighteen. Really, this was my first party, period, because I'd never been the kind of popular girl with friends who got invited to everything. More like the opposite.

So maybe, just maybe, my expectations were too high.

And that made my downfall hurt that much more.

I didn't usually wear makeup apart from a little mascara and lipstick, and even that was just once in a while. But that night, I did myself up. Eye shadow, blush, lip liner, everything to accentuate the sexy angel costume I'd bought that morning at a shop in Queen West. At first, I worried it was excessive. Maybe a little too provocative. But that was what I was going for, wasn't it? To get Trey's attention. And to do that, I needed to look like the grown woman I thought I was.

I smiled when I saw myself in the mirror. My thin white dress gripped my body and showed off what I might flatteringly call my curves. I donned the little wings and tried to gather my courage. I was getting more and more nervous with each minute that passed.

I walked outside and down the stairs, clutching the handrail tightly. Some guys were gawking at me. That helped my confidence a bit. One of them walked over to the bottom step and looked up. He didn't have time to say hi, though, because my brother came up behind him and pushed him out of the way.

"What the hell are you wearing?"

"A costume."

"That's not a costume. That's… You look like a model from one of those…you know, that shop with the chicks in their underwear. The, uh, dammit…"

"Victoria's Secret?" I guessed, trying to help with his confusion.

"Yeah, that one. Now go upstairs and change."

"No can do," I replied.

"You're my little sister, and I'm not going to let all those animals see you like this."

"By 'those animals,' I presume you mean your friends? Do they know what you think of them?"

"Harper," Hoyt hissed.

"Hoyt," I said back, not blinking.

"What's going on?"

I tensed up as I heard his voice, and when our eyes met, my knees trembled.

"Hey, Harper."

"Hey, Trey," I whispered, cheeks burning.

He was dressed as Peter Pan. And he was adorable.

"Say something, dude! Tell her she can't go dressed like that with all the morons that are going to be there," my brother ordered him.

Trey looked me up and down with an impassive expression, and

I felt disappointment spread through my body. I don't know what I expected, but it wasn't indifference.

"Don't be a jerk. Let the girl be. Everyone knows she's your sister. Nobody's going to dare bother her," he said.

That word stuck in my chest like a sharpened dagger. *Girl.* I hated it. It sounded so patronizing, so disrespectful, so… I wished I could turn invisible just then.

My brother wasn't convinced, but he finally agreed, and soon he'd walked off, following a brown-haired girl in a pink bikini with a mouse tail pinned to her rear end. Apparently he couldn't focus on two things at once.

"Have fun. I'll be here if you need anything," Trey said before turning toward a fairy in a push-up bra who came over with two glasses, handing him one just before they took off.

As for me, I stood alone in a corner watching everyone drink, dance, and hook up.

Luckily, Hayley and Scott showed up not long afterward and rescued me from that increasingly uncomfortable situation. I knew some of their friends, and I was able to have fun with them without it turning into an effort.

A few hours later, the party was at its peak. The room was full of people, bodies twisting under the faint light to the rhythm of music that sounded like a bombardment. I caught sight of Trey dancing with a girl in a nurse costume who seemed determined to give him a thorough physical examination. She was stunning, and I felt insignificant alongside her. Really, there was no one there I could compete with.

But he looked away from her, and our eyes met. There was something in his expression I couldn't put a finger on. I turned around, ashamed that he'd caught me staring, and tried to focus on the people there around me. But I couldn't follow the thread of the conversation. My mind kept turning back to one thing. Him.

I regretted being there, regretted being stubborn, regretted my absurd determination to cross the country just to be at that party. Sure, I wanted to see him one last time, but the price was too high, and I could only stand to suffer so much.

Had I really believed he'd notice me?

I tried to ignore him the rest of the night, but I couldn't. Every time I heard his voice, his laugh, or saw him dance, I turned.

Unrequited love is a disease that has no cure, and the only treatment is disappointment. Waking from the dream, realizing it wasn't as beautiful as you'd imagined.

But Trey would never disappoint me.

He'd never get the chance to.

I wouldn't let him.

Or so I thought.

It was late when I found him walking out of the bathroom, stumbling, glassy-eyed. After years of observation, I knew instantly something was wrong. He hurried upstairs and even pushed aside a friend who tried to tell him something.

I don't know what made me follow him and knock at his door. I don't know what made me go inside when he shouted that he wanted to be left alone. I don't know what made me shut the door when he looked up from his bed. But what I do know is what I felt when I looked back.

"Hey," I whispered.

His disgusted expression softened. "Are you okay? Do you need me to find Hoyt?"

"No. I just saw you come up here, and…I wanted to make sure you were all right. Are you?"

I leaned against the doorframe, aware that he was watching me.

He sighed and tried to force a smile. "I'm fine. Thanks for caring."

I knew he was lying. His face was a kaleidoscope of emotions, none of them good.

"Sure. I guess I should go back downstairs."

"No worries."

I grabbed the knob. And inside I felt a tingle, as I always did when I heard his voice or saw his face or his perfect smile. There was a string that united us, and I felt it tense, making it impossible to separate.

In the middle of these chaotic thoughts, I heard him ask me, "Are you having fun? At the party, I mean. It's different from high school, right?"

"Sure," I said over my shoulder. "It's not bad. But I'm getting tired, and if I hear five more minutes of techno, I think I'm going to lose it. My ears are killing me."

He laughed, sounding more lively now.

"I know how you feel." After a pause, he continued. "You can stay here and hang out with me for a while if you like."

Without thinking, I replied, "Sure."

He waved me over, and I walked slowly to the bed, sitting timidly on the very edge. I looked around at his things: his shelves full of books and comics, the flat-screen TV on his dresser, the video-game console and cartridges. There were drawing materials and a speaker playing music on his desk. Everything was clean and orderly, everything smelled good—citrusy, but also masculine. Next to the closet were suitcases and boxes, reminding me that he was leaving in a few days. The thought of it was painful to me, and I tried to ignore it.

"You must be excited that you got into MIT," I said.

"Yeah, it's a big opportunity." He sat up on his pillow. "What about you—college, all that adult stuff?"

He was slurring and looked a little tipsy. I knew he'd been drinking. I now wondered how much. Not that it was any of my business. Anyway, he seemed relaxed now. The wrinkles were gone from his forehead, and he was more interested in me than whatever had caused him to run away from the party earlier.

I'd made him smile. That meant a lot to me just then.

I told him a bit about my new life in Toronto, my classes, and how happy I was to be newly independent. I told him about my little apartment and my neighbors. The older woman on the first floor who spent all day staring through her peephole. The piano teacher on the second floor who listened to blues until after midnight. The big family on the top floor whose children ran back and forth like crazy all weekend and had put any maternal instincts I might have thought I had on hiatus.

He grinned as he listened, especially when I laughed, and I couldn't stop doing it, just as I couldn't stop myself from talking. We had never talked that long and had never spent that much time alone. We'd never been just us, the people we really were, together.

It was like a dream.

My fantasies taking shape.

And I didn't want to wake up.

"What about your friends?" he asked.

"I've made a couple, but I don't have time to go out, really. I signed up for too many classes."

"Any boyfriends?" I was surprised this would interest him. "You can tell me. I won't say a word to Hoyt."

I blushed. For some reason, I wanted to impress him, to act older and more experienced, but some things are impossible to fake. I'd never been with a guy. And it was mostly his fault. Compared to him, most guys weren't good enough to give them an opportunity. My mind and heart had always belonged to him. His least gesture fed my dreams and fantasies for months on end, and all I wanted was to stop being invisible to him. That hope was the only thing that kept me afloat.

"No, I don't have a boyfriend."

"You must have gone out with someone, though."

"Yeah, I mean, I've been out a few times."

I looked away so he wouldn't see I was lying and adjusted my hair. Suddenly I felt a sharp pain—it was caught on my earring. I tried to pull my hair loose, but it kept getting more tangled.

"Is something wrong?" Trey asked.

"My hair's wrapped around my earring and I can't get it loose."

"Here, let me help."

He sat up and grabbed my ear before I could say anything. I tried to ignore the heat I felt when he was so close. Tried not to notice his tongue as he bit down on it in concentration.

"I can't do it like this. It's really caught up in there and I can barely see. Come on, get up."

He grabbed my hand and pulled me over to the lamp, where he bent over, squeezing my earlobe. After a few tries, I felt the hair come loose from the hasp. When I looked up, I saw him smiling with satisfaction.

We were so close that I could feel his breath warming my cheek. He looked at my lips for a few tense moments that I wished would last forever.

"You look beautiful tonight," he murmured.

Now all the sounds and music on the other side of the door seemed to recede. I grinned. I couldn't help it. I couldn't believe this was happening. My heart was pounding, my nerves were raw.

"What's so funny?"

"You've just never said anything like that to me. You've never noticed the way I look before."

"Believe me, I've noticed the way you look many times. You're gorgeous."

"How much have you had to drink?"

"A lot, but not so much that I don't know what I'm saying."

I could see he was watching my lips as I talked.

"You honestly think I'm pretty?"

"You're pretty, you're perfect, I'm crazy about you. Tonight, especially." He reached out and ran a finger across my cheek. "And you're especially adorable when you blush. If I didn't think it was wrong, I'd give you that kiss I've been holding back all night."

I felt fireworks go off inside me, felt the burning of hope, of anticipation. And nothing else mattered to me just then. He wanted to kiss me, and I wanted him to kiss me. I refused to think about anything else, even to notice that feeling in the pit of my stomach warning me that I was letting my desire get the better of me, that there was something else I needed to pay attention to.

"Then do it," I murmured.

He smiled wearily and shook his head, then leaned his forehead toward mine and rested his hand on my waist.

"Don't say that."

"I want you to."

"It wouldn't be right."

"Says who? It's just a kiss."

"Just a kiss," he repeated softly.

"Just one little bitty kiss."

I felt his lips on my forehead, his hot breath tickling me, and I started to melt. He ran his other hand down my back, moved downward, kissed me on the cheek. On the ear. Traced out a path down my jawline. I closed my eyes, absorbing all of it: the gentleness, the wariness, the perfection of that instant.

I didn't care if it was right or wrong.

He stopped on my lips. He was going to kiss me. He really was. I had to grab onto that stupid lace-up shirt he was wearing to keep from falling over as I waited for it to happen.

His mouth brushed against mine, just a bit. And then it came: he took the leap, and he was there next to me, floating in the abyss. He clutched the back of my neck and covered my lips with his. There was no hesitation, only determination. He held me as though he was scared to let me go.

He tasted like alcohol, tobacco, and something sweet. And in an instant, he became my favorite flavor.

I stood on my tiptoes and wrapped my arms around his neck. He pressed into me stubbornly. There was no turning back. I had dreamed of this so many times, and I wouldn't let anything stop me from getting what I wanted now that it was finally happening. Not my insecurities, not my fears. Not my utter lack of experience.

Because I was just a girl, and love is complicated. And there's no instruction manual to help you understand it.

His caresses became bolder, his hands reaching parts of me no one had ever touched before. I didn't stop him. I couldn't, and I didn't want to. There are risks that are worth it. I pulled him closer. Closer, and closer still. I convinced myself that what we were doing was real.

There are gaps in my mind. I don't know how we went from standing up to lying in bed. I tried to memorize each second of it, but he distracted me with his soft fingers and the little noises escaping his throat. And the way he gazed at me, as though he'd never seen anything like me in his life. His hands exploring every inch of my body tenderly; the hunger, the emotion in his kisses.

I trembled when his naked body covered mine. From desire. From lust.

I could see a question in his eyes. Without speaking, I answered yes. He looked at me for an eternity, and I saw an infinity reflected in him, everything, even those shadows that had caused my heart to pause.

But then our mouths touched, and I let myself go.

I wanted to give everything to him, and he accepted. Timid, delicate, contained. Our bodies joined. It was perfect, absolute, complete, profound. And I cried. The pain I felt made it so real. I had given up before, years ago, when I was innocent and a dreamer and gave him that first piece of my heart. Now I was offering him the last, with open arms. Now I was entirely his.

We lay there, saying nothing, his hand on my belly, his head on my arm. Then he fell asleep. The party was still going on downstairs.

I wondered if my brother and sister were looking for me. But I didn't care. I just wanted to stare at his face, so relaxed, hear his measured breaths, watch his eyes shifting beneath his eyelids. Imagine he was dreaming of me.

The sun started to rise, and the walls brightened. I woke with a powerful urge to go to the bathroom. I got up noiselessly and looked for my clothes. I was getting dressed when Trey moaned. He sounded like he was in agony. He sat up, trying not to fall over, leaning against his pillows.

That's when he saw me.

His eyes were bloodshot as he looked me over, and I felt so uncomfortable I had to cover up. Even before his lips moved, I knew everything he was going to say—knew his questions, his doubts, the terror that had overtaken him.

He jumped up and ran toward me.

Then the shouts began. The words that were hard as fists. The unbearable cruelty of his coldness. After everything I had given him.

That wasn't Trey. That wasn't the guy I knew, the guy I had slept with. Or maybe it was him, more than ever.

What the hell do you think you're doing here?

Get the fuck out of here.

You're just a little girl. Don't you understand what could happen?

Are you trying to get me in trouble?

Don't ever come near me again.

And I could do nothing. I couldn't even react as he grabbed my arm and threw me out of his room.

12

Because It Was You

The bad weather seemed here to stay as the darkness of night pressed in on the windowpanes. The thunder growled, the lightning carved furrows across the sky, and strange shadows crisscrossed the walls.

At least the wind had calmed, along with the drumming of the rain on the roof, which was now a soft, hypnotic mutter.

Trey didn't say a word as I told my story, and he looked down the whole time, his fists balled on his thighs, his knuckles white. His lips were downturned; the muscles in his face were rigid.

It all felt so distant once I'd finished and I saw him looking so defeated.

"I don't know what to say!" he shouted, barely visible in the glow of the embers. Then he cursed and sank back, overcome by sadness. "I don't know how I was capable of such a thing."

"It was a long time ago. Just forget about it."

"I remember…"

"Trey, seriously, you don't have to."

"I need to talk about it."

"Okay." I gave in.

"I remember seeing you on the stairs. Talking with Hoyt. I was having a good time. All those people were there for me. Then my phone rang and…it was my grandfather. My mother's heart had given out. She'd died…" Those words seemed to crush him beneath their weight. "I've always been a coward, and when something overwhelms me and I don't know how to deal with it, I run. I'm trying to fix that part of myself, but that night…that night, too, I ran away. I remember I got hammered and I smoked a bunch of weed. But that didn't make the pain go away, so I took some pills." Ashamed, he concluded, "I didn't usually take that shit, Harper, I promise."

"I believe you."

"After that, everything's blurry for a bit, and then it goes completely dark."

All sorts of emotions were gathering inside me. For him, that night was a black hole. For me, it was the aftermath of a bombing, and I was still feeling the aftershocks.

I stared at a ribbon of smoke rising up the chimney so as not to have to look at him, and with just a thread of voice, he went on.

"The next thing I recall is waking up and seeing you there. And I lost whatever last bit of reasonableness I had. I wasn't thinking, I just reacted. All that mattered to me then was the thought that someone might find you in my room. It never occurred to me that you and I had…you know. I just never even thought of that."

I nodded. His words were sincere, and he didn't have to try harder to convince me. Overcome with emotion, he apologized. "I'm sorry, Harper. I can't tell you how sorry I am. If I could, I'd go back in time and change everything."

"Yeah. Me too." I breathed in and out and tried to be completely honest. "Or not everything. I would only erase the part where you woke up and screamed at me. All that came before that… I liked it."

I could tell my words surprised him, and my cheeks suddenly felt hot. I was grateful it was dark enough that he might not be able to tell.

"Come on, you can't really think that! You slept with an idiot who was so fucked up he couldn't remember anything, and…" Now the gravity of what had happened had struck him. "My God, it was your first time! Someone should beat the shit out of me!"

"Don't worry about it. There's only one person who has the right to avenge me, and that's me. And I'm not going to do it."

"Did I… Was I gentle with you?"

"Very, very gentle, and very caring," I admitted timidly, almost starting to sweat. "And I liked it. I mean, it wasn't like in novels, where the virgin has four orgasms in a row and everything's perfect. But it was nice. It was nice because…because it was you, Trey."

"What does that mean?"

"I was so hung up on you back then, and you'd never give me the time of day. I was invisible to you. You were always surrounded by the hottest chicks and that made me feel like a zero." What followed I didn't want to say, but it seemed like the perfect night for confessions, so I went on, "And when you told me all that stuff in your room, I…"

"I did, though."

"You did what?"

"I did notice you. You were the only thing I ever saw when you were around. What I said to you before I got angry… I meant those things, Harper. I wasn't lying. I liked you. I thought you were gorgeous. Perfect. You grew up and you turned into a dream for me. I couldn't take my eyes off of you, and when you came up to my room…I guess I let my feelings get the better of me."

His confession had surprised me and had brought back to me how incredible that night had been, how sweet. The thought of it stung me. Looking at his lips, I wondered if I had imagined his words.

"I let my feelings get the better of me, too, Trey. But it was wonderful."

He was moved, and almost shouted, "You really think so! I feel so relieved."

"How come you never said anything?"

He ran his hands through his hair. "The first and only time your brother ever busted me looking at you, you were seventeen. And he told me he'd kill me if he ever saw me doing it again."

"What way?"

"What way do you think?" he asked mischievously.

"You're lying. You didn't even know I existed."

"What, you want proof?" He turned toward me. "August. Discovery Islands. I went with you and your family to Sonora for a few days' vacation. On the second night, really late, you went down to the pool in a robe. I was there. I saw you."

"You were there?"

"Yeah. I couldn't sleep, so I went out for a walk. I was going to go over and say hi, but you threw off the robe and jumped into the water before I had time to speak." He chuckled. "I hadn't realized until then how much you'd grown. Like…all over. You know what I mean. And I just stood there in the dark gawking at you like a dummy. Ever since that night, you were always on my mind."

Flattered, I thought back. "That was the summer when I'd just turned…"

"Sixteen."

"I had no idea."

"I've always been good at hiding my feelings. That doesn't mean I don't have any."

That was true, I saw now. The feeling was real, and the struggle to suppress it must have been titanic. But there he was now, revealing everything of himself to me.

"If you'd ever told me, I don't know, maybe…"

"I couldn't, Harper. You were just too good, too good for anyone. Especially me. You still are." Sorrow hid his face, like a cloud pushed by the wind until it blocks the sun.

I tried to peer inside him, to see his soul. But I realized the man before me was a stranger. I'd never truly known him. Not if he could close himself up so tightly that I'd never even realized he was interested in me. Knowing this knocked me off-balance, and I wondered how many other things I would now have to question.

Ten years, and I hadn't truly known him for even one of them.

Maybe that meant the love I'd felt for him had never been real, either.

Maybe I had fallen in love with a figment of my own imagination.

Maybe I'd woven an idea of him out of nothing.

"This is too weird for me," I whispered.

"What?"

"Being here talking to you like it was just nothing."

"Why's it weird?"

"Because I hated you for so long, and I still have that bitter taste in my mouth."

"Sure. I get that."

"No, you don't," I exploded, standing up. "You made me love you, and I did. Then you made me hate you, and I did. And you never knew either thing was happening. Now I feel empty because I no longer have a reason to hate you. Or I do, but I can't blame you, because you didn't even know what you were doing."

He stood, too, and tried to step toward me, but stopped when he saw my expression.

"I don't know what to feel now, Trey. I'm angry and I'm upset that I'm angry, but I can't help it, it's still there inside me, and I don't know how to dislodge it."

"What I did was wrong, whether I remember it or not. I hurt you, Harper. And you have a right to feel what you feel. Four years is too long to have to hold on to that."

"It is." I felt the tension in my body loosen. "I should have come to see you and talk to you instead of hiding and licking my wounds, but I was so ashamed…"

"Then talk to me now." I shook my head. I was exhausted. "I don't mean just about that night. What I'm trying to say is…you can be angry if you need to, but give me a chance to fix it. Give me time. Don't push me away. Let me have a chance." He smiled. And I did, too. It was impossible not to when he looked at me that way. But it was a weak smile, a broken one. "Give us a chance to be friends."

"The quality of mercy is not strained;
It droppeth as the gentle rain from heaven
Upon the place beneath. It is twice blest:
It blesseth him that gives and him that takes."

—William Shakespeare,
The Merchant of Venice

13

Everything Was Smoke

The next morning, I felt sick. The events of the previous days had taken their toll on me, and my body was protesting the emotional and physical burden I'd subjected it to. My mind was so exhausted that if I closed my eyes, I could almost see my neurons on the point of short-circuiting.

I didn't know what to feel, what to think, what to do about the situation. I didn't know if that heaviness I felt was sorrow, anger, something else, or all those things together.

Luckily, we had electricity now, and when I jumped out of bed, my absolute first priority was to take a long, hot bath.

I opened the tap, and the tub started to fill. The wind had softened, the rain now a meek drizzle. The sky was clear apart from a thin veil of clouds pierced in places by the sun. At last, the storm was lifting.

I submerged myself in the hot water. I don't know how long I stayed there, lost, my head bursting with thoughts I couldn't get rid of or let go. I kept thinking the same things over and over, analyzing them from every possible point of view, but instead of coming to any conclusion, my uncertainty only grew.

Filling my lungs with air, I sank my head underwater. Beneath the surface, I could hear my mind more clearly.

I was thinking about my future, my expectations, trying to figure out what to do with my life. I couldn't make any decisions. Couldn't step back or move forward. I was hiding in a cell of my own creation.

Smoke—everything around me was like smoke. Impossible to breathe. But as I opened my eyes under the warm water, it started to clear away. And I felt my facade cracking. There was a truth there that I couldn't ignore. I'd always cared about what others thought of me, even if I pretended otherwise. And that desperate need for acceptance was what made decisions so hard for me.

Even when I rebelled against my father, choosing to study literature, I didn't do it for myself alone. No, I was thinking of my mother and how much she would have liked for me to follow in her footsteps. And when I focused all my energies on being the best student, it wasn't for me, it was to show everyone else that I could do it.

All those faceless people I let control my life because…

Because why?

I didn't dare think of the real reasons I'd slept with Trey that night. What I was trying to show, and to whom. The resentment I felt now. The forgiveness I was incapable of offering him.

I was scared to know. To see how deep my errors ran, to have to try to accept them. And yet, if I couldn't do that, how could I accept others' mistakes?

How could I forgive Trey?

I went back to my room wrapped in a towel. I took a clean pair of shorts and a not-too-wrinkled T-shirt out of the closet and dressed.

Trey was in the living room, sitting at the table with his laptop open and piles of paper, pencils, markers, and rulers. He looked up. I couldn't help but stare at the glasses on the tip of his nose. They looked good.

"Hey."

"Hey." He smiled. "There's coffee. You want some?"

I went to the kitchen and poured myself a cup. I made him one, too, and took it back out there. I guess it was intended to be some kind of peace offering. An open door inviting him to try to be friends, the way he had asked me the night before.

He thanked me, and I could feel him watching me as I returned upstairs. I threw my clothes and sheets in the wash. Then I walked around the house until I got bored enough to go back to the living room. I charged my phone and tried to call my sister. Service was choppy, and with that weak signal, I couldn't get through. I couldn't even get my messages to send.

Thankfully, Trey's laptop charger worked on my computer, so I could turn it on. I looked through my folders, thought of all I had to do, scrolled through my unread emails. I opened a half-edited manuscript and glanced at the most recent notes. I thought about turning in an assignment I had due, then wondered if I'd even go back to my internship.

Sharing this space with Trey was easier than I had thought. Though we barely talked, the silence was comfortable. The only problem was how much he distracted me.

I looked over at him every time he drew the lines in what must have been a blueprint or made measurements and calculated dimensions. He was concentrating so hard that lines appeared on his forehead, and he rubbed his nose and temples compulsively when he was trying to figure things out. Because the ink from his black marker had gotten on his fingers, he soon had black streaks all over his face. That tickled me.

For a moment, I was blinded by the light that entered the window. I stood and ran over to the door. The sun was out. I stepped outside. The rain was gone, the sky had patches of blue, the light was bright and warm, the damp grass smelled delightful. There was even a rainbow in the sky. I closed my eyes and took a deep breath of the cool, clean air. I could hear the sea again, serene.

When I opened my eyes, Trey was standing there watching me.

"I'm hungry."

I could have said something more poetic, but my hunger was stronger than my inspiration.

"Everything we had in the fridge is spoiled," he said. "In the cabinet, there's just a packet of pasta, a jar of tomato sauce, some powdered mashed potatoes, and I think a jar of mushrooms."

I frowned.

"You think the roads are okay? I know a restaurant in town where the food is to die for."

He grinned. "A hot cooked meal. Now you're speaking my language. Besides, I need to go to the town hall to get the blueprints for this house."

"Let's give it a shot, then," I said.

I was ready to get out of there, almost as if I were afraid the world had vanished during the storm. I needed sun and air. And fries and chocolate cake. I'm a simple woman—I've never asked for much to be happy.

Trey had driven to the island in a huge black SUV. One of those monstrous things with a grille on the front and lights on the roof and an exhaust pipe sticking up in the back.

"Are you trying to compensate for something?"

He smiled and shook his head. "You try and drive a regular car through Kluane National Park, the Saint Elias Mountains, or the Rockies and see how far you get."

"Did you do all that?"

"More than once. I like all that stuff: climbing, snowboarding, dogsledding… If you can do it in the mountains, I'm up for it, especially in wintertime."

"What about staring at the countryside from a comfy seat on a porch, with a cup of hot chocolate in your hands and a wool blanket across your legs?" I smirked.

"I like that, too," he said.

We got into his car and drove off. The roads were muddy, and much of the terrain was flooded. Where I had seen fields of green grass before, there were now lakes connected by channels of water. No matter where you looked, you could see the sun shining. When we got to town, we saw the damage: fallen branches, broken signs, gaps in the road where the water had rushed through. Access to the port was blocked, and a group of men was busy there with concrete blocks and construction materials. It had been worse than I'd thought.

The town hall was a building of wood and red brick next to the church, which was all white apart from its faded gray roof. We went inside and shut the creaking door behind us.

A woman sitting behind the information counter stood up, smiling so wide her eyes seemed to almost disappear. After a few niceties, Trey told her what he needed. She told him to fill out a form, then led us to a room on the upper floor, where she dug through the plans on a shelf until she found the correct blueprints, which she helped us copy.

We decided to walk to the restaurant, since it was close by. Trey seemed lost in worrisome thoughts that wrinkled his forehead.

In a moment of weakness, I observed his faded jeans, his tight white shirt, and his tan. There was something special about his hard, masculine features, which were handsome in a classical way. I shivered, realizing how much he attracted me and how irritated that made me feel.

Turning back to the road, I tried to think of a way to dispel those four years of resentment. Because I had the feeling there were parts of him I hated and others I accepted. And that contradiction was making me turn in circles when what I needed was to move on.

"There it is," I said, pointing at the restaurant.

The worry vanished from his face. "I hope it's as good as you say, because I'm dying of hunger."

"Want to bet on it?"

I pushed open the door, and the delicious scent of fish and spices surrounded us. The place was full, and no one could stop talking about the storm. A group of fishermen were talking at one table about how much money they stood to lose if access to the port wasn't restored. They were also concerned about damage to the potato fields on the island's north.

I felt sorry for them, victims of circumstances they couldn't control. From behind the bar, Ridge lit up when he saw me. "Are you all right? I called you several times, but your phone was off."

"My battery went dead, and we didn't have power. And even when I charged it, the signal out here is garbage."

He laughed before looking at Trey with curiosity.

"Ridge, this is Trey. He's friends with my brother-in-law."

"Nice to meet you."

"Same," Trey said, shaking his hand.

"When did you get here? The port's closed and even the helicopters won't be able to land until the afternoon."

"Two nights ago, on the last ferry."

"And you found Old Bay? You must know the area well."

"I've been here a few times."

Ridge nodded. I had the sense that he was evaluating Trey, trying to decide whether or not he could trust him. He opened his mouth to go on speaking, but I interrupted him.

"Do you think you could whip us up something to eat? We're starving."

"Sure." He glanced around. "There's a free table over there by the window. Carlie will be over soon to get your order."

We thanked him and took our seats. The window looked out onto the port and the vastness of the Gulf of Saint Lawrence. It was stunning.

Carlie came over in her usual bad mood, but as soon as she saw Trey, her attitude changed. Amazing what a little testosterone and a handsome face can do.

We ordered the daily special of mussels, lobster rolls, and salad. For dessert, we had a blueberry flan with lime sauce.

"Don't hesitate to call me over if you need anything else, I'll be right over there," Carlie said in her snake-charmer voice. Naturally, she didn't even bother looking at me.

As soon as she walked off, Trey turned his attention to me. "Have you known Ridge long?"

"Two and a half days, basically."

"Really? I'd have thought it was more. He certainly seems interested in you. And me, but in a different way." I could sense the sarcasm in his words.

I flapped my eyelashes at him like a Victorian lady. "What do you want me to say? I have that effect on people. They see me, and they just adore me."

Trey leaned back in his chair, and I shifted nervously.

"It's not what you think," I went on. Carlie appeared, but said nothing as she dropped our drinks at the table and walked off again. The bitch. She batted her eyes, too. She had more of a knack for it than I did. "Ridge is like that with everyone. He's a bit of a philanthropist and an animal rights activist. He's…he's a good guy."

Trey looked at me with curiosity as I took a sip of my soda and asked him, "So you said you've been to the island a couple of times?" He nodded. Another thing I was finding out about him was his tendency to keep silent, to answer with vague movements you might miss if you blinked. It made me nervous, and that made it hard to keep my own mouth shut. "When was that?"

"The first time was right after I moved to Massachusetts. The second time was a few months later, when Scott tricked me into thinking we were coming for a guys' trip, but I actually spent the whole weekend painting and putting furniture together."

That was typical Scott. The memory made Trey grumble as if he were still irritated by it, while I pursed my lips and tried not to laugh.

Carlie reappeared to drop our dishes off on the table. We ate like wolves, only stopping to catch our breath or sigh with satisfaction. Everything was delicious, but I ate the mussels so fast I barely noticed. Then I took a bite of lobster roll and was unable to stop myself from exclaiming, "Thank you, God!"

I closed my eyes. When I opened them, Trey was gawking at me. I cleared my throat, feeling a bit embarrassed.

"Why'd you come here the first time?"

"For the house. Hayley saw an ad for it in Prince Edward Island and she twisted our arms until we came here to look at it."

That was weird. Hayley usually told me everything, right down to the most insignificant details of her life, but she'd never said anything about that.

"What were you doing in Prince Edward Island?"

This made him uncomfortable, and the color drained from his face. He set down his fork and said, "I…uh… Honestly, this isn't the time…"

"Harper?"

14

Finding My Place in the World

I turned to where I'd heard someone shout my name and saw Adele and Sid walking to our table.

"Hey!"

Adele hugged me so tight she squeezed a giggle out of me. I hadn't expected such affection from her, and it made me feel a little awkward. I was almost moved to tears as I hugged her back.

"Honey, are you all right? That storm was worse than anyone expected, and we were worried about you. We went by your house and it was empty. I almost made Sid knock the door down."

"Almost," Sid interrupted her with a smirk. Adele gave him a playful slap on the chest. "Luckily we saw tire tracks going in the direction of the village, and I managed to convince her you had probably come down here."

"You're sure you're okay?" she repeated. "You must have been scared, all alone there."

"Relax, I'm fine. Plus, I had an unexpected visitor." Trey stood up as I introduced him. "This is Trey, a friend of mine. This is Adele and Sid. They live on the island."

"Pleased to meet you."

"The same, young man," Sid said, reaching out his enormous hand.

"Oh, but you're eating!" Adele almost shouted apologetically. "I'm so sorry for interrupting you."

"It's fine. You can join us if you like."

"Yes, please do," Trey seconded me, to my great relief.

We didn't need to say it twice.

Sid pulled over two empty chairs, and we moved our plates aside to make room for them. Carlie came over, playing nice again, and Trey leaned in close to me.

"So first you introduced me as your brother-in-law's friend. Now I'm your friend. Should I be getting excited about what comes next?"

I looked away, abashed, my defenses crumbling at my feet. Maybe I needed a break from them, though. Maybe there was no reason to keep them up. Maybe the line between bitterness and forgiveness is thin. Maybe it's easy to imagine what you'd do in this or that situation when you're living it in your mind, but when it actually happens, you have no idea how you'll react. Because there are many shades of gray, and many colors in the mix, too.

"That depends," I said softly.

"On what?" His face was very close.

"You think I'm going to make it that easy on you?"

"I'd be disappointed if you did."

"Well, far be it from me to disappoint. I'm going to try to make you proud." Looking at him, I saw something in his expression I had prayed to find there before.

"What do you do, Trey?" Sid asked.

"I'm an architect."

"Ooh, a creative type. I like that. Have you worked on any projects we might know about?"

"No, sorry. I'm just starting out."

Trey described his work and everything he hoped to do in the future. It was hard to listen to him. I was distracted by his good looks, his voice, his pronunciation, the elegance of his hands when he gestured, the echo of his laughter. But then he said something that did catch my attention: a plan he was working on to raise funds for some of the First Nations communities in the Maritimes to improve their dwellings, schools, and public buildings through the profits of his architecture projects.

I was impressed. I had no idea he was someone who would willingly give his time to others. I'd always thought of him as frivolous, living a life of girls and parties, blowing money on cars and trips like the stuck-up rich kid he'd always been in my mind.

I was sitting next to a virtual stranger. He was so different from how I remembered him. So much more complicated. And I wanted to know him now, to peel back all the layers until I knew the deepest parts of him.

Sid seemed to think highly of Trey, too, and offered to help him in the future in any way he could.

"Sid, that would be amazing. Thanks."

"No worries, man. I'm Mohawk on my dad's side, Paiute through my mother. I would do anything to help my brothers and sisters."

Sid went on to tell us a bit about his life. He'd been born on the outskirts of Brantford, on the Six Nations reservation. In his teenage years, he went to live with an uncle on his mother's side who made his living doing odd jobs on a ranch. In his free time, he did wood carving, sculpting traditional figures and symbols that he'd sell to tourists. He taught Sid how to work wood, and Sid took to it, and he liked being paid for his creations. Soon carving was how he made his living.

"So what brought you to Petit Prince?" Trey said.

"I came here for a relative's funeral and I stuck around a while to help out the family. Then Adele showed up in my life and, well, we just stayed."

"You left everything behind, too?" I asked.

Sid shook his head and scooped up a spoonful of blueberry flan. "I didn't leave anything. I found everything here."

He leaned over to Adele and kissed her on the cheek, and I thought my heart would melt.

Ridge came by with a bottle of liquor and a tray of glasses. I realized the place had almost totally emptied out.

"How about a drink for you all? On the house."

"That's very generous. Thank you, Ridge," Adele said with a smile.

"Hey, Peter, come on over here and join us," Ridge said to a customer having his coffee at the bar.

They pulled over another table, and Ridge served us. Peter turned out to be very nice. He was from Petit Prince, but two decades ago, he left the island for college. Once he graduated, he moved to New York, where he worked for a PR agency until he had two heart attacks back-to-back and decided to rethink where his life was going. He'd been home for less than a year, and now he grew potatoes and fished for lobster.

The door opened, and an older woman of medium stature with white hair and big blue eyes walked in. Her expression was stern, even annoyed, as she called out: "So this is the generation that's supposed to take this country forward? Thank God I'll be dead by then and won't have to see it."

Ridge laughed, a little buzzed. "Come on, Emma. I've got a bottle of moonshine set aside just for you."

"If it's as bad as that fish you cook, I'd just as soon drink the dishwater."

"You're heartless."

"I've got my teeth, though. At my age, that matters more than a heart."

We all cracked up, and the longer we sat there, the more I lost track of time, forgetting my worries and my constant, painful self-awareness. Sometimes, to find the answers you need, all you have to do is relax. Being there, I realized I wanted to feel the way those people did. They weren't afraid of anything. They were happy with their simple lives, with moments like this one, with the honest pleasure of sharing a bottle of liquor.

I wanted that: a modest life.

I wanted a new beginning.

I wanted to be strong enough to achieve it.

I wanted to fill the emptiness in my life.

"I'm going to go take a walk," I told Trey.

He looked up from the blueprints he'd gotten at the town hall. He'd been going over them for more than an hour, drawing new additions, making measurements. I'd been watching him, but I couldn't make head or tail of what he was doing. For me, it was just lines and more lines.

"You want some company? I could leave this for a bit."

"Nah, no need. I'm just going to go up and down the beach."

"Okay."

I walked out barefoot, stepping down from the porch to the damp grass, which tickled my feet. Once I was on the sand, I traced out the line of the shore, enjoying the coolness as my heels sank in. It was afternoon, and the sun had begun to drop on the horizon. I was ready to declare an end to the day and get some rest.

The sea murmured softly, and I got lost in memories that had been dormant for a long time, moments I had pushed aside to avoid the feelings they provoked in me. My dreams when I was a little girl and I still believed in magic and the impossible felt within reach. The time when I felt loved and protected, and a good-night kiss and a gentle look were all I needed to drive my fears away.

But suddenly there were no more kisses, no more smiles, and the fear came back. Fear of the dark, of solitude, of a world that had stopped all at once. Cold, unreal, without a trace of magic. Without meaning, without a center, because she had left it.

Ever since childhood, there were things I didn't understand: my father's cold looks, his shouting, his constant disapproval. Like an eraser, they blurred me at the edges and made me something vague and distant from what I truly was. As I grew older, I tried to rediscover all that. I drew myself from different perspectives, in different colors, trying to find an image of who I was that he would approve of. I never did, and I got lost on the way.

Maybe Grandma and Hayley were right. That was just a mirage. Trying to be everything others wanted from me, trying to be appreciated, valued, and loved, I distorted myself so much I couldn't recognize the real me behind the mask.

But I needed to find that person now, rediscover her, *listen* to her. Ask her what her dreams and desires were. Understand her. Get to know her. Help her to stop being a defenseless little girl. Learn with her to make my own decisions without thinking of anyone but myself.

Swimming against that current of thought, I reached the pebble beach. I remembered there what Adele had said. After a strong storm, you might find glass on the shore that had been cast up by the powerful waves.

Instead of thinking, I let my mind go blank and looked for mermaids' tears among the stones.

I found a small green one and weighed it in my hand, stroking its edges with my thumb. It was round, but slightly rough. I put it in my pocket, along with several others I came across afterward. Not a bad haul.

In the distance, I saw the first star of dusk against the gray and purple shadows of the sky. If I didn't hurry, night would fall before I made it back.

I went inside and saw the table had been set for dinner. Delicious aromas came from the kitchen. Trey had been heating up the leftovers from the restaurant that Ridge had boxed up for us.

He was in the kitchen, leaning against the counter next to the oven, concentrating on something in his hands. I didn't realize it was my book until I saw him turn a page. A million butterflies took flight in my stomach when he grinned at something.

I cleared my throat and he looked up, startled. He hadn't known I was there.

"Hey," I said.

"Hey! I didn't hear you come in."

"I realize that."

He smiled and closed the book, holding it up for me to see.

"I hope you don't mind. I saw it on the mantel."

"Not at all. You can borrow it if you like, but only while we're here. I never part from it."

With a curious expression, he told me, "It's not my usual kind of reading, but it's good." He handed it back to me. "How many times have you read it?"

"I lost count a long time ago. But lots."

"You can tell. The book feels like it could disintegrate at any time."

"It's in that shape because it's a family heirloom. My mother gave it to me when I turned five. It had belonged to her before, and to my grandmother a long time before that. Mom used to read it to me at night. That's my favorite memory of her. For lots of reasons that are hard to express."

Trey's eyes filled with compassion.

"I think I'm starting to understand some things. Like why your brother used to always call you Pumpkin."

"You did, too."

"Yeah, because Hoyt did it and I thought it was funny, but I never knew what the story was. It's because of the main character and her red hair, right?"

"Yeah. I used to like to pretend I was her. I'd paint freckles on my face and talk in a high-pitched voice. Hoyt would pretend to be Gilbert because I didn't have anyone else to play with." I laughed, but with a touch of sadness. "Then my mother died and he had to take care of me. He used to read me a few pages of this book every night, the same way she did."

"I can understand why it's so special to you."

All at once, I was impatient for him to understand me, and I explained, "It is, but it's not just because of what it means or the people I associate it with. Or because it made me realize I wanted to be a writer. It's also the story itself. It's Anne. I feel like we have things in common, and the things we don't, I wish we did. I wish I could be more like her."

Trey turned his head to me, and I felt he was looking inside me, seeing into my soul. I'd had that impression more and more frequently lately. He reached out and grabbed the book I was holding tight to my chest, and when he did, his fingertips brushed my cleavage. When he withdrew his hand, I felt a burning there.

"You know what? I think I will read it."

"Seriously?"

"I've never been more serious in my life." The oven's buzzer sounded and he turned it off. "So wait—you just said you want to be a writer?"

I felt faint. "No."

"Yeah. You literally just said it."

"Okay, I said it, but I don't feel like talking about that with you."

"Why not?"

Trying to think of an answer that wouldn't require me to confess anything, I drew a blank, and I finally blurted out, "Just because."

He grinned mischievously. His mischief was infectious. But he didn't pry; he just took dinner from the oven while I watched him, and my stupid, innocent heart remained attentive to his voice, his every word and movement…those eyes that seemed to see every single thing I tried to hide from him.

We sat at the table, where Trey opened a bottle of Riesling he'd found in a small wine rack in one of the cabinets. It was exquisite, and a perfect pairing for the fish.

Setting my fork down and wiping my lips with my napkin, I said, "This morning, when you were talking with Sid about your job and the projects you had in mind…"

"Yeah?"

"I had no idea about all that. All those things you're describing, they…they just…"

"Spit it out, Harper."

My feet were dancing nervously under the table. "I just assumed you'd end up working for your dad, designing fancy apartment buildings and five-star hotels for oil billionaires. Piling up money so you could blow it on stupid shit like one of the Kardashians."

He almost spit out his wine, and he laughed so loud it echoed through the room. "I'm really starting to worry about the image you have of me."

"Well, don't, because it's starting to be obvious I have no idea who you are."

"There's something we can do about that," Trey said, turning somber. "Ask me whatever you want. Shoot."

I sat back and thought it over before beginning, "You're working on a project to raise money for First Nations communities."

"Yeah."

"Why?"

"Because I've read a lot about the situation on the reservations. The folks living there just want the chance to preserve their culture and identity for future generations. The government does next to nothing for them. So someone else needs to step in."

"And that someone is you?"

"Me and other people. I'm just one of many."

"Why?"

"I just answered that question."

"I mean why are you worried about what happens to those people?"

He lifted his napkin from his lap, dropped it on the table, and took a sip of wine before refilling both our glasses.

"I visited a couple of the Mi'kmaq reserves four years back. I saw them from the inside, and I learned what matters to the people there and how important their roots are to them. I couldn't just look away."

"That was four years ago. Was that the same time you went to PEI with my brother and sister?"

"Yeah, but that's another story. A much longer, more personal one."

"One you don't want to tell me."

"One I don't know how to tell you, Harper."

He got up and opened a window. I, too, felt it was getting a little stuffy inside. As the fresh air streamed in, I heard him walking behind me, then felt his hand on my shoulder. An electric shock traveled from my feet to the top of my head.

"Come outside. It's nice. I'll pick up all this later."

I grabbed my glass and followed him out to the porch, where we sat on the steps. It smelled of cut grass, damp air, and salt. I could see the dark outline of the coast lit up by the moon and the reflections of the stars in the clear sky on the surface of the water. There were millions of tiny bright spots over our head.

The waves were breaking against the rocks. Time seemed to have stopped. Is it possible for two people to communicate while saying nothing? I was starting to think so that night. Glances and timid expressions seemed to give birth to a real connection, an invisible thread joining the lives of two beings. Uniting us, one stitch at a time.

"What else do you want to know?" he asked me.

Enjoying the view of his profile as he looked straight ahead, I said, "If your main work is nonprofit, what do you live on?"

"I got lucky, and an environmental foundation bought my cap-stone project."

"Wow. It must have been really good."

"It's a marine research center, designed on a limited budget with recycled materials, everything sustainable and off the grid. Its focus is on recovering endangered species. They paid me enough that I don't need to be in a rush. Let's put it that way. And if things get tight, I've almost got them on the hook for another project I finished last year." He took a sip of wine. "Though, truth be told, I wouldn't want to sell it."

"Why not?"

"Maybe it's just a stupid dream, I don't know… But I'd like to do it on my own, from beginning to end. It's good enough that I think I could find investors for it."

"Are you going to tell me what it is, or do I have to force it out of you?"

"It's a model for a small town, but dedicated to culture. With art schools focusing on painting, music, sculpture, writing, galler-ies, concert halls, gathering places, and student residences. I know it's ambitious. But there's nothing like that in the world! I don't want recognition or anything like that. If I wanted my name in the papers, I'd just design skyscrapers and luxury hotels and corporate headquarters. I want to do this, because…because without art, life would be a mistake."

His dreams—his mind—had captivated me. His kindness. His sensitivity. And his intelligence, which I saw glimmer in that quote he'd just used to express his thoughts.

"Friedrich Nietzsche said something like that, didn't he?"

"Bingo."

I felt a wave of emotion, something completely new, in my abdomen. It rose up into my chest and throat, almost oppressive in the way it flooded all of my senses.

"Why are you looking at me that way?"

"No reason," I responded. But my cheeks were burning.

I didn't tell him I was trying to figure out how to convince myself that the guy next to me was the same one I had met one September afternoon when I was just twelve years old. The one who had broken my heart. That broken heart I had struggled to piece back together and that was now throbbing harder with every detail of his soul Trey gave me a glimpse of. That heart that was revived thanks to a hope in him I'd never fully let die.

"Harper, seriously, you're making me nervous."

"I'm not doing anything!"

Just then, a shooting star crossed the sky.

And I made a wish: *I want to find my place in the world.*

I knew it was stupid to make a wish just because some rock that had caught fire in atmospheric gases had appeared and would soon burn up and vanish. It didn't make sense, but still, I put every part of myself into that wish. I couldn't help it, the same way a moth can't help flying toward a flame. Trey was lost in thought, and in the dark, his face was hard to make out, but it didn't matter because I knew every detail of it.

He surprised me with the words, "I'm afraid you're going to make me start thinking you like me again."

"You wish," I responded.

"Or that you never did stop liking me." There was a trace of amusement in his voice.

"Again, you wish. But tough luck."

"Getting back to things you want to know about me," he said, "no, I'm not going out with anyone. In case you were wondering."

"It never occurred to me to ask," I lied.

"Sure." He leaned back and stretched his legs. "Just so you know, I'm not just single. I'm also open to offers."

I felt a heat in my chest, and I knew it wasn't just the wine. "If you think one's coming from me, you can keep waiting."

"Well, that's too bad."

"Why?"

"You'll have to find that out for yourself, Pumpkin."

"Call me that again and you'll regret it."

"Are you threatening me? If this is going to get physical, maybe we should try a date first."

"Or not."

"Fine," he replied, "we can get physical without one. But only because you insist. Just so you know, I like the sound of a date."

"No physical contact and no dates!" I shouted.

"Fine! I mean, not going out or not having sex first feels like rushing it to me, but if you want to just go for it, we can get married."

I laughed under my breath. We were flirting. I don't know how we made it to this, but we were flirting. I was on fire. "Technically, we've already done one of those things."

"It kills me that I can't remember," he muttered, frustrated. Then he leaned in, and the light from the living room glowed in his eyes. I held my breath as he said, "I can't stop thinking about it. That you and I…"

I heard a ding. For a moment, I didn't realize it was my cell phone. But when I did, I leapt up.

"Oh my God, cell phone reception! Civilization!" I shouted, going inside. I thought I could hear Trey laughing behind me.

After the emotion of the past days, my sister's voice nearly made me cry. We talked for a long time, and with each second that passed, I had to bite my tongue harder not to tell her about Trey. But he was there to do something nice for her, and I couldn't reveal his presence without spilling the beans about what Scott had in mind.

"You sound different," Hayley said.

"Really?"

"Yeah. Your voice, your tone, the way you're phrasing things… I don't know, you sound happy. Content. Like actually happy, not just faking it."

I took a second to think over what she'd said. She was right. I was happy.

"Yeah, I feel good, Hayley. Maybe it's the place, or maybe it's the people I'm meeting, but…either way, thanks for forcing me to come here."

"You say that like I really coerced you."

"No…"

"But if you'd gotten stubborn, I would have."

"Sadly, I believe you."

"Either way," she said, "you must be doing something right to feel that way. So whatever it is, don't stop it."

"I promise."

"I've got to go, I think Scott's drowning."

"Are you serious?"

"Yeah, or getting eaten by piranhas," she said in a flat, dry tone. "Actually, I think a jellyfish stung him. I'll call you later. Love you."

"Love you, too."

I looked at the phone with a bittersweet feeling before falling back on the cushions and looking at the ceiling. I stayed still there, thinking. It's amazing how differently you can start to look at the world when you find out how other people see it.

Thinking about my sister made me think about Hoyt, and I sent him a text to tell him I'd be out of town a few days, that I needed to disconnect. I didn't give him any explanation, because otherwise I'd have had to lie, and I didn't feel like it.

I smiled when his response came a few seconds later.

Hey, you can count on me, you know that, right? I'll always be on your side. Love you, Pumpkin.

My eyes fell closed. It was all I could do to stand up and go brush my teeth.

There wasn't a sound in the house. When I crossed the hall, I saw Trey lying there on his bed. I could hear his breathing, and my nerves made me shake all over as I walked over to his doorway. He was sleeping there with my book open on his chest. It was adorable.

But I couldn't just leave him that way, so I tiptoed in, trying not to make noise, picked the book up, and laid it on the nightstand. Then I covered him up with the comforter at the foot of the bed. I looked at him a few seconds and noticed the deep circles under his eyes. They weren't the kind you get from physical exhaustion; they were from another kind of exhaustion, the kind loneliness can cause. I knew that because I'd seen them under my own eyes too many times.

I turned off the night.

"Good night," I whispered.

"Good night, Pumpkin," he murmured, half-asleep, once I was in the hall.

I smiled. And my foolish heart smiled, too.

15

The Truth Is, I Don't Understand Myself

Trey wasn't there when I got up the next morning. His car was gone, too. If all his drawing materials weren't still spread out on the table, I'd have been afraid he'd left Petit Prince forever.

Without him, it was too quiet between those four walls.

I sat on the porch and watched the sun come up in the clear sky. I stayed out there long enough to finish my second cup of coffee, telling myself how much I liked the tranquility there. The lack of bustle, the lack of work and stress, the lack of worries.

When I first arrived, it had gotten to me how there was nothing to do. Now I wondered how the hell I would return to my routine once I was home. What would I do if I couldn't feel the sun on my face, breathe the fresh air, walk slowly with no real place to go? How could I return to a place where nobody noticed the weeks or months passing until the leaves fell in fall or a Christmas tree reminded them that time hadn't really stopped, that it was always slipping through your fingers like sand.

My thoughts were contradictory, hard to grasp, uncertain. Had I really lost my mind after just three days here?

Maybe it was something in the water, or maybe in the air, some strange substance that was changing me the same way it had changed Ridge, Adele, Sid, and even Peter.

The sound of an approaching vehicle brought me back from my reverie. A minute later, Trey was walking up the porch steps with his briefcase. He looked like a tourist in his Bermuda shorts, his T-shirt, his tennis shoes, and his sunglasses.

"You went into town?"

"Yeah. Ridge told me there's a scanner and Wi-Fi at the library, and I needed to send a couple of emails and file for permits for the renovation."

He went inside, and I followed him in.

"So you're finished with the plans?"

"Yeah. We can do it. We don't have to touch anything structural, and the blueprints for the new addition are complete. My part's done."

I smiled and held it until I thought it looked real. If he was done, that meant he'd be leaving. The idea nauseated me slightly.

"I finished your book, by the way. Thanks for lending it to me."

"You read the whole thing?" I asked. "And you liked it?"

He was gathering his pens, ordering them in a box. With a slightly flustered expression, he began, "Yeah, it's good. And I can see why it has to unfold the way it does, because of the historical context and all..."

"But..."

"But all those people are assholes! Right from the beginning, everyone treats Anne like dirt just because she's an orphan and she's different. I realize things get better and by the end it's happily ever after, but she has to go through hell before they accept her! She had to change to fit in. And Gilbert, especially—what a dickhead."

"He's not a dickhead," I protested, trying not to laugh.

"Maybe you look at him from a romantic point of view and the ending justifies everything, but trust me, he is. *We were born to be good friends, Anne. You've thwarted destiny enough.*" He imitated Gilbert's shrill voice. "That loser was dying to get her out to the stables and lift up her petticoat."

I covered my mouth to keep from laughing, but couldn't stop myself. There was something adorable about Trey being mad at a book. His eyes had a killer look in them that I found alluring. He was fascinating and enigmatic at the same time, and his anger had something innocent to it. All of that drew me closer to him.

"What's so funny?" he asked.

"Nothing. I just didn't expect the story to really affect you. Because of you saying you don't normally read that type of book." I sat on the couch and he flopped down next to me, close enough that our bare arms touched.

"I read it because of what you said. How you were like Anne in a lot of ways and how there were other ways you wished you could be like her. I wanted to know what that really meant."

"So…?" I asked.

"Honestly, I think I understand what the book means to you." He rested his hand on mine and stroked my fingers. It was more tender than anything he'd done so far, more tender than anything he'd done since that night years ago, and my body wasn't ready for it. "Harper, you don't need to be like anyone else, least of all a fictional character from another time. You're amazing. Why should you be any different?"

"You think I'm amazing? You barely know me."

"We've spent a couple of very intense days together. In other circumstances, I'd say they were the equivalent of months, no?" He leaned his head back and looked up at the ceiling. "Yeah, I think you're amazing, intelligent, and lots of other things. The question is, why don't you think the same?"

I didn't know what to say. His hand was still holding mine, and in my mind, there was so much going round and round that I couldn't find anything to hold on to.

"Did you know the author was from New London and lived in Cavendish later?"

"Yeah," I replied, surprised. "How did you know, though?"

"I googled her."

I smiled and he wove his fingers into mine. "So now that you're done with the house, I guess you'll be going?"

"I don't have to be back in Montreal until after Labor Day. I was thinking I would stay here until then. But that was before I knew you'd be here. Maybe you'd rather I head out earlier..."

"No. You can stay. I was thinking that was when I'd go back, too." Outside, I could hear the cawing of the seabirds.

"Harper?"

"Yeah?"

"Are we good?"

"What do you mean?"

"After what happened, what you told me—are we all right?"

"Yeah. I guess so."

"You guess?"

"We can't change the past," I told him. "And we can't just forget it like it never happened. Maybe with the passage of time..."

"Maybe we can't forget the past, but that doesn't mean we have to let it control us."

He was right.

"And I don't want to."

For the first time in ages, I felt light, relaxed, unafraid. We were so close that I could feel his breath on me as he sighed. My eyes wandered down to his lips and remained there until I noticed he was looking at mine, too. The moment was thick with tension.

Trey was like the sun just then, warm, brilliant, drawing me toward him. But I knew it was dangerous, going too close to the sun like Icarus.

Well, at that moment, I was as happy as Icarus on his way up toward the sun, without the least notion that if I didn't slow down, I might fall to my death.

I wasn't thinking. I still couldn't really grasp that he was here and that the past two days had been real. As real as the intense stare he was giving me just then, looking as though he wished to memorize every detail of me.

"Hello? Are you two home?"

"Is that Sid?" Trey asked.

We got up and walked outside. Sid waved as he walked over. His skin was glimmering with sweat and he was panting.

"You all right, Sid?"

"I've been out on the beach looking for driftwood. When it storms, a lot of it washes up on the beach, and I found a pretty big piece down there. I was wondering if you'd help me bring it home."

"Sure. Anything you need."

An hour later, a heavy, nine-foot piece of wood was leaning against the wall of Sid's workshop, while he and Trey were lying flushed and wheezing on the grass outside.

"You actually came all the way from Old Bay carrying that?" Adele asked.

"I didn't… I didn't think…it would be so…hard," her husband babbled.

"I don't know what's harder, that branch or your head."

They were an odd couple, so different on the surface that it was hard to believe they were so close. And yet I also couldn't imagine them apart.

"Trey, sweetie, are you okay?"

"I will be as soon as I can get my lungs back inside my body," he struggled to respond.

"Let's go in and make them some iced tea before they die," Adele said.

She invited us to stay for lunch and wouldn't take no for an answer. She roasted sliced turkey and artichokes with delicious stuffing, and we talked about any and everything, and time flew by without us realizing it. After cleaning up, Sid took Trey to his workshop to show him his sculptures and his new chain saw. He talked about it as if it were his firstborn son.

Adele made more iced tea and we drank it in the salon next to an old fan that offered slight relief from the heat. The temperature had gone up fast after the storm, reminding us that summer wasn't over.

With a roguish grin, Adele asked, "So…are you and Trey a couple?"

"No!" I couldn't believe she'd just come out with it like that.

"You seem to get along well. How long have you known each other?"

"He's my brother's best friend, so I guess around ten years. Why do you think there's something between us?"

"Because he watches you like he can't stand the thought of letting you out of his sight. And that makes me think he's afraid of something. And I'm wondering what exactly the story between you two is."

I looked away from her and toward my glass, a bundle of nerves. I'd never spoken to anyone about my feelings for Trey. For years, I'd kept them a secret, something that belonged to me and me alone. And doing that made me idealize him until he was this perfect being who lived only in my mind and who I could gaze at, enraptured, and pray to like an idol. Then I learned he wasn't so perfect, that he was anything but perfect, and I hated him. Now I knew he was flesh and blood, real, human. And it was funny that Adele should tell me he looked afraid, because I was afraid, too. Afraid he'd leave, afraid he'd stay. Afraid of what I might feel. Afraid of feeling too much, afraid of not feeling enough. Afraid of what could come next.

To Adele's inquiring look, I responded, simply, "It's complicated."

It wasn't that I didn't trust her; it was that there was somebody else involved. It was Trey's story, too. It was ours, and I wanted it to stay that way. Free from other people's judgments and opinions. In part, because he'd played the villain, and I needed to turn him into the hero redeemed.

In her smile, I could tell Adele understood.

"You and I have a great deal in common," she said before changing the subject.

We said our goodbyes late in the afternoon and walked back home along the edge of the cliff, where there was a green blanket of grass that contrasted beautifully with the red of the rocks. Those colors were accentuated by the sun that was starting to set, sending orange rays across the blue sky. We turned onto a path leading downhill, feeling free and easy.

I took off my sandals when we reached the pebble beach. I liked feeling the rocks under my feet as I walked. We weren't in a hurry, and I enjoyed listening to the rush of waves.

"You really want to be a writer?" he asked.

"I don't want to talk about that."

"Why, would you have to kill me afterward?" he joked. I rolled my eyes and he tried again, "A writer, though? Seriously?"

"Are you always this persistent?"

"Only when something really interests me." He came around in front of me and started walking backward. "Come on, tell me more. What do you want to write about?"

"I've been writing for years. The problem is, I never finish anything."

"Why?"

"For a million reasons. My studies, my job, life and the roads it takes you down. A lack of time. I don't know!"

"You suck at making excuses. Now tell me the truth."

Since when did he know me so well he could tell when I was lying?

"I said I don't know."

"I don't believe you."

His insistence was starting to irritate me.

"Fine. A writer has to have things that I don't have, like talent and good ideas and…" A bitter taste rose up in my throat. It was pride. Because the truth was, I did believe I had talent. I knew I had good ideas. None of that was the problem. "A writer is the sum of their experiences. And I don't have many, honestly."

"Then you should go out and look for them."

"If only it was that easy. I know people say you just need the will-power, but it's harder than that."

"Sure, you're right. But sometimes you have to close your eyes and take a risk."

I took a deep breath, feeling more and more lost in all the dispa-rate thoughts whirling in my head. This subject was like a thorn in my side, and every time he opened his mouth, it sank in deeper.

"Have you ever done that? If so, maybe you can give me some advice."

"Let's see. I could be working with my father at his studio right now designing luxury apartments that cost thirty thousand a month for rich jerks. But instead, I'm tempting bankruptcy working on proj-ects to improve other people's lives. So yeah. I think I can give you advice."

There was frustration in his voice. I stopped and stared into his eyes. I felt bad now for trying to dig at him that way.

"Sorry," I said.

He came close and pushed my bangs aside, not losing his smile.

"My grandfather says we end up here by chance, because we hap-pened to be born. But everything else is a choice. Yesterday, when you said that book made you want to be a writer, I wasn't just listening to you. I felt you. The excitement, the urge. Then I saw you trying to suppress that, stuff it deep inside you, just like you're doing now. And I don't get it."

That made me think.

I didn't understand, either. He was right: writing was my dream. It had been since I was a girl. I'd just left that longing floating there. I'd tried to make it disappear. Yet it was still there, a ghost coming to visit me when I let down my guard, whispering that I'd never be complete until I made it happen.

As if someone had just turned the key to a lock, something opened up subtly within me.

The answer to the question why.

I was scared to fail. There was a stigma against failure in my family. And if I messed up, I'd be telling them they were right about me. And I couldn't stand that, and I couldn't stand thinking that I was letting the rest of the world, especially my father, decide for me instead of doing it myself. Tears stung my eyes, but I didn't want to cry in front of Trey.

"I guess I'm scared of trying and realizing I've got the desire but not the ability. I'm scared of rejection letters, of not being good enough, of not being able to accept the ups and downs."

He was so close that I was waiting for something to happen, but instead his questions continued. "Is your fear really that strong? Do you really want to spend your life editing and publishing other people's novels and dreaming of the book you'll never actually write?"

Where did he get off? I suddenly saw him as a six-foot-tall Jiminy Cricket, even if his body looked like a Greek god's and his smile was to die for. I shook my head in response.

"No," I said softly.

"Trying to forget your dreams so they won't destroy you isn't the solution. My grandfather taught me that. He always says you have to keep fighting like a warrior even if you're afraid you'll lose the battle. Fate is always on the side of those who believe with all their heart."

A warrior? Fate? What the hell was he talking about?

I thought about those words as we walked on. They sounded a little mystical, but there was something very basic in them that was true. It was strange for him to use such lofty language, though. It wasn't like the Trey I knew.

"Your grandfather sounds like he's full of good advice. I'd like to meet him some day."

We reached the dunes. We could see the house not far from there. I crouched down to put my sandals back on and saw a tiny glimmer. I squealed when I saw it was a blue piece of glass. I lifted it up to look at it closely. It was slightly rough on one side, resembling a shard of ice. Precious.

"What is it?" Trey asked, behind me.

"A mermaid's tear." I looked back over my shoulder. "They're little pieces of glass that spend decades in the ocean. The sand and the currents polish them until they look like this. They're treasures. Adele uses them in her art."

"Why are they called mermaids' tears?"

"It's a legend. They say these pieces of glass are the tears of a mermaid crying for the sailor she loves but can never be with because she was banished to the bottom of the ocean."

"Damn. That's sad."

"Love shouldn't hurt, but it does."

"Not always, Harper. What hurts isn't love; it's everything around it that tries to stifle it."

I turned back to look at him. "That's pretty."

"I can't claim the credit for it, I read it somewhere. But I agree with it. So is that why you came here?"

"Is what why I came here?"

"To try and get over someone. Maybe you needed time or distance to get over a boyfriend."

"No!"

"Are you sure? Because if it's that guy you were going out with, your brother says he's a jerk. A brown-noser with no personality of his own. And a person like that doesn't deserve a minute of your time."

I smiled again. I had the feeling that smiling was all I did when he was around.

"No, it's not him. I do need time and distance, and that is why I'm here, but it's nothing to do with Dustin. It's way more complicated and important than some dumb ex."

Seeing that he really cared, that he was attentive and maybe even worried, I realized I could tell him anything, and that with a little luck, he'd understand me. Just maybe. I mean, he had, hadn't he, a few minutes before? In fact, I wasn't sure anyone else had ever understood me so well.

I sat on the sand, and he did the same. I closed my eyes and listened to the sea and tried to find the words to tell him this was a crucial moment in my life, a moment that might change everything.

"I don't know if you know this, but my grandmother left me her house and the bookstore."

"Hoyt mentioned it."

"Do you and my brother spend all your time talking about me?" I growled.

That seemed to make him uncomfortable. "He *is* my best friend," Trey said, "and he talks to me when he needs to. And he's worried about you." He sank his fingers in the sand and brought up a handful. "And to be honest, I listen closer when you come up."

He grinned. I shook my head. What was I going to do with him? His flirting disconcerted me, and I wondered how real it was. I didn't want to get overexcited. I couldn't afford to.

"Let me put it this way," I said. "Imagine your future is all planned out and you're sticking to it. And then one day something changes. A new road opens in front of you. So on one side you have the so-called important things, stuff that really is tempting: a wonderful world where you can be someone and make a name for yourself. Respect, admiration, comfort. And the other road isn't so flashy, but there are other things there that maybe matter more."

"Like…?"

"Memories, identity, roots…dreams. Hopes. And not having to worry about repairs because you're too poor to afford them!" He laughed, but I tried to ignore it. "Well, I'm standing at that crossroads, and I have to choose. Either I go back to Toronto and keep studying and working at the publisher or I stay in Montreal and leave everything behind to run the bookstore."

"Wow. Those really are two totally different paths!"

I looked out at the sea to watch a bird flying low over the water's surface.

"So what would you do?" I asked.

"No answer I can give you will help. The solution depends on your priorities, on what you really want. You have to get your own ideas in order, think about your dreams, decide what's important for you."

"It sounds so simple when you put it like that. But what if I choose wrong? What if I throw all my eggs in one basket and regret it and then it's too late to change my mind? What if I have no idea what I actually want?"

"We've all asked ourselves those questions," he said in a caring tone, seeming to understand how complicated the situation was and how hard it must be to live in my skin. "But ask yourself, Harper: What do you want more than anything in the world?"

I needed a few seconds to respond. Then something emerged from me without my even thinking of it.

"I want the opportunity to be happy."

"See? You do know what you want."

"And I want to understand myself. Because I don't. I—I don't know who I am. I feel like somewhere along the way I forgot. Or maybe I never did know. And if I don't know who I am now, how will I know who I want to be in the future?"

I felt sad, nervous, edgy, exposed after sharing all my thoughts with him. All the thoughts I never said aloud. He grabbed my hand and held it. But he didn't try to give me answers. And him just being there and waiting made more and more words rise up within me.

I stood. I had to move, had to do something. I walked to the water's edge. He followed me.

"I keep thinking about the consequences my decisions could have. That's what I do all the time, keep turning the same subject over and over. It feels like so much effort, but in the end, all that ruminating gets me nowhere. I feel stuck. I feel like I can't move without knowing all the answers in advance, and even when I do take a step, all I can think about is what others will think of me, and it's like I'm trying to show them... I don't know. Something. Why do I care so much what others think of me? Dammit, I'm just a dreamer. A dreamer who will never turn her dreams into reality. Who will never fill the void inside her."

Trey wrapped his arms around me. He pulled me in tight, as though he wanted to protect me from the surrounding world. When he spoke, his lips just barely grazed my earlobe. "That's not true, Harper. You just... You just have to believe in yourself. I know what I'm talking about. I know how you feel. Trust me."

I closed my eyes. No one had ever held me like that before. Emotions flooded me, making my hands shake. "Why should I trust you? Or is that another story you don't want to tell me?"

He grinned sadly, and I felt the heat of his body through my clothes. "I'll tell you anything you want to know. Just let me find the time, okay?"

I nodded, no longer capable of speaking. A heartbeat was echoing in my ears. I didn't know if it was mine or his.

"But promise me you won't fall in love with me out of pity," he whispered timidly.

I laughed and tried to hold on to that splinter of joy Trey had managed to find. And the feeling of it spread through my arms and legs like a warm, restoring bath.

This wasn't a trivial moment. Nothing that was happening to me there was trivial. Nothing at all.

16

Leave a Mark on Their Lives

I want...

I couldn't sleep, and I kept repeating those two words over and over. *I want, I want, I want...* They reverberated inside me. It was painful, but I didn't know how to stop it.

I sat on the windowsill and leaned my head against a pane of glass. Outside, the night swallowed everything.

You just have to believe in yourself, Trey had said. But I also needed to get my thoughts in order, meditate on my dreams, choose which of them mattered most. And that meant no longer being so scared of rejection that I strove to satisfy people, to impress them and live up to their expectations.

Accept all the times I tried to say no and said yes instead.

I thought of all I had accomplished up to then. Being a model student with grades that had brought me the admiration of my professors, an internship at a prestigious publisher that a lot of people would have sold their soul for...and? What else? Those two things summed up my entire life. Study and work. Every damned hour of the day.

And my father still didn't see me.

Because that discomfort in my chest was always about him.

I felt terrible.

Nothing I ever did would be enough. Nothing.

Another what-if occurred to me. Another maybe.

And I started panting, and my lungs burned.

Why was I still trying to deny it?

I would never win him over. I'd never get his acceptance. Or his admiration. Or his... love.

For sixteen years, I'd been trying to make a place for myself in his life. How much longer would I have to keep going before I could convince myself it would never happen?

To hell with him! I was the one who mattered!

I tried to dig around in myself and find a shred of happiness, no matter how tiny, for all the things I had, for all I'd done, without any help from anyone. And what I found was nothing.

Emptiness.

Just plain emptiness.

I didn't have friends. Not real friends, not the kind you go out to dinner with, take vacations with, the kind who want to share your thoughts. The closest were my brother and sister. But I hardly ever saw them; we just talked on the phone.

I was totally, horribly alone.

Alone and empty.

I had deceived myself, thinking it wasn't that way. Had used my time wisely. Had set goals, overcome challenges, kept climbing upward. I'd imagined myself in a big office. My name in the papers. My photo in one of those lists of most influential people. Touching the sky. Being a star. None of it would be enough to make him say those four words, the four words that mattered most to me: *I'm proud of you.*

I walked over to the bed, tossed the pillow aside, and picked up my book and my grandmother's letter. I reread it. I hadn't done that since I'd left Montreal.

...when I look at you, I still see that little girl who would rather put books in order on a bookshelf than go play with other kids. The one who enjoyed making recommendations and dreamed of writing her own stories one day. I still recognize her in you and I still see the flickers of that old wish in your eyes. And that's why I want to give you the chance to get that hope back.

I put the letter down and glanced around the room, trying to find my computer. Then I sat on the bed and turned it on. My hands were jittery as I opened a hidden folder. I hadn't looked at it in years. I picked the first file on the list. One hundred twenty pages of a love story set in a fantastical universe, with gates to other dimensions and people with psychic powers. I grinned as I recalled how I'd come up with the idea after binging on all the seasons of *Heroes* and falling in love with Milo Ventimiglia.

I opened another and scanned the first few paragraphs. Dear Lord. I didn't even remember this one; I must have been nine or ten when I started writing it. Next.

Dear Mr. Darcy, how much harm you did to my idea of love, I thought, after skimming the sad prologue to yet another of my manuscripts.

I lay back and rested the laptop on my belly and started to read my most recent attempt at a novel. A nearly finished project that I abandoned at the last minute out of...fear? Indecision? It felt like a century since I'd written the last word. Now I couldn't remember what had stopped me.

I looked up, rubbed my tired eyes, and glanced at the clock. For three hours, I'd been absorbed in pages I myself had written. In those words, I had found so many parts of myself that I could have used them to build a second me. And that encouraged me.

I closed my eyes and took a deep breath. I wasn't lost. I'd just forgotten where I was hiding. For so long that I might as well have disappeared.

I got up feeling giddy with hope, like a rocket that was about to take off. And I knew. I'm not sure how, but I knew. I knew it in my body. I knew it in my heart. And I stopped falling, and the void beneath me disappeared, and my feet were on the ground. The veil had lifted, and I was walking tall, and at last I was getting somewhere.

Like a rocket, I flew out of the room. My heart was pounding out of my chest. It was late. I should have been asleep hours ago, but I needed to tell him. Out loud. I needed to tell *him*.

His door was cracked. I pushed it open.

"Trey?" I wasn't sure he heard me, so I walked close to the bed. "Trey?"

"Harper? Are you…are you all right?" His voice was groggy, hoarse.

"I know what I want."

"What?"

"I know what I want to do."

He felt around for the lamp on the nightstand and turned it on, then blinked several times and rubbed his eyes, not quite able to believe what I was telling him. I climbed into the bed on my knees, smiling like a lunatic. I couldn't help it—I was euphoric. So euphoric that I didn't notice he was clothed only in a skimpy pair of boxers. A little patch of fabric and then skin, muscles, a patch of hair around his belly button, and five stars, each bigger than the one before it, trailing down his side.

That wasn't there four years ago!

I tried to ignore the tingle I was feeling as well as my memories of the night we'd made love. He was squinting and smirking, but I could tell he thought I was acting weird.

"I know what I want to do," I repeated. I waited a few seconds to make it suspenseful, then burst out, "I want to write. I want to live surrounded by books. I want to move other people with my words. I want to leave a mark on their lives. I want to create memories and feelings. I want to give people things to dream of. I want to make their hearts race. I want all that. And I want to do it in the only place I've ever actually been happy. My grandmother's bookstore."

Trey sat up and leaned against the headboard, seeming unsure what to say as he looked me over from head to toe.

"See? You do know what you want. You always did. You just needed to remember where you left that part of yourself."

"I did! I found it! I can feel it. I can feel that tingle in my fingers telling me to write. That's what I want to do. Not think about the future or other people. Who cares what anyone thinks? I've had enough of being the good little girl who just swallows everything, who always says yes, who bends over and lets everyone get their way."

"Damn straight. Just because other people like to have an opinion doesn't mean they have any idea who you are or what you need."

"Well, to hell with them!"

"That's right! To hell with them! No one can choose your road. It's yours and yours alone."

He understood me. And that made me happy.

"You're a know-it-all, but I like that," I said.

I felt something tug at that thread that had connected us those days, and suddenly my head was empty. And maybe that's why I did the first thing that occurred to me. Stupid as it might have been.

I bent over clumsily and grabbed his chin and kissed him. Just for a second. And he kissed back, and I felt him sigh.

I pulled away as quickly as I could, realizing what I was doing, and jumped out of the bed.

"Thanks," I said, walking out of the room.

I didn't know what time it was when I woke. My head hurt, and I was hungry, but nothing could wipe away that warm feeling, sweet like honey, that filled me up inside. I walked out of the bedroom barefoot and headed downstairs.

No one was in the living room or kitchen, and when I peeked out the window, I saw Trey's SUV wasn't parked outside, either.

I was disappointed, but I got over it quickly. In my new life, there was only room for positive emotions. I poured myself a cold coffee and drank it out on the grass. It was perfect. The sun toasting my skin, the waves breaking in the distance, the whistle of the wind over the sand. I'd miss all this when I had to go back.

I sat for a while on a boulder, aware of how few moments like this I had left. I felt an unfamiliar inner peace and enjoyed the instant, truly living it. Without a past or a future. All present.

Back inside, I took a shower, then put on one of the dresses I'd stuffed randomly into my suitcase. It was a tiered dress, sheer on the outside, cream-colored, with a print of flowers and leaves. I sat on the bed with my computer, intending to look back at the man-uscripts, notes, and documentation I'd been holding onto a long time. Some of my ideas struck me as worth rescuing and working on again.

It was stirring, but also intimidating, the idea that I was taking a step, changing my life, working on something that would make me happy.

After taking a glance at everything, I started to trust in my abili-ties, and I was ready to prove to myself that I could do it. But I knew the publishing world and how hard it was for a writer to stand out enough to get that first shot. Let alone the second. Let alone main-tain your reputation and name enough to get a third.

It wasn't easy to survive there.

You're here today, but tomorrow you might be gone, and no one will give you a second thought. One minute you were surrounded by people, getting compliments, feeling important, feeling special. The next, it was silence, oblivion. The phone stops ringing, the doors stop opening.

But I pushed all that aside and focused on the main thing.

Chapter 1

In the morning, when I wake, a thin layer of white covers the grass up to the edge of the lake...

Sometime later—I don't know how long—I heard a car coming down the road. I could tell by how loud the motor was that it was Trey. Our kiss from the night before flashed in my mind, and I could feel the aftershocks in my body.

Suddenly, I was embarrassed to see him. To face the fact that I had put my lips on his without even asking his permission.

As I was looking around for where to hide, the door opened and he was standing there beaming on the threshold, shaking a greasy paper bag. He tossed it to me, and I caught it in flight.

"It's grilled turkey and cheese. Eat it, it's getting late."

"Late? Are you in some kind of rush?"

He reached into the back pocket of his jeans and took out two folded pieces of paper, looking like a child on Christmas morning.

"*We* are. We've got two tickets for the ferry. It leaves in an hour. Throw enough clothes in your bag for a couple of days. We're going to PEI!"

A thousand questions passed through my head, but he was gone before I could ask them. I jumped up, tore the sandwich wrapper, and took a bite. With my mouth still full, I went to his room. He'd opened a suitcase on the bed and was stuffing T-shirts inside.

"So you just up and plan a trip to Prince Edward Island without asking me?"

"You don't ask people before you give them a gift, Harper. You just do it, and the other person accepts gracefully."

"So this is a gift? What's the occasion?"

"There are things to celebrate. I finished my blueprints, and you made your big decision."

"Trey, I don't know if I want to go to PEI. The day after tomorrow is Labor Day, and I need to go home after that. I like this place, and I think I'd rather stay here until then. Hang out with Adele, go back to eat at Ridge's…" I lifted the hand with the sandwich in it, and a piece of lettuce fell out. I caught it before it touched the ground.

"I get it, and I'm not going to force you, but I'd really like you to come with me. We'll go out, have fun. We had a bad start here. Here, and maybe in general. We barely know each other, and I'd like to change that. Make it better."

"How?"

"By getting to know you and letting you get to know me. I'm not as bad as you think."

"I don't think you're bad, Trey. Maybe just something of a mystery."

"Well, maybe I don't want to be a mystery anymore."

He looked nervous as he said this, but only for a moment, then he was back to his jaunty old self. I wondered how it was possible for everything to change between us in just a few days. All of a sudden, the villain wasn't such a villain, and the princess had to admit she wasn't such a princess, either, and she'd come down from the tower where she was imprisoned, and she wanted to live. It had taken her a long time. She'd had to realize she'd always had the key, but that a part of her hadn't wanted to leave because she felt safe behind bars. That she'd gotten used to the ambiguity, the chaos in her mind, even as it was slowly poisoning her heart.

But now she was strong, and she was ready for a plot twist in this story that had been sad since the beginning. She was tired of thinking so much, tired of turning over the same things, looking at them from different angles and perspectives and trying to find an answer. Enough examining the possibilities only to push them aside and forget about them. She wanted to live them. She wanted to be open to everything.

She no longer hated her memories or her desires. But she did hate how scared the word *us* made her. And the longing that shook her when he wasn't there. The need for him. And not knowing if they both felt it, or only her.

He dropped a pair of socks, and I leaned over to pick them up.

"Fine. Let's get to know each other. Even if I doubt there will be many surprises after everything we've told each other," I said, holding out the socks to him.

He smiled in reply, but there was something in his eyes I didn't know how to read. He grabbed my wrist and pulled me close. That pressure made me shiver. He had that mischievous expression again that put me on tenterhooks. My poor heart was tired of pumping so much adrenaline.

"There's one condition, though," he added. "I've planned these days out, so I need you to trust me and go with the flow."

I remembered how Trey had ground my heart into dust years ago. Now he was holding that dust in his hands and molding it, shaping it like clay, trying to give it back its original form.

As if it were that simple.

But maybe it was? Because it seemed to be working, and in a strange way, that made me feel vulnerable, because if he could put me back together, that meant he could break me again. I knew it was stupid to think of things that way, that it didn't make sense because we weren't the people we'd been in the past. We had changed, and this time…

This time was different. Real. Something was happening between us. What, though? I was scared to ask.

"You've made plans, then?"

"Yes!"

He bent forward, and I closed my eyes as I heard him whisper, "Trust me. Do you think you can?" His voice sounded sweet as molasses.

"Yeah."

"Are you sure? Because it seems like you're waffling."

I grinned and pushed him away slightly. It wasn't fair, how handsome he was, how irresistible. I needed a break and walked toward the door.

"Harper." I looked back over my shoulder. With a devilish smirk, he said, "About that kiss last night…"

The heat in my breast, in my neck, in my cheeks made me stop. I had tried to tell myself I'd forget it ever happened. Apparently he hadn't.

"Kiss? I have no idea what you're talking about."

He bit his lower lip. And it took my breath away.

17

Do You Believe in Fate?

It was Isak Dinesen who said, "The cure for anything is salt water: sweat, tears, or the sea."

I don't know why, but I remembered that when I was on the ferry looking at the sea, those words sank into me, and I found myself in them. The sweat on my skin when I woke from nightmares. The tears spilled with countless emotions I couldn't manage to express. The sea that surrounded me, restoring my calm, healing me as I struggled to bear the pain of that process. Because salt burns and stings, but it also helps the wound scar over.

I sucked in a deep breath of sea air. A few days before, I'd made the same trip in the opposite direction, yet I already felt I was different from that person who had looked at the waters with suspicion and fear. Before I knew where they were taking me.

I was starting to realize that this was what courage was: moving forward, confronting uncertainty, facing whatever lies ahead. What I had thought was my comfort zone was just a comfortable prison I had gotten used to by stifling my urge for freedom.

Now I could feel that freedom. It was still vague, but I could sense it taking shape, growing stronger, within me. There was a weightlessness to me, as though I were floating after the chains that had held me to the ground had broken.

Can a whole life's inertia just vanish in three days? Before Hayley opened the door to that corner of the world for me, I would have said no. I didn't believe in love at first sight or sudden revelations that appear out of nowhere like a magic trick. For me, that was the stuff of books, fiction and fairy tales, not something that could ever happen in the real world.

But I was wrong.

Three days can alter the course of a whole life. Just like that. And nothing special has to happen. Sometimes the simplest things can make the most powerful changes occur, bringing meaning where there was none before. Sometimes, something happens or someone shows up, and your eyes open in a way they never have. Like that walk with Trey the afternoon before. He'd gotten me to strip my soul bare, to realize what was missing in my life and who I wanted to be.

He had no idea how important that had been for me. How he'd saved me from myself, made me feel hope again.

"You must have something really nice on your mind to be smiling like that," he said.

"Indeed." I grabbed the rail to keep from losing balance. The waves in that part of the gulf were big. "Do you believe in fate?"

He offered me one of the chocolate bars he'd bought in Petit Prince before we left. I unwrapped it and took a bite. He did the same, eating half of it in a single bite.

"I don't think fate is behind everything. Or that every step in our lives is predestined. Because that would mean we were incapable of choosing, and I don't like the idea of not being in control of my own life."

How different we were, I thought—how different and how similar at the same time. "Well, I do believe in fate. And I also believe in coincidences and lucky accidents."

"Lucky accidents? What's that supposed to mean?"

"Lucky accidents are these things that might seem bad at first, but they end up leading to something good. Like, I don't know, your car breaks down in the middle of the highway and only one car stops to help, and out of it steps Chris Pratt."

He didn't seem convinced. "What are the chances that would ever happen? One in a few million?"

"Still, like you just said: there *is* a chance. And fate and hope go hand in hand."

"I think what you're calling a coincidence or a 'lucky accident' is a series of circumstances that depend on a person and their environment," he said. "That's all. There's not some genie that's granting your wishes. The universe isn't tracing out a plan for us or trying to give us cosmic signs about what we should do." He turned around and leaned his hips against the railing, back to the sea. "What you call fate is just us and the decisions we make. If your car breaks down and you're stranded on the highway, the luckiest accident you could have is for a tow truck to show up."

"Well, I like the idea of fate. But I also like the idea of life being a choose-your-own-adventure book where the story changes depending on the choices you make."

"Wait, so you're saying each person can have several different fates?"

"Exactly!" He got it. Or he got me, at any rate.

"Do you think it's fate that brought us together on this island?" he asked.

"I'd like to think so."

He leaned in, reached over, and stroked my cheek with the tip of his fingers. "Well, then, maybe I'll end up believing in it, too."

It was late afternoon when we reached Souris. We'd brought his SUV on the ferry, and we drove it out past the city, heading toward the west. I did as I'd promised, trusting Trey and letting him take the lead without asking any questions.

The sun stained the sky orange, and I stared at it through the windshield, enjoying the play of colors as the darkness started to gather. The wind coming through the window ruffled my hair. It was cool and smelled of damp earth. I closed my eyes and took a deep breath, and when I opened them, I found myself surrounded by pastures and magic forests.

The roads were practically empty. The island didn't have any big cities like the other provinces of Canada, but its rural countryside was simple and charming.

We talked about everything and nothing while the music played softly in the background. We shared the same favorite group, and since I was no longer scared of looking silly in front of him, I turned up the volume and sang at the top of my lungs.

Long before we got there, I realized we were headed to Charlottetown. I remembered the roads from my own trip a few days ago. But I didn't say anything. I liked the look on Trey's face when he was thinking he was going to surprise me.

But surprise me he did.

We parked next to an information center for tourists and walked through the center of town before getting dinner on the patio of the Water Prince Corner Shop. We ordered fish cakes and fried clams, then headed to the famous ice cream shop COWS on Queen Street. I ordered the apple crisp flavor; he picked maple walnut. We ended the night sitting outside at a bar listening to live music.

"Another?" Trey asked after downing his second shot.

My throat was burning and I couldn't get my vocal cords to work, but I nodded.

He pushed his way through the crowd and headed toward the bar. He was taller than everyone, and he was noticed, especially when he walked past the women. One of them tried to get his attention and I frowned, trying to pretend it didn't bother me. He didn't even notice her. He seemed oblivious to how sexy he was, or at least acted like all that attention didn't matter to him.

That was one more proof that he wasn't the boy I used to know...

He was different. Now he was...

He was...

He was a hurricane. Fire. Rain splashing a window. Sand blown up by the wind. Sweet wine. Chocolate melting on your tongue. Sunlight. Words spoken on the porch. The savor of a kiss. Throaty laughter. The soft touch of fingers on skin. Music, silence, air. Heartbeats.

That was the alcohol talking. I'd never been able to hold my liquor.

Late at night, we went back to the car and Trey drove to Fitzroy Hall, a handsome bed-and-breakfast where he'd reserved two rooms.

Lying down, I thought to myself that it had been a perfect night. I realized that there was so much more to being alive than I'd thought about. Life meant talking, laughing, listening, smelling, tasting. Touch. New experiences.

The next morning, we got up late, had breakfast, gathered our things, and went to the car. I was curious, questions dancing on the tip of my tongue, and it was getting harder and harder to hold them back.

"You ready?" Trey asked me.

I nodded, feeling excited.

I watched the city speed by as we left it behind on the highway. The sky was clear, and the sun was hot through the windshield. It's strange how things change sometimes. And how others never do. Everything I felt was still too intense—the good and the bad. I was diving into my feelings as if into a deep pool, reaching the bottom, holding my breath. Sometimes the pressure vanished and I could breathe again, but sometimes I was trapped down there for days.

An idea occurred to me just then, a thought loud as thunder: my decision was going to have consequences, direct and indirect ones. People would react to it, and I didn't know how to face their reactions.

"You're quiet," Trey said. I turned to him and nodded. "A penny for your thoughts?" he continued.

"You'll have to do better than that. A penny won't get you much nowadays."

"Fine, name your price. Just let me know what's going on in that head of yours."

I took off my sandals, curled my legs up in the seat, and hugged my knees.

"I just keep thinking about how I'm about to become the owner of a small independent bookstore, and I don't even know if I can pay the bills. And how I picked that over being someone."

"You are someone. And you're not just going to be the adorable owner of a cute little bookstore, you're also going to be a professional writer, and one day when you're rich and famous and millions of people are buying your books, you'll realize you did the right thing."

I felt almost embarrassed at his inexplicable faith in me. "I hope so, because my father's going to disinherit me. I'll be exiled from the family home and probably forced to change my last name."

"You really think he won't support you?" Trey asked, unsure whether or not I was being serious.

"I know he won't."

"I mean, I get that at first it will be hard for him to accept. It *is* a big change. But when he sees how happy you are…"

I shook my head. "No, Trey. My relationship with my father is complicated. He rarely agrees with what I do or how I do it."

"Why not?"

I shrugged and started gnawing at a little strip of dead skin on my lower lip.

"I don't know." He reached over and clutched my hand, and his fingers touched the bare flesh of my thighs, but intimate as the gesture was, I didn't bat him away. "I've always wanted to take the reins in my life, but in the end, I back down. I've never managed to take the last step. I've never known how, or maybe I have, but I was too busy worrying about what other people would think to consider my own needs and desires. That's the truth. And having him constantly in my head held me back because my father's never approved of anything about me. There's no making him happy. At least I never have and I doubt I ever will, and as long as I can't, he'll go on treating me like the worst mistake he's ever made."

"I had no idea. Your brother and sister never mentioned that."

I forced a smile and turned to him. This was the first time I'd been honest with anyone about it. "It's different for them, you know? I love Hoyt and Hayley, but I can't help envying them, too, even hating them a little when I see how well they get along with him. I'd have done anything, literally anything, to connect with my father, even just once. But I'm over it. I'm too tired to keep trying."

"I'm so sorry, Harper. I had no idea things were like that."

"No! It's fine! I'm fine!" I tried to be more enthusiastic than I actually felt. "I've been following my plan B for years without ever even trying my plan A. Well, now that's over. I want to do what I've always dreamed of: write. Write as if each page might be the last one I wrote before I died."

He didn't respond, and I didn't need him to, and him knowing I didn't need it thrilled me. He slowed down and came to a stop on the shoulder, leaving the motor running. And that man who had burst into my life unexpectedly and had made me believe in my dreams bent so close to me I could feel the heat in his exhalations.

His lips rubbed mine, almost without touching them.

And from instinct, I closed my eyes and waited.

I felt him again, but surer this time, pressing into me with passion as his hands held my face. It was sweet and delicate, tender and devastating. I yielded to that kiss, and I gave back as much as I got. I don't know how long it lasted; I didn't know kissing a man could feel like that. When his tongue wrapped around mine, I was certain I never wanted to kiss anyone else that way again.

I realized something then, and the realization gathered force as we continued touching each other: I loved him. And knowing that terrified me.

I pulled back, almost out of breath, though it took all of my strength not to leap at him. "I think this was a mistake," I said.

He smiled as if he knew something I didn't, a secret, and rubbed my cheek with the back of his hand. "I love those pretty things you say," he said, giving me one last peck. "Now close your eyes and promise me you won't open them again until I tell you. We're about to arrive somewhere. I want it to be a surprise for you."

"I cannot fix on the hour, or the spot, or the look or the words, which laid the foundation. It is too long ago. I was in the middle before I knew that I *had* begun."

—Jane Austen, *Pride and Prejudice*

18

My Destiny and Yours Crossed

"Okay, you can open them."

My eyes had been closed so long that for a moment, all I could see were bright flashes over a blurry background. I had to blink several times to see clearly.

Then I saw a house with white walls, a green roof, and a delicate fence surrounding a garden full of flowers and vegetables. My mouth fell open in surprise when I noticed a covered carriage with a horse and a girl in a brown, ankle-length dress, a white apron, and lace-up boots, all in the style of another era. Rounding off the costume was a straw hat and long braids tied at the ends.

We got out of the car and she approached us with a broad smile. "Hi, my name is Layla. Can I help you?"

"I'm Trey Holt. I called yesterday to make a reservation for a guided visit."

"Of course. I was waiting for you."

Her, the house, all of it confused me. I felt as if I'd stepped into a dream, as if I were floating in some vague space between past and present. But I wasn't. I could hear a rushing sound in my ears, and my eyes filled with tears. They rolled down my cheeks and fell like huge drops of rain.

I couldn't believe it. I was at Cavendish. I was at Green Gables. The real farm had never existed, but this was the re-creation of Avonlea that had been built on the island decades ago. My whole body prickled with joy, but a second later, the sorrow hit, quick and hard like a wave from out of nowhere, nearly knocking me over.

There are things you never forget, things that live inside you forever.

Moments that come late.

That should have belonged to someone else.

I turned around and started walking away.

I needed a second to breathe. To pull myself together.

Because I didn't want to lose that battle with guilt, but I just couldn't help feeling frail and fragile.

In that moment, a whole world came back to me and vanished at once.

I didn't know where I meant to go, but I had to try to escape the hole opening up in my chest, all those feelings welling up inside of me.

Trey hurried over and took my hand, stopping me and turning me toward him. He looked worried at first, then when he looked closer, utterly baffled.

"Are you crying? Why?"

I shook my head, unable to find the right words. "It's...all this." I groaned, waving my hand past the landscape around us.

"Because I brought you here?" he asked, more and more upset. "I'm sorry, I thought you'd like it. The other morning I got curious, and I tried to find out more about your book, and I learned about this place. I thought it would be nice. After all you've told me, and everything that story is supposed to mean for you..."

I sobbed, and the tears fell like a waterfall down my face, burning my cheeks.

"I'm so sorry. Please, don't cry. If I'd known you wouldn't like it, I'd never have brought you here."

"I'm not crying because I don't like it. It's the sweetest thing anyone's ever done for me."

"What is it, then?" His face was full of uncertainty, and I wanted to kiss him again and make it all vanish.

"When my mother got sick, she promised me we'd come visit here together. I think she wanted it to be just the two of us, so I'd have that memory of her."

"Did you ever make it here?"

I shook my head, but through my grief I could see something special in the way he looked at me, as if I were the only person in the entire world.

"No. A few days before we were supposed to come, my father came to my room. He told me my mother was sick, that if things got any worse, she might die. I had no idea, and that scared me. And he said Mom had only agreed to make the trip because of me, because I was a spoiled and selfish little girl, and that if anything happened to her, it would be my fault."

"How old were you?"

"Six."

"Jesus!"

I heaved again, trying to get some air.

"He forced me to tell my mother I didn't want to do it. I was so young, and my father scared me back then. So I did as he asked. She died thinking she didn't matter to me." I blew my nose.

Trey hugged me, and I squeezed his shirt in my fists. I was wailing. I couldn't stop the storm that had broken out inside me. I was reliving that entire time as though it had just happened.

"Of course she knew you mattered to her. Trust me."

"How do you know?"

"Because mothers never stop loving their children. They always forgive. No matter what you do."

His response moved me. And hurt at the same time. But somehow, it allowed me to crawl out of my grief toward something else. I felt his lips on my hair. A kiss that turned my tears of sorrow into tears of bittersweet joy.

"Harper?"

"Yes?"

"Why does your father hate you?"

"I don't know."

I felt relieved, grateful to be held by him. And we stayed that way for what felt like days.

"Forget him," he told me, his voice angry, grabbing my shoulders and stepping back to look me in the eyes. "Screw him. He can go to hell. You don't need him."

"I thought you liked him."

"I could never like anyone who treated you that way," he said, wiping the tears from my cheeks.

Even now, it's hard for me to express what that day meant to me.

We visited the house and looked at all the different rooms, which were decorated with furniture and mementos from the era. I shouted with joy when I entered Anne's room and saw her brown dress with the puffed sleeves hanging on the closet door. The kitchen, the sewing room, Marilla and Matthew's bedrooms, the actors walking around dressed as characters from the book… All that was like being inside a bubble outside of time, where the normal rules of logic didn't apply.

The other visitors felt the same. I could tell by the looks on their faces. For a brief moment, we felt it was all real, that the world we had visited in books actually existed.

After walking through the stables and around the property, we headed for the trails, where the story came to life beneath the trees of Lover's Lane and the Haunted Wood and on the banks of the Lake of Shining Waters. I thought of my grandmother, how much she would have liked knowing that in real life, the area was just as pretty as she could ever have imagined.

A few minutes away from the farmhouse was Avonlea Village. It was touristy, but cute, with quaint shops and charming little houses. It didn't look much like the town I'd always visualized, but I didn't care.

We had pizza at an Italian restaurant called Piatto and bought a big bag of candy at a chocolate shop. Trey liked chocolate as much as I did, and we ended up fighting over the ones that had the toffee center. It was funny to see him acting like a child, running after me as I tried to escape and gobble them down. I stuffed a handful in my mouth and nearly choked on them.

We rested a while on the lawn in one of the gardens before heading to New London, where I saw the house in which Lucy Maud Montgomery was born. The place where her entire world took shape.

In the afternoon, he recommended going back to the hotel so we could shower and get ready for dinner. I thought it was a brilliant idea. I'd been sweating, and I had grass blades and little bits of chocolate in my hair.

We returned to Cavendish, not far from Green Gables.

"Is this our hotel?" I asked.

"Yeah. Do you like it?"

I nodded, mouth hanging open, eyes wide as saucers, staring at the imposing white building that I assumed was the center of the complex. All around it were pretty little cabins. The whole place was like something from a fairy tale.

A nice women greeted us in reception and accompanied us to our rooms on the second floor. Dragging my suitcase upstairs, I felt a tingle in my body like a premonition. Looking over my shoulder, I saw Trey and was surprised to find his head hanging low, his features stiff with worry. But as soon as he noticed I was observing him, all that disappeared. He smiled and winked.

When we entered the room, I jumped on the bed and lay there a few minutes staring up. But what I saw wasn't the white ceiling above me. Instead I saw dozens of images, shooting past one after the other like a slideshow. I was happier than I'd ever been, and all I could think about was savoring every minute of that night and the day that would follow. Every second next to him. That man who had turned my dull gray world into one that was alive and moving.

I rubbed my lips, remembering when he'd kissed me. And I wondered what I should think of it. We'd been acting like two friends. But then there were moments when we seemed to be stripping each other bare.

Or no. That wasn't true. Not really.

I was the one who was stripping myself bare.

I had opened my chest for him like a window and shown him the bleeding heart inside. He had seen everything I was. My light. My darkness. My dreams and desires. My secrets. It was as if he had a superpower and could force out of me all the emotions I tried to keep under control. Opening up inside me the space I needed to keep from suffocating.

Trey, though, was closed up. I hadn't noticed that until just then. Sure, I knew things about him. He'd talked to me about his projects, things he was doing and things he wanted to do. How he loved the mountains in winter and the beach in summer. How he planned to design and build a home one day on the shores of one of the Great Lakes, where he'd live surrounded by dogs when humanity no longer had anything to offer him.

But I knew there was much more there under the surface. I'd

caught sight of that something more once or twice, but just hints of it, like that moment on the stairs.

I got up and walked to the bathroom. After a quick shower, I looked at myself in the mirror. My skin was tanned, which brought out my eyes. I didn't need any makeup, I thought. I pulled my hair back in a ponytail and smoothed out the bottom of the flowery dress I'd put on. Then I rubbed my belly, trying to calm myself.

I heard a knock at the door. When I opened up, I couldn't help but gawk a moment at his body in those black jeans and that black button-down shirt. Then I saw his recently shaved face, so smooth it was hard not to reach up and touch it. He smelled nice, and he was so handsome it hurt. He could probably tell I was thinking that. His smile told me he knew everything, while I knew nothing about him.

"You look dazzling," he said.

"Thanks. You too."

"Ready for dinner?"

I nodded, elated.

We got in the car, and five minutes later we were parking next to a country house with cedar siding and white windows. It must have been a farmhouse at one time—the curving roof gave it away. There were planters overflowing with gardenias on the sills of the upper windows. Creeping vines climbed the walls, and all around were big flowerpots with bushes and flowering plants. The lighting was scant, giving the place a romantic feel.

As soon as we were inside, I fell in love with the place. The dining room was small and intimate, and the decoration eclectic, combining old and new. On the walls were paintings by local artists for sale, and there was a bouquet of roses on each table.

A waitress walked us over to a window table set for two and soon returned to take our order. We chose the grilled vegetable and goat cheese salad with vinaigrette, pork loin with mustard and roasted apples, a bottle of red wine, and a couple of appetizers.

"This place is beautiful," I said.

"You like it?"

"I love it! I know I promised not to ask questions and just go along, but…did you already know about the hotel, this restaurant, and everywhere else?"

"No. I've never been here. This is my first time in Cavendish."

"Then how'd you…?"

He leaned over and reached into his back pocket, taking out a piece of paper that he slid toward me with his fingertips.

"Two things helped me: the internet and the desire to see that smile on your face," he said. As I looked down at the paper, I thought I should let my hair down so he wouldn't see the blood rising in my face and making my ears glow. When I unfolded it, I saw a list.

"You don't want to keep the rest of your plan a secret?" He shook his head, so I kept reading to satisfy my curiosity. Everything was there: names, telephones, distances, right down to the last detail. He'd spent a long time preparing the itinerary. It had taken effort, not to mention money. I looked up at him. "Trey," I said, "this must have cost a fortune. Let me pay my part of it."

"No. I told you it was a gift. A gift is something you give someone, not something you ask them to go halfsies on."

"As a gift," I replied, "I accept it, but still…this is too much."

"It's not, though. I want to do everything for you. I want to make up for how I treated you, even if I know I'll never be able to."

"Trey, I don't need you to make up anything."

His expression was pained. "I screwed up bad. And it started long before that night."

"What do you mean?"

"I should have done something about my feelings as soon as I started to realize I liked you. I shouldn't have dragged it out like that. What happened was my fault. I hurt you, and what I did was wrong, and I can't stop regretting it. It was a mistake, and I made it worse when I threw you out like that, Harper. I realize I can't change the past, as much as I'd like to. But I can try to do better now."

"Trey, don't punish yourself…"

"I can't help it! I can't stop thinking over all that I said. And the fact that we did it. That I was your first time. And that I can't remember it! I don't remember what it felt like to touch your body, I don't remember what your skin smelled like when it was close to mine. I don't remember your caresses. I don't remember what it felt like to kiss you intimately, or to be inside you. And that hurts me because I liked you, Harper. I've wondered so many times what it would be like to be with you."

I was speechless and felt a dull ache invading those wounds that I thought had healed. The tense silence stretched on as our eyes met in a stare. I did remember every second of it: his body, his aroma. I remembered his lips, our intimacy, his teeth, his nails, his moans. Our caresses. All we managed to say to each other in silence. All I felt. Him. The void at my feet. How simple it was to jump. Getting lost in his breathing and the beats of his heart. Reaching the summit. Holding each other and tumbling over the edge.

I had a strange feeling, as if my eyes were windows and he could stare into me and see me replaying these images in my mind. And I had a knot in my throat, because everything he'd said had been in the past tense.

But then he spoke again, his voice gravelly, intense: "I still like you. I still think about what it would be like."

His comment took me off guard. I'd never felt so exposed, so vulnerable. The tension in the air was like electricity. Emotion piled on emotion in my chest: happiness, desire, hope, fear…oscillating, vibrating, overlapping. I was afraid my ribs weren't strong enough to hold them all in, that they'd explode and send shock waves rippling through the room.

Everything seemed to disappear. The room, the other diners, the entire world. I was silent, not because I didn't know what to say, but because I did know, and I wasn't ready to open up like that. I was scared to think of *us* when I didn't even know if an *us* was possible.

We stayed there contemplating each other, trying to decipher each other, for more time than I could reasonably count. Then I looked at the paper and realized our dinner was the last item on the list. I was sure we were supposed to be there another day. Was I confused?

"I was thinking tomorrow we could improvise," he said, as if he could read my mind.

I liked that idea. Just letting ourselves go.

We turned our attention to our meal. The music playing in the background was nice, and the food was to die for. I knew everything, down to the smallest gesture, would linger forever in my memory.

"Tell me about your mother," he said after we shared a slice of carrot cake with buttery icing. I hadn't seen that question coming, and I needed a moment to respond.

"Most of my memories of her are like postcards. I might see something that calls up a scene, and then for a second or two, she's back. But that's it. I was really little when she died."

"I wish you hadn't lost her so young. It wasn't fair. Not for either of you."

"You're right," I whispered, trying to suppress the tears. "She was a special woman. That's something I remember about her: the way she could light up a room, the way her laughter drowned out everything. I remember her braiding my hair. I remember her voice when she used to read to me. But in a strange way. Like I couldn't tell you if her voice was high or deep. It's different. It's like…"

"It's a feeling."

"Exactly!" I exclaimed. He understood me better than I understood myself. "What was your mother like?" I knew I should be careful touching that subject, but I hoped I could break through his shell and find out more about him after the confessions he'd made to me before.

"I think they're waiting for us to leave," he whispered, as if I hadn't asked.

It was true: the tables around us were empty, and the waitress was standing at the bar. We asked her to bring the check, and we left not long afterward. When we got to the car, Trey said we should go to North Rustico, a nearby town he'd seen photos of in his research. On the drive over, I was lost in thought, and he made no effort to interrupt me.

We parked by a café called Blue Mussel, bought a couple of ice creams, and walked to the lighthouse, which wasn't far. The views there were gorgeous. In one place, the sea pushed inland, forming an estuary that joined the beaches of North Rustico, Anglo Rustico, and Rusticoville. The buildings were few, the lights were dim, scattered like fireflies in the night, and the moon shone in its pale halo in the clear sky. Where the sea met the horizon was absolute darkness.

Trey and I stood there breathing the sea breeze, calm, in peace. It was pure tranquility.

"Tell me what you like," he said.

"I don't know. Movies, music, books…"

"I don't mean simple things like that."

"What do you mean, then?"

"Let me give you an example. I like to lie on my surfboard and stare at the sun while the waves rock me. I can even fall asleep that way. I like walking on newly fallen snow, getting out in it with my dog, rolling around in it until we're both soaking wet."

"You have a dog?" I was surprised. He had told me he liked them, but this was the first time he mentioned owning one.

"Yeah, he's a beautiful Alaskan malamute named Sisuei. That means 'blaze of fire.' I called him that because his golden eyes glow like fire."

"Well, that's something you two have in common. Yours glow, too. They say dogs and their owners end up resembling each other, but I never thought it was true."

He chuckled, but I don't think it was my comment that did it.

"He's amazing. He's just two years old and he's already huge. He's smart, intuitive, a little bit mischievous. A friend's taking care of him right now."

I liked how proud he seemed of him, and said, "I've always wanted a dog, but we were never allowed any pets at home."

"I'll introduce you to Sisuei."

"I don't think I'm good with animals. My neighbor has this cute little mutt and he hates me. He growls and barks every time I see him."

"Sisuei will like you."

"What makes you so sure?"

"Because he's just like me."

"Tell me more of your likes," I said.

"When I'm in the mountains, I like to get up and watch the sunrise. Something about that moment, the first light of the day, the silence… I don't know, it's just calming. I like driving, too. I can do it for hours without getting bored as long as I have some decent music. It's relaxing." He took a bite of his ice cream and licked his lips. "Do you know Andrée and Geneviève Grandbois?"

"Are you talking about the chocolate makers?"

"Yeah, Chocolats Andrée and Les Chocolats Geneviève Grandbois. They're both on Mile End. And I swear, between Waverly and Park, the air smells like chocolate. That's why I rented my place on Jeanne Mance Street. I like that scent."

"Are you for real?"

"Yeah. And don't look at me like I'm nuts."

It was hard not to, so I turned my eyes toward the ocean covered in shimmering reflections. I couldn't believe so many stars were visible in that sky. I licked off a sliver of ice cream and savored it, thinking of what a puzzle Trey was, and how hard it was to fit those dozens of pieces together.

"I had no idea that's where you lived. I barely know anything about you."

"You don't have to know a bunch of details about someone to know them. You've learned more about me in four days than some people who have been around me my whole life." He seemed to disappear for a moment, but then, just as quickly, he was back. "You never answered me. What do you like?"

I had to think for a few seconds.

"I like going to Fairmount first thing in the morning, when the bagels just come out of the oven. That first bite, when they're still hot... Mmmm. I like going underwater and opening my eyes. Feeling like I'm in a bubble where the only thing audible is my heartbeat. Getting lost for hours in a bookstore, any bookstore, just to touch the books' spines, open the first page, read it, smell it. It's magical! Going to the aquarium to see the seals. I do that when I feel alone or sad. They're so funny that they always make me laugh. I like crying during romantic movies. I like going to the botanical gardens and getting lost among those living sculptures; it makes me feel like Alice in Wonderland. You must think I'm a weirdo, like I have this fixation on being other people, but I promise you, that's not it. It's just that I did that when I was little. I had so much imagination. Too much, maybe. It's possible that I still do. And I love to walk, too, without picking where I'm going in advance, just taking off and getting lost."

Suddenly, the moment seemed to freeze, with me staring at him and him staring at me. To break the spell, I pulled my bangs behind my ear.

"I like walking, too," he said softly, as though it were a confession. "Especially in the morning, when nobody's left their house yet, and I can think."

"What do you think about?"

He shrugged. "Things. Ideas. Like how the world needs more people who mean what they say and say what they mean. Or how much time we waste looking for explanations for life instead of simply living it. How it's a mistake to believe only in what you can see and hear. Or wanting things to be the same when you're not even the same. How time passes, but pain doesn't, but if you stop thinking about it, the hurt doesn't hurt so bad... Maybe you're right and the universe makes plans for us without checking with us first, and it was a happy accident that my destiny and yours crossed." He came closer. "I want to be open with you. And that scares me, because if you see everything that's inside me, you're not going to like all of it. And if you don't, maybe you'll want to turn your back on me. And that terrifies me."

A second. That's how long I needed for my perspective to change. For my mind to stop thinking about everything that *could* happen and center on what *was* happening.

Him and me.

Us.

I wished it would last forever.

The light penetrated my deepest shadows. And the truth was there, as if it had fallen from heaven. Bright and clear, suffusing me inside and out.

A new excitement had taken hold, and I wasn't nervous and I wasn't resentful. As the ice cream melted in my mouth, other things seemed to melt away, too: my doubts, my suspicions, all the distance that I had put between us.

It was foolish to go on denying the truth. Love happens, even when you don't want it to. There's no magic potion you can take to fend it off, no formula logic can use to protect the human heart. And the heart is trusting, even stupid, even foolish. It doesn't learn from its mistakes. It gives everything; it jumps in with open arms and eyes closed.

And just then, my heart went running toward its master, unable to stop or even slow down what was growing inside it. A feeling I'd thought was lost, but that had actually never gone away. It had only been hibernating, waiting for this moment to emerge, placid, unhurt.

This moment.

A moment of hunger.

A moment of desire that outweighed everything else.

Feeling him. Letting destiny decide if forever was possible.

Gambling. Because the risk was worth it.

I stepped up on my tiptoes and cupped the back of his head with my hand, making him bend down so I could kiss him. I didn't look away from him, but at last I had to close my eyes. To feel him, feel all of him, more intensely. His body next to mine. His hot breath on my lips.

I opened my mouth, lusting for him, leaned into his chest when I felt my knees go weak, let him hold me up in his strong arms—let our bodies come together, one molecule at a time, turning into one.

When he let me go, the world was spinning around us so fast that I couldn't move. I hid my face in the gap between his shoulder and neck and inhaled his scent. We kissed each other on the lips, on the temple, on the chin, as I struggled to make myself believe this was real. I felt his palms on my face as our eyes met. Connecting.

Everything was right now. Every piece was in its place.

We couldn't keep our hands off of each other as we returned to the car. We couldn't keep our hands off each other in the car, in reception at the hotel, on the stairs, in the hall. At the door to my room, we devoured each other. We separated, faces and lips flushed, and I could see the desire burning in him, all the things he wanted to do. He was holding back, and I was, too.

Neither of us knew what to say. He reached up, stroked my cheek with his knuckles, gave me a brief last kiss.

"Good night," he said.

"Good night," I whispered back.

I turned to open the door.

"Harper?"

"Yeah?"

"Does this mean you and I…"

"Yeah. I think so."

His smile was the last thing I saw as I shut the door.

The last thing I saw when I closed my eyes.

19

Does It Have a Name? Is It Going Somewhere...?

I've always been a good girl, but what I wanted was to be free. I couldn't say how many times I'd fallen, how many times I'd risen up from the ground broken, how many cracks I bore, how many pieces of me were missing. I was sunny on the outside, but inside the storm was always raging. Now, though, I felt myself falling upward, and I was poised to land in the present. A present that was full of dreams.

I didn't want to stay there with the door closed, watching life through the peephole. I wanted to cross the threshold. I wanted to decide about things and not worry about the consequences. I wanted to live for myself, to do things on my own. To depend on me and no one else. To love, to yearn. To accept that this is who I am, this is who life has made me. Maybe I'll feel alone, maybe I'll suffer when I don't want to. But how long the pain lasts depends on me.

Loving doesn't mean the other person loves you back. But that's also not a reason to give up on it.

Love exists whether we want it or not.

It's love that chooses, and you just have to follow along.

I'd never have reached that point with Trey if I hadn't been led along by his words, by his way of understanding me, by that ease with which he looked into me and saw things I didn't know existed. At the same time, he'd taught me that I didn't need him to pass through that door. I didn't need him or anyone else. Just myself. Because there's only one person who knows what I'm thinking, what I'm feeling. One person who always laughs and cries with me. And that's me.

We can't always wait for someone to put out a safety net for us before we jump.

If you want to be happy, you have to try.

I don't know how long I stayed in bed thinking all this over. I could have stayed there even longer, floating in the calm waters of my emotions. It was the first Monday in September, Labor Day in Canada.

I kept following my thoughts as I showered. The rational and the irrational ones. Some were clear as daylight; others were confused and tangled. I had taken a step the night before with Trey. That had set something in motion. And I wasn't going to stop it now.

I dressed and grabbed my things. After a few tries, I managed to get my sister on the phone. I couldn't keep her on the line long, but I could tell that she was happy. She told me how scared and excited she'd been to swim with the sharks. That despite her claustrophobia, she'd enjoyed her deep-sea diving class that Scott had gotten her. Then she started in with the questions, and I had to bite my tongue not to let it all out.

"So, you're going to keep the bookstore? Are you going to write, too?"

"Yeah. That's the plan."

"My God, Harper. You can't imagine how happy that makes me. Deep down I knew it. I knew that was the decision you'd make. You're a compulsive romantic, and there's nothing you can do about it. You're emotional, and sensitive, and you were born to be free. To dream." She sounded prouder of me with each loving word, and that made me weepy. "We'll celebrate when we're both back, okay?"

"Yeah, that'll be amazing. Hayley?"

"Yeah?"

"How come you didn't just tell me what to do before?"

"Babe, I did tell you, lots of times. But you didn't listen. You needed to see it for yourself."

I nodded even though she couldn't see me. And I closed my eyes, imagining her gentle face.

"Harper, you know I'm here for everything you need. The same goes for Hoyt and Scott. We're your family."

She was trying hard to wring the tears out of me, but I held on until we said goodbye a short while later. Then I sent a message to Hoyt. He responded with a selfie from the beach that warmed my heart. Was that an octopus he had on his head?

Trey wasn't in his room, so I went downstairs. I tried to be cheerful, but I was trembling inside.

Trembling from uncertainty.

Trembling because I had no idea how to act around him now.

Trembling because my feelings were growing too big for me to handle.

"Have you seen my friend?" I asked the receptionist as I turned in my key.

"I think he's outside."

"Thanks."

I walked onto the porch, nerves frayed, and found him. He'd brought his car around to the entrance and was leaning against it, waiting for me, in torn jeans and a shirt with rolled-up sleeves. His hair was in sexy disarray.

He had been looking at his phone, but now he glanced up as I came to meet him. I wasn't sure what to do or say. How to act. He stepped forward, too, and his eyes descended briefly to my lips before he kissed me, pulling me close and making all my fears and doubts disappear.

There really was a him and me—an us.

I realized then that we had always known each other, somehow, but that before had been the wrong time, and without realizing it, I'd been waiting for him. I realized that the hatred I had felt for him was a way of not forgetting him. Of holding on to him until I could love him the way I should.

"The dining room's full, but I found a café a few minutes away that doesn't look bad," he said.

"Cool. I'm dying of hunger. I need something in my system ASAP."

"Same," he said, and I felt his fingers travel from my waist to my hips, where they paused, slightly jittery. He seemed hesitant to pull away.

I wanted him. I wanted, wanted, wanted him.

I recognized then how much desire can hurt. Can shake you. Can stick the knife in and twist it. And I felt a tickle on my skin, a dampness between my legs. I felt my fingers twitching, I felt need. All at once, like a bomb going off.

I never knew my body could feel that way. A sensation as soft as a whisper and powerful as an avalanche. My body. Alive. Desperate. Hungry.

We left Cavendish on the highway to New London, crossed Stanley Bridge, and soon were parking in the lot of a small restaurant called Sutherland's. We took our seats on the terrace and ordered coffee and sandwiches.

We didn't talk much through breakfast, and even in the car we were hesitant.

We took off, not sure where we were going. I liked that: improvising, being free.

After New London came Kensington, where we stopped to visit a haunted house on a hill. It was a theme park, a bizarre Tudor mansion built at the beginning of the 1890s that had a koi pond and a petting zoo. Its first owner had been a rich Englishman known to the locals as Doctor Jack.

According to legend, Doctor Jack rented out rooms in the mansion and attracted many visitors. Some of them disappeared and were never heard from again, and it was said that their ghosts remained there, wandering the halls at night.

We didn't see any ghosts, but we did find some hilarious keepsakes in the gift shop.

Later, we ate in Summerside at a pizza place close to the port. There, we met an old couple who told us we should visit the lighthouse on Cape Egmont and the Bottle Houses, which a former lighthouse keeper had begun building in 1980.

That was enough to arouse our curiosity, and we headed out. I don't know how long we spent there. It could have been twenty minutes, or it could have been two hours. Trey was fascinated by it: out of recycled bottles, one man had built a house, a tavern, and a chapel. It had taken thousands of bottles cemented together, of different shapes, sizes, and colors. If no one had gathered them, they'd just have ended up in a landfill.

Trey observed and admired everything, right down to the last corner, noticing the smallest details. Especially interesting to him were the places the structures had been repaired. And, of course, we were dazzled by the symphony of light pouring in through the colored glass.

I got tired and sat down to rest on one of the benches around the property to watch him walk back and forth taking pictures with his cell phone. I took mine out, too, to check my email and saw I had two missed calls and a text message from Frances. I'd had it on silent. Dammit.

Hey, Harper, I just wanted to tell you I'll have to leave earlier than I thought. My sister's ill and she needs my help. I wish I could be here when you get back, but it doesn't matter.

We'll see each other soon. Don't worry, I've left you a list of instructions with everything you'll need to know. Take care. I love you.

I dialed her, but the call went straight to voicemail.

I had talked to her a few days before, the same morning Trey showed up with the tickets, but I hadn't told her anything about my decision about the bookstore or about my relationship with him. I wanted to do that in person. But I still felt the need to talk, for her to listen to me, so I could share with her all those feelings I had.

I tried her one more time, then put my phone away.

When Trey finally came over, my mind disconnected from everything else and focused on him. He awakened so much in me…

As a joke, he bowed and invited me to accompany him. The sea breeze curled around us as we walked to the lighthouse. The afternoon was pretty, the sun an intense orange. We held hands as we walked along the cliffside. The views at the end of the cape were incredible. The vast ocean, the waves breaking against the rocks, the bright-red sand, and far out, a whale. I pointed to it, but couldn't utter a word because I had rarely seen anything so beautiful.

Trey smiled and wrapped an arm around me, and I leaned my back into his chest. His mind seemed to be elsewhere, and his preoccupied air made me think of a defenseless little child I wanted to protect. Something was going on with him, and that something had to do with me or with us. And that scared me, because in four days, I'd fallen hopelessly in love with him. Or maybe I had been since the first moment I saw him.

"It's after five, and we're two hours from Souris. We've missed the ferry," he said.

"I don't mind spending another night here. We can probably find somewhere to sleep."

"You're thinking about sleeping?"

His voice was like molten chocolate spilling over me and warming my skin, my muscles, my bones.

"You're not?"

"I just meant there are lots of things we could do awake."

He slipped a hand under my sweater and caressed my stomach, my ribs, climbed until he was just millimeters from my breasts. Then he moved downward, just with his fingertips, and every line they traced burned like fire. He was torturing me.

The ground shifted. What were we doing? Who were we? Where were we going? I still needed answers; I hadn't learned to live without them. I turned and looked at him, and asked, "What is this?"

"I don't understand."

"You and me, what are we doing? Is it real? Does it have a name? Is it going somewhere? Is this just something that happened because we were on the island together? Will it vanish once we leave?"

He let go of me, and I felt so small in that moment. His face was grave, serious, as he responded.

"Look, I had no idea this was going to happen. But it is happening, and it's real. It's one hundred percent real. As to what we should call it or where it's going…I can't tell you that, Harper. I don't think it even depends on me. I have other things to take care of, and until that's done, I can't think beyond the now."

I felt a sharp pain in my chest as I asked, "Are you talking about someone else? Another girl?"

"No! I swear I'm not. You're the only one, Pumpkin. I think you always have been."

"Is it my brother, then? Because when he said what he said to you, that was a long time ago. He's not going to do anything. I'm twenty-two years old, now, I'm an adult. You're his best friend. He'll probably be happy for us." I was stumbling over my words.

He shook his head. "I wouldn't let your brother come between you and me."

"Then tell me what's going on, because I don't understand. What things do you need to take care of?"

He bent over and kissed me, once, twice, three times. Soft little kisses, gentle, intimate. Then he leaned his forehead against mine.

"Nothing. Don't worry. I just…I just want to do things right."

"Me too."

"I feel like we should try not to think too much, just let time pass and see what it brings us."

I couldn't reply when I saw how sincere he looked. I only had two options: end everything just then, end the torture, but also the joy— or accept whatever he was offering me.

Maybe there wasn't a name for what we were sharing or a map to keep me from getting lost. But I chose. I chose to walk the tightrope, chose our kisses, chose our touch. Chose him.

For as long as it lasted.

For as long as neither of us walked away.

For as long as he needed to resolve his issues.

For as long as holding on to him hurt less than letting him go.

I opened my eyes slowly. My eyelids felt heavy. I saw Trey driving, one hand on the wheel, the other arm hanging out the window. The wind was ruffling his hair, and the rays of the setting sun were reflected in his glasses. I memorized his profile, every contour, every inch.

He turned and looked at me. "Hey there, sleepyhead."

"I didn't even realize I'd drifted off."

He reached over and rubbed my bare leg. Trying to shake off my drowsiness, I saw a landscape I didn't recognize.

"Where are we? I thought we were going back to Charlottetown to spend the night."

"That was the plan," he said with a mischievous grin, "but then I remembered there was something I wanted to show you."

"And what would that be?"

"You'll see. We're almost there."

I kept the questions to myself from then on. Despite his good mood, there was evident tension in his shoulders, his expression, even the way his fingers were gripping my thigh. I reached down and wound my fingers around his, squeezing them until he relaxed.

The road was bordered by shrubs and trees that opened now and then to give a brief view of the sea, which, as the sun set, turned from blue to black. A long bridge appeared before us, with an island on the other side. As we crossed it, I could feel Trey getting nervous again, and soon enough, I was nervous, too. At the end of it was a sign.

"Lennox Island? Where are we exactly?"

"In the north."

I saw another sign: WELCOME TO LENNOX ISLAND. FIRST NATIONS.

"What are we doing here?" He didn't answer.

A shiver ran up my spine. I tried to let things be, despite my anxiety. If there was one thing I'd learned about Trey, it was that he obeyed his own rhythms. Sometimes he was fire, sometimes he was ice. He could close as quickly as he opened up, and you never had time to prepare yourself.

We crossed the island and reached an intersection on the opposite shore. To the right was a church with yellow walls, a dark roof, and a small cemetery beside it. Trey turned left and kept driving. We passed colorful houses and took a dirt road into the woods.

Finally, he stopped at a small house with gray siding, black shutters, and white trim. He turned off the motor and stared briefly before announcing, "This is it."

The door opened, an old man stepped onto the porch, and we got out. I could see the family resemblance between him and Trey. A woman walked out behind him and her face lit up instantly. Her gray hair was pulled back in a bun. She must have been seventy, at least, but she was very agile for her age.

"Trey!" she shouted, hurrying over to Trey. They hugged each other. "I didn't know you were coming."

"Hello, Elaine. Sorry I didn't get in touch. It was a last-minute thing."

"I don't mind. You're always welcome. Who's she?"

Trey waved me over. "Elaine, this is Harper. She's Hoyt's sister."

Hearing him say this surprised me, but I guess it shouldn't have. If they were as close to Trey as they seemed, maybe they were close with my brother, too. Telling myself that made me feel a bit more comfortable.

"Hi. It's nice to meet you."

Elaine smiled at me warmly, and I smiled back. She was a cheerful woman, and it was hard to resist feeling at ease with her. Trey guided me toward the house. As we approached the doorway, where the man was still standing, Trey offered the man his hand.

"Hello, Grandpa."

"Trey."

"Harper, this is my grandfather. You can call him Nicholas."

"Welcome."

"It's a pleasure meeting you, sir. Nicholas, uh, Mr. Nicholas…"

I don't know if I imagined it, but he seemed to be amused.

Elaine invited us in and started preparing dinner. She'd been marinating a piece of meat that she now took out and began cutting into small pieces.

"Can I help?"

"Sure. Four hands are better than two. Grab that basket of potatoes and peel me a couple."

I sat down at the kitchen table and got to business. She finished cutting up the meat and started it cooking on the woodstove, then took her place next to me, pulling pea pods from a bag and stripping them.

She spoke as quickly as she moved, telling me about all the vegetables planted in her garden, the special care each of them required, and her medicinal herbs for ointments, oils, and healing creams.

I listened with interest, but my attention was really on what lay beyond the window, where Trey and his grandfather were sitting on a stump and conversing. Serious. Hardly moving.

I wondered why Trey had been so hesitant to tell me about his family. I'd been surprised that his grandparents were Mi'kmaq. He'd never mentioned it. But still, I couldn't imagine he thought his origins were something to hide from me.

"Are you and Trey seeing each other?"

The question put an end to my speculation. I blushed, embarrassed that my mind was wandering and also because I hadn't expected such a personal question.

"Us? Going out? Well…um…" I chuckled. "See, the thing is…"

"You don't have to feel uncomfortable. It's none of my business, anyway."

"No, it's not that. It's more complicated. Sorry…"

She looked back down at her cooking, as though to tell me it didn't matter.

"I've known Trey for a long time, but up to now, he and I… What I mean is, like…" All this dillydallying was starting to get on *my* nerves; I couldn't imagine how the old woman felt. "We ran into each other a few days ago, after a pretty long time, and I just can't really say if what we're doing is going out. If it makes sense to say we're together. If we have, like, a relationship. I just don't know."

"Of course."

"Maybe it's too early to think about getting serious, you know?"

"I don't. That's for you all to decide."

Her meditative expression, her words, something about her just invited me to open up to her.

"I guess, yeah. Actually I did ask him, and he told me that we had to let time tell us what the future has in store."

I couldn't believe I'd admitted that to her, and I could tell she hadn't expected it. "He told you that?" she said. "And then he brought you here to meet us?"

I nodded, grinning meekly.

"Pretty much. Your grandson isn't what I'd call transparent, and I think he's confused about himself and about what's going on in his mind."

Elaine burst out laughing. "Oh, honey, that's an inborn trait of the men in this family. If you try to understand them, they'll end up driving you crazy. And just so you know, Trey's not my grandson. But I love him as if he was."

"He's not? Sorry, I just assumed…"

"Don't apologize, it makes me happy that you did. I'm Nicholas's second wife. The first one died not long after his only daughter was born."

"Trey's mother, you mean?"

"Yeah. Her name was Marianne. I guess you know that, though."

She gave me a sweet look before taking the potatoes away to wash them. Of course, I had no idea what Trey's mother's name was. I had no idea about anything to do with Trey or where he'd come from. I'd seen his dad a few times at different events: he was arrogant, full of himself, and from what I'd heard, a womanizer. I'd never liked him, and I was ashamed to admit that some of my prejudices against Trey were really because of his father.

I was trying to choose between grilling Elaine about her

step-grandson or respecting Trey's privacy, since there was so much he hadn't trusted me enough to tell me. My principles, my conscience, told me not to dig any deeper. I didn't have the right.

I hated being such a good girl.

And I hated not being able to turn my mind off.

20

Nothing Lasts

After a dinner in near-silence, Trey asked me to take a walk with him. Night had fallen and it was humid, and the fresh scent of plants surrounded me.

For a while, neither of us spoke. I was being rebellious. I needed that sometimes, to act like a child and have my little tantrums. I was looking for the least excuse to argue. I was frustrated. I hadn't realized I felt that way, and it was driving me mad.

There was no logic to my impulses. Or maybe there was: I'd had my life all planned out, and he had turned it upside down. He was forcing me to move through unknown territories without a map. And now I wanted to know more, explore, try things.

And I wanted to know what he was thinking.

The house was closer to the beach than I'd imagined. I was surprised to see it appear before us, the sea calm, the waves soft and murmuring, the stars high in the sky, the rhythms of the night hypnotic.

Trey stopped and stood with his hands in the pockets of his jeans and drew a nervous breath. He spoke softly. "My mother was Mi'kmaq, and my grandparents are, and their parents, and generations before."

Something absurd entered my mind—but I wondered if it could be true.

"Trey, were you embarrassed about that? Is that why you never wanted to talk to me about your mother?"

He smiled and shook his head. "No. I'm proud of who I am. I never talked about her because there are things about me that you might not like. And if you don't like them, you'll pull away…"

I closed his lips with my hand, unable to believe he would really think something like that of me. Unable to imagine what I'd done or said to make him think I might behave that way.

"Me? You thought I'd judge you because of your family?" I brought my hand over to his cheek and stroked it. "Who you are and where you're from don't matter to me, Trey. All that matters is what you make of your life."

He kissed me.

"You're killing me," he said. "I feel like I'm losing it. Like I'm going completely crazy."

"In a good way?"

"See?" He laughed. "That's exactly what I mean. You're priceless. Incredible."

I blushed. I wasn't. Not even a little. Was he blind? Stupid? Who knew. At any rate, there was no way I was driving him as crazy as he was driving me!

He took my hand and dragged me to the shore, to a boulder that jutted out into the water. I could hardly see him, just his outline against the glow of a slender crescent moon. He sat down and motioned for me to sit on his lap. When I did, and when he wrapped his arms around me, I thought to myself that there could be no better place in the world.

He kissed my temple, and his face remained close to mine as he started talking.

"My parents met in the spring of 1990, at a folk music festival in Vancouver. They fell in love, and two weeks later, they were living together. My mother got pregnant, they got married, and I was born. Things went well between them at first. My father got a job in a major architecture studio and quickly made a name for himself. With fame came money and hangers-on and a lifestyle and social position that he liked a little too much. There was just one problem. Suddenly he was ashamed of my mother. She wasn't *classy* enough to hobnob with the stuck-up women his friends were married to. They talked bad about her behind her back, and my father knew it. He wanted her to pretend to be someone else."

"Poor thing. She must have felt terrible," I whispered.

"She didn't. She was strong, and she never renounced who she was."

"So what happened?"

"They argued constantly. I remember them fighting at all hours, but I was too little to realize why. One day I came back from school and Mom was gone. I didn't understand how she could abandon me, and I kept asking about her. I wanted to go find her. I needed to see her again. That was when my father started to talk about *those people*… Of course he was talking about *my* people. He was nasty about it, and he never let me forget that a part of me was *like them*. He kept repeating that my mother had chosen *them* over me."

I turned to look at him and saw the pain in his face with every word.

"How cruel of him."

"He never let up, and I started thinking like him. But that turned me into someone insecure, ashamed of my mother, and I hid that part of my life. She stopped existing for me. She was like a ghost."

"She never tried to see you again or make contact with you?"

"Yeah, she did, many times. I didn't know that then. My father had taken out a restraining order against her, saying she'd threatened to kidnap me. It was a lie, obviously. She went to my school, showed up at my house, and eventually she got arrested. She spent time in jail because of it."

A dark cloud of curses was forming on the tip of my tongue. What kind of man could do that to his own son?

"The years passed," Trey continued, "and I still hadn't seen her. But then I turned fourteen. There was a woman watching me in the park where I was hanging out with my friends. I started noticing her. I remember she was wearing beaded earrings. Then one day she came over and called me by my name. I recognized her then…"

"And what did you do?"

"I took off running. I saw her twice again, the next day and the day after that. She was waiting for me outside. So I hid." He sighed and passed his hand across his forehead. "I mean, I hated her because of what my dad had ingrained in me. A few years later, Dad and I moved to Montreal, and I met your brother and sister. And you. It was a new start, and it forced me to forget everything that came before. When people asked about my mother, I always said she'd died when I was little."

I didn't know what to say, and I didn't want to judge him. So I limited myself to remarking, "It must have been very hard for you, living like that."

"It's easy. You just turn into an asshole and you stop thinking about anything but yourself." His voice was as fragile as rice paper.

"Don't say that."

"No? Think about it. A week ago you thought I was a piece of trash."

I felt bad and turned away.

"I'm sorry, Harper. I didn't mean…"

I couldn't see his expression, and I was glad, because that meant he couldn't see what I was feeling then, either. A tear streamed down my cheek.

"I know. It's fine. It's true," I said. "But I don't see you that way anymore."

He hugged me tight and rocked me softly back and forth beneath that black velvet sky and the stars that shone like pearls. I don't know how much time passed before he spoke again. "So at the end of my second year of college, in the summer, I went home for a few days. I remember I was just about to go to San Francisco with some friends. My dad and I got into an argument; I don't remember why. It got heated and he ended up blurting out the truth. How he'd lied to me about my mother and how she'd never left. He had forced her to go. He'd threatened her, blackmailed her, lied to her... He did everything he could to get her away from me. After that, I couldn't stop thinking of her. I did some investigating and found out she lived here with my grandfather and Elaine. But a year passed until I gathered the courage to call. We only talked for a few minutes. I didn't know what to tell her."

My heart ached for him as he stroked my back distractedly. I wanted to say something, to console him somehow as he tried to pull himself together. But I didn't know how.

"She wanted us to see each other. She told me she had a heart problem and she couldn't travel anymore. I think she invited me to visit lots of times, but I always made some excuse. Time passed, and I kept telling myself that next time, I'd do it. But the feelings my father had provoked with his lies still ran deep, and something in me refused. She died four months later. The same night you and I..."

He let me go, stood up, and walked a few feet away. I let him. But the thread that united us kept getting tenser, and finally I couldn't resist the pull. I came up behind him and hugged him. My hands joined at his chest, and he covered them with his own.

"I still haven't forgiven myself," he said.

"Trey..."

"I don't think I ever will."

"Don't torture yourself, please."

"It's just…life changes from one moment to the next, and we know that, but somehow it's so hard to figure out what that means. I was an idiot, you know? All I thought about was myself. But then I lost my mother, and what I felt… I just don't know if I can describe it. I came to Lennox for the first time for her funeral, and I discovered this place. I sat right here on this rock and stared at this same shore. And I realized what an asshole I'd been. And I understood what it meant when we say nothing lasts, Harper. Everything can change at the drop of a hat, everything can end in the blink of an eye, and you have to take advantage of every moment."

Happiness and sorrow are so close that sometimes you can feel both of them at once. And I did then. I was happy because I was with him, and I felt special when he shared his secrets with me. But I also felt sad because I saw him wounded, struggling with his demons, and there was nothing I could do.

He reached up and touched my face.

"I feel like a bad person for the way I acted with my mother, and I understand if you—"

"You're insane if you think I'd leave you for what you just told me."

"I run away, Harper. It's a bad habit. I wouldn't blame you for wondering if I'll do it again."

"How many ways do I have to tell you this? I'm not going anywhere, and I feel certain that you aren't, either. You could have vanished at any moment, but here you are."

"I'm still here."

"You're still here."

"You too."

"Yeah."

"And us both being here, that means something," he said pensively.

"Do you think you're ready?" His voice, his attitude changed. The bad boy who melted my heart was back.

"I might be." I pulled him tight to me and asked, "What exactly is that something you're talking about, though?"

I could see the stars in his eyes. The stars, and not much else.

"I'm talking dates, I'm talking physical contact… In fact, if I remember correctly, you already signed on for that."

I grinned, feeling flushed. With my hands on his chest, I could feel his heartbeat, quick and strong beneath his ribs.

"Does what we've been doing these past two days count as a date?" I asked.

He nodded slowly.

"Because if that's the case, I guess we should move on to the physical contact. That's the next logical step in the relationship, no?"

"It certainly is," he whispered.

"Good. Because there are some things you apparently don't remember and I'd like to remind you of them."

"Are you sure about this?"

"I've been sure since I was twelve years old. Every time I've ever been with anyone, I've thought of you. So yes, I'm sure."

He dove in, his lips covered mine, his tongue intertwined with mine. He nibbled, groaned, grabbed my ass, and pulled me tight to him. I was touching him all over, unable, unwilling to suppress my desires. I wanted him to understand how much he mattered to me, how much I needed him.

Our bodies were so close, they could have been one as I felt under his T-shirt and touched his skin. He did the same, touching the lace of my bra. Our bodies were on fire. I was aching, each of his caresses a sweet torture. We were getting impatient, ready to see those corners of each other that were still hidden, when a gust of wind struck and we realized the weather was about to change.

"We should get back," he said.

"Sure."

But instead of that, he kissed me again. Again. Again. Only after that did he take my hand and guide me back. I could hardly see, but he seemed to know every inch of that terrain, and I followed him, unafraid of where I might step.

Soon we were in the clearing where the house and garden lay. The lights were off, and the only sign of life was the barking of the dogs. He grabbed our luggage from the car and started walking around the house.

"Aren't we going to sleep inside?" I asked.

"I don't know if you realize this, but there's only one bedroom, where Grandpa and Elaine sleep. And the sofa isn't exactly big."

"We're not going to sleep outside, are we? Because if that's the case, I'll pass. There must be spiders and ticks and all kinds of creepy-crawlies out here."

Trey laughed. "We're not sleeping outside. We're sleeping over there."

I squinted my eyes and saw a white outline against the under-brush, and as we approached, I could see a small white camper van. I stopped, flabbergasted.

"We're sleeping in a camper?"

"It's not just any camper."

"Uh, it is, though."

"Don't worry, it's quite comfortable—real bed and everything." He mounted the few steps, opened the door, and put our things inside. "Come in. It's quite spacious, you'll see."

"I need to go to the bathroom first."

Trey sighed, but patiently, and walked me over to a little wooden shack under the trees. He pushed the door open and turned on the light inside.

"This one's for us. It's got electricity and running water, as you can see."

"Hot water?" I asked, with strained hope. I was desperate for a shower.

"Yeah. The water heater's in the back. I'll turn it on."

"Thank God," I murmured. It's not that I was a fancy-pants, but my contact with nature hadn't gone much further than the parks in the various cities I'd lived in. "Why's your grandfather have a bathroom out in the woods?"

"Grandpa built the house when he remarried, but it's not big enough for more than two, so when Mom moved back here, he bought the camper for her. And now it's mine when I come here to visit."

This would be fun, exciting, I told myself. I was going to spend the night in a camper with Trey in the woods on an island. I had an idea for a book now. A suspense story, full of love and sex.

I kept thinking silly things like that while I showered, and even when I climbed into the clean sheets Elaine had laid out for us, I couldn't stop. She'd left a note wishing us a good night. What a lovely woman.

I looked up at the roof of the camper, lit up by the lantern Trey had taken from a trunk that he used as a table. Outside, an owl was hooting and the wind was rustling the trees. I thought I could hear plunking sounds—scattered at first, then rhythmic. I listened closer. It was starting to rain.

The door opened and Trey came inside wearing nothing but a towel around his waist. In the soft light, I could see water droplets shining all over his body, dripping down his arms, his chest, and his belly, falling and soaking into the white cotton of the sheets.

"It's raining," he said.

"I realized that," I responded, not taking my eyes off of his body.

I was almost ashamed of the scenarios that played out in my head. When I looked into his eyes, I realized he must have known what I was thinking. He was serious, very serious. I felt exposed as he kneeled on the bed, his eyes telling me of his intentions, of promises of future kisses and caresses, of knowing, smelling, tasting each other in a perfect embrace.

Sparks of tenderness flew.

Madness overtook us.

My body yearned for his.

And his shouted out for me.

I got on my knees in front of him, grabbed the edge of my T-shirt, and pulled it over my head. He observed every inch of my nakedness as though peering into my soul.

"I can't believe I ever forgot this."

My nerves were raw, waiting for him to touch me, to see his hands on my body. I wanted to feel him. I wanted to know him again.

I wrapped my arms around his neck and pulled him closer to me. My hands on his firm back, his tight waist, his abs contracting as I tore off his towel. It was all so different from that first night. He was so different. I was.

His lips touched mine, and we fell down on the bed, panting. I moaned as he touched me. He tickled my belly button and reached into my underwear, and I arched my back. I could feel him smiling as his lips traced a line from my neck to my stomach to my thighs. He kissed them, giving me goose bumps.

I felt it all: every soft touch, every stroke, so sweet it was painful. I melted in his mouth like molasses. He took me to the limit, tormenting me. I wanted to cry, to beg him to free me so I could touch the sky. Over and over, he took me to the edge and then drew back.

Then he climbed back up me, leaving a trail of kisses that led to my lips. I could feel his torso heavy against my breasts. I trembled in anticipation, wriggled my hips, tempting him, and he groaned into the hollow of my neck. Then he slipped inside, slow, but deep.

And just as the storm broke out above us, a storm of kisses, caresses, and moans broke out in the camper: whispers, breathing, groans, hips grinding, bodies touching, rocking, swaying, faster and faster, harder and harder, letting go.

Outside, the rain kept falling.

21

Between You and Me,
There's Nothing But Us

I had the feeling I'd done and lived more things in a week than in the rest of my life combined. And that past life looked so far away from me in that tiny camper—that tiny space of belonging—where our bodies lay, full of peace.

I closed my eyes and held my breath when he moved, grabbing my waist and pulling me in to him. I could easily imagine a world inhabited by just the two of us. Two people lucky enough to find each other. Two people whose kisses and whispers told each other they had decided not to part. To give it a go. To see what would happen. To keep trying a thousand times if necessary until they got it right.

I smiled. When he exhaled, I could feel it on my neck, a perfect rhythm, like a soft pounding of drums. Outside, the birds were flitting about and chirping. One of them lighted on the camper. I could hear its tiny feet scratching the metal. The forest was full of life.

Trey kissed the back of my neck, and I turned around to look at him. We didn't say anything. There was no need to, there were no words that could explain what we felt. Sometimes the lips, the hands can say it all… As we traced each other's features in the bliss of the day after, a day that had followed a night that still felt as fresh as though it had only just began, I thought of how precious moments were: a thing could break, a thing could disappoint you, but a moment preserved in time was something that would last forever.

"Breakfast is ready!" Elaine yelled from the cabin.

"You hungry?" Trey asked.

I nodded, finding the question funny, somehow.

I didn't want to leave our little habitat of twisted sheets now smelling of our bodies. But all good things must come to an end. We both had another life and other places to be.

I dressed and went straight to the bathroom, then I packed my travel bag and followed Trey into the house. Nicholas and Elaine were sitting at the table already.

We had a huge breakfast of eggs, bacon, and pancakes with maple syrup. Then we loaded up the car. I hugged Elaine goodbye and shook Nicholas's hand. From the twinkle in his eye, I could see he was a man of kindness.

He reminded me a great deal of Trey.

"I hope you both come back soon," Elaine said.

"We will. I promise," Trey said, pulling her in close to him.

As we drove off, I was absorbed, my head leaning toward the open window, contemplating the landscape as the wind blew through my hair. I couldn't stop thinking, reflecting, trying to figure out the meaning of all that was happening.

The barrier that had separated me from Trey the night before had collapsed when he'd told me about his mother and his regrets. His sunken shoulders, his evasive eyes, the heavy silences that pointed at secrets unconfessed, were no longer a part of him. I could see that in his relaxed bearing, in the lightness in his smile.

As he drove, I wondered why he'd thought there was anything in his past I'd ever hold against him. How could I judge him for something he'd been pushed, almost forced to do? And who was I to say whether anyone was a bad person? Anyway, for me, he wasn't one. For me, he was marvelous: complicated, maybe, a little macho, maybe, but still, he was exactly what I needed.

He pulled off and stopped the car.

"Come with me. I want to show you something."

I got out and followed him down a narrow path, about two hundred yards into a clearing with views of the sea. He stopped and stared out at the horizon.

"Over the last hundred years, this island has lost more than three hundred acres of land. The water's swallowing it up. See that church over there?" In the distance, there was a bell tower. I nodded. "My mother's buried over there in the cemetery. The community had to spend a fortune to build a rock wall to protect it. Otherwise the sea might have destroyed it."

"Really?"

"In the long term, there's no stopping it, but I'm working on raising money to help people with this kind of problem... It's not an overnight solution, but I don't want a quick fix anyway. I want something sustainable."

"That's amazing, Trey. I mean it. It's just wonderful."

"Sure. Well, I just wanted you to see it."

It was moving to see how shy he was, and I hugged him around the waist, standing there with him a while, just watching the waters of Malpeque Bay.

"Tell me about your mother," I whispered.

After a pause, he began, "You told me the other night that your memories of your mother are like postcards. Mine too. I didn't...I didn't really know her. I just know the things Elaine and my grandfather told me about her. She liked music and art, and she worked as a tourist guide for visitors on the island. She was good at it: she knew all the history, the customs, the old legends. And people enjoyed listening to her. Everyone here loved her. Her death was a big deal for them."

He brooded for a minute, then shook it off. His mood seemed to shift just like that. He smiled wickedly at me and grabbed my hips.

"Don't you realize I'm trying to behave? Trying to be polite, a gentleman, and all that. But you're making it awfully hard on me…"

By now, his hands had crept into my waistline and were toying with the hem of my panties.

"If this is going to work, I need you to be yourself," I said.

He kissed me deeply, then said, "Fine," drew a breath, and went on. "If I'm being myself, then I'd have to tell you all I want to do is fuck you and look in your eyes and see you telling me how bad you want it. I want to stare at your face while I'm doing it and see you dying for more."

Who needs poetry when the man of your dreams is whispering nasty thoughts in your ear? This was the most romantic moment of my life, and I loved it. No one had ever talked to me that way, and it made me feel alive, powerful.

"Is there much traffic on this road?" I asked.

He caught the drift of my words. And a few minutes later, we were making love in the back seat of his car.

We made it back to Petit Prince late in the evening, and we were exhausted. We stopped briefly at the grocery store and afterward went straight home.

I felt strangely calm, almost as though the little time I had left on the island would never run out. Summer was reaching an end. September had started, and soon autumn would be setting in.

As soon as I walked in, I headed to the bathroom for a shower. I'd been in a spell those past few days, even if I remembered now and again all the things I'd have to do when I got back to Montreal, and those thoughts upset me. I wasn't ready, but I had to admit I might never be, and even that visceral fear couldn't stop me.

There's a phrase I love, one that gives me hope and strength when I think about it: *Everything passes.* I used to dip my head under the water and repeat it to myself like a mantra.

Trey took a shower of his own while I went to the kitchen to make dinner—the last meal we'd share in that house. Burritos with grilled vegetables.

I cut everything up into little slices and roasted it with a little oil, heating the tortillas in the oven. In ten minutes, everything was ready.

I laid our dinner out picnic-style on the porch, with a blanket and pillows to make us more comfortable. The night was gorgeous. Alongside the dishes, I poured us each a glass of wine. Once more, I savored the beauty of the landscape, waiting for Trey to appear. His hair was damp, he smelled of soap, and I felt a shiver up my spine. He sat across from me, crossing his long legs. The candles I had lit made his eyes twinkle and cast deep shadows across his face.

During dinner, he told me more about the Mi'kmaq, including legends about their gods that I tucked away in that part of my head where I liked to keep ideas for future stories. I couldn't help it; I did it without thinking. Every detail awakened my imagination: a phrase, a song, an image…and then the gears started turning. And the pieces of the enormous puzzle that is a novel started to come together: people, scenes, dialogues…

I still don't know how to explain it. How a book is born. How it develops, grows, weaves together. It's something that just happens.

As we finished our bottle of wine, we planned the next day.

Our farewell day.

The day we'd return to the real world.

"Now you can go ahead and tell me how my sister found this house."

Seemingly out of nowhere, he replied, "For a long time, I didn't tell them the truth about my mother."

"Are you talking about my brother and sister?"

He nodded. "I never told them, and I never told Scott. The day after the party, though, after Hoyt took you to the airport, the four of us had lunch together, sort of to say goodbye. I guess they could tell something was up with me, and you know how they are. They wouldn't stop pressuring me. So finally I let it out."

"What did they say?"

"Nothing. They didn't say anything. They just packed their bags and bought plane tickets and dragged me to Lennox for the funeral. No one reproached me, no one was angry with me, nothing."

I could tell the memory was bittersweet, and for a moment, it seemed to have sucked him in. I knew he was thinking about them.

"You really care about them, don't you?" I asked.

"They're the closest thing to a family I've ever had. We ended up staying on the island a few days, and once, when we'd gone out to Charlottetown, Hayley saw the ad for this house in the window of a real estate agent. It was love at first sight. She made us catch the ferry that same day to come see it."

"That's Hayley for you. I struggle sometimes to understand how a person that rational, that methodical, can be so impulsive at the same time. I've always wanted that self-assurance of hers, that resoluteness."

"You have those things, though, just in your own way."

I took a sip of wine and smirked. I wished I could see myself the way he did. "What happened once you saw the house?"

"She never told you?"

"No."

He cradled his glass in his hands. "There's not much to tell, really. Scott bought the house, but he kept it a secret until he'd renovated and furnished it. He used Hoyt and me as free labor. It was the perfect engagement gift. He was always the romantic one, out of all of us."

When we were done eating, we lay back and looked up at the sky. Trey reached over and pulled me on top of him and held me.

"So now what?" I whispered.

"What do you mean?"

"You. Me. Montreal. Us."

I slid off him, and he toyed with my hair as he responded, "Honestly, I just assumed we'd turn into one of those corny couples that I've always hated."

"I'm serious!" I said.

"Me too! We can call each other all the time, go to the movies to feel each other up, kiss late at night on some deserted street while I walk you home after a date. Stay over at each other's places. I could make you breakfast!"

"I like how you think."

"Do you? Because there are more ideas where that came from. I'm talking lovemaking... Every night. And at all hours of the day." He leaned over and kissed the corner of my lips. "I could be the only person allowed to kiss you here." He touched my breast. "And here." He slid his hand between my legs. "And here. Especially here."

I wanted that, too. I wanted to be a corny couple. I wanted him to kiss me all over. I wanted him to kiss me other places, too. I had imagined it so many times that the dream had worn thin. I turned and kissed him, tasted him, reached into his pants and elicited a moan.

He got up and pulled me up, too. We stumbled into the house, our lips joined the whole time. He kicked the door shut, and I threw my arms over his neck. I felt wide awake and hungry—hungry for him. We took the steps one at a time until we reached the top, threw each other against the wall, felt our way along until we found his room.

He undressed me as my hands sought out his belt buckle. Our

clothes wound up on the floor, and I felt every inch of his beautiful bare body as the throbbing inside me grew more powerful. I was in control. I pulled him toward the bed and he sat back, propped up on his arms. I loved him so much it hurt. He grabbed me around the waist and pulled me into his chest.

Our bodies met.

Our eyes got lost in each other.

My muscles tensed as I took him inside me.

I made love to him slowly, my mouth seeking his, drinking in his exhalations and groans, losing myself in the sensation of it.

"I wish I could spend my whole life this way. I'm crazy about you," he whispered.

"And I'm crazy about you."

"I don't know what's happening between us, but I don't want it ever to end."

My lucky accident.

"Between you and me, there's nothing but us," I said. "And there's no reason it ever has to end."

"Childhood memories are sometimes covered and obscured beneath the things that come later, like childhood toys forgotten at the bottom of a crammed adult closet, but they are never lost for good."

—Neil Gaiman, *The Ocean at the End of the Lane*

22

Farewells Are Necessary. They're the Prelude to Seeing Each Other Again.

I woke at dawn. Trey was sleeping like a log next to me. One of his arms was serving as my pillow, and the other was wrapped around my waist. I could get used to waking up like that every day.

His face was the pure reflection of peace, and I couldn't take my eyes off it. I buried my nose between his neck and shoulder and inhaled his scent, and I loved how electric, now nervous it made me feel, all those sensations I couldn't control. And the knowledge that they wouldn't go away, that they were here to stay because he was here to stay. I held on to those feelings to keep from falling into sadness.

Because it hurt, leaving Petit Prince, but at the same time, there was excitement in it. A strobe light of emotions, flitting back and forth, until I could hardly tell one from the other.

What a huge, mysterious inner world we human beings harbor…

These feelings are all that life is, really. Once you learn that, once you internalize it, the knowledge never leaves you. And you stop being scared. You just accept that there will be good days and bad. Good moments and bad. That life will always be that back-and-forth for you, at least if you're like me. That you can hold those two extremes inside you, impossible as it seems.

I kissed Trey on the throat and got out of bed without making noise, taking leftovers from the fridge to make a breakfast of tortillas and eggs.

I didn't rush. I ate calmly and stared out the window. By the time I finished my coffee, it was cold. Then I went to the bathroom. I turned on the shower and heard the water striking the porcelain. I stripped slowly and stood beneath it. The heat overtaking my body was pleasant. I squeezed shampoo into my hand and washed my hair, and though my eyes were closed, I knew the shower door had slid open. I could hear it and feel the rush of cold air. Then it shut, and it was warm again.

He forced my hands down and rubbed my scalp with his own hands, then guided me under the water and washed away all the foam. From behind, he hugged me and kissed the back of my ear. His fingers traced little circles on my skin as they edged their way toward my breasts.

"My precious mermaid," he whispered.

His hands slipped downward, and I felt a whirlwind of desire between my legs when his fingertips reached their destination. His touch was soft but passionate, his movements rhythmic, growing in intensity as my breaths grew shallower.

I abandoned myself to pleasure. Then he turned me around. I opened my eyes, and he was there. Pure, ferocious desire overtook me. The warmth of him. Fire.

My hot Trey, I thought with a smile.

We made love under the water. When it was done, we held each other. Fragile. Invincible. Two hearts together as one.

We packed our bags and took them out to the car. Then we cleaned up inside and turned off the gas and the breaker box. The house was silent, cold, and neat, and looked as if nobody had been there at all.

I felt as if there was a stone in my chest as I heard the lock click and Trey took out the key.

We held hands as we walked to the beach toward Adele's house. I've never liked goodbyes, and that one was going to make me sad indeed. I'd admired her since I was little, and now I adored her as a woman, a real person.

The blue house sat perched like a tiny lighthouse on the cliff. A few minutes after taking the path, we had reached the top. Sid saw us from yards away and raised a hand in greeting.

"What a surprise," he said.

"We came to say goodbye," I replied.

"Well, I'm sad to see you go."

Adele came out with a smile on her face, wiping her hands off with a rag as we approached. She hugged me tight.

"You look gorgeous."

"It must be the sun. I've gotten a little bit of a tan."

"It has a magic effect on people here on this island."

She was right, I thought. After standing back to look at me a moment, she turned to Trey with a strange grin on her face, as though she knew something I didn't.

"We're going," I said, unable to hide my sorrow.

"Oh, honey, you say that like you were telling us goodbye forever. Listen, now. You can think of this as your new home, and I hope you'll come visit as often as you wish. You'll always be welcome."

I couldn't help but feel moved. I hugged her again, catching her off guard and making her stumble, and we both laughed until we had tears in the corner of our eyes. I don't know why, but I seemed to be special to her, too.

"Come, I have something I want to give you."

She guided me to her workshop and opened a drawer in a white cupboard, taking out a cardboard box that was tied with a lavender ribbon. She handed it to me with outstretched arms.

"Don't open it until you're gone."

"What is it?"

"A surprise."

I nodded. "I've got something for you, too." I reached into my pants pocket and pulled out the piece of red glass I'd found just after arriving on the island. "I want you to have this."

"Harper, it's yours. I can't accept that. If you knew how rare they were…"

"I do know, that's why I want you to have it. I'm sure you'll do something beautiful with it."

She looked at me, and then at the carmine tear in the palm of my hand before grabbing it and squeezing it.

"Thank you."

"Adele, I'm going to miss you. You…you've helped me in ways you can't even imagine."

"You made your decision, didn't you?"

I nodded. "Yeah. I'm not going back to my old life. It's not for me. I got used to living in it, but I didn't feel it was mine. It was just habit or resignation that made me believe it was right for me. I mean, I don't regret studying literature and I don't regret my internship at the publisher. Those were wonderful opportunities, and I learned a lot. But… these days here opened my eyes, and I've realized I want more than that. More freedom. More happiness. More…life. Do you understand?"

"Of course I do. Years ago, I had that very same feeling. Now you see, it's not so complicated, right?"

Her expression was bewitching—the same expression that had drawn me in as soon as I met her—and I knew right away she was talking about Trey and me.

"No, not anymore. To tell the truth, nothing could be easier."

"Well, I'm happy for both of you. You make a beautiful couple."

Sid drove us back home. We had lost track of time, and the ferry left in less than an hour.

"See you later," he shouted from the open window after dropping us off.

Trey got into his SUV and started the engine. I waited a moment before leaving in my own car. I needed to look back at the house one last time. I took a deep breath. It smelled of the sun and the sea. Birds were flying back and forth, cawing constantly, diving down toward the water to catch fish. The sky and the ocean melded on the horizon. The sound of the waves was almost deafening, even from there. I tried to memorize it all, down to the last detail, so my imagination could treasure it forever.

We dropped in at Ridge's restaurant to say goodbye. Nice as ever, he packed us a bunch of food to go and invited us to come back whenever we wished. He walked us to the port. The sight of him, shrinking as we floated out into the sea, was the last image I had of that island that had changed my life.

Two hours later, we reached the wharf in Souris. Trey drove his car out of the ferry's hold and slowly down the ramp. I followed him out in mine and parked it in the lot at the port, where I could have someone from the rental company pick it up for a fee.

I got in Trey's car. We had a long drive to Montreal. Seven hundred miles, easily. An adventure.

"You ready?" he asked me.

"I'm ready."

He stomped the gas, the motor roared, and we took off. We passed the hours talking, listening to music, holding hands, getting to know each other.

He told me some things I hadn't known about, like his spats with my brother when they were young and stupid—in his words. It was funny, hearing about the trouble they had gotten into. Each situation was more ridiculous than the one before it.

We stopped a couple of times. Once to fill up and once at a Tim Hortons to grab a bite to eat. I watched the sky go dark, watched the lights of city after city recede into the background. On a desolate stretch, in utter darkness, I asked him, "Where are we?" trying not to yawn.

"We're almost to Edmundston. We'll stop at a hotel and catch some rest there, I think."

I stretched my arms out and rubbed my sore muscles.

"That sounds good. Every inch of my body feels tight."

He grinned, looking at me out of the corner of his eye. "Maybe I can do something to loosen you up."

I shook my head. Soon we saw a sign marking Exit 26, and we pulled off, parking in front of a cute little Days Inn with blue walls and white columns. We got out and stretched our legs before taking our bags out of the back and entering reception.

A pleasant-looking girl behind the counter gave us a room on the second floor.

Trey let me shower first, and I stayed a while under the water. I shaved my legs—I'd been putting it off a few days—and rubbed myself down with lotion when I got out before putting on a pair of cotton shorts and a T-shirt.

I found Trey lying in bed scrolling through the channels with the remote. He whistled when he saw me, eyeing me up from head to toe.

"What are you trying to do to me?" he asked.

I threw the towel at him that I had been using to dry my hair. He got up, walked past me, gave me a kiss, and smacked me on the butt. I looked at the little dimple in his cheek and thought I might die.

The bed creaked when I sat down on it. I opened my purse and took out the tiny box Adele had given me. I carefully untied the ribbon to keep from tearing it and lifted the lid. There was a red envelope inside and a necklace. I lifted it up and looked at the bit of cobalt-blue glass polished by the sea, held in place by silver wire. Next to it were several charms: a seahorse, a star, and a mermaid holding another tiny piece of glass in her hands.

My eyes got misty, and I had a lump in my throat as I put the necklace aside and opened the envelope. Inside were a couple of photos. One was identical to the photo I'd seen in Adele's workshop at her home: her, radiant, smiling, holding one of her prizes. I turned it over and saw her message:

> *Thank you for giving meaning to all those years of work. The admiration's mutual, my little mermaid.*

I had to cover my mouth with my hand when I looked at the next one. I don't know when it was taken, or by whom, but there we all were: Adele, Sid, Trey, Ridge, even Peter and grumpy old Emma.

And me.

I looked so happy, I could hardly recognize myself. It was from the lunch we all had together after the storm. I turned it over and saw another message on the back.

> *Farewells are necessary. They're the prelude to seeing each other again, and that means there's no need for sorrow when you and I say goodbye.*
>
> *Come back soon, dear.*

Trey came out and sat next to me. When I looked over at him, I saw the water dripping from his hair.

"Fun day, wasn't it?"

"Yeah," I said, still staring at the photo. "Do you remember who took it?"

After a moment's thought, he responded, "I think it was Ridge's sister. What was her name?"

"Carlie."

"Yeah, her. I saw her snapping pictures with her phone."

"I'm going to miss them. All of them."

Ruefully, I put the photo away.

"You know we can go back whenever we damn well please, right? We can turn around right now if that's what you want. All you've got to do is say the word."

But when I looked up into that handsome face—the word *love* dancing on the tip of my tongue, when I uttered it after kissing him—*I love you*—too softly for him to hear, because I was too scared to shout it—I knew we couldn't turn around. Not yet. And so I handed him the necklace and asked, "Do you mind?"

He nodded, and I turned around and let him part my hair in the back and clasp it. Then he planted his lips on the spot his fingers had touched and left them there for several seconds.

We got into bed. Trey turned off the TV and the lamp on the nightstand, and with the curtains drawn, I could barely see. I cuddled up to him, and he hugged me, letting me rest my hand on his chest. Our legs wrapped around each other. Tired as I was, though, I couldn't sleep when I closed my eyes. My mind was too busy trying to absorb the happiness that being held by him brought me.

"What will you do when you get back?" he asked, running his hands through my hair.

"I don't know. I've got so much on my plate that I don't know where to start. I guess the first thing is to go see my grandmother's lawyer to get his help with the paperwork. I need to go to Toronto, too: settle up with my landlord, get my things… I need to talk to my professors, to the publisher, to let them know I won't be finishing my internship. My God, I've still got manuscripts to go through! I should at least correct those and turn them in before I call it quits."

"Don't worry, you'll get it all done. You just need to organize yourself a little."

"It sounds so simple when you say it like that."

He laughed. "Look on the bright side. You're not one of those people anymore who lives without living. On autopilot twenty-four hours a day. Chained to the phone, to your email, to your job… Never able to stop and rest or really feel anything. You're the master of your time now, of your life. That's amazing."

"I guess you're right," I said, kissing him on the chest.

"I'm always right. Always."

"Easy now—don't be so humble. You should think more highly of yourself," I joked.

"You're right. Sorry. I forgot to add that I'm also perfect. Just look at this face and this body. I'm a ten out of ten. And smart, to boot."

"Smart I'll give you…" I said. "Everything else, too. Always right, handsome, generous, and a little naughty…"

"Naughty?"

"You know it's true. One of those guys who acts tough and walks through life like he doesn't give a damn about anything. I know a secret, though. You're a softy, deep down. You're sweet as chocolate."

"I'm not sure if that's a compliment."

"It is," I said, adding, "I like myself a naughty boy."

His fingers moved slowly down my ribs to my waist and drew tiny figure eights on my hip. The symbol for infinity.

"Okay. So I'm sexy. I'm sweet as chocolate. And I can fuck like a god."

"Exactly!" I shrieked. "Just own it! The whole world is thankful you exist."

The game came to a stop there. I thought it was all funny, but he must have been starting to get uncomfortable, because he needed a moment before he spoke again. "Jesus," he said finally, "you must think I'm completely fucking full of myself."

"Not at all. You need to do something about that *fucking* mouth, though." As he tickled me in response, I said, "Seriously though. You're self-assured. I like that."

"So what else do you like about me?"

"I like how everything's just okay when I'm with you. You make me feel like everything's possible."

"What else?"

"I like how you look at me."

"Like you were a drop of water and I was wandering thirsty through the desert?"

"Yeah. And I like the way you kiss."

He bent over me and did it, slowly, softly. "I'm glad. Because I'd happily kiss you every day, every hour, every minute…every second."

"And I love being in bed with you and talking. Or not talking."

"Tell me more."

I reached around and touched the small of his back, arching to bring him in closer to me. This was getting exciting.

"I love looking at you. Touching you. Feeling you."

Trey's phone buzzed just then, and I could see the light from it glowing on his face. He looked at it briefly, then put it away, holding me tight and burying his face in my neck. The phone buzzed again. And again.

"Couldn't that maybe be important?" I whispered.

"It's your brother," he murmured. "He's been writing me for days and I keep ignoring him."

"Why?"

"Because I don't want to lie to him, and I don't want to tell him I'm with you. Not until I'm sure."

"Sure of what?" I held my breath.

"Sure of you," he replied. "Sure of us."

"Of me?"

"I can't tell him I've lost my head over his sister and I don't give a damn whether or not he likes it! Not until I'm sure this is real for you."

"It's real."

"How do you know? What if everything you felt these past few days was just your imagination? Maybe everything is just you idealizing me. Like a pleasant dream. Maybe when you're back in your routine and everything's normal again, you'll…"

I silenced him with a kiss and wrapped my legs around his hips. And in that kiss, I tried to encapsulate everything I felt for him. Everything in my heart, everything in my body and soul. I pushed him over and sat on top of him, pressing my forehead into his, mingling our breaths. I couldn't see his face, but I kept my eyes open anyway, riding him back and forth. Deeper. Harder. I had to, I didn't have the words to calm his uncertainties, so this was the only way I knew to tell him this was real.

Sometimes words don't work, and we have to find another language to express ourselves. Especially when it matters. Especially when you need a person to know that what you have is forever. I used my lips, my skin, my hands, our moans to speak to him. My body shouted to him that I couldn't imagine living a single day without him. And I could tell that his body was saying the same.

At some point I froze and collapsed on top of him, and I heard him singing to me. He stayed inside me as he held me tight, and I envisioned an entire film about the two of us divided into chapters. Perfect scenes. Intense dialogues. A happy ending, and an epilogue showing how everything stayed beautiful into eternity.

What I didn't see was the bump in the road that turned everything upside down. Every story has one, or more than one, the way an earthquake has aftershocks that can shake the foundations of the tallest building until you're certain it will topple over. Unpredictable twists and turns you can't control, destructive as natural disasters. Unbeknownst to us, we were in the eye of the storm.

She was a romantic, sentimental child, with a pref-
erence for solitude, few friends, and a propensity
to be moved to tears when the roses in the garden
bloomed...

—Isabel Allende, *The House of Spirits*

23

That Person Who Makes You Want to Do Everything Again

It was past 11:00 a.m. when I finally got back. I left my suitcase on the floor and looked at the walls with new eyes. This was my home now. I opened the windows to let in a little air and put a James Bay album on the old record player. The music filled the entire room.

As I threw my dirty clothes in the wash and put away my things, I realized none of Frances's old belongings were there apart from her favorite cup, which was in the drying rack, and a shawl hanging on the coat-tree.

Time seemed to run backward, like a video on rewind or the sand in an hourglass rising miraculously upward, and I could briefly see Frances and my grandmother within those walls, happy, laughing, their arms around each other on the sofa while I colored with crayons, kneeling on the floor. All those memories, down to the last detail, came to life in my mind. My time there had been the happiest I'd ever known, and there was a bittersweet contentment in finally being back there.

Is it possible to miss yourself? Yes. I knew. I was doing it right then.

I took a deep breath and focused on the here and now. No more ruminating, no more thinking in circles, no more running away. I looked for a metal box my grandmother used to store her buttons in. I emptied it out and put inside the book my mother had given me when I was a girl. I needed to see it for what it really was: a keepsake, but also just a thing. I couldn't use it as a sanctuary every time I felt alone. It wasn't a refuge, it wasn't therapy, and turning it into that had been harmful for me. It was time to give it up.

No more hiding it under the pillow.

Trey was right. I didn't need to pretend I was someone else, especially not a character from a book. All I needed was to be myself.

I also put away my grandmother's letter in the same box. When I closed it, I felt lighter.

Then I plugged in my computer and made a few calls while I waited for it to charge. I got hold of Hayley and managed to talk to her for a few seconds. She was somewhere in New Caledonia. Hoyt answered me on the first ring, "Little Pumpkin!"

"Hey, big brother."

"Where the hell have you been?"

"I was trying to think through some things. Don't worry, though. I'll tell all."

"I hope so. Did you find what you were looking for?"

"Yeah. That's…that's why I'm calling. I've decided I'm going to stay here in Montreal, for good."

He waited a moment to respond, and I could hear murmurs in the background. "I'm glad to hear that, Harper. I like the idea of having you here close."

I tried to remain calm. "Next week, I'll go to Toronto, just to get my things and take back my apartment keys. I've got to talk to my department head at school and my boss at the publisher…"

"I can give you a hand if you need."

"No, I can handle it on my own."

"Okay."

"Excuse me, sir. You'll need to turn off your phone. We're about to take off," a woman said.

"Are you on a plane?" I asked.

"Yeah, Dad wants me to make a surprise visit to the New York office. I'll be back in a few days. If you want, we can have dinner and you can tell me everything?"

"Yeah, call me, I have something I need to tell you in person."

"What?" He sounded slightly alarmed.

"Nothing bad. Relax."

"Sir, your phone."

"You should listen to her or they'll throw you off the plane."

"Right. I'll see you soon then, Pumpkin. Love you."

"Love you, too."

I hung up and looked at my phone, feeling nostalgic. It would be nice to live close to my brother and sister again. I dialed Frances, but it went straight to voicemail.

"Hey, Frances. I hope your sister's better. Call me when you can. I need to tell you some things... I've decided to keep the house and the bookstore. I'm scared. I'm nervous, too, but something tells me this is what I need to do. Really, though, I wanted you to know I was back, and... I just want to talk to you. I love you, Frances. Take care, please."

I smelled spices coming through the window. I looked at my watch: it was 1:30. There was nothing to eat in the house, so I threw my computer in my bag and headed out.

I'd put in my earbuds and was listening to music and making a list of things to do in my head. Correct my last few manuscripts, buy tickets for Toronto—the sooner, the better—deal with the inheritance papers...

I went into a takeout place and got a veggie sandwich with yogurt sauce before walking to the bookstore. The soft, late-summer breeze warmed my skin, and I smiled, feeling relieved—feeling like myself.

"Someday" by We Are Harlot started playing. I loved that song, and I hummed it to myself along the way.

I stopped at the front door and just stood there for a long time, staring at my reflection in the glass before taking the key out of my purse and opening the door. My heart was pounding out of my chest.

I took one step, then another, gazing at nothing in particular, reabsorbing details I already knew from memory. The place seemed to be embracing me, welcoming me, and I touched the shelves, the antique cash register, the books piled on the tables, feeling the magic throbbing there. I could hear the rush of blood in my temples telling me what I already knew: this was my world.

There in my sanctuary, surrounded by calm and quiet, I cleared off a table and took out my laptop and food, and sat down, feeling bliss amid the scent of new books and lemon air freshener.

A knocking on the glass startled me. I looked up and saw Trey waving from outside. It was almost nighttime. I must have been sitting there for six hours, at least.

I opened the door and stepped aside to let him in. As soon as he'd crossed the threshold, he lifted me up and pressed his lips to mine. I was happy, but also nervous. Being there with him made our relationship so real that it almost scared me.

"Something wrong with your phone?" he asked.

"Were you calling me?"

"I've been calling you for hours. I wanted to take you to dinner."

"Sorry. I usually keep it on silent when I'm working."

He kissed me again and set me down, and I stumbled away, wondering if I would ever manage to keep ahold of myself with Trey around. He gave the shop a once-over.

"I like the place," he said.

"I'll need to make some changes and bring it up to date a bit. And I need to set up a little writing corner since I'll be spending so much time here."

"I could lend you a hand," he said, then grabbed me, squeezing my buttocks. "Or two!"

"I love how romantic you are."

His face changed to that of a little boy caught doing something wrong. I loved that, especially because I'd never seen him do it with anyone but me.

"I've never, uh… I've never had a serious relationship. Like with anyone. So I'm not sure if I know how to do it. How to, like, be romantic and say sweet nothings that sound like poetry. I can learn, though, I swear!"

Maybe he didn't know, but he was a good guesser. I couldn't imagine words that would have stirred me more.

"Being romantic is overrated. Someone slamming you against the wall and giving it to you has its charm."

And in the blink of an eye, he had gotten to work. His body was tight against mine, holding me off the floor, his hips between my legs, his eyes looking sly but beautiful at the same time.

"That I can do," he said.

I laughed—I couldn't help it—and a warm feeling spread through my chest that was nothing like what I'd ever experienced before. I thought I had known what desire, pleasure, and love were… But I hadn't, not until he showed me. You have to give everything, you have to feel that other person doing the same, striving to satisfy you even more than they want to satisfy themselves…

I knew then, as he kissed me, that I would spend my life with him. Doing everything. Talking, laughing, dreaming, traveling, sleeping, having sex…

I kept my arms wrapped around his neck as he stumbled over to the table with me and leaned me back on top of it, lost in our passion. Our bodies were inflamed, we couldn't hold back, we were lost in each other, and then…

And then the bells rang, sounding sharper than I remembered them. I'd forgotten to lock the door. We sat up and tried to arrange ourselves as best we could.

"Excuse me, are you open?"

A woman was gawking at us, seeming to realize she hadn't picked the ideal moment to come in. Trying not to crack up, embarrassed, I told her, "Sorry. We're, uh…we're doing some renovations. We'll be open next week."

"Thanks. I'll come back then." She turned around, but then paused, and added, "Sorry to interrupt you."

Before I could answer, the bells rang again and we were alone. Trey broke into cackles, deep and forceful, that echoed through the bookstore.

"You think she'll really be back?"

"I hope so," I said.

"It's dinnertime. You want to come over?"

"Sure," I said. I wanted to know everything about him, wanted to use each moment with him to discover something, and what is more personal and intimate than someone's home? It's a reflection of who we are, and it shows our identity in a way few other things can.

On the way there, I recited briefly what all I'd done that day, mainly reading and correcting manuscripts. I told him the stories in all the books, the parts I'd liked, the parts I thought didn't work. How bad I felt for marking mistakes or making suggestions, because I wasn't sure that I knew enough or mattered enough to tell other writers how to do their jobs.

"I don't know much, but it seems to me a degree in literature and creative writing plus two years working at a publisher—plus the fact

that you're a writer yourself—qualifies you to make those ki
judgments."

As we walked, I could feel him glancing over at me, and I did th
same—trying not to catch his eye and failing. He reached out and
grabbed my shoulder affectionately, pulled me toward him, squeezed
me. "We're here," he said, pointing to a tall, narrow Victorian house
with a stone exterior and a turret on the right corner that made it
look like a castle.

"It's beautiful," I said.

"Architecturally speaking, it's a masterpiece. It's one of the oldest
buildings in this neighborhood, but it's very well preserved." We
walked up the stone steps to the door, which he opened for me.
"Ladies first," he said.

The interior was nothing like what I'd imagined. It was open, like
a loft, and the decor was modern. There were no walls separating the
dining room, living room, and kitchen, and the room felt gigantic and
free. A wooden staircase climbed to the second floor.

"I can't believe this place, Trey."

"Thanks. Unfortunately, it's not mine. It belongs to a friend who's
living in Europe. I take care of it and he rents it to me for next to
nothing. I'm sorry to say the fridge isn't well stocked, but I'm sure we
can whip up something nice. Will you help me?"

I nodded, removing my purse and tossing it onto the sofa. Then
I froze. A gigantic dog had appeared at the top of the stairs. It
was gray with white spots, and its golden eyes were glaring at me.
It must have been Sisuei. I gulped. He was much bigger than I'd
imagined.

"Relax," Trey said behind me. "He's chill, he's a regular gentleman.
He won't even come down till I tell him. You want to meet him?"

"I think so?"

"Sisuei, come."

wn and jumped up on his back legs, trying to

turned to me. He sniffed me, walked in a

staring at me with curiosity. Then he groaned

y hand with his nose.

waiting for you to pet him."

for real?" I asked.

"Yeah. He loves to be scratched behind the ears. You're lucky. He usually ignores everyone."

"You probably tell all the girls that. Do you take him for walks in the park when you're looking for a hookup?"

With a seductive look, he walked over, put his hands on my hips, and said, "First of all, you're the only girl I've officially introduced him to. And second of all, Sisuei doesn't know how to fake his feelings. He always shows his true colors."

I crouched down, not quite trusting the dog, and stretched out my hand to pat his enormous head. His hair was a little stiff on the ends, but soft and woolly underneath if you sank your fingers into it.

"Hi, Sisuei. I'm Harper. It's a pleasure to meet you. Trey told me about you. He said you're a very good dog."

Sisuei barked happily and tried to lick my face. It tickled.

"Come on, dude, leave her alone. You're covering her in slobber," Trey said.

Sisuei seemed to understand what he was saying and sat back. He was so pretty I could hardly stop looking at him.

I followed Trey into the kitchen. We washed our hands and he offered me an apron. While he cut vegetables and a chicken breast into strips to stuff the puff pastry, I got to work making the salad. I wasn't much of a cook, but a simple vinaigrette I could handle, and I fancied it up with some honey and mustard. It was a variation on a French recipe my grandmother used to make.

Trey stuck a finger in the bowl, and I slapped him away, but before

I could, he'd already lathered it in dressing. He then stuck it in his mouth and sucked it.

"Disgusting," I said.

"It's tasty," he murmured, not ashamed in the least.

We had a glass of white wine while we waited for his tart to cook. Trey showed me the rest of the house. We lingered a while in the room that had become his studio. It was full of blueprints: hanging from the walls, in folders, in dozens of cardboard tubes, laid out on a draftsman's table, on a desk next to his computer.

As he showed me his projects, he started to shine, and I felt I could understand his passion, which was similar to mine when I talked about writing. Being passionate about something—I think we can all understand that. It's something we all want, and when you feel it, there's no denying it. It keeps us alive and it brings us close to the people who are the same as us in a kind of perfect communion. Jack Kerouac said it best: "The only people for me are the mad ones, the ones who are mad to live, mad to talk, mad to be saved." That's what we were. Mad to be saved. Mad about each other.

We had a relaxed dinner at the island in the kitchen, and Trey spoke to me for the first time about his father. They barely talked anymore. Even though they lived in the same city, they'd only seen each other a few times that year, and the experience hadn't been pleasant. He kept saying it didn't matter, but the way he repeated it told me it did. So did his eyes, which revealed his pain, his need to run from something he hadn't yet told me about.

And my heart, which I'd felt growing stronger those days, turned to an object made of glass that could fear, suffer, and break.

I talked to him about my father as well. I told him things I'd never told anyone, and he listened to me in silence. Before I knew it, I was revealing all the things I had hidden without realizing it: the tears spilled in hiding, the mornings when I hadn't wanted to wake up, everything I'd been willing to do to get him to look at me the way he did at others. The things I would still do...

"Will you tell him?" he asked me.

"That I'm going to stay?" He nodded. "Why? He'll find out either way, and if someone else tells him, I won't have to deal with his reproaches."

"Harper, you need to get past your fear of confronting him."

I rubbed my cheeks, trying to distract myself. I knew it was ridiculous to keep being afraid of my father when I was twenty-two years old, but the feeling ran so deep that I didn't even know how to face it. I only knew how to run away.

"I know, but..."

"But what?"

"Confronting him isn't really what I'm scared of," I confessed, at last starting to understand myself.

"What is it, then?"

"I'm afraid if I do it, I'll find out why he doesn't love me. And a truth like that can really hurt."

"Trust me: lying hurts way worse, and silence can hurt even more than that."

By now we were sitting on the couch. Trey brushed a strand of hair out of my face and tucked it behind my ear. He liked to do that, and I liked him doing it. It was a tender gesture. I leaned my head to the side and pressed his hand into it.

"Look at us," he said.

Just then, Sisuei hopped up onto the couch and rested his head in my lap. I petted him. I was more comfortable with him there, and I closed my eyes, listening to his soft groans. When he nuzzled me closer, I bent over and buried my nose in his fur, hugging him, and feeling a little stupid. I looked at Trey out of the corner of my eye.

"What?" I said defensively.

"Nothing."

"I know you're thinking something. What is it?"

He took a deep breath. "I've always felt like something was miss-ing in this house. And I never knew exactly what. Now I do. It's you."

That remark made me want to kiss him, drag him off to bed, tell him all the reasons I needed him, too. But instead I started laughing like an idiot. As though he understood, Sisuei's ears began to move.

"Don't laugh, dammit!" Trey said. "I've never even thought any-thing like that and you're making me feel like an idiot!"

A romantic song started playing on the stereo, and I leaned in to him, not sure what I was doing, just wanting contact: eye to eye, mouth to mouth, skin to skin. My desires mingling with his. We were like two treasure hunters exploring each other's bodies with no map or compass, just following our instincts.

We didn't let each other go until the sun rose. Our fingers danced over each other's nakedness while the music played. I heard "Love Somebody Like You" by Emma White, and the notes seemed to float around us.

"I got you something," he said.

"A present?"

He nodded, slipped away from me softly, and stood. Walking to the closet, he pulled out a drawer, reached in, and grabbed a black paper bag. He sat down beside me and handed it to me.

Nervously, I glanced at him before peeling off the gold sticker hold-ing it closed. My grin grew into a smile as I brought out a book, a novel, called *The Readers of Broken Wheel Recommend* by Katarina Bivald.

"It's about a young woman who starts up a bookstore in a small town and how reading changes her and her new neighbors' lives," he said.

I ran my fingers over the cover in gratitude. "Thanks, I didn't expect this. I'm so excited!"

He kissed me on the forehead.

There was something else in the bag, so I reached back in, pulling out an assortment of different-sized notebooks tied together with a ribbon.

"Those are for you to write down all the ideas that occur to you." Then he pulled out something else, a rectangular black box I hadn't noticed. "And you can use this to write them with."

My lips quivered and I had a knot in my throat, and when I opened the box, tears welled in my eyes. It was a Montblanc Le Petit Prince pen with my name engraved on it.

"Trey, this is too much."

"I know it's silly, but since it had the same name as…"

"The island," I said.

"Yeah. I saw that and I just had to get it."

"I don't know what to say."

"You don't have to say anything. These are just the kinds of things any writer deserving of the name should have."

I wanted to tell him all I felt in that moment, all that those gifts meant to me. All that he meant to me. But words escaped me. There just weren't any that said enough. What phrase could capture the feeling that without understanding why, you just wake up one morning and there's someone next to you who makes you want to live? This is how the best things in life come to you, out of nowhere, without warning. And you realize that loneliness only exists because you've refused to open the door and let that person in. The person who's always there, through rain, through shine.

There weren't any words to tell him that I wished that every clock in the world would stop and make this moment eternal. That if I could choose, I would wish for us to be reborn as two cats so we could have nine more lives together. For everything to remain as it was. Our eyes met, and I touched his cheek and ran my fingers down his neck, then pulled him close and stopped a few millimeters from his mouth, inhaling his breath. I kissed him until my heart was pounding and my entire body was tense. And the smile he offered back to me was a promise of bright sunny days and long nights of conversation, laughter, and sex.

24

You Can Get Everything You Want in Life If You Can Handle a Little Fear

I barely saw Trey the next two days. He was busy with clients and had to dash down to Syracuse to give a talk on bioclimatic architecture. I spent the whole week buried in books I had to shelve and manuscripts I had to correct.

Late one Saturday afternoon, Mr. Norris, my grandmother's lawyer, came to see me at the bookstore to sign some documents. He was a nice man with elegant manners who reminded me of a movie star in the fifties. And that made me think of Adele, whom I'd almost forgotten since I'd come back.

On Sunday, I got a message from Hayley. They had just landed in Florence, where they'd be spending a couple of days. Then they'd continue on to Paris, and would fly back home from there on Thursday. I was dying to see her. I had a million things to tell her, and I wanted to share all the new things I was feeling. Until then, I'd have to content myself with a four-legged furry friend who liked to climb on the sofa and stare at me.

I don't know what I was thinking when I told Trey I'd take care of Sisuei while he was away. I didn't know the first thing about dogs, and I could hardly take care of myself. Trey must have realized this, because his expression was skeptical when he said yes.

I looked over at Sisuei, and his ears stiffened. He was a pleasant creature, and after just a few hours together and one walk around the block, I felt like we were the best of friends. When he saw I wasn't taking him anywhere, he groaned softly, and I chuckled. I got it. I was starting to get bored, too.

"You know what, Sisuei? Today we're going to have lunch outside. That way you'll get your ass off the couch for a while."

He followed me into the kitchen as I looked out the window. The day was sunny, and it was hot for that time of year. I made a salad and a couple of sandwiches and tossed them into my backpack with a blanket before rolling my bicycle outside.

It took me a moment to feel comfortable pedaling with Sisuei's leash around my wrist. I was too scared of falling to relax. But Sisuei was a good companion: he stayed beside the bike and was attentive to my movements, and he knew what I was going to do before I did. I was supposed to take care of him, but he was taking care of me, and I could have hugged him, I was so grateful.

We went to the Montreal Botanic Garden, one of the prettiest places in the city. Nearly two hundred acres of plants, flowers, and greenhouses. After paying, I walked straight to the Chinese Garden, which was my favorite. I found a peaceful spot and sat down to eat. Sisuei didn't even blink as he observed me, mouth watering.

Have I ever told you I can't say no to anyone?

I tore off pieces of the sandwich for him, hearing Trey shouting at me in my head that I was only supposed to give him dog food. But those little pellets were disgusting-looking and they smelled like liver. According to him, they had all the nutrients a dog needed, and the sugar and fats in human food was bad for dogs. But what was the harm in a little chicken and tomato? They were natural, plus I always bought organic. And they must have tasted way better than his food, which looked like rabbit droppings.

"If you don't tell him, I won't," I said to the dog as he devoured one last bite and almost swallowed one of my fingers. I stroked him behind the ears, and he licked my cheek.

It was a little gross, that trail of saliva on my face, but it didn't keep me from loving him more and more with every second that passed.

When we were done, we both lay down on the grass, and when we got up, we walked beneath the trees. Sisuei kept pressing his nose into my hand, trying to get me to pet him. I didn't know why he needed my attention all the time, but I liked it. I could get used to having a dog, walking him, the constant companionship. Even Trey didn't make me feel as necessary or important as Sisuei did when he gave me one of those looks full of longing. I'd never had an experience like that before.

We returned home at dusk. When we turned the corner for our street, Sisuei became frantic, and soon I realized why: Trey was waiting for us in the doorway, sitting on his suitcase. He stood as soon as he noticed our presence.

"What are you doing here?" I asked.

"I can't tell you how much I love such a passionate welcome-home," he said, and I laughed, letting him embrace me and relishing his scent. I closed my eyes, feeling an almost unbearable throbbing beneath my skin. "I came back early. I couldn't stand spending another night away from home. I missed you too much."

He kissed me slowly while Sisuei walked around us in circles groaning like a puppy. Trey let me go to give him some attention. He barked and jumped around, and when he finally calmed down, we entered the house.

We had dinner and wound up on the floor on a pile of cushions watching a movie. Then we went for a walk so Sisuei could do his business before bed.

We went to La Fontaine, and in the park, Trey took Sisuei off his leash so he could run around. We walked the path, not talking, as if words no longer had a point. The only sound was the rustle of leaves in the wind and the water in a nearby fountain. Now and then, Trey would look over at me or kiss me for no reason, first soft, then so passionately that I would writhe with frustration when he pulled away.

I sighed and looked up into the black, empty sky.

"It's so empty. It's nothing like Petit Prince," I whispered.

"It is, though. It just looks different." He wove his fingers through mine and spun me around to face him. "Do you miss the island?"

"A little, yeah. I miss the freedom I felt there. The…feeling of home."

"But you can be just as free here. You can be happy, you can have everything you want if you try."

Curious, I asked him, "Do you?"

"I feel like I do. Sometimes." He shrugged. "I want them, at least."

"Having and wanting aren't the same thing. They're not even close to the same thing."

He shook his head. I could tell there was something he was trying to say, but he couldn't find the way.

"I know, you're right, but I know what I want, and I know I'll always fight for it, and in a way, that's much more important than having it." He pulled my hand until we were standing under a tree whose leafy branches fell like curtains, concealing us. He held my face and stared at me. "I know I want to enjoy my life. That every minute of it counts. That I need to do what I love, what moves me. Be free. Choose. Choose how, when, where, why, with whom. But I already know the answer to that last one. It's with you."

Knowing he wanted me like that made me feel sure of myself. Knowing he needed me—that was a new feeling, and it was addictive.

"Why do we always end up having these serious, intense conversations?" he asked. I shrugged, and he shook his head. "Just so you know, I'm not usually like this."

"Oh, you aren't? What are you usually like?"

"A dumb jerk."

I giggled. "I doubt that. I see you as a deep, sensitive, romantic man."

"Romantic? My idea of romance used to be telling a girl I liked her tits and ass. I thought that was the best compliment you could give. But I have to admit, it usually worked."

"You never said anything like that to me," I said, pinching him.

"With you I just think it. All the time. But when I open my mouth, all that comes out is how much I like your smile, the sound of your voice, the smell of your skin, your contradictions, your craziness. It just emerges involuntarily."

I scowled at him.

"You think I'm crazy?" I asked.

"Crazy about me!"

"Dear Lord, you're just as bad as I am."

Looking like a mischievous child about to play a prank, he whispered, "You bet I am," and leaned in close. "I'm crazy, too. Crazy about touching you, about kissing you all over, about fucking you. I think about that all the time, too."

I blushed. I wasn't used to a man talking dirty, and it lit a fire inside me.

I realized something then, as his stare burned into me: I was still free. Freedom had followed me here. It lived inside me. And I understood something else, the meaning of a word I had never really grasped before then. Home.

Home isn't a place, it's the person or people who love you.

That night, at that moment, home was that tree we were hiding under.

And later, it was my bed, our kisses, the wild, ferocious fire between us.

Flames, lust, impatience, possession.

Primitive, instinctive sex.

And afterward, his arms were my home as I fell asleep, exhausted. His breath on my neck. The calm after the storm.

My home was him.

As long as it lasted.

The next day, I went to Toronto.

Leaving the airport, I watched through the window of the taxi as we headed toward my apartment in the Annex, a student neighborhood near the university. I thought and thought, went over each and every step I had to take. First I'd go to school and talk with my advisor. I knew dropping out would disappoint him, but I was sure of my choice, and that was enough for me. I didn't need a bunch of extra letters coming after my name to make myself feel special.

Then I'd go to the publisher to announce my departure. I'd hand in the revisions that were due and close that stage of my life with a smile.

When I entered the apartment, I was pleased to find it just as I had left it.

I picked up the letters my landlady had been sliding under the door and took a glance at them. There was nothing interesting apart from an invitation to a poetry reading at the White Rabbit, a bohemian café. And that had already taken place the Friday before.

I threw my suitcase on the bed and called the moving company I'd hired to confirm what time they'd be coming to pick up my things.

Then I went outside and caught the streetcar down Bloor Street to campus. There were students all over, walking, reading on the grass, laughing, conversing. I watched them, thinking how I'd never been like them; I was the type who was always in the library studying. If I made a list of the people I'd talked to with any regularity in Toronto, I doubted I could come up with more than a handful.

A part of me regretted not trying harder. Not looking for friends, not going out more. I wished I'd done that instead of spending four years working my fingers to the bone to show myself I could do something—something I could hardly even remember the point of anymore.

I entered the imposing Jackman Building, with its fake marble pillars, and headed to Professor Cook's office. When he saw me come in, he smiled, took off his glasses, and laid them on his desk, watching me sit down.

"Let me guess: I'm not going to like it, right?"

I shook my head and shrugged, already apologetic.

"I think I could use a coffee and a sandwich to help me absorb the blow. Are you hungry?"

"Honestly, yes."

We left the building and walked to Subway. I ordered a chicken teriyaki sub, chips, and a juice. Then we went to a park nearby and sat on a bench. I told him about my worries and fears, my personal situation, and where I actually saw myself in coming years.

Professor Cook listened to me while he ate, giving the impression he understood.

"You must think I'm making a huge mistake…"

He took a deep breath, balling up his napkin.

"Harper, you're one of the best students I've had in all my years of teaching. I know for certain that you would have a bright future as a researcher. Your paper on the feminine image in medieval Spanish literature was brilliant. Your study on censorship in your second year knocked me off my feet. If you go into publishing, you'll bring a new vision with you, one we all need at a time when rushing things to the market means every book turns out the same. You remember that when we talked about that in class, I found your analysis of it very sharp. And yet…" He paused for a moment. "And yet, I don't think you're making a mistake. University is a place you come to learn what your dreams are, to start understanding your goals. If you want to write, Harper, write. The world needs more minds like yours, sensitive, critical, and people will want to know your thoughts. All of us need to find our place in the world. If that's yours, you need to go for it."

I was deeply relieved, and I smiled at him, and he smiled back. We said our goodbyes not long afterward, and I walked to the registrar's office to officially resign from the program.

Later, I went to the publisher. Simon & Schuster was on 166 King Street East, thirty minutes away on foot—a long but necessary walk to shake off my nerves. I was so lost in thought, still tossing over everything Professor Cook had said, that I hardly realized I'd made it there until I saw the offices in front of me. I climbed the steps and walked through the door. My heart always skipped a beat when my feet touched that blue and yellow carpet. I walked toward Ryan Radcliffe's office. His assistant, Gwen, was sitting at her desk.

"Harper!" she said when she saw me.

"Hey, Gwen, how are you?"

"Good, thanks. Busy as ever, but you know how things go around here." I nodded. They were always going full-speed, but the collegial atmosphere made up for the pressure. "What about you? We've missed you here. Especially Ryan. You were spoiling him."

"Sorry. I needed time to work out some things."

"Don't mention it. I understand. It's not easy, losing someone you love that much."

"Is Ryan in his office?"

"Yeah, I'll tell him you're here."

Gwen lifted the receiver and dialed his number. Seconds later, Ryan Radcliffe opened the door to his office.

"Harper, come in."

He invited me to sit down and took his place behind his desk.

"I'm happy to have you back. How…how are you?"

"A lot better, thanks."

"I'm glad to hear it. We sent flowers for the funeral. I hope you got them."

"I did. They were gorgeous. Thank you."

"It's nothing. You've found your place here. You're one of us now."

Oh God! This was going to be harder than I'd hoped. I blinked to stop myself from crying. "Ryan, I need to tell you something…"

I didn't go into details. I didn't even tell him I was planning to become a writer. I wasn't completely honest in that moment, and I don't know why. I used my family as an excuse and said I needed to start over close to them. In his face, I could see he didn't understand me, but he knew there was nothing he could do to change my mind.

I handed him a stick drive with all my work finished and tried to tell him all it had meant for me to be part of his team and how much I had learned in my months there.

As soon as I was outside, I had to lean against the wall to catch my breath. I'd gotten past my insecurities, but that didn't mean they were gone forever, and the symptoms now were coming back to haunt me. I looked up in the sky and sucked in as much air as I could. I'd done it. I'd said goodbye to my present and to what I'd always thought would be my future to try to become the person I thought I could be.

I was out of my mind.

I started laughing, so hard I had to sit on the ground. The people walking past must have thought I had utterly lost it.

The sun was starting to dip behind the buildings, and the cool air raised goose bumps on my skin. I bought a burrito from a food truck on the corner. I left the bag on my kitchen counter when I got home and changed into a pair of sweatpants and a ratty T-shirt. I opened all the windows to air out the apartment, which smelled of dust and damp. Then I sat on the fire escape with my phone and dialed Trey's number.

I waited impatiently for him to pick up. On the fourth tone, I heard the following: *I'm sorry, the number you have dialed is not in service, unless you are a wonderful and very sexy girl I'd love to have on my sofa right now.*

I giggled and covered my mouth with my hand when I realized a woman in the next building over was watching me.

"What would you do with that naked girl on your sofa, then?"

"My intentions are bad. Always. I'd make her orgasm until she passed out."

"Well, what a lucky, sexy girl she is, then. How about if you take your clothes off and open the door right now. Maybe you'll find out she's got a bad streak, too, and she's standing there waiting for you…"

"Are you for real?" he said.

"Only if you can figure out a way to teleport me over."

"Dammit!" He sighed. "It's not nice to play with my feelings like that."

"Don't tell me you actually went to the door?" I laughed, imagining him doing it.

"Yeah, ha ha, very funny."

I wished just then that I really had gone there, that I could watch the door open and see him appear. "I love to know you're missing me."

"I never said I was missing you."

"I also love you getting all pissy like a little boy. Let me guess—you're going to make me pay for this?"

"You better believe it. How did everything go today?"

"Well. I think. I don't know. What I mean is…I know I did what I had to so I could be fair with myself, but it felt…weird."

"You're weird. That's one of the things I like about you. And I've realized something about you. I think I know what you need."

"You do?"

"Yeah," he said. "You need to do different things from before, connect with the new you. How about if we take off for the mountains this weekend? Get some clean air, some exercise, some together time."

"You know I'm not big on exercise."

"I didn't say what kind."

All right, then. Any plan that included him was up my alley.

"I'd love to. But my brother and sister are coming back this week and I'd like to see them. It's been a while, and…I need to tell them about us, too."

"Harper, about that… If you don't mind, I'd like to be the one to tell Hoyt. He's my best friend, and I want to do it the right way. It matters to me. You get that, don't you?"

I agreed. I was excited to share something that made me so happy with him and Hayley, but I understood the position Trey was in.

"Of course. It makes perfect sense." Excited at the thought of seeing him in just a few days, I asked, "Will you come get me at the airport?"

"I'll be there."

"Good night, Trey."

"Good night, babe."

That *babe* had sounded so sweet, I nearly hyperventilated. All I needed was his voice to make me feel free, crazy, chaotic, unpredictable. And also scared, dependent, exposed. If only I could find balance and stop oscillating from one side to the other. Going constantly up and down. Struggling with the fear that was always lurking just behind me.

Suddenly I remembered a phrase: *You can get everything you want in life if you can handle a little fear.* My mother used to say that when we got scared of new things. The first day of school, riding a bike.

My mother.

I saw her for a moment, her wild blond hair pulled into a long braid, her vitality seeming to multiply itself as she clapped for me and shouted while I pedaled one foot after another until I made it all the way around the fountain.

Maybe it wasn't so bad, being afraid.

Maybe it was one more part of the motor that kept me living.

Maybe it was necessary, because feeling pain is better than feeling nothing at all.

25

I Would Have Asked
Him to Stay

I saw him as soon as I walked through the glass doors. He was leaning against a column paging through a newspaper, wearing a white shirt with rolled-up sleeves, gray jeans, and black sneakers. To say he was handsome would be the understatement of the century.

He looked up, at me, through me. I tried to act normal, not like a person hopelessly in love; but I was one, and I failed. The words *I love you* danced on the tip of my tongue, but I held them back.

Trey walked toward me and raised a finger, motioning for me to walk toward him. I hurried over and threw myself into his arms. His lips covered mine with a hot kiss.

"Hey," he whispered.

"Hey."

"Everything good?"

I knew what he meant. I had just said goodbye to an important part of my life, and I still felt like I was wandering in a cloud, and nothing seemed quite real.

"Yeah. I think so."

"Then let's go celebrate."

He guided me to the car and put my suitcase in the trunk, and we drove away.

"Where are we headed?"

"I thought we could get dinner somewhere relaxing and then have a drink after. Maybe go dancing."

"Dancing?"

"Yeah, dancing. Is that weird? You say it like it was something for girls to enjoy and for guys to force themselves to do so they can get laid afterwards."

"No!" I shouted. "It's just... I've never gone out with a guy who liked to dance before."

He raised an eyebrow. "Have you gone out with a lot of guys?"

"Why is that any of your business?"

"Just curious..."

He smiled, and I did, too. It was fun, talking nonsense with him, not thinking of anything, really, and certainly not of tomorrow. It was liberating.

"Well, what's clear to me is you were never going to get anywhere with those guys. You were obviously waiting for me."

"Now that's self-assurance," I said. I looked over at him, and he returned the gesture as we waited for the light to change. "What about you... Have you been with lots of girls?"

He rested his hand on my thigh and rubbed it softly.

"One-night stands. Friends with benefits. Nothing exclusive, nothing serious. I was waiting for you, too."

I leaned over and gave him a quick kiss.

He had waited for me.

I had waited for him.

Maybe we'd always been waiting for each other, even since before we had met.

———

We decided to go to L'Gros Luxe, a bar close to my house. It wasn't busy, and we took a corner table by the window and ordered a few dishes to share.

"So, when will your things get here?" he asked.

"Tomorrow, if the moving guys are on time."

"Let me know if you need any help."

"It's just a couple of boxes of books and clothes. I'll be fine."

He gave me a surprised look. "You hired movers just for clothes and books? You don't have any electronics, posters, appliances? How many books are we talking?"

I dipped a carrot stick in dressing. "I guess…thousands? I did inherit a bookstore, remember? My grandmother picked me for a reason. Being surrounded by books is heaven to me."

"I thought I was heaven to you."

"Trey, don't get offended, but if I had to choose between my books and you… You might well come up short."

He bent over, reached under my shirt, and stroked my lower back while I studied every inch of his lips.

"Books aren't everything. You know that, right? A woman has needs, basic needs…" I had to admit, he knew how to get to me. "A book can't kiss you, a book can't caress you. A book can only go so deep…"

"I don't know about that."

He responded with an inquisitive look. I was having fun. He liked being in control, but he also liked pretending nothing mattered to him, and it was entertaining, watching him go back and forth between expressive and indifferent.

"Well, you'd have to show me," he said, "because what I'm imagining right now is very, very weird. I'm trying to keep an open mind, but…"

I laughed and stuck a piece of celery in his mouth to get him to be quiet, but he chewed around it and said, "I'm glad you find me funny."

We paid and walked outside holding hands, very close, ignoring the entire rest of the world. Trey hadn't been kidding about dancing, so we went to Les Foufounes Électriques, a club and concert hall in the Latin Quarter.

With him everything was fun, even walking down streets I knew by heart, his arm around my waist, him leaning in to whisper something every few steps, unable to keep away from me. It was hard for me, too, to go for long without staring at him. His eyes intoxicated me. He had a childish tenderness, but with a manly firmness that could inflame me inside in an instant. He seduced me with his easygoing attitude, which hid an impulsive, passionate heart. He was life distilled, and everything paled beside him, beside the mirage of what we could be someday.

He made me laugh with his games and his stupid, often shameless questions, which I answered without the least bit of embarrassment. He liked that about me, and he'd give me kisses on the neck to hide his hoarse, sexy laugh when people passing by started to stare.

"Hey," someone said, "sorry. Excuse me, can you help me with something?"

We turned and saw a couple on the opposite sidewalk. The guy waved.

"Hi," he repeated, crossing the street toward us. "We're looking for MTelus, the concert venue. We were told it was close to here, but I think we've missed it."

"Have you heard of it?" I asked Trey.

He nodded.

"Yeah, it's the former Métropolis." He let my hand go and approached the couple. "It's close by. We're going to a place right next door. We can walk there together."

"Wow, that would be great," the girl said.

She was blond, with bright, expressive eyes, and very pretty. When she turned, I saw a tattoo on her neck, a little bird taking flight. The guy was tall, with brown hair and a friendly smile. I thought I might have seen him somewhere before.

"We've been walking in circles for a while, and we were starting to think we'd never find it," he said. "By the way, I'm Nick, and this is my wife, Novalie."

"Nice to meet you," she said.

"A pleasure," I responded.

"It's this way," Trey said. "I'm assuming you're not from Montreal."

"We're not even Canadian. We live in Boston, but we spend a lot of time in Bluehaven. We're in Canada for our honeymoon, traveling from coast to coast," Nick said.

"Congratulations! Why'd you pick Canada, though? Didn't you want somewhere warmer, with exotic beaches and daiquiris?" I asked.

"We've got a little sailboat, and we go out a couple of times a year, usually to the south. This time, we wanted to do something different," Novalie said.

"Well, I hope it's been special," I told her.

"It's been amazing. Are you both from Montreal?"

"Yeah, and we both live here. Trey's an architect and I own a bookstore."

"You own a bookstore?" Novalie asked, excited. "My aunt has one in Bluehaven. I like to help her out whenever I visit her. It's such a special place for me. You can't imagine..."

Nick looked at her over his shoulder. By now, the men had moved ahead of us, and she and I were walking together.

"I inherited my shop from my grandmother. She died not long ago."

"I'm so sorry."

"Thanks." I shrugged. I felt so comfortable with her that I made a little confession. "The bookstore was her life, and she held it together through thick and thin for decades. I hope I can do the same. It means a lot to me. I basically grew up in the place."

"I'm sure you'll do great."

"It's kind of a calling for me."

"Why just 'kind of'?"

"Because my other thing is writing. I'm going to try to do both and pray that I've made the right decision."

Novalie's green eyes didn't blink as she looked over, trying to see something inside me. "You know, since I was really little, I've always liked dance. Ballet. My mother was a dancer. She was really good, and I always wanted to be like her."

"You said *was*."

"Yeah, she died years ago."

"I'm sorry." She and I had more things in common than I would have guessed.

"After her death, I gave up dancing. It wasn't until I started college that I enrolled in a dance academy. It was nothing big, just a way to scratch the itch while I was studying comparative literature. Then, when I was finished with school, I had a revelation, and I ended up starting my own ballet school. It barely sustains itself, but I don't regret it because it's what I was meant to do. When you do something because you like it, it's always the right decision."

"You're right. And it took me too long to figure that out. By the way, I studied literature, too."

"For real?" I nodded. "You and I seem to have a lot in common," she said.

"Harper," Trey called. "They've got two extra tickets for Bring Me the Horizon tonight at MTelus. You want to go?"

"Please do," Novalie said. "We were supposed to take my friend Lucy and her boyfriend, Roberto, but they missed their flight," Novalie said.

"Yeah, why not? We were already planning to get a drink and go dancing," I replied.

"Cool!" Nick said.

"Nick's a musician," Novalie told me as we kept walking. "He teaches at Berklee. He tries to catch as many concerts as he can. He says it's the best way to discover new sounds and styles and appreciate the nuances... I don't really know what that means. Half the time what he says goes over my head."

"The same thing happens to me when Trey goes into detail about his projects. All I see is blueprints and they might as well be hieroglyphics."

"Yep. That's exactly what I feel when I see sheet music."

We laughed.

"So who is Bring Me the Horizon?"

"You've never heard them?" she asked. "You'll love them if you like death metal, screamo, that kind of thing..."

"Screamo?"

Novalie giggled and covered her mouth before reaching into her pocket and pulling out a little white package. "Here, you might need these."

Inside, I found a pair of earplugs. "Are you kidding?"

She shook her head.

When we got there, we had to wait a few minutes to get inside. Trey and Nick had hit it off and were chatting away about their pets. They seemed to be competing to see which dog was cooler, Sisuei or Ozzy, Nick's Labrador.

We flashed our tickets and went inside. The place was packed, and we struggled to make our way toward the stage. Fifteen minutes later, the lights went down. The crowd shouted until every voice was one deep roar just as the band came onstage. My heart was racing. Though I didn't mention this to Novalie, I'd never been to a concert like that. The closest thing I'd been to was an open-air folk festival! Those are the breaks when you have no social life or group of friends to do things with.

The lights came up, the screams grew louder, and the band started playing the first chords. The sound coming from the amplifiers was deafening.

That night was probably the most fun I had ever had. I laughed and shouted until I could barely speak.

And I danced. After an hour, they played a slower tune, almost sensual, if music that heavy can be called sensual. I felt Trey's hands on my hips and his body against my back moving softly back and forth. I was stiff at first, but then I gave in, and my muscles loosened.

The music echoed through my head, then through my entire body. As he gripped me tighter, I turned around and looked into his eyes. Our foreheads touched, our lips came together, and we swayed to the rhythm, fluid, body to body, speeding up as the drumbeats started pounding.

We kissed, our hearts beating a thousand beats per minute, holding onto each other tight. If I had known all the stupid things I would do after that night was over, I'd never have let him go. I'd have held him until our bodies were one.

I'd have asked him to stay.

Stay.

Please stay.

"All it takes is a thought, just one thought for the world to come tumbling down, and with it the whole set, the curtains, the masks, and then the dead come back from the grave, the ghosts, and everything you thought was buried, hidden behind a smile."

—Laura Esquivel, *The Colors of My Past*

26

Sometimes the Truth Hurts

I've wondered at times what happens to those magic moments that we push aside because they're so sad. Those moments that are our truth, that tell us who we really are, with no masks, no disguises, no camouflage—just bare flesh. They're so hard to get at, so hard to create, and then they vanish as soon as we lie down in bed.

But maybe they haven't gone anywhere. Maybe they just turn vague in our minds, linked to some image or memory that will allow us to bring them to life again when we need them. Maybe they hide on purpose, offended because we didn't hold them in high enough regard, because we took for granted that they'd last forever.

We always think when we find happiness, that it will never abandon us. But that's vain, and often it's not in our hands.

Anytime I got the chance, I liked to go to the Notre-Dame-des-Neiges Cemetery. The first time was for my mother's funeral, and since then, I've visited her whenever I've had the opportunity.

The last time I went was for my grandmother's funeral.

And now I was there again, at her grave. The mound of red earth had been covered by a granite slab and a tombstone. I laid the white tulips I'd bought for her down on the stone and sat on the blanket I'd brought with me so I could spend some time by her side.

It was strange: I thought the fear and pain would overwhelm me, but I felt calm, as if she really were there and there was no point in missing her. That wasn't true, though. I did miss her. I missed her terribly.

I opened my purse and took out some chocolates. I unwrapped and chewed one as I stared at her name engraved on the tombstone. Then I lay back on the grass and enjoyed the silence I had always found so pleasant there, beneath the one ray of sun that had managed to penetrate the thin cloud cover. Time passed as I let my emotions roll over me. I imagined her appearing by my side to awaken me from a bad dream in which the world had gone on without her. I had always been able to count on her love: selfless, sweet, eternal. Learning to go on without it was going to be hard for me.

I savored my memories, then I stood up and kissed the tombstone and traced out the letters of her name with my index finger.

"Goodbye, Grandma. I'll see you again soon."

I didn't bother drying my tears as I walked to the center of the cemetery, following one of the paths worn by visitors' feet that zig-zagged between the tombs and mausoleums.

It was a pretty place, in its way, almost an open-air museum, with sculptures that included copies of Michelangelo's *Pietà* and William Wetmore's *Angel of Grief.*

A light breeze shook the trees, bringing me the scent of damp leaves. The clouds were no longer white—they'd turned gray and were darkening by the minute. A raindrop fell on my forehead.

I hurried on to my mother's grave. It lay amid blossoming trees under a statue of an angel praying. Dad was Catholic, but he hadn't brought me up religious, and as far as I knew, his religious sentiments went no further than that statue. If he ever had believed in anything, it must have died with my mother and remained buried, along with his good intentions, inside that granite crypt.

"Hey, Mom," I said, kneeling in front of her tomb. I pushed aside some dried leaves that had fallen there and laid down a bouquet of tulips. A fine rain was falling now from the dark sky, but the branches overhead protected me from the worst of it. "I've got a lot to tell you. I don't even know where to start."

"You could start by telling her how you're going to ruin your life by becoming a goddamned cashier."

I leapt up, terrified, and turned to see him there—my father, observing me with that contempt he had perfected over many years. He was holding a huge bouquet of wildflowers. He left it at the foot of the angel, kissed his hand, and touched the place where my mother's name was engraved.

"How did you find out?"

"There's nothing I don't know, Harper." His way of speaking made me feel exposed.

"Listen, you may not like the path I've chosen, but I'm an adult and this is what I want to do."

He raised his arms in exasperation and let them fall to his sides.

"When are you going to learn? It's not about what we *want*, it's about what we ought to do. Our place in the world, who we are. Sometimes we're obliged to do things whether or not we're inclined to. You should know this by now."

"But…you always said we should try to find something we could devote ourselves to one hundred percent, and that's what I'm doing."

"I wasn't talking about running a bookstore. I meant—"

"The company, investing, the family name," I finished for him.

"Exactly."

"I'm no good for that."

"Then what are you good for? What have you done to make up for the…?" He closed his mouth and struggled to swallow the words burning his lips. "It's best if I go."

He turned on his heels and walked away, seemingly indifferent to the rain.

"Has it ever occurred to you that you could try encouraging me instead of always talking down to me?" I shouted, full of anguish. He looked back with a grimace.

"So that's what you think, that I talk down to you?"

"Never, not once have you said anything kind to me, or even anything pleasant. I know you can be nice, I know you can even be sweet and caring, because I've seen you do it with other people. But with me, you're incapable of it. It's as if you hate me, and I can't figure out why."

He turned and walked back, his hair and blazer soaked.

"Maybe if you would stop screwing up for once…"

"I am. I have." I brought my hand to my heart. Raindrops dripped onto it from my hair, which was damp now and smelled strongly of my shampoo. "And you should feel proud of me. I'm living my dream. I'm happy."

He clicked his tongue, disgusted.

"You don't even know what that means."

"Mom taught literature and philosophy, she adored that bookstore, and she wanted to write one day when she was done teaching. I'm just trying to be like her…trying to be the person I really am."

"Don't say that."

"Why does it bother you so much?"

"Just shut up."

I was surprised by the aggressiveness in his words. Something told me I should listen to him, but I couldn't stop myself.

"Is it so wrong for me to want to be like her, follow in her footsteps?"

"Harper, shut up."

"My mother believed in dreams, believed that you didn't have to see them clearly, that just feeling them was enough."

"And what good did it do her?" he hissed, just as thunder rolled across the sky. "Dreams, longings, her pie in the sky... None of it was tangible or logical. None of it was real. If she'd been more reasonable, she'd still be here with me and not there, under the dirt."

I blinked, unable to believe what I was hearing.

"What are you saying? What's that supposed to mean?" I didn't understand, and as he turned to go again, I screamed, "Why do you hate me this way? Just tell me for once, dammit!"

His back turned, I could see his shoulders rising and falling with his breath. His voice cut into me like a knife.

"You took her from me. You took the person I loved most. You took away the love of my life and left my children without a mother."

"What?"

He turned, trembling.

"When she got pregnant, we found out something was wrong as soon as they did the first tests. She was very sick. The doctors said she needed to start cancer treatment immediately, but she didn't want to because you were there inside her. I told her to get an abortion, to think about it, at least, to think of her children, to think of me. I begged her until my throat was raw to get rid of you, to get better. I told her we could have more children later. But she refused. She told me she couldn't. And when you were born, it was too late. The cancer had spread. I don't know how she managed to even hold out for the six years that she did."

All of a sudden, it was as though I couldn't hear his words, as though they were just meaningless sounds, grave, crackly. Nothing made sense. I saw the pain on his face and felt the air around me grow thin.

The truth doesn't just hurt sometimes, it can break you inside like glass. I felt the solid earth beneath me give way, and sorrow and despair wrapped their hands around my neck.

"Why didn't anyone ever tell me?"

"She made us all promise, and I could never say no to her. But that's over with. You want to know why I can hardly stand to look at you? Because she died so you could live. And I don't think I'll ever forgive you for that."

"Dad…"

"She left. You stayed."

I was frozen as if in a block of concrete. The smallest movement was impossible. I closed my eyes, unable to take in what I was feeling, worried I might literally lose my mind.

"So it doesn't matter what I do, and it never did. The problem isn't my decisions; the problem is me."

He didn't answer.

"So what about Sophia? What did she do that was so wrong?"

"She supported your mother. She let her kill herself."

"I'm sorry."

"Sorry's no good. She's still there, under the ground. And no one can ever bring her back."

"Still, I'm sorry."

I felt the world vanish around me.

I wished it would end.

Wished I could stop feeling what I felt.

Wished I'd never existed.

"I'm sorry," I repeated a third time, unsure what else to say, because the words that could console the two of us hadn't yet been invented.

"I'll believe you when you show it."

"How? I'll do whatever you ask."

"You already know. And you owe it to me."

I nodded. Desperation twisted its knife in my heart, making the wound bigger and bigger.

It was true. I owed it to him.

27

Hopefully You Find Yourself Someday

I went back home and cried. I cried as I'd never cried before. Until dawn. My soul shattered, my heart in pieces. I curled up in bed as if I were six years old again, had just lost my mother, and was hugging the pillow waiting for the sun to rise.

Eventually I fell asleep.

I woke up muddleheaded with swollen eyelids that were almost impossible to open. I struggled out of bed because I had to, because I needed to go to the bathroom. In the mirror over the sink, my face was pallid and tear-streaked, a white mask framed by red hair kinked from a night spent in hell. I looked at myself, but I saw someone else, a girl who had taken her mother's life with her selfishness and her longing to live. A person who had broken her father's heart, condemning him to loneliness, unhappiness, the greatest pain a person can experience. The pain of losing someone you love and knowing you can never have them back. I hated myself, and I wished I could disappear forever.

Tears clouded my eyes, burning them, and sobs wrenched the muscles in my chest. What a strange feeling despair is. It bowls you over like an earthquake, making you beg, shout, and curse the world, hoping it will stop.

My father's words kept resounding in my mind. I needed to feel loved by him. I longed for it; I had ever since I was a girl. But he never would love me, and now I knew why. The truth. The hard reality I just had to accept and that caused me unspeakable pain.

My mother had died, and it was my fault.

Mine.

Mine alone.

I went back to my room, where I heard an irritating hum. My phone was vibrating in my purse, which was still on the bedroom floor where I'd left it the day before. I ignored it. I just wanted the time to pass quickly and leave this agony behind me. I didn't want to go through this. Nothing could ease the pain. Nothing.

I lay back on my pillow, alone and lost, insecure, full of fears and doubts.

Once more letting someone else tell me what my life should be.

My phone woke me. I'd been sleeping on and off, now dreaming, now opening my eyes, in a kind of limbo. I looked around. It was dark except for a soft light coming through the curtain from the streetlamps. Night had fallen. Maybe I'd been in bed a day, maybe two.

I dragged myself up, grabbed my purse, and took out my phone. I wasn't sure whether to unlock the screen. I was scared of the number of missed calls and messages I'd have.

Twenty calls.

Eighteen messages.

All of them from Trey.

Oh, Trey. I'm so sorry…

I lay back again and looked at the ceiling.

And thought and thought and thought.

About the same thing over and over.

Much longer than I should have.

It was my fault my father had become a sad, bitter man. He was right, I owed him. I owed him compensation, and I knew what it would cost: my dreams, my hopes, my longings…

Everything I had been.

Everything I was.

Everything.

Me: one simple word that defined something so complex.

And it wasn't hard to make the decision. I should have done it long before.

I gave up. I was beaten. I had no right to take my place in the world because it never had been mine anyway. I'd occupied it unfairly, hurting other people and making them suffer. But at least I could make up for some of it, even if it would never be enough. Even if doing so meant writing myself into an unhappy ending.

My phone buzzed again. Another message.

This time I opened it. But I didn't read it. I couldn't.

I took a breath and held it as I typed, my heart aching with regret and guilt and most of all, cowardice—my strongest trait:

What we have can't be. I'm sorry, but it's best if we not see each other again. Goodbye.

I turned off my phone and threw it against the wall. I rubbed my chest, trying in vain to relieve the pressure. Then I dragged my tired body into the sheets to let my mind rest. At last I knew what I had to do. Wait to feel the pain. And soon it came. An aching all over. For Trey, for the void my mother's sacrifice had left inside me, the desolate ground where nothing could now be built, where nothing would grow.

Because I myself was nothing.

Boom, boom, boom…

"Harper, are you there? If you're there, open the fucking door. We have to talk. I promise you, you can forget about me leaving until you let me see you."

I leaned my forehead on the door, feeling the walls close in like a pair of merciless hands. I wanted to see him, but I couldn't.

"Fine," he said. His voice had changed as he'd stayed out there waiting for a sign. First it was sweet, now it was hard and scared. "I'm calling Hoyt and Hayley. I don't want to, because this is between us, but you're not giving me another option."

Hoyt and Hayley? Hayley was coming back that night, and Hoyt must have already been in Montreal. Neither of them knew about Trey and me or what had happened with my father. And they couldn't find out, or things would get more complicated.

I had made my decision.

It wasn't fair for me to push ahead, happy, thinking only of myself, as though nothing had changed when it obviously had. I slowly turned the lock and opened the door. Trey was sitting on the stairs. As soon as he saw me, he stood. He looked as terrible as I did. His hair was a mess, his eyes had deep bags under them, and I could tell he hadn't slept. I stepped aside to let him in. He walked past me without looking at me and came to a stop in the middle of the living room, where he stood with his hands in his pockets.

I closed the door behind me. I'd been a fool to think I could get him out of my life with a mere text message. Trey wasn't the type to give up easily. He needed to understand every single detail about how things worked and why.

We observed each other in silence. I had to leave him and try to make everything go back to how it was before. As if he'd never existed. As if he hadn't come back into my life. It would hurt him, but I had to abandon him, hard as it was, especially knowing it would be forever.

I sat on the couch. He did the same, but far away from me. I felt relieved and shattered at the same time. I could feel the tension in the air. He was nervous. He took a deep breath and rubbed his face before speaking.

"What's going on, Harper? What was that message about?"

I shook my head, looking for words that were lost.

He went on, "My grandfather says a brave person is scared of his enemy, but a coward is scared of his own fear."

His grandfather had an answer for everything. I managed to look up and meet eyes with him. My hands were trembling. I felt sick, and the ticking of the clock was so loud I thought it would drive me mad.

"I can't keep going with you, Trey. I need this to end."

He paled before my eyes and looked up at the ceiling.

"Why?"

"Things have changed."

"In two days?"

"Yes."

The tears on my cheeks felt like drops of acid.

"Why?" he asked, his voice cracking. "And don't answer with some stupid phrase everyone uses, like 'It's not you, it's me.' No bullshit. Tell me the truth."

I nodded, fighting to keep my emotions under control—the very things I'd never managed to keep my grip on.

"Okay," I whispered. "I know why my father never loved me. It was my fault my mother died. They found out she was sick as soon as she got pregnant with me. Everyone told her to abort so she could get the treatment she needed, but she refused. She decided to have me, and that's why she died. My father can't forgive me and I need him to. I realize it might never happen. But if I try to be the person he wants me to be, maybe time will bring us a little bit closer. Do you understand?"

Trey sighed, struggling to get out from under the weight that was crushing him, and I felt even worse about myself, about him, about everything.

"No, I don't understand. I don't understand what the hell that has to do with us." He got up off the sofa and started pacing back and forth. "I'm sorry you had to find that out. It's tragic. If I try to put myself in your shoes, I can't begin to imagine what you're feeling. Your…your mother sacrificed herself for you, she took that decision because, evidently, you mattered more to her than anything. And then your father goes and blames you for her death. You should be grateful to your mother, and instead you think you owe him something? How do you expect me to understand that?"

He brought his hands to his head.

"Trey, it was *my* fault. She chose me. And because of me, Hoyt and Hayley grew up without a mother. Because of me, my father lost his wife…"

"Your fault? Harper, stop carrying the weight of the world for a minute and think about what you're saying. You didn't do anything. And even if you think you did, what does that have to do with us?"

"If I stay with you, I can never be the person my father wants me to be."

"Are you listening to yourself? What about the person you are? The person you really are?"

"There's no such thing as the person I really am. I've never really been anything."

He sighed.

"That's not true. You're real. You're someone who dreams of working in her grandmother's bookstore and turning it into somewhere magical. The girl who wants to write books and make the world live through her stories. The girl who sees a future with me at her side. You can't close your eyes to all that, Harper."

"I have to, though. If I want my father to accept me, I have to make a break with everything."

He shook his head. I could see he didn't like where the conversation was going.

"How the hell do you think you're going to get him to accept you?"

"I'll work for his company, I'll go back home, and I'll live there. I'll try to be more like Hayley…"

He looked at me as if he didn't know me, and I could see it took superhuman strength for him to try to remain calm and patient.

"Fine. You're making the worst mistake of your life, but fine. What about me, though? Why can't we stay together?"

I was exhausted. Every ounce of my strength was gone. And each question he asked me pulled us further and further apart, and I was dying inside.

"Because you would be a constant reminder of everything that could have been, and I can't take that. Every time I see you, I'll think of how it's felt being with you, and it will be torture, knowing I'll never feel that way again. I need to start from zero, Trey. I need you to forget these weeks. Forget everything that's happened between us. Just go back to that Halloween four years ago when we saw each other on the stairs. Let that be your last memory of me. I can't go on seeing you."

He shook his head, unable to accept what I was saying.

"You think one thing, and you say another. You believe one thing, and then you act differently. You're a pure contradiction. Chaos. You swore to yourself you'd never make a decision based on others' expectations again, that you'd follow your own dreams and wishes. And now, look at you: you're giving your life up for someone else."

"You don't understand. You don't…understand me."

He raised his arms and let them fall to his sides, powerless.

"I'm trying. I swear to you, I'm trying, but you're like an unsolvable riddle. I keep getting more and more clues, but none of them lead anywhere, and I'm afraid they never will."

"Well, if you can't understand me, Trey, at least trust me. This is for the best. It's over. It's over, dammit!"

He stepped over and took my hands.

"Harper, babe, you have a problem. It's that you're constantly feeling, and it's so intense that you're unable to stop suffering in this illogical way that's eating you alive. You're being carried away by feelings you can't control: guilt, desperation, anguish... You can't make important decisions in the middle of that whirlwind. You're setting yourself up for disaster."

The anguish on his face was so intense that it was as if he was bearing all the pain for both of us. Tears rolled down my cheeks. I couldn't stop them. He tried to hug me, and I turned away. If I let him, I wouldn't be able to stick to my decision. When I looked back at him, his eyes were two deep wells of sorrow.

"Do you love me?" he asked.

"Trey..."

"Do you love me?"

"That's not it."

"Just answer the fucking question!" he shouted. "Do you love me?"

"Yes," I responded, bitterly but honestly.

"It's not true," he whispered. "Until you accept yourself, until you stop feeling guilty for everything that's happened around you, until you trust in the person you are and learn to love yourself, you can't love someone else. So I'm sorry, Harper. You don't love me."

That poisoned arrow hit me straight in the heart.

"I do love you, but I don't want to hurt you, and I know I will. Sooner or later, I will."

"You're already hurting me. Don't you see? Do you think me being far away from you is somehow going to be good for me?"

"Trey, I can't survive if I try to do this halfway. Torn between what I love and what I feel I have to do. I need to choose."

"And let me guess: you've chosen."

"Yes," I moaned.

If my life was a book, the most dramatic chapter was being written right then.

"For someone who usually thinks about things so much that she's paralyzed when she's forced to do something, you sure are letting some ridiculous impulses carry you away."

"Maybe you don't believe me, but this has nothing to do with impulses."

"If I leave now, this is it, Harper. We're done forever. I can't just leave and come back into your life every time you change your mind. I can't."

"I understand."

Then there came a moment—he shook his head so slightly, if I hadn't been looking close, I could have missed it—when I knew he had understood. He understood there was nothing he could do to save me, that I didn't want to be saved. He rubbed the back of his neck and said, "I guess that's all I can say."

"I'm sorry, Trey."

"Yeah, me too. You know something? No one is more lost than the person who doesn't want to find themselves. I hope you do, Harper. Hopefully you'll find yourself someday."

I tried to resist the agony taking hold of me. I felt like a fish flopping desperately on the shore. I was scared, and I couldn't keep going. Time froze for a moment, and then he turned around and walked toward the door.

Weakened without realizing it, victim to my own desperation, I said, "You're going, just like that?"

He turned, and I saw a tear on his cheek.

"What would be the use in staying? Would something change if I begged you not to destroy what we have, to fight for what you truly love?"

I couldn't get out even one word. The feelings were there, but I couldn't articulate them. I was crushed.

"Goodbye, Harper," he said. "And don't worry, I won't tell anyone about what happened between us. You can relax and act like we never met. When I go out that door, I'm going to do everything I can to transform back into that shallow son of a bitch I was that Halloween years ago."

Something cracked inside me, in my chest, the way the ice of a frozen lake cracks under your feet just before you sink in. The door opened and closed, and he disappeared.

My despair turned to rage. I cried, punched the wall, was thankful to the physical pain for taking my mind off my feelings. I fell to the floor, weary, and remained there a long time, I don't know for how long, until it stopped. Until the emptiness lifted me up and took me away.

28

What You Don't Know Can Hurt You

The next few days I spent shut up in the house. I didn't have the strength to do anything.

After what my father said, I couldn't stand to look in the mirror. All I saw there was pain, and the realization that I was still the person I'd told myself I'd left behind, the vulnerable, insecure little girl I'd never wanted to be.

I avoided my brother and sister all week. I wasn't ready to see them, let alone to tell them I'd finally decided to work in the family business. I didn't know how to justify changing my mind, especially so suddenly, and I didn't know how to look sincere when I'd be lying to their face about what I really wanted.

On Sunday night, I had to drop the self-pitying act, though, because they showed up at my house with Chinese takeout and a bottle of wine.

I hardly remember anything about that night. I hardly remember what reasons I threw out to justify the ridiculous plan I'd come up with. What I do remember is the skepticism on their faces, the worry, their silence, which seemed agreed upon, as I struggled to smile, even though all I wanted to do was cry.

On Monday morning, I took my fanciest clothes out of the closet: a slim black dress and a tailored jacket. I pulled my hair back soberly and put on makeup. Then I went downtown to the Weston Corporation head offices.

I announced my presence in reception, and a few seconds later, they sent me to the elevator I would take upstairs to my father's office. Alex, his secretary, shook my hand and told me to wait a few minutes. I sat on the leather sofa in the vestibule, the same one I had sat on so many times as a child. I was nervous. Alex's phone rang, and she picked up. When she set it down, she told me I could go inside. My father was ready to see me.

As I walked through the door, my entire life compressed to a tiny, insignificant dot. My father was sitting behind his imposing desk. No hellos, no questions. He just looked me up and down and nodded. He knew why I was there, and if he was surprised, he didn't show it. Maybe Hoyt or Hayley had already told him I was coming. Or maybe he knew me well enough to assume that after our meeting in the cemetery, I'd have no choice but to come pay my *debt*.

He called Alex and she hurried in, a gentle smile on her face and respect in her eyes.

"Mr. Weston."

"Alexandra, my daughter will start work here today. I need you to get her an access card and an office on the eighth floor. She's going to be Dustin Hodges's new assistant." I almost said something, but why bother? I'd sold myself, body and soul. He went on giving instructions. "Give her one of the interns to help her settle in and tell Mrs. Daniels to show her the ropes in the department and give her a rundown of what her duties will be."

Alex couldn't hide her surprise.

"Of course, Mr. Weston. I'll get right on it. Ms. Weston, it's a pleasure to be working with you. Welcome aboard."

"Thanks, Alex. But call me Harper, please."

She walked out, and I attempted to follow her, but my father called out, "Wait."

Before I could stop myself, I started babbling, "Dad, I don't know the first thing about finance. I can't accept a post with any real responsibility. I should be working in the mail room or running errands or something, starting from the bottom."

Dad put some documents in his briefcase as if I weren't there, and when my litany of doubts and worries was over, he started walking out, saying in passing, "We're having dinner at home tonight. Bring your things over and you can have your old room back. I'll tell the staff to have it ready for you."

"Sure."

In just a day, everything had changed. My surroundings lost their color, the world turned gray. The magic drained away, and all I could do was tell myself the hopes I'd harbored had never really existed. All I could do now was act—act like it didn't hurt, act like I wasn't utterly destroyed inside. Act like I was fine and nothing mattered. The truth was, sorrow and pain were tearing me apart, and all my ambition and determination was gone. I was an empty, soulless shell.

We sold my grandmother's house and bookstore three weeks later. I'd be lying if I said it wasn't one of the hardest moments of my life. I cried every night from regret. And every morning, I'd wake up and miss the girl I'd been. The one who wasn't so torn, so indecisive. The one who had saved me from ruining my own life. The one I hoped was still alive inside me and would come back someday, maybe.

Time passed, and I got used to my new routine. My job was to do everything Dustin asked of me. Take calls, greet clients, take notes at meetings, draw up contracts... I tried to do everything right, tried to learn, and didn't complain at his attempts at flirtation. For some reason I couldn't put my finger on, Dustin thought everything between us would go back to being the way it was. He gave me flowers every day and invited me constantly to dinner, and my rejections meant nothing to him. Soon I'd run out of excuses.

The only positive thing was that I was seeing more of Hoyt and Hayley. I usually went to lunch with them at a nearby restaurant. That was my only happy moment of the day.

Hoyt started spending his evenings at the family home in Léry now that I was staying there. We'd have dinner with Dad and watch a movie or read in the library.

Things with Dad were better than they had ever been. Our relationship remained cold, sometimes tense. But now he could at least stand my presence, and when he didn't think I could see him, he would watch me with curiosity.

On the weekends, I'd walk through the gardens on the property, letting my mind wander, recalling the few happy moments I'd spent there among the flowers and trees.

Hayley and Scott came to visit almost every Sunday. Dad would barbecue lunch himself and drink beer with the guys like a regular, everyday person. Gathered like that, we seemed like a real family, and that made me feel, however briefly, like a real person.

Sometimes you fall apart, and to keep going, you have to pick up the pieces of yourself first. I tried to do it, but they were so heavy I could barely take a step. Only with time did it get easier. And yet, my heart ached. The pieces of it were sharp, and I couldn't figure out how to hold them together, and all I could do was try to cope, try to forget.

I tortured myself, wondering all the time what I would be doing if Trey were there. Wondering if he'd met someone. If he missed me as much as I missed him. Probably not, because he had vanished without a trace. Three months had passed since we'd broken up, and he hadn't made the least effort to get me back. It was selfish of me to think he should, after what I'd done, but I couldn't help it.

They say time heals all wounds, that distance makes you forget. But it's not true.

Time is distance.

Distance is longing.

And what you don't know can hurt you.

The days flew past, and I let them carry me along. In my desolation, the only thing that kept me afloat was books, which at least helped me disconnect from reality.

One day at work, I took out the latest book I was reading, A.J. Finn's *The Woman in the Window*, a mystery with lots of suspense. For now, I'd vetoed all love stories. As I read, I unwrapped a turkey and cabbage sandwich and looked at it with disgust.

"I'd throw that away before it mutates and eats you."

I looked up from my so-called lunch and saw my brother standing in the doorway of my office with a pleasant grin on his face. I laughed and did as he said.

"I thought you were taking the day off," I said.

"So did I, but Corbin's sick and I have to present the new renewable energy project we're working on in Tokyo." He loosened his tie. "Now that you've thrown away your sandwich, are you up for grabbing a bite with me?"

"Tacos?"

"Sure, with extra guac."

"What about an ice cream after?"

"With chocolate and colored sprinkles," he said, grinning.

"I love how well you know me."

"I'd be a terrible brother if I didn't."

It was nice having him nearby, spending time together. He was less like a big brother now and more like a friend—a friend who protected me, who liked to boss me around, but whom I wouldn't change for anything in the world.

It was cold, and snowflakes were floating in the air as we walked to La Capital, a nearby restaurant that made the best tacos in town. We ordered a sampler as well as quesadillas.

"I think I'm going to take the next step with Megan," Hoyt said, taking a sip of his soda.

"What's that supposed to mean?"

"I'm going to ask her to go out with me."

"Isn't that what you've been doing for months now?"

"We've been going out, but we haven't been *going out*… We've always seen each other with other people, as friends. I'm going to try to take her on an actual date."

"You've been hung up on her for this long and you haven't even asked her on a date?"

"I told you I like to take things slow and do it right. I really like her."

"Well, if you keep taking it as slow as you have, don't be surprised when she ends up going out with someone else."

He nodded, tense.

"I know, dammit. But when I'm with her, she just does something to me, and I can't act. I've never had that happen with any other woman."

"Imagine someone telling me years ago that my brother, the heart-breaker, was going to be here whining about how he's too scared to ask a girl out," I joked.

He shot me a killer glance that made me laugh.

"What do you know about it, Pumpkin? You've still got Dustin barking up your tree. Are you ever going to accept his marriage proposal and free him from his torments?"

With horror, I replied, "My God, no. I'm not planning on going out with anyone, let alone Dustin. I only tolerate him because of Dad."

My brother's face changed.

"Remember when we were talking on the phone recently? You had just come back from your mysterious trip, and I was on a plane headed to New York. You told me you had something important to tell me. What was it?"

I felt my pulse start racing. That seemed like a lifetime ago. At the same time, it could have been yesterday. I thought of Trey, my brother's best friend. That was what I'd wanted to talk to him about. I'd wanted to tell him how much Trey meant to me. That I was in love with him. That for some strange reason only fate could know, we were together, and I needed to shout it to the entire world.

"No idea. I don't even remember. Probably just something stupid."

Hoyt's face was serious. He didn't believe a word of what I was saying. The mood was tense, and getting tenser with every breath. He reached across the table and covered my hand with his.

"It doesn't matter the day, the hour, or how busy I am. When you're ready to tell me everything, just call. I mean everything. There's nothing you could do that would make me stop loving you, Harper. Nothing."

His phone was lying on the table. It lit up with a message. He took a look and started typing a response, at ease again.

"That look on your face tells me it must be Megan…"

He chuckled.

"Nah, it's Trey. He's just letting me know he's parking. He's coming in to give me a hand with some specs on the presentation. Some of this stuff I have no idea about."

It took me a minute to soak in what he'd just said. Trey. He was going to see Trey there. I started trembling. I wasn't ready to see him. I never would be. I shot to my feet and put on my hat, scarf, and gloves.

"Sorry, Hoyt, I need to go. I forgot I have to make clean copies of a couple of contracts Dustin's got to have for this afternoon."

"This shouldn't take long! Stick around and we can walk back together."

"I can't. I just don't have the time. You're paying, right?" He nodded and I kissed him on the cheek. "Thanks. You're the best brother in the world."

I hurried out so fast that I ran into a guy coming in. I murmured *sorry* and crossed the street in the middle of traffic. I didn't see an oncoming car and it screeched to a halt to keep from hitting me. I thought I'd have a heart attack by the time I was on the other side. When I stopped to catch my breath, I saw him, looking at his phone and walking up the sidewalk.

The feeling was like being punched in the stomach. But I couldn't stop staring. He was thinner, with a short beard. I thought of all the times I'd kissed that face. He was as handsome as ever, maybe more so. Three months it had been since I'd last seen him, and I still missed him with such intensity that there were days when I didn't think I could stand it.

I turned around before he could see me and scurried off without looking back. In that moment, it was either keep walking or fall over and die. I needed distance. I needed to feel I wasn't falling to pieces inside.

I lost track of time as I wandered from one place to the next. The city looked gorgeous with Christmas decorations in the shop windows and lights festooning the streets. The holidays weren't far away now.

The snow fell harder, and the cold seeped into my bones. I stopped a second to get my bearings, and that's when I noticed it.

I had stopped directly across from the bookstore.

My spine tingled as I saw the boards covering the window and door. I guess they wanted to protect the glass. Otherwise, nothing had changed. It was dirtier, more desolate, but the same. No one had touched anything.

I peeked through a gap in the boards and almost whined from sorrow. Inside, nothing had been touched. I could see the cash register in the shadows, the hundreds of books piled up all over. The tables, the armchair, the lead-crystal lamp.

I didn't get it.

It had been months since I'd let my grandmother's lawyer take care of the details. He'd put the bookstore on the market, and not long after, he'd found a buyer. I didn't ask him to tell me the details. It hurt too bad.

I tried to get a grip on myself when I saw the looks of worry from the passersby. But I couldn't help it. That had been my only true home, and my favorite memories, my happiest moments, my dreams, my hopes, my childhood were all locked up inside there. Along with the ghosts of the women who had mattered to me most.

If I stayed there, I'd lose every last trace of that false peace I'd told myself I'd found because I needed it to survive my new life. I turned around and left.

I ran away like a little girl fleeing the monsters in her closet and under her bed. I ran away from reality. I ran away as if you could run away from pain, as if it were really possible to run away from yourself.

29

Every Action Causes a Reaction

The new year began, and with it I got a gift. I'd worked hard to learn my job well, and my father gave me a promotion with more responsibility. He moved me to public relations. That meant I no longer had to work for Dustin.

I was excited. I thought that meant I was free of him and that constant harassment he thought was love. And it was true that I no longer saw him during work hours. But I still had to put up with him elsewhere. He spent more time at my house than his. My father invited him to everything. He even celebrated Christmas and the new year with us.

Hoyt liked to joke that Dustin was my father's secret love child, and he accused me of having an incestuous relationship with him. I didn't think it was funny at all. In fact I hated it—the very idea disgusted me.

"He just makes my skin crawl," I said to Hayley in the bathroom of a restaurant one day, strutting around the way Dustin did and imitating his voice: "'Of course, Mr. Weston. You're absolutely right, Mr. Weston. Brilliant, Mr. Weston.' He's the biggest ass-kisser I've ever seen. Does he not know there's a thing called pride, dignity?"

Hayley cracked up laughing as she washed her hands.

"Yeah, honestly, I don't get it."

"What?" I asked.

"Judging by the way he treats him, Dad doesn't like him much more than we do. But he still takes him everywhere. For some reason I can't figure out, he's obsessed with the idea that Dustin's the right guy for you and he can't stop waving it in your face."

"I know! Well, he can keep waiting. I've spent months and months trying to make him happy, but I've got my limits, and one of them is Dustin. I can't even stand him looking at me."

Hayley looked up at me in the mirror. "I know you gave up your dreams because you think you owe Dad something."

"I told you…" I began to reply nervously. But she interrupted me.

"Harper, I'm not dumb. I may have let it slide, but that doesn't mean I didn't notice. I've spent my entire life watching you strive to get his attention. And here you go doing it again. But, honey, he's not worth it. So why do you keep killing yourself over him? You never wanted this. You wanted to write."

I looked away and forced a blithe smile to lighten the heavy atmosphere. Hayley hugged me. I needed that contact, that human affection, and it made me let down my guard. I closed my eyes and leaned into her.

"I hope you'll tell me the truth someday," she whispered into my ear.

"But what if what I have to say changes everything between us?" I struggled to make it through that sentence, remembering it was my fault Mom had left her an orphan when she was just ten years old.

"Harper, if you told me right now you were the witch from 'Hansel and Gretel' and you'd just eaten them both, I'd figure out how to help you hide the bones."

Hearing that was bittersweet, and it moved me beyond words. I turned around to hug her back, so tight that she shrieked that I was breaking her ribs.

We went back out to find Dad, Scott, Hoyt, Megan, and of course Dustin, my nightmare, at the table.

And there was someone else there. Not that it should have

surprised me. Everyone knew my father, and whenever we went out, someone came over to greet him. I don't know how, but even before I saw him, I could feel who it was. There was just something in the air. And maybe in my heart, too.

It was him.

I froze. All at once, I could hear nothing. I was terrified. I wasn't ready for this. I never would be.

"Trey!" my sister shouted.

He turned around with an enormous smile that vanished when our eyes met. He went pale, and I must have, too. I was sure we looked like two ghosts there in the crowd. My whole face felt dead.

"My God, it's been forever since I've seen you. I didn't even get the chance to thank you for your help with the house on Petit Prince. It's looking gorgeous."

They hugged.

"I just did my little part. It was really your husband's idea."

Trey. Hearing that name made me dizzy, like I was tumbling over a cliff. He wouldn't stop looking at me, and I couldn't, because everything that wasn't him had disappeared. I took a step forward. Then another. I felt like I was walking over a bottomless ravine and could only breathe easily if I reached the table.

"Harper, aren't you going to say hi to Trey," my sister said, giving me a slight shove that had the force of an atomic bomb.

"Yeah, uh, of course. Hey, Trey," I barely managed to say.

"Hi, Harper."

I tried to close my eyes and trap the sound of him saying my name, so I could hold onto it forever, deep in my heart.

"Why don't you have a seat with us?" Hoyt said. "We were just about to order drinks."

"Yeah, man, stay a while. There's room for both of you," Scott chimed in.

Both of you. The sight of Trey had so stunned me that I didn't notice *her*: a woman with long dark-brown hair. She was incredibly beautiful.

"Harper, sit beside me, babe. That way we can make some space for them," Dustin said.

Trey's eyes darted over at him and then back at me. I saw he was tying up loose ends, and I wished the earth would swallow me up. I wanted to scream at Dustin to shut his damn mouth for once. To tell Trey there was nothing between that imbecile and me, that there never would be, and he didn't need to worry about it.

But I didn't. What was the point?

Trey wasn't mine anymore. I had left him five months ago, and he had clearly gotten over it. Probably he was just looking at Dustin out of curiosity. I had assumed he was hurt, but he was probably just struggling to believe I'd gone back with such a loser.

"Thanks, but we've got movie tickets and we're running late," he said.

"Ah, that's too bad," Hoyt replied. "You've been a hard man to get ahold of lately."

"Work, work, work, you know how it is."

"Cut the excuses. Let's hang out some time. Actually…" He snapped his fingers as he remembered something. "You know what? I'm taking Megan to Petit Prince next week. Hayley's leaving us the house. You should come along. Both of you. It'll be fun."

It was agonizing, thinking of him taking her to the island. Our island. Our secret. I could tell Trey was looking at me as my brother talked. That he was nervous. The girl sensed something between us, too. I could tell by her face. She seemed to know things about me, and the possibility that Trey had talked about me, about us, made things even more uncomfortable.

"I don't think I can. Sora and I…"

"Trey, don't make me beg," Hoyt insisted.

"I'll call you."

It was all I could do not to take off running. I needed to escape that pain that was drilling into my chest—the pain, the insecurity, the anguish, and still worse, the jealousy. I was so jealous it burned.

Seconds later, Trey said his goodbyes and left the restaurant holding hands with the girl. I got away from Dustin, taking the chair across from him and making sure my father noticed. And he did. We stared at each other a long while. I don't know where I got the courage. Maybe because I wasn't entirely myself. Something in me was vanishing.

I spent the rest of the night in a fog and was the first one to stand when Dad said he was tired and ready to go back home.

We didn't exchange a word on the way back to Léry, and even in the hallway on our way to our rooms, all he managed was a curt *good night*.

I took off my boots and lay in bed, feeling as if someone were torturing me with electric shocks. But the only person torturing me was myself, and I had been that whole evening, replaying every second of my encounter with Trey in my head.

I'd deceived myself with the ridiculous belief that with time my feelings for him would lessen. I was wrong. Five months hadn't been enough for the wounds to heal. And deep down, I knew five years wouldn't be, either. Not five years, not five decades.

He was a part of me, and he always would be. Next to him, I'd learned who I was and all the things I was capable of. I'd learned what a strange, beautiful place the world could be. That magic existed and wishes come true. That dreams can become reality.

I had broken up with him to try to forget the beauty of being with him and find meaning in the life I had chosen. And it hadn't worked. My father mutely tolerated me at best, and a little voice still whispered to me that even with a hundred lifetimes, I could never make up to him what he'd lost.

I had sacrificed everything for a debt I could never repay.

I walked over to the window and opened it. The cold outside was glacial, but in my room it was stifling. I hit the windowsill as hard as I could. From rage. From stupidity. From cowardice. From despair. Because I hadn't thought about myself.

Because I'd thrown out of my life the one person who gave it meaning.

Because he had turned the page and now he was sharing his world with someone else.

I realized then that errors have consequences and every action causes a reaction.

"I shiver, thinking how easy it is to be totally wrong about people—to see one tiny part of them and confuse it for the whole, to see the cause and think it's the effect or vice versa."

—Lauren Oliver, *Before I Fall*

30

Time Passes. Then One Day You Wake Up.

I felt like a lit candle just about to go out, when the flame loses intensity, shrinks, and writhes, trying to avoid the inevitable end.

For days, I'd been moving in the shadows, with no light, no color. My routine had become a series of mechanical acts, my voice a whisper I barely used.

One by one, I picked up my thoughts and memories and locked them in a little box in the most secret part of myself. I ran from the chaos into the arms of self-control.

And like that, without light, without color, spring came.

The first Sunday in April was a clear day after weeks of rain. The sun was bright and warm through the windows. I got out of bed and pressed my nose to the glass and saw birds flitting around and boats on the lake drifting away from the coast.

It was a beautiful day for an occasion as sweet as it was sad.

There was a knock at my door, and my brother slipped in before I could even say hi. He gave me a tight hug, then examined me with a worried look.

"Is it just me, or are you skinnier?"

"I'm the same as I've always been."

I sat back on the bed and Hoyt sat down beside me.

"Don't do this to me," I said.

"What?"

"Stare at me. It makes me nervous."

"I see someone woke up on the wrong side of the bed."

I forced a smile and lay back on the mattress. He was right. I was in a bad mood. I had been for a long time.

Out of nowhere, he started tickling me like a crazy person until I shook and rolled back and forth, trying to get away from him. Since we were kids, he'd always known how to get under my skin.

"Come on, Pumpkin, give your Uncle Gilbert some sugar. Just a teeny tiny kiss." Again with the *Anne of Green Gables* references.

"Stop!"

"No."

"Hoyt!"

"I'm not stopping."

My stomach hurt from laughing so hard.

"Fine, fine, I give up."

Hoyt stopped and pointed at his cheek, and I gave him a little peck.

"I always hated you tickling me when I was little, and I still do," I said.

"You love it."

"What I liked was you playing with me."

"Not me."

"Liar."

We both lay back and stared up at the ceiling.

"Today's her birthday," he whispered.

"I know."

"I'm going to the cemetery. You want to come with?"

I grew tense. I hadn't been back there since I'd learned the truth about her death from my father. I had tried, but I'd never managed to make it past the gate.

"Sure."

I don't know where I found the strength to do it. Maybe I was just resisting giving up completely and saw it as a challenge I could face.

"We should tell Hayley, too," I said.

"I already called her, but she wouldn't pick up. It's always a hard day for her. She usually struggles to get through it."

Guilt ate into my heart. A guilt inseparable from my father's words, attacking my weaknesses, making me feel insignificant, blaming me for tearing the family apart. I was playing a dangerous game, thinking that going there with Hoyt and Hayley might help, but I had no other choice. The bitter memories were chasing me like ghosts, and I was afraid they would catch up to me.

Hoyt patted me on the leg and got up.

"See you downstairs, okay?"

"Sure," I said.

Hoyt drummed his fingers on the wheel. I realized he was anxious, but it was getting on my nerves. We had been stuck in the lot for a while, in a long line of cars at a standstill behind a bus full of tourists that had gotten stuck between two other vehicles.

"I don't get it," my brother grumbled. "Why the hell would tourists come waste their time at a cemetery instead of going to a museum? It's weird."

I shrugged. I liked to visit cemeteries. At least, I used to.

"I mean, these places are kind of like museums," I responded, to his evident skepticism. "Think about it, there are mausoleums here that are hundreds of years old, sculptures from the Victorian era, famous people with elaborate tombs that are basically works of art... You can see why people are interested."

"There are no dead people in museums."

"Yeah there are. What do you think a mummy is? Or those animals they have in natural history museums? You know those are real animals. Grandma only told you they weren't because she didn't want you to start crying."

Hoyt waved me off. He hated being reminded of how sensitive he'd been as a little boy. He used to cry when he stepped on an ant. He was still that way, I thought. He just knew how to cover it up better. That was what our family did best: cover things up.

We bought some lilies at a flower stand, and Hoyt started walking over the paved path to the grave. I watched him, incapable of moving, and swallowed. When he noticed I wasn't with him, he turned, his expression preoccupied.

"Are you okay?"

"Yeah," I lied in a thin voice, faking a smile.

He walked back toward me, took my hand, and pulled me forward softly. We walked beneath trees whose branches cast shadows on the damp grass. Soon we were there. The bright spots of sunlight on the ground quivered when the wind shook the trees, and I could see bits of dust, pollen, and little insects hovering in the light. It was so pretty, we couldn't help but stop and stare.

"Hello, Mom. Happy birthday," Hoyt said, laying the flowers on the ground. Then we stood there in silence for a while, remembering her.

"You know when I was eight I decided to let my hair grow long because I was jealous of how Mom used to braid yours and Hayley's?"

"Are you serious?" I said, grinning.

He nodded. "She would spend hours brushing your hair, sometimes until you fell asleep. And then she'd sing to you."

"Yeah, I remember that."

"She loved your curls. They were just like hers," a voice behind me said. I turned and saw Hayley. She said hello and patted Hoyt on the arm. "Sorry I didn't get back to you. I wasn't sure if I could come. If I could take it, you know. Especially not with Grandma here, too."

"Don't worry," Hoyt I said, taking her hand. "I'm glad you're here. Maybe we both need each other to get through it."

All at once, I felt like an intruder between the two of them, as if I shouldn't have burst in on that moment that had always belonged to just the two of them. They were twins, they'd been together since before they were born, they had a connection I could never compete with. They shared feelings, memories, losses. A lonely childhood where the only thing they had was each other.

And it was my fault.

I was sad. Furious. I looked at the grave. She shouldn't be there. She should be up here, and I down there. Fate had made a mistake, letting me live and her die.

And even that was a step too far. I simply shouldn't ever have existed.

"I'm sorry." The words came out of me of their own free will, cutting me in two. "I'm so sorry."

I started hyperventilating. For months now, I'd been undergoing a slow, painful torture, and I couldn't take it anymore. I couldn't keep it in. I couldn't go on pretending that nothing was happening when it was.

I cried, sobbed, was beyond all consolation. Furious with myself. Desperate. Brokenhearted.

"Harper, what's going on?"

My sister tried to make me look at her, but I couldn't, and shoved her aside.

"What is it?" Hoyt asked.

"It looks like an anxiety attack," Hayley said. "Harper, honey, relax. Everything's all right. We're here for you."

I kept shaking my head and walking backward.

"It's not all right, nothing's all right, it's all my fault." I flailed around with my arms, then wiped my nose. "It's my fault."

"What is?" Hoyt asked with fear in his voice.

"Everything. Mom's death. Dad being alone. You having to grow up without her. She couldn't even be at your wedding, Hayley. I know how much you would have wanted that."

"But, honey," she said, coming closer, "she was there for me. I do wish she could have come, but she was there in spirit. I know that. Why are you saying all this now, though?"

"Because there's something you don't know."

"What?" Hoyt asked.

I closed my eyes and let it all out.

"I came here to tell Mom I wanted to be a writer. And Dad was here, and we got in an argument about the bookstore, the house… I kept asking him to finally tell me why the hell he hated me so much. And he did. He told me it was my fault Mom had died. Her cancer… They could have cured it if she'd accepted treatment. But…she didn't because she was pregnant with me. If…if she'd gotten an abortion, she could have recovered. She'd have been there for your birthdays, she'd have met Scott and Megan. She'd be a grandmother one day… And now, none of that will happen because I screwed it up."

Between the hiccups, the panting, the tears, the trembling, I could barely speak. Hoyt and Hayley just stood there and stared, eyes wide.

"Dad told you that?" Hoyt said. "What else did he say?"

"That he would never forgive me."

"That son of a bitch."

"He said…I owed him, I owed you. I said sorry, I asked him to forgive me, I really am sorry, I said, but it wasn't enough for him. He wanted me to show it."

"Show it? How?" Hayley asked.

"By being the person he always wanted me to be. And I tried. I went home, I took a job at the company, I forgot my dreams, writing, the bookstore… I broke up with Trey, and now he's with another girl. I don't matter to him anymore. All I want is to disappear."

"Trey?" they asked in unison.

"What does Trey have to do with this?" Hayley asked.

My brother didn't even blink. So many emotions were running through him that he was in a daze, but then a moment came when he understood. He brought his hands to his head.

"I'm going to kill him. I'm going to string him up by his balls and…"

"Hoyt! You're standing at your mother's grave!" Hayley reproached him.

"No!" I shouted, rushing to Trey's defense. "He didn't do anything wrong. He helped me. A lot. He wanted to tell you, he wanted to tell both of you, but he didn't have time. I broke up with him first and made him promise he wouldn't tell."

"Did he sleep with you?"

"Hoyt!" Hayley shouted.

"What? I need to know. I can't believe that bastard was doing it with my little sister and didn't tell me. My best friend! Fuck!"

Hayley ignored him—to her, he was acting like a child—and she concentrated on me. "So you're telling me you and Trey…?" I nodded. "For how long?"

As I tried to pull myself together, I realized how strange the situation was. I had opened my heart to them, and the only thing they actually seemed to care about was me going out with Trey. I turned around and walked away. And then I understood. It was as predictable as the ending of a story. How could I have failed to see it?

I turned back to them. "Why weren't you surprised when I told you about Mom?" They looked at each other, clueless as to how to respond. "You knew, didn't you? You knew. And you never said anything."

"Harper, we couldn't. We promised we never would. It was a secret. You were never supposed to know," Hayley said.

"Why?"

"Because of this!" she shouted. "Because you'd blame yourself when you'd never done anything. You deserved to live without that burden."

"Yeah, Pumpkin," Hoyt interrupted her. "This isn't your burden to bear. There is no guilty party here. It's just a tragedy, and that's that."

"You knew," I repeated, more for me than for them. "Since when?"

Hayley looked at Mom's grave, as though asking forgiveness or seeking permission. Then she looked at me wearily.

"Mom told us not long before she died. She knew Dad would blame you, he already did before you were born, and she was scared he would turn us against you. But we understood, and we promised her we'd take care of you just as she would."

"But it wasn't fair. It wasn't fair to you, having to deal with that responsibility when you were so little."

"What about you, though, Harper? You were the youngest one, the most sensitive, the most vulnerable, and you didn't have a mother or a father. Even Grandma couldn't see us as much as she'd like."

"I'm sorry."

"Don't you dare tell us you're sorry again. You didn't do anything," Hoyt reminded me. "You should have come to us and told us what was going on before you made a decision. Not just about Dad, about everything. And everything includes…"

"Hoyt, drop the thing with Trey, okay?" Hayley said. Hoyt scowled at her and murmured something I didn't hear.

"Fine, I'll do it," I said. "I'll tell you everything this time. The whole truth."

Hayley came close and hugged me. I leaned against her and closed my eyes, trying not to cry again.

"How about we go to my place and order some food?" she said. "We can talk there. Anyway…" She parted my hair to look me in the eyes. "I have something for you."

"What?"

"You'll see."

31

The Letter

Hayley lived in a nice apartment close to Notre-Dame Cathedral. Hoyt drove us there in his Jeep. The whole time, I stared out the window, feeling my life was about to change again and uncertain whether I could take it. I was tired mentally, physically, and spiritually and wasn't sure where I'd find the energy to go on.

At one minute, I felt everything with profound intensity, and at the next, I was utterly indifferent, as though there had been a short-circuit in my brain and all the wires were melting together.

I knew they were both looking at me. I knew they were both worried. I tried to smile, to say something that could wipe that maudlin expression off their faces, but I couldn't. For the first time in my life, I had stopped pretending everything was all right. Because it wasn't. Not at all.

Outside, people were strolling on the streets, in the parks, on patios, enjoying the sun that was getting brighter and hotter by the minute.

I closed my eyes. It was stupid, but I missed my life in Toronto, so simple, so uncomplicated. Studying, going to class, going to work at the publisher, surrounded by people who made me feel part of something. But what I missed the most was Petit Prince. There, I had felt at home. I missed Adele, Sid, Ridge…all of them. I hadn't heard from them, I hadn't even tried to get in touch, not a postcard, not even a text just to see if everyone was all right.

Consciously or unconsciously, I always pushed everyone away. That was the reality.

Scott was sitting on the sofa watching tennis when we went inside. He waved, distracted, and said, "Everything okay? You're all looking a little rough."

"Everything's fine," Hayley said, bending over to give him a kiss. "Sweetie, can you order us some Japanese food from the place on the corner? And maybe open that Chardonnay we brought back from that little village in Provence?"

Scott seemed confused, but he duly stood up and vanished into the kitchen while I settled down on the couch. Hoyt took the recliner next to me, and Hayley, after turning down the TV, sat across from me on the coffee table.

Unable to contain myself, I burst out with, "Can you imagine what my life has been like, lugging around that secret? Every day, I used to ask myself why my father hated me, and I tried every way I knew how to get him to love me. I didn't understand what you two had that I didn't, and I envied you, and I used to wish I could just stop caring about you and all you had. I only truly felt good when I was with Grandma and Frances and I could pretend they were my only real family."

I could see my words hurt my sister as she hid her face in her hands and sighed. It wasn't fair, blaming them. They were two more victims. At ten years old, they'd had to take responsibility for me and for a secret too heavy for two children to bear.

"I'm sorry," I whispered.

"It's fine. It's normal for you to feel that way."

"If I'd only known…"

"If you'd known, instead of just asking yourself, you'd have been certain he hated you and why. I don't know which is worse. But Harper, we promised," Hayley pleaded. "We all promised her. It was her last wish."

There was nothing else to say. In their place, I was sure I'd have done the same. Scott came back with the four glasses and the wine, served us, and sat beside Hayley, putting an arm around her.

"Well, now that we've cleared that up, let's get to the other thing. How in the hell did you end up with Trey, and why did neither of you tell me anything?" Hoyt asked.

"Did you just say Trey? Trey and Harper?" Scott butted in.

I looked around at all of them. Why did they find it so strange? It almost offended me. Oh well. This was the moment to clear everything up and tell the truth.

The truth—what a complicated word. So subtle, so open to modifications and interpretations. So liable to change depending on who's telling it.

"I was going to tell you… I was going to tell both of you when you got back to town." I bent forward and rested my elbows on my knees. "Remember when I called you, Hoyt? You were about to take off for New York… Well, it was about Trey. We ran into each other at the end of last August in Petit Prince."

Hayley frowned, then started tying together loose threads, then finally understood. She smiled at me, shaking her head.

"In Petit Prince? What the hell were you doing there?" Hoyt was still in a bubble.

"I convinced Harper to go spend a few days there because she was so stressed out. Grandma had just died, she needed to decide whether to sell the bookstore, and she couldn't do it here with Dad pressuring her. That's why we didn't tell anyone," Hayley explained.

"And what was Trey doing there?"

"Blueprints," Scott responded, chuckling. "Seriously. I asked him if he could take a look at the house to see if the renovations we were planning were feasible. I didn't say anything because it was supposed to be a surprise for Hayley. I had no idea Harper would be there."

"By the way—it was a lovely surprise."

Irritated, Hoyt blurted out to her, "So it was your fault."

"It's nobody's fault!" I screamed. "What is your problem? You talk about Trey like he was an ex-con and not your best friend."

"He and I had an agreement: hands off my sisters."

"Who do you think you are to say who can and can't hang out with me? What's next, you want me to ask your permission to leave the house?"

"Harper, you're being unfair," Hayley said. "And Hoyt, you're being a dickhead."

He mumbled something and crossed his arms, his stare furious at first, then relaxing into a kind of muted worry.

"Sorry, I just…I don't want anyone to hurt you."

"I know." I grabbed his hand, and he pulled it to his heart, which I thought was almost comical. "Hoyt, it's not what you think. And I was the one who treated him wrongly."

I could see he didn't believe me. For him, I was still a sweet little girl who couldn't even hurt a fly. He clicked his tongue and conceded. "Fine, tell me the story. But spare me the intimate details."

"You mean sex, or…?"

"La la la la la," he said, covering his ears. "For God's sake, I don't want to hear that word coming out of your mouth."

I couldn't help laughing, maybe because the tension between us was finally disappearing. I tried to put my thoughts in order, remembering that he didn't need to know *everything*, especially what had happened at that party years before. I decided to focus on the essential.

"Trey showed up at the house the day after I got there. It was a surprise for both of us, but whatever, we didn't think there was any harm in spending a few days together. And we got to know each other better and better, went for walks, had some meals... We got to trusting each other, and in the course of our conversations, he helped me realize I'd always wanted to be a writer and convinced me to stop being afraid. He encouraged me to keep the bookstore and to hell with what Dad thought. He talked about his projects, his plans for the future. And about his mother and how wrong he'd been to reject her."

"He told you that?" Hoyt asked.

"Yeah, he even took me to meet his grandfather. And so one thing led to another, and... you know. It happened. We came back to Montreal together. We decided to give it a try and see where things went. And honestly, those were the happiest days of my entire life. We had the idea of organizing a dinner where we could break the news to you. Trey wanted to tell you in person, Hoyt, so he could look you in the face and promise you he wasn't just fooling around."

Hoyt nodded. That affected him.

"And that's when you bumped into Dad at the cemetery," Hayley concluded.

"Yeah, and everything went to shit. I pushed Trey away. I was destroyed. I told him what we had was over, and I never saw him again until that night in the restaurant when he showed up with that girl. So I guess he's turned the page. I mean, what did I expect him to do? It's not like I left him with anything to hope for."

"And you?" Hayley asked.

On the verge of tears, I responded, "I still love him... so much it aches."

Hoyt cursed, stood, and walked to the window. When he turned back around, his face was full of pain and understanding.

"I can talk to him, Harper."

"No," I said quickly. "I don't want you mixed up in this."

"But…"

"No! I don't even know what I'm feeling right now. I don't know what I'll do. I have so much to think about."

"Harper…you're hurting. I can try to fix this."

I stood, desperate.

"I need you to promise me you won't do anything. Neither of you. Promise. I am where I am because you made a decision for me without my permission way back when I was a child. You may not have realized it, but you were controlling my life instead of letting it belong to me."

I had stopped being merciful, and for a moment, they didn't know how to respond. But it didn't matter. I'd had to break myself into pieces and sift through the shards to find the strength to defend myself. And I wasn't ready to relapse. I had to live for me now.

"You're right," Hayley admitted. "We promise you we won't do or say anything."

"Thanks."

"What are you going to do, then?" asked Scott, who had been quiet the whole time.

I had to think about it. I took a sip of wine, swirled my glass, stared into it. All I knew was that I'd been living in hell for months now, ignoring myself until I'd stopped being who I really was. I had sacrificed so much—and for nothing. I'd been chasing a mirage, unable to understand that you can't force love, and you can't win it like some employee-of-the-month award. Not even if it's your father's love you're after. Love is something that's born in the heart. Your bloodline, your DNA have nothing to do with it. It's impulsive, illogical, visceral.

And sometimes it's just not there.

I felt the world falling away around me.

I'd lost what my grandmother had left me; I'd lost the dream of writing. I'd lost Trey. And I had no way of getting them back. Maybe I should just take the money I'd made from the sale and start over somewhere, I thought. Give myself the chance to finally get to know myself and find acceptance and recognition.

Hayley walked out and soon came back with a cream-colored envelope, offering it to me with her hand outstretched and reminding me that she'd told me in the cemetery that she had something for me. I put my glass down and accepted it.

"What is it?" I asked, sitting back down.

"Grandma gave it to me when she got sick. She told me Mom had left it for you, but I should only give it to you if you one day found out the truth."

I opened it and took it out carefully, scared of what it might contain. It was a letter. Handwritten. Beginning with the words *Dear Harper*.

I'm writing this letter for you with the deepest wish that you'll never, ever have to read it. If you do, it means he wasn't brave enough, and he couldn't manage to appreciate what we made together.

Honey, whatever your father tells you, it doesn't matter. It doesn't matter how he makes you feel. Nothing is your fault. For six years now, I've been trying to get him to fathom it, to see things from my point of view, to understand me. But I've failed.

Sometimes grown-ups are scared, honey. We're scared of being alone, of suffering and not knowing what to do with all our suffering. We're scared of losing what we love, and that makes it impossible to enjoy the moment or create memories we can take solace in when the future comes. Fear makes us sad and selfish; it blinds us to the beautiful things life gives us. That's your father's problem: he's scared, and he pretends to be angry with you.

That's right, my darling. I said he's pretending.

The person he actually blames for all this is me. But he's never been brave enough to admit it. Maybe because I was already dying then and a part of him was ashamed to hate his wife when things were nearly over for her. Or maybe because he needs someone to be the target of his bitterness when I'm not there.

Whatever it is, you've never been responsible for our problems. You have to believe that.

I'm sorry I forced you into this battle. Maybe it was selfish to bring you into the world and then abandon you so soon afterward. But ever since I first heard your heartbeat at the hospital, I couldn't imagine the universe without you in it.

I regret nothing. I could never have not had you. Just one look at you tells me I did the right thing.

I know I'm leaving you in good hands. Your brother and sister love you, and they'll always protect you. You'll take care of each other, because that's what family does. I wish I could be with you to watch you grow up and grow wiser. I wish I could give you the same advice your grandmother gave me.

Try to find a balance between your head and your heart. Don't take life too seriously. If you don't know which path to choose, always go for the one that makes you smile. Laugh at yourself, and remember that the only person whose opinion matters is the one who looks back at you in the mirror. Fight for what you believe in, don't break, don't bend, and never regret anything. If you don't like something, change it. If you've made a mistake, fix it. If you love, show it.

The only thing worth regretting is not saying or doing what you feel. Sometimes, life gives you a chance to change your destiny, and you can't let it pass.

Don't let anyone get you down. Swim against the current if you have to, but don't stop moving forward.

I know someday you'll do all the things I couldn't. You'll do them for both of us. Live as if every day was your last, be happy, free, and fulfill your dreams. I know you will.

You're strong. Brave. Beloved. Everything. Don't ever forget that, and don't let anyone tell you otherwise.

I love you crazily. All three of you.

My children: you are my world.

Love,
Mom

Tears slid down my cheeks. For a second, I felt she was there with me. Her words had lodged in my soul, and somehow they had taken all those fragments of my shattered self and glued them back together, making me whole.

I dried my eyes with my shirtsleeves and said, "Thank you," to Hayley, and to the rest of them, "I love you so much. I don't think I've ever told you enough."

"We love you, too," Hayley said.

"Ugh," Hoyt said, trying to hide his emotions. "Now's one of those moments when I ask myself why I couldn't have had a brother. Another guy to act normal with me when you girls are getting all mushy."

I chuckled, jumped up, and threw my arms around his neck, kissing him all over his face.

"Thank you, Hoyt. I mean it. You're the best brother in the world, no matter how much you act like a jerk."

"Are you all right?" Hayley asked.

"Yeah," I said, "I needed this." I pressed the letter to my heart. She watched me, and I could tell she wanted to know what was written there. "Here, take this. It's for the two of you, too."

"Seriously?" she asked.

"Yeah."

Hoyt walked up beside her and they read it together. I tried to take a snapshot of the image in my mind to hold on to forever. Then I gathered my things and left.

I needed to be alone for a while and to digest all that had happened. I walked with my senses more awake than ever, letting every word of my mother's letter soak in. A part of me wished I had read it before, but then I remembered her advice. And I told myself it had arrived at just the right moment, when I really needed it most.

Remember at the beginning, how I said it all started with a letter, a gift, and a guy as lost as I was?

Well, now I had the letter.

32

Sink or Swim

Taking risks wasn't something I was great at. The same goes for following my impulses. I've always been scared of the uncertain, of doing something rash, of consequences, of being wrong, of things not turning out as I'd hoped. What am I saying? I've always been afraid of everything.

I was an expert at hiding my feelings. At least from other people. They were always still there inside, though, quivering, multiplying, expanding. And they always cut into me, causing wounds that never quite healed.

For hours, walking through the city, I repeated my mother's words in my head. With every step, I felt my wounds finally beginning to heal and the sharp edges of my feelings smoothing out like mermaids' tears under the ocean—softy, shiny, precious, so clear you could see right through them. They gave me a different vision of the world, one that was nonetheless incredibly real.

And in that world I had a purpose: to live. For my mother. For me. For both of us. She had given me a beautiful gift—my life—and secrets, lies, errors, and my own insecurities had wasted it for years in unhappiness. But there was still time to change. I could still start over. Connect with my own life, be a part of it. Flow. Follow my heart.

With every step I took, another fear fell away. Another mistake. Another doubt. Another regret. Another obligation.

When I stopped, there was nothing left but myself. My mind blank, my heart unburdened. For the first time, I had no plans, just a certainty: I wasn't going back to my father's home.

I was tired and my feet hurt. I looked up and saw a sign for a hotel on the next block.

I walked there and asked for a room, went up and took a shower, put on a robe, wrote my brother and sister and told them not to worry about me. Then I ordered a bunch of food from room service and spent the evening watching TV.

At some point—I don't remember when—I fell asleep.

No more insomnia, no more bad dreams.

Alex looked up and sighed with relief when she saw me. Then she stood, walked over, and stopped me in the hall.

"Where have you been all morning? Your father won't stop asking about you. He's losing his mind because you weren't at the PR meeting."

"Is he in his office?"

"Yeah, but if I were you, I wouldn't go in. He's in a terrible mood, and he said no one should bother him."

"Luckily I'm not no one."

I walked past her and opened the door without hesitation, not even bothering to knock. My father was sitting at his desk. When he looked up, I saw his expression change to furrowed brows, squinting eyes, disgust, impatience, and behind them, a fear and insecurity I'd never known how to make out before.

"What do you think I'm paying you for? To do nothing? Don't think you're special. You're an employee like anyone else. You can't just come and go as you please. You have obligations, and this morning's meeting was a wash because you didn't show. Are you never going to do anything right?"

I took a deep breath and didn't break eye contact with him. It was hard, but I kept a grip on myself.

"I'm quitting. And I'm moving out."

"What?"

"You heard me. I'm done."

"Are you out of your mind?"

"Maybe. It's possible."

"Harper, I'm advising you…"

I shook my head and walked toward him.

"Do you never get tired of being so bitter all the time? Isn't it exhausting, being so angry?" He opened his mouth to reply, surprised at my resentment, but I didn't give him the chance to speak. "It's not my fault Mom died. It was her decision. She never regretted it, and I'm not going to regret being alive now. She was right when she said you were a man who couldn't handle pain and suffering. They made you sad and selfish and they blinded you to all the good things life's given you." My voice was trembling, but I didn't let up. "I'm going to live my dreams, and I'm going to be happy. For her and for me. Because, in case you didn't know, that's what life is—trying to be happy. That's the whole point. I'm…I'm sorry you never learned that. And I'm sorry you think it's my fault you're miserable, but there was no way I could have changed anything!"

He didn't say a word. He'd gone pale, and his hands were shaking.

"I give up. I'm not going to keep trying to win your affection. I know it's impossible, and I'd rather swim alone than sink with you." To my surprise, I managed to smile at him. "I'm going to be a writer, and I'm going to do whatever I can to get my grandmother's bookstore back. That's my dream, and it was Mom's dream, too."

I turned around and walked out without looking back.

"Harper?"

Dustin's voice stopped me just as I reached the elevator. He walked over with that same patronizing, condescending expression I'd always hated and, when he reached me, grabbed my elbow and tried to drag me off somewhere more private. I jerked away as if his fingers burned like acid, and I didn't care if it hurt his feelings. The poor idiot. If he didn't get away from the Westons, he'd soon be a lifeless puppet with no backbone whatsoever.

"Harper, you can't keep doing this. You need to grow up. You need to start focusing on the things that really matter: your dad, the company…"

"You've got something in your teeth."

"Really?" He hid his mouth with one hand and started digging around with the other. "Where?"

"No, I just wanted you to shut up. Now listen. You're the one who needs to grow up. No one here gives a damn about you. Least of all my father. You'll never be good enough for him. Do you honestly think he wants us to be together because he likes you? I'm sorry to burst your bubble, but he only wants to see me unhappy and he knows with you I will be. You're a good guy deep down. I know you are. Get out of here while you still have time, before it eats you alive."

The elevator doors opened and I walked inside. Dustin just stood there gawking at me. As the doors slid close, I raised my hand and said, "Bye now!"

That same afternoon, I got my things from Léry and moved to a modest apartment on the Plateau that I found in the classified ads online. It had a little living room with a kitchen, one bedroom, and one bathroom, but that was all I needed.

I called Hoyt and Hayley to give them my new address and tell them not to worry. Then I called Mr. Norris to make an appointment. I'd need his help to get Shining Waters back.

"Are you telling me you don't know who bought the shop and the house?"

"What I'm telling you is they were purchased through the shell company whose name is on the contract, the same company that made the bank transfer, and they were acting as intermediaries. The owner is someone else."

"Yeah, but who?"

"That's private. There's no way of knowing."

"Can't you just ask? Have you told them I have very personal reasons for wanting to buy them out?"

"Theoretically, I could try, Harper, but there's something called confidentiality…"

"What about public records? There must be something on file. They'll have to pay real estate taxes. There must be a name, an address…"

"I've tried. There's nothing."

I sighed and sank back in my chair. I didn't want to lose hope, but there seemed to be no way to find the new owners of the bookstore. Mr. Norris bent over his desk and attempted to look reassuring.

"I'll keep trying. I promise."

"Thanks."

I walked out of his office still clinging to a desperate hope and walked toward the Plateau. My mind was clear, my heart was alive and healed. Or almost. There were still some memories that made it ache. But the ache wasn't something bad, because it reminded me of the person I loved most in the world. I needed to think of him now and then. The recollection of him made me whole.

I stopped on the sidewalk in front of my grandmother's old house. Nothing had changed, despite the passing months. It even seemed as if someone was living there. The entryway was clean, so were the windows, and there were flowering plants on the balcony. Someone had even put up a new mailbox.

I crossed the street, pulse racing, and rang the doorbell. I needed to know who was living there.

I waited.

Nothing.

Silence.

I knocked and knocked again until there was nothing left to do but accept that no one was home. I looked in the mailbox. No letters with the new owner's name. But I wouldn't give up. Whoever lived there might be the owner of the bookstore, too, I thought. I sat on the steps, ready to wait as long as I had to.

The hours passed, and the cold sank in. I shivered. All I had on were jeans and a thin jacket over my wool sweater. The temperature was low for the end of April.

I stuck it out until the sun set and I could no longer feel my feet. Then I started worrying I'd catch cold. I got up, numb, and walked off, sad that I hadn't found what I was looking for, but hopeful, because if someone was living there, maybe I could talk to them, and all wasn't lost.

I walked to the bookstore before returning home. Someone had painted graffiti on the plywood covering the windows, and some of it had gotten on the frames. I was angry; it was my fault that the place was falling into the ground. I couldn't understand why someone would buy it and then just leave it abandoned.

I couldn't take the nostalgia.

The idea that I had lost all that forever.

I spent the next few days trying to find out all I could about the buyer or buyers. I asked the neighbors, dug through the mail a second and third time…and found out nothing. Whoever it was didn't seem to spend much time at either place. At the bookstore, no one ever answered the doorbell and the lights never came on, and at the house, no one opened the windows or even moved the curtains.

My impatience was killing me.

Luckily, the impulse to write had returned. My head was full of ideas, thoughts, emotions that were begging to be expressed.

I bought a desk at a secondhand shop and set it up under the window at the apartment. Next to it, I placed a bookshelf and an apple-green rug I found at a flea market. That corner, with its views of Baldwin Park, was the nicest spot in my apartment. I spent hours and hours there, typing nonstop. Putting my story on the page. Reliving it from another perspective, with the necessary distance to make it art.

My work was my refuge, and not even the uncertainty about what the future might bring could lessen the pleasure of my newfound freedom. I was living outside of time, paying no attention to the hour, without a routine. It was chaos, and I loved it.

I learned to feel good. To care for myself. To enjoy every last moment.

I learned to think in the now. Not to rush. To be happy.

But I never did learn to forget him, to stop missing him. To erase the impression of his hands touching me and his lips covering mine.

Him. Just him.

And every night, when I got in bed and the silence overtook the room, I'd fall asleep thinking of his eyes, his smile, of all we'd had. And it hurt. It hurt bad.

May started, the weather changed, and the temperatures rose in southern Quebec. I traded my desk for the damp grass and the shadows of the trees. Lying back in the park, I'd squint and stare at the bits of sky visible between the leaves.

I was trying to decide how to end my novel, and I wound up thinking about the differences between real life and fiction. But also about how similar they were. How they both have a beginning, they both descend into confusion, they both have conflicts, trials and errors, harmony, resolution. How both can have a happy ending, how all love stories deserve one, whether they're imagined or whether they really happen.

Except for mine, of course. My own love story had just broken off in the middle.

Forever.

Forever: a word that could describe the greatest happiness or the vilest sorrow.

Out of the blue, a guy walked over, a few years older than me, interrupting my thoughts and getting in the way of my sunlight. I moved to the side. I was like a lizard, trying to soak up every ray. Shielding my eyes, I saw it was my brother.

"You know you're sitting on an anthill, right?" he said.

"No, I'm not."

"You'll see when all the ants crawl in your ears and start eating you from the inside out."

I smirked.

"Those kinds of jokes only worked when we were little," I replied.

"You say that like you ever grew up, shorty."

"Yeah, yeah…" I sat up. "What are you doing here?"

"Megan's away on a trip and I didn't feel like eating alone."

"Well, I guess I'm proud to come in second."

He sat down next to me, apparently unworried about the grass staining his costly tailored suit. He opened a paper bag, took out a couple of sandwiches, and offered me one.

"Thanks. I'm starving, actually." I took a bite of pastrami. "And this is delicious."

We smiled at each other and talked with our mouths full. I guess we'd never really learned our manners, or else acting like children brought us back to the old days, and we were trying to relive them.

"How's it going?" he asked, pointing at my laptop.

"I'm almost done, but I don't know how to tie it all together. You know me—always indecisive."

"I've got an idea. Just kill everyone. A giant massacre, no mercy."

"I can't kill them! It's a story of love and love lost."

"So is *Romeo and Juliet*, and everyone dies in it."

I rolled my eyes, tore off a little scrap of bread, and threw it at him, hitting his cheek.

"Why are you so weird?" he asked.

"Why are *you*?"

"I guess it's in the genes. Thank God I got the good ones."

"Yeah, and I got the good-looking ones," I responded, crossing my eyes.

I giggled and gave him a hug, and as I rested my head on his shoulder, he told me, "I saw him." I knew who he meant. "We ran into each other in a bar downtown."

I waited a few seconds, trying to absorb the news. Losing him had hurt me, and I'd had to bury my feelings for him to keep them from haunting me. But the wall I'd built to protect myself was weak and full of cracks, and it was hard to keep my emotions from seeping in.

"How was he?"

"Good. I mean, he looks good. We talked a little while, but I didn't get much out of him. He isn't spending much time in Montreal. He's more or less living on Lennox Island. He's super-involved in the reservation there."

"I love that place."

"The thing is, though…he's changed, or something's changed

between us. I think he's avoiding me on purpose. Me! It sounds stupid to say this, but I miss him!"

That made me feel guilty. I knew how important Trey was to my brother.

"I'm sorry, Hoyt. It's all my fault."

"Don't worry. We're adults, and these things happen. He disappeared for a while when his mother died, too, but eventually he came back. He always ends up coming back."

"Was he…was he with someone?" I asked.

"Do you really want to know?"

"Yeah." I was masochistic in that way.

"He was with the same girl." He paused, contemplating me. "Why don't you just call him and try to see him, Harper?"

"No!"

"You could fix what you had."

"He told me if I let him go, he was never coming back. Anyway, he's with someone else. He's put it behind him."

Hoyt shook his head. He wasn't the type to give up easily.

"I'd be happy to go find him and drag him here by the balls."

"You know how mad that would make me. And you promised you wouldn't."

He threw up his hands. "I'd do anything for you."

"Then trust me and let me resolve things my way."

There was a battle going on inside him. He was a natural protector and couldn't sit still when the people he cared about were suffering. But he respected me too much to overstep my bounds. I knew he had given up when he reached into the inner pocket of his jacket and took out the letter our mother had written me, handing it to me.

"Hayley and I talked, and we decided you should keep it. Mom wrote it for you. Here. I need to go. You're good, right?"

"Better than good," I said.

33

You and Other Natural Disasters

I went home not long after Hoyt left to make myself a coffee. While the water was boiling, I reread my mother's letter. I had always regretted not remembering her better. And what I could recall, I sometimes questioned, unsure whether it was real or I had made it up as a little girl to try to feel better.

But that piece of paper was real. Better than a memory. These were her words, and her hand had written them for me. *If you don't like something, change it. If you've made a mistake, fix it. If you love, show it.* I repeated that like a mantra, like a prayer, making the message a part of me.

I went to my bedroom, opened a drawer in my dresser, and took out my metal box. I picked up my book and held it a few seconds, feeling the old, wrinkled cover. Then I tucked the letter away between its pages.

When I went to put it back, the tickets to Green Gables that Trey had given me fell out of it. I had kept them as a memento of one of the most beautiful days of my life.

I'd lived in a haze those past few months, like a machine, focused only on breathing, eating, sleeping, and working, keeping myself alive… But that was over, the spell had broken, and now I couldn't stop thinking, remembering. And I wanted to scream. To scream until my voice was gone. To scream out all my frustration and impatience. To scream because I wanted to live.

I put the tickets back inside the book and closed the box, then went back to pour my coffee and sat in front of the computer intending to write all afternoon. At night, I'd go to my grandmother's old home and keep guard in front of her door.

It was a waste of time, I knew.

I was starting to think a ghost had moved in there, or an invisible man.

I could hear the clock: *tick-tock, tick-tock, tick-tock.*

I toyed with my pendant and tried to concentrate on the blank page, watching the cursor blink hypnotically.

I needed an ending. A good one. Something believable, something fully ripe, something that would leave a mark.

I thought and thought, and poured myself another coffee, hoping to find answers in the last sip. But there was nothing there, and when I finished it, my stomach ached.

Doubts appeared, insecurities. Maybe there was too much of myself in the story, and that's why I couldn't come up with a happy ending. But a sad one just wouldn't do. I already had a sad ending with Trey, and what are books for if not to dream of something better?

Eventually, I realized it wasn't coming to me. I just couldn't put the words together and make them mean something. My mind had traveled elsewhere, very far away from there.

I couldn't stop thinking of Trey and how stupid I'd been to give him up. I regretted so much having ruined our relationship... I failed him when he gave his all for us, and it killed me to think that I could never tell him how sorry I was and that I'd do anything to be with him again. Not that I had a right to—to burst into his life and start overturning things now that he'd managed to rebuild it with another girl.

And it wasn't fair to her, either.

Damned empathy! Why was it so hard for me to just be a selfish bitch like so many others?

I put some music on to distract myself and opened the windows. The breeze shook the curtains and it smelled slightly of ozone. Thunder rumbled far away. A storm was coming.

That just brought me more memories.

I took a carton of ice cream out of the fridge and sat on the fire escape. I needed to clear my head, and chocolate almost always did the trick.

I could hear the rain hitting the roof before I felt it on my bare arms. The wind made the trees bend and blew wet dead leaves across the ground. The blanket of gray clouds lit up, and a loud crackle followed.

The storm struck the city with force, dark and beautiful at the same time. But all I could think of was that other woman who now stood between Trey and me. I remembered that first night, when I almost beat him with a candlestick, and I couldn't help but laugh. How we'd pretended we couldn't stand each other when we were dying to tear off each other's clothes.

I wished I could go back to that moment and start over. But miracles and time travel didn't exist. I'd lost him, because I was an idiot. *The only thing worth regretting is not saying or doing what you feel.* I was about to bite down on another spoonful of ice cream when I remembered those words from my mother's letter, and for a moment, I thought someone had whispered them in my ears.

And maybe she did. Maybe her spirit spoke to me in that moment, and it was just the motivation I needed.

My heart started pounding. Something changed inside me. All the pieces of my mind were now working, moving together in rhythm, but taking off in a different direction. And I understood what those words truly meant.

I did feel remorse—how could I not have? It hurt worse than any torture. And yet, in a way, I had been wrong. I was regretting the wrong things—my actions in the past—when I should have been regretting what I was doing now, like sitting on my ass on the stairs pitying myself because I had a broken heart.

And changing the way I looked at things changed the entire picture.

I dropped the carton of ice cream, hurried inside, and started to write.

The words flowed out of me like water, and I couldn't stop, the phrases absorbed me, one after the other and on to the next page, thinking of nothing but the scenes as they unfolded in my head. And time kept flying by faster and faster.

Hours passed, dawn broke just as I was typing the last word, and I followed it up with three periods…

I looked up from the screen with a smile on my face. Fulfilled. Euphoric. Then I took a deep breath and closed my eyes. I just needed one more thing. And magically, it appeared. The perfect title.

I scrolled back to the first page and typed:

You And Other Natural Disasters

Because that's what Trey Holt had been for me: an earthquake, a natural disaster, a hurricane, a volcano spitting lava, the perfect storm. I had survived it.

I had lived to tell the story.

"The free soul is rare, but you know it when you see it—basically because you feel good, very good, when you are near or with them."

—Charles Bukowski, *Tales of Ordinary Madness*

34

The Gift

I thought I might fall over dead with every step I took on the bridge from PEI to Lennox Island. I didn't know if I deserved his forgiveness—probably not. And maybe that wasn't even what I wanted. I just knew I needed to tell him the things I really felt that night, months before, when I broke his heart and pulverized mine.

I couldn't keep it all inside. If I did, I'd never move forward. And I had to. With or without him.

The cool air in my lungs roused me. The sun was rising over the trees, but beneath the branches, the fog in the woods refused to lift. My feet sank in mud. My nerves were making me nauseated.

The door opened.

Nicholas was sitting on the porch with the same expression I remembered from before. He was smoking his pipe and blowing smoke from his lips. I noticed the strange shapes it made before it dissipated, paused, and tried to smile as best I could.

"Good morning. I'm not sure if you remember me. I was here a few months ago. I'm Harper, Hoyt's sister. I'm looking for your grandson, and I was wondering if…" Before I could finish, Nicholas exhaled more smoke and pointed to the corner of the house.

"Thanks," I said.

I walked around the back of the cabin, saw the camper, and felt my throat close up. Then a ball of gray hair hurried out and leapt at me. I opened my mouth to shout but couldn't when its sticky, grainy tongue started licking me all over. I tried to turn away, shouting, "Stop! Stop! Sisuei, that's enough!" I was laughing all the while.

The dog moaned with joy and kept jumping around me, tongue flapping out, pressing his muzzle into me. I kneeled down, reached out, and hugged him, sinking my nose into his soft fur. He was so pretty.

"Hey, big guy, who's a big boy, you're a big boy, aren't you?" I said, holding his head so I could look in his eyes and scratching him behind the ears. He really had grown.

He barked once and tried to lick me again, and I responded with more pets, hugs, and kisses. Then I felt Trey behind me.

I stood and turned, slowly, trying to keep my legs from trembling.

Trey was there in the middle of the clearing, wearing nothing but a pair of half-buttoned jeans. He was barefoot and had a towel slung over his shoulders. He was breathing hard, and his eyes were full of questions.

I whispered his name: "Trey."

He stepped toward me, but then stopped as if scared. I looked past him. The girl I saw him with that night appeared behind him with two cups of coffee.

Time stopped when I looked back at him, and any hope I might have harbored vanished like mist scattered by the wind.

I'd lost him. I really had.

It's not that I hadn't known the possibility was there; I'd imagined every possible version of the story. But still, the confirmation was like a blow to the stomach. I looked at him, and he looked at me. I tried to say something. I'd had a whole speech prepared, but now it was meaningless. I pursed my lips, tried to gather all the courage I had in me, and did what I came there to do. Tell it straight.

"I know it's too late. I know I ruined everything between us. But there's something you need to know. I was wrong. I messed up a lot of things, and I regret all of them. I pushed you out of my life when you were the most important person in it. I gave you up. I lost you, and now it's killing me. You made me realize who I truly am. You helped me to feel again and to want things I'd never have allowed myself to want on my own."

His face was the very picture of uncertainty. I saw his Adam's apple move up and down as he swallowed, and there was so much vulnerability in that gesture that I felt even weaker. I continued.

"I miss you so much on some days that it feels like I can barely move. I'm sorry I sacrificed what we had. Especially because it was for nothing. It's hard, and it hurts, and on some days, I think the pain will never go away. I'm not perfect, Trey, and I never will be. That's the truth of it. I failed you, and I failed myself, and now I have to live forever with the thought of what things would be like if I'd acted differently." My voice cracked. "You were right, I'm like a riddle without a solution."

I looked at the woman, then back at him.

"I'm sorry if I'm putting you in a difficult situation, but I need to be selfish and impulsive for once in my life and get all of this out so that I can move ahead. I know what I did, I had my reasons, they were wrong, and now here we are. It's possible I'll make a mistake again, that I'll be weak, that I'll have doubts and insecurities. It's happened thousands of times already. I'm just like that and I don't know if I'll ever change because it's who I am. And that's the truth. But I know I'll always put myself together again, and I know this new version of me is better than the old one. I'm happier, I'm more alive, and I'm more in love…with you."

I sniffled and wiped away my tears.

"I know I don't have any right to come bursting into your life like this. But I needed to do this to feel complete again."

I pulled up a smile from somewhere deep inside myself, while he stood there motionless, his fists clenched, his eyes full of pain that I had caused.

Sora took a few steps.

"Trey," she whispered, with something urgent in her tone. I think she wanted him to react.

I felt small and lost. But also brave, for the first time, because I'd opened myself up without reservation. And sad, too, because the ending I'd been so scared of was now written. And evidently, it wasn't a happy one.

I turned around and walked away.

I'd be lying if I said it didn't hurt. That it was hard to admit that he hadn't followed me. That I didn't hear the echo of my name in the air or feel a hand on my wrist holding me back.

I'd be lying if I said it didn't hurt to realize that I'd been talking about an *us*, but all that was left was an *I*.

I lost it. The tears came out so hard and fast that I couldn't see.

Period.

Sometimes love crosses your path, awakens you, and then it goes. Whether you want it to or not. And there's no one to blame, except maybe your own stupidity.

"Can't you just make the right decision for once without making every single wrong one first?"

His voice stopped me, and I turned. He was looking at me with a face that was part-anguished, part-infuriated.

"What's the right decision?"

"Staying here."

I took a step toward him, he took a step toward me, and we were drawn together like two magnets.

"You want me to stay?"

He nodded, smirking, just barely, but that was all I needed to come back to life.

"You were just standing there, though, immobile, not saying anything, and I thought you didn't care, and…"

He interrupted me. "You needed to say all those things, and I needed to hear them. I needed to know that you had missed me, too. That you still love me, that your life had been terrible without me, too."

I approached him slowly. "I'm sorry."

"Why'd it take you so long?"

I didn't even know myself, but I tried to tell him, stumbling over my words. "I thought I was doing the right thing at first. The best thing for everyone. And when I realized I'd screwed up, it was too late, and I didn't know how to fix it. You said you'd never come back, that you couldn't just keep coming and going while I waited forever to figure things out. You were gone, and I didn't have the right to come looking for you."

His hands cupped my face, and he kissed me. And the tears that emerged from me now were tears of relief. Of joy. I could feel his heart beating against my chest. How I'd missed him. But then something occurred to me.

"Wait," I whispered, pulling away. "This isn't right. Not like this. You…you're with that girl. This isn't fair for her. And it isn't fair to me, either."

Trey looked at me like I'd lost my mind. Then he understood and laughed. What the hell was he laughing about?

"Are you talking about Sora? Harper, Sora and I are nothing."

"I saw you together, though."

"Sora's family. Her mother and my mother were cousins. We met a few months ago, when she moved to Lennox Island. She's a lawyer. She's been helping me out with the legal aspects of my project. That's all."

"But she…"

"She's a friend. She's the only friend I've been able to talk to about you."

"You told her about me?"

He grinned and wiped away my tears with his thumbs.

"Every day. About how much I missed you, about the awful death I wished on that boyfriend of yours. I hated it when I saw you with him."

"Trey, I didn't go back to Dustin. I didn't even want him in the restaurant with us, but he wouldn't stop following me around."

He leaned in toward me. I could feel the heat of his breath. There was a spark there, lighting us on fire. Our bodies still reacted that way every time they touched. And once again, I felt that tingle in my belly.

"So now what?" I whispered.

"You decide," he responded, looking me straight in the eye.

It was a dare, and I could feel my mouth dry out. Decide. That word had always been a nightmare for me. I took a deep breath. Everything I wanted was there in front of me. I had found myself now. I knew who I was. And so did he. And he accepted me with all my defects.

"You and me. Together. Forever. Here or anywhere in the world. I don't care as long as we're together."

He pulled me tight to his chest, and said, "I can think of one place we might go." Then he let me go and took my hand. "Come with me. There's something I've been wanting to give you for a long time."

"What?"

"Something that belongs to you, but that I didn't know how to give back to you."

I was confused, but I let him drag me into the camper, and I kneeled down on the comforter while he looked in his trunk. He took out a large manila envelope and handed it to me.

I looked at him timidly, and he motioned for me to open it. I undid the hasp and looked at the documents inside. I brought my hand to my chest, my eyes struggling to take in all the clauses and conditions.

It was impossible!

The world started spinning beneath my feet.

"You bought the bookstore!"

"And the house," he replied, a little nervously.

"Why?"

"I knew what they meant to you, and I couldn't let you lose them. I just figured I'd hold onto them for you, and some day... I don't know, maybe I just needed something of you in that moment. I didn't know how to let you go."

"But...where'd you get the money from?" Before he could answer, I knew. "No, Trey! You didn't sell your project!"

He ran his hand through his hair and gave me a look that was meant to calm me down, but it was just too much. "I handed it over in exchange for the company buying those two properties for me."

"That was your dream, though. Your legacy. You were going to find investors and do it on your own. You wanted it so bad, remember? 'Because without art, life would be an error.'"

"Without you, life would be an error."

"Don't say that. Don't...don't just give up like that." My mind started racing. "We can still fix this," I said. "I've got the money. I haven't spent a cent. If I transfer it to you and you call those people, you can still get it back."

He shook his head, making me feel worse. "They've already started building. There's no going back now."

"But..."

"It's fine. I'm okay."

"I still have to give you the money back, though."

"That I can live with."

"Trey! It was your project, your dream, and you gave it up for me."

"Harper, you still don't get it. You're my dream. I would do anything for you, no matter what the price. The only project I actually care about, the only one I'll never give up, is you and me being together, and all the things we can build."

"You want a future with me?"

"I guess it sounds nuts, but yeah."

"You're a disaster," I told him.

He laughed and said, "I love disasters. And I love you. I guess I'm just crazy like that."

I lost myself in the gold of his eyes and couldn't resist any longer. I jumped at him, captured his lips between mine, pressed my body desperately into his.

And as I melted in his arms and his hands climbed under my clothes, we became that happy ending we had begun writing all those months ago.

Life isn't about waiting for the storm to pass…It's about learning to dance in the rain.

—Vivian Greene

Epilogue

A Guy as Lost as I Am

"*You and Other Natural Disasters*," Trey says, his forehead furrowed. "I still don't get what that title has to do with me."

The first copies have just arrived at the bookstore. I'm nervous, because tomorrow it goes on sale all over the country. Just the thought of it makes me panic.

"It's a metaphor," I tell him, taking books out of their boxes and setting them out on the table.

I run my fingers over the cover of one copy and feel as if I'm starting to float. I still remember like yesterday when Ryan called me to make an offer on my manuscript just a few weeks after I sent it to him. I couldn't believe it. I still can't.

"But it's a good thing, right?" Trey asks. He just can't let the issue go.

I turn and look at him. He's so handsome that I fall into a trance every time I do it. We've traveled a lot this past summer. To the mountains, to the beach, even briefly to Bluehaven to visit Novalie and Nick. The sun has tanned his skin and lightened his hair, and he looks better than ever. I'm sure I'll never tire of him—of the ticklish feeling that overcomes me in his presence, of his deep voice, his mirthful laugh, his golden eyes that seem to know everything about me.

"It's the best thing," I reassure him.

I look at the clock and realize time is getting away from us. In the bookstore, everything appears to be in order. Since Trey redesigned the interior, it's brighter and much more spacious, with comfortable furnishings and modern touches, and thanks to him, our clientele has doubled.

I walk to the cash register and take the keys out of the top drawer under the counter. Trey shifts in his chair. He's hunched over and strangely quiet, and I ask him what he's doing.

"Reading."

I run over and snatch the book out of his hands. "Not yet. Please."

He grabs my wrist and pulls me into his lap, kissing my neck. I melt when I feel his lips on my skin.

"You can't just hide it from me for the rest of our lives," he whispers.

I know it's silly, but I still haven't let him read it. Our story is in those pages, but so are other things, thoughts so private, so harsh, so ruthlessly honest, that I don't yet feel ready to share them. I'm scared they might hurt him or make him feel guilty for stuff that's actually my fault.

"Just wait a little longer," I whisper.

"Okay."

He smiles, gives me a squeeze, and nibbles my earlobe.

We close the bookstore and walk to my grandmother's house, which is now our home. It goes without saying that the phantom owner I was stalking all those weeks was Trey.

He took care of the place, visited often, kept it clean, and watered the plants. But he never dared move in. When I asked him why, he told me he couldn't help seeing us in every corner, and it was too hard for him.

That made me fall even more deeply in love with him, impossible as that is to imagine.

Sisuei greets us at the door, barking and jumping nonstop until Trey finally shouts at him to be still. He sits and stares at me with a sad look on his face. I'm a softy with him, and he's sly enough to pick up on that. When Trey's not looking, I give him a treat.

We take our suitcases outside and lock the house.

Trey puts everything into the trunk while I open the side door of the SUV and let Sisuei into the back. He can hardly keep still, even in that tiny space, and whips the windows and the seat backs with his tail. I pet him, trying to calm him down. He loves traveling. Finally, when I pat his head, he lies down.

I turn on the music just after Trey starts the engine. "Ready?" he asks.

"Yep."

"Great, let's go."

I squint at the blue sky, trying to control my heartbeat. We've got a long journey ahead of us.

From the ferry, I can see the coast, and my nerves suddenly feel raw. As we approach, the colorful houses take shape before my eyes. I can see the roads, the church, the town hall, and, further to the left, a gray silhouette: Ridge's restaurant.

"You look happy," Trey says, standing by my side. I smile at him from the heart.

"I am."

I reach up and touch the glass pendant and the silver mermaid hanging around my neck. It's the first time we've been back to Petit Prince since that week that changed the course of our lives. And it's a special visit, for all sorts of reasons.

The ferry soon docks, and we're the first ones off the ramp. Dozens of meaningful moments return to my mind, bringing me to the verge of tears.

"It hasn't changed a bit!" I say.

We park and walk to the restaurant with Sisuei running circles around us. Even from the road, we can hear the voices and music inside. I pull at Trey and walk faster, until I can smell the food and feel something I can't quite put my finger on until the door opens—the feeling of family.

"You're here!" Hayley shouts when we appear.

Scott waves, but doesn't take his eyes off the sports channel on TV.

There's a frenzy of hugs and kisses on the cheek. Hoyt picks me up off the ground and tickles my ribs until I start shrieking.

"Jesus, grow up!" I shout.

Megan slaps him on the shoulder, and he turns around and does the same to her. *Welcome to the family*, I think.

Adele walks over with Sid. I jog up to her and hug her tight. I can barely speak. But then, what is there to say?

"You look gorgeous," she tells me.

"You too," I respond.

"I see you're wearing your necklace."

"Always."

Ridge comes out of the kitchen and notices me, and I give him a hug. There's a new face here, too—a pale girl with brown hair and big eyes who observes us timidly. She's pretty.

"Who's that?"

He blushes and smiles.

"She came for the ocean, but I think she's staying."

I hug him again and tell him, "She's a catch."

At the table, it's all shouting and laughter. It's Thanksgiving, and it was my idea for us all to celebrate together. Chaos erupts as we pass the plates back and forth. Looking around, I realize everyone I truly care about is there. I savor the moment and wish I could hold on to it forever. Hide it away in a little box, an instance of happiness, the kind of

happiness these special moments radiate—moments that are insignificant, but at the same time bring meaning to the entire universe. I wish
I could record the laughter and listen to it over and over when I feel my
wounds from the past, when the harsh memories start hurting again.

The world is prettier now. And I'm a part of it, not just a bystander.
At some point, I realized that you have to live every minute of life to
the fullest, and that there's no point in investing time and energy in
things that don't make you happy.

Hours later, I'm still thinking of this as I look up at the sky full of
stars. The waves break on the shore, wash up over my bare feet, roar
softly and nearly lull me to sleep. Trey comes up behind me, and his
hands wrap around my waist, warming me all over.

Time stops in a way that only happens when he's around.

Far off, the darkness flashes briefly white. And the scent of rain
is in the breeze. We hold each other and watch the storm approach.
The thunder roars over our heads and the stars disappear. On the
horizon, we watch a lightning bolt shoot downward toward the sea.

The first raindrop falls, then another. Big ones. Soon, the rain is
pouring. Our clothes and hair are soaked, but we don't care, despite
the cold. I look over my shoulder and kiss him, and he takes a deep
breath, rocking me back and forth, our feet sinking into the sand. The
beach is witness to our happiness, to a story that had begun long ago.

His hands guide me in a kind of slow dance, and he tells me, "I
think I understand now."

"What?"

"The title of the book. The truth behind it. What you and I are."

"A potential disaster area?" I joke.

"No. Two survivors who have made it through the storm and can
dance now under the rain."

And that is how a guy as lost as I am makes me fall even more in
love with him. Impossible as that still seems.

Read on for a sneak peek
at more from María Martínez in

Where There
Are No More Stars
Left to Count

1

Maybe Antoine was right and it was my fault. It had been weeks since things had started going badly for us. Too many arguments, and always about the same thing: My attitude. I wasn't the same person I used to be. I was cold and uninterested. Absent.

And it was true, in a way. The past six months had been torture for me. The operation, recovery in the hospital. Returning home and the weeks of rehab. My grandmother's constant reproaches, how easily she made me feel bad for everything that's wrong with the world. Probably the polar ice caps are melting because just once, I did something without her permission.

Just because I wanted to.

Once, and the punishment was brutal.

Deep down, I think she was happy about the accident. The satisfaction on her face every time she said *I told you so* or *If only you'd listened to me* was a cruel pleasure she liked to wallow in. Her eyes shouted *You deserve it* every time they caught me in their stare, and then, with a condescending smile, she would forgive me under the sole condition that I sacrifice every second of my existence to her.

No one should be responsible for making another person's dreams come true. It's impossible to live up to the expectations of a person who has failed to achieve her own dreams and desires.

But the hardest thing for me to bear was the uncertainty.

The wait was consuming me inside and I was incapable of thinking of anything else.

Maybe Antoine was right and I was pushing him away just as I was everyone else. Still, I would have appreciated a little empathy from him. A little more patience and compassion. I had known Antoine since I was fifteen, when his family moved from Paris to Madrid for work, and he began to take classes at the Royal Conservatory of Dance, where I was studying, and I knew he was emotionally stunted. Not just that: he didn't even know how inept he was at trying to put himself in someone else's shoes.

Despite that, I'd learned to love him along with his defects. As a friend at first, and something more a few years later, when we both entered the National Dance Company as soloists. At twenty-two years old, the strongest relationship I'd had, apart from with ballet, was with Antoine. That was the only unconditional love I'd allowed myself.

For that reason, I was scared of losing him. I needed his affection. And I was scared, closing my eyes and holding my breath when he curled up tight to me beneath the sheets and, still sleepy, slid his hand between my legs. He pressed his hips into my buttocks, and I could feel he was aroused. I took a breath and let it out slowly, concentrating on his fingers, how they caressed me, the warmth of his chest against my back. The way he pulled me tight.

I opened my eyes and looked at the hands of the clock.

His finger tried to work its way inside of me. I flinched and grimaced. I tried to relax, but I couldn't—I couldn't feel anything at all.

"I've got to go," I whispered.

Face beside my neck, Antoine grunted, nibbled my shoulder.

"Come on. Look what you're doing to me."

He pushed into me again. I was starting to get agitated.

"I'll be late."

"Just a quickie," he said, using his French accent like an aphrodisiac. But it got on my nerves.

I jerked away and got up, glancing at the clock again and feeling anxiety in my stomach. I grabbed my dress off the chair. Still in bed, Antoine huffed and lay on his back, staring at me.

"Are you for real? Dammit, Maya. We never do it anymore, and I...I have my needs."

I pulled my dress over my head and glared back at him. "Never? What was yesterday, then?"

"Getting it on in a bathroom with our clothes on doesn't count."

I rolled my eyes and sat down to tie my shoes, looking for a moment at the scars on my leg. Their color was lightening, and the swelling was starting to go down. Or at least that's what I thought—I didn't dare to actually touch them. I stood and grabbed my cellphone off the table.

"Are you seriously leaving?" he asked, as if it weren't obvious from the fact that I was heading for the door.

"I can't stay any longer, OK? I've got a doctor's appointment in less than an hour."

He jumped up, looking surprised, and I couldn't help but eye up his nude body. A whole life devoted to ballet had transformed him into a perfectly proportioned, walking sculpture. And yet, I felt nothing.

"It's today?" he asked, and I nodded, feeling a hint of panic at what I knew he'd say next. "Shit, I'm sorry! I completely forgot."

"It's fine."

"You want me to come along?"

"No need," I told him. "I'd almost...rather go by myself."

He looked relieved, and that made me feel bitter as he came over, wrapped his arms around me, and kissed me on the forehead.

"Everything will be fine, you'll see. You'll dance again, you'll go back to being principal, we both will, and we'll travel the world together. They'll talk about us the way they did about Fonteyn and Nureyev. You and me on stage, Maya—we're something else."

He grabbed my chin and forced me to look him in the eyes—those eyes so green it was hard to believe they were real. I smiled softly. It was true, onstage we were so in synch we moved as one body, one mind, and we trusted each other completely. Never once had I feared that he'd drop me.

If only the same was true in our personal relationship.

"I'll let you know," I said.

"Sure, just text me. I've got class and then rehearsal today, so I'll be back late."

"OK."

I gave him a quick kiss on the lips and hurried into the bathroom, washing up a little and taking a look at myself in the mirror. My eyes were so dark I could hardly see my pupils. My brown eyebrows framed them, just as my brown hair framed my face, still with a few tangles in it I hadn't managed to brush out.

I leaned in close and thought about how different I looked from the rest of my family. My grandmother, my aunts and uncles and cousins, my mother…all of them were blond with light-colored eyes, their features a reflection of my grandmother's Ukrainian side of the family. Even on my grandfather's side, the Spanish side, most people had pale skin and straw-colored hair.

I was the exception. And whenever I noticed those differences, I couldn't stop thinking about how somewhere, there where similarities. Traits that resembled another person. Him. Wherever he was.

I walked off down the hall and heard voices in the living room: Matías and Rodrigo, whom I found at the breakfast table. They formed part of the corps de ballet and shared the apartment with

Antoine. It's funny how small the ballet world is, like a little army you serve in and give your all to. You work sixteen hours a day, six days a week. You eat, sleep, and breathe ballet.

Maybe that's why we dancers rarely associate with people outside the world of leotards and point shoes. You have to be in it to understand it. We spend almost all our time together, training together, rehearsing together, touring together.

"Good morning!" I said.

"Good morning," Matías replied.

Rodrigo stood and pulled a chair close to the table. "Want a coffee?"

"No thanks. Caffeine's the last thing I need today."

I looked around for my bag and found it on the sofa. Then I grabbed an apple Matías handed to me. He was always so attentive. I thanked him with a peck on the cheek.

"Today's the big day," he said.

"Or the worst day," I responded.

Matías was my best friend, the only one I could tell everything to without any worry of being judged. I could share my worries with him, the loneliness that comes with that disciplined, competitive lifestyle. I could cry in front of him; I could show him all my shortcomings, even the ones I buried deep.

"It's all I know how to do," I told him. "I can't lose this."

"You won't. Worst-case scenario, Natalia will put you with the corps de ballet until you get your rhythm and confidence back. Then you'll be principal again."

"You really think that?"

"Of course I do. Ever since she came on as director of the company, she's done everything in her power to keep you in the ensemble. She's been following you since the conservatory days."

I nodded, wishing with all my might that he wasn't wrong.

I started dancing when I was four, and I hadn't done anything since. I'd given up all other studies to focus on ballet, climbing slowly to a summit everyone thought I was predestined to reach. I had what I needed to achieve it. And even if the fear of injury is something that stalks every one of us, I never thought it would happen to me, and not in such a ridiculous way.

Acknowledgments

When I reach this point, I always feel words aren't enough to thank all the people who undertook this voyage with me.

Thanks to Planeta—my team, my home.

To Irene, for her trust, her eagerness, and for being much more than just an editor.

To Esther, for opening the door, letting me fly, giving me the keys.

To my friends forever: Nazaret, Tamara, Yuliss, and Victoria.

To Alice Kellen, for sharing this crazy world with me.

To Elena, Dunia, and Lorena. Your support and care are priceless.

To Daniel Ojeda, who's always there.

To Miriam Iglesias, for every smile (my *birthday present*).

To my Estrellitas, thanks for so many things.

To Bea, for pushing me to write this story.

To my daughters, who made me the heroine of my own story. I love you very much.

To my parents, for teaching me that only brave people can be good people.

And to you, my readers, the most important ones of all.

Thanks.

About the Author

María Martínez is the successful Spanish author of *You and Other Natural Disasters*, *The Fragility of a Heart in the Rain*, and *When There Are No More Stars Left to Count*, among other works. She writes sensitive stories that address the complexity of emotions and issues like family and identity. When she is not busy writing, she spends her free time reading, listening to music or watching series and movies. Her favorite hobbies are getting lost in any bookstore and having fun with her daughters.

Facebook: María Martínez
Instagram: @mariamartinez.itsme